ALLERIA
(Chronicles of the Moon Born, 1)

Chantal Noordeloos

Grendel Press

Cover Design by Olga Panfilova
Edited by Kasey Kubica

Published May 2024
ISBN: 978-1-960534-14-9 (Paperback)
ASIN: B0CXVCN5P9 (eBook)

Written by Chantal Noordeloos
www.chantalnoordeloos.com

Published by Grendel Press LLC
www.grendelpress.com

ALLERIA

SERENWERDD
WHITE OCEAN
NORTH SEA
RAS AL HAS
TRIBARI
RAS AL MAD
PLAINS
PLAINS
SWAMP
MOUNT FIRE BREATH
YOUYA
DRY LAND
SHOUWEI
BOLICHENG
WESTERN MOUNTAINS
JINZI
YUCHENG
GANGKOU
PLAINS
SPAR
FAIR FOLK WOODS
DOORN
AMBERDE
GOLDEN HOLLOW
WOLFMAW
WEST SEA
WESTPOORT
DRY LAND
GHOST WOODS
JEBEL FAHI
BHAGA
JOBARA
MIRROR FALLS (WAT
TURINIQ
NHEMER HAV'N
OOTH
KHMER
GHEVEL
FARPOD
DESERT

EPKUV
CHAKYL
BILDUU
FROZEN TUNDRA
BATO
AISIK
FROZEN TUNDRA
FROZEN TUNDRA
NDRA
LOST VILLAGES
ES'D
SEVEN GODS MOUNTAINS
KOFL
JABARI
FARAJI
FARUSH
SOUTH PORT
NEVERFALLS
ANDS
CLOUDCHILL
MTUMWA
LAKE ELORA
SYLVA
BROKEN BRANCH FOREST
PLAINS
SWAMP
BORDERLANDS
HELFYRTH
FYD
ZURI
HICE
EAST SEA
PLAINS
TINKS
MARSHES
ANTIRA
SILVER CITY
SWAMP
EAST PORT
DRY LAND
MIRROR LAKE
FARZEE
AMERAL
TEMPLE OF
TARNISZ
MOON TOUCHED CANYON
EFTAL
HERLOO
MISTAG
LOCH EMERALD
HOGE BERGEN
NISH
PLAINS
KLEINE
STEDE
SUN TOUCHED CANYON
DORISH HARBOR
HIP'EL
TUN 'IL TOU
DORINTH
PARSI DESERT
LAVERIA OTHAR
OQUA
EA
QUAEE DESERT

To Stefana,
Who always speaks her mind, and dances like no one is watching.
I'm grateful you're my friend

PROLOGUE

11 YEARS AGO

Some new beginnings start on rainy nights in places far away and hidden from sight. This particular story began on such a night in a place called the Shadow Marshes, and it started with a witch, whose hunched figure threw a log on the waning fire, where it caught light with a soft hiss and a crackle. Her thin hand, covered in liver spots and thick, blue veins, pulled an ornate, cold-iron poker from a rickety stand and prodded the wood gently. The light of the flames cast red and gold shadows on her wrinkled face, while dainty wisps of smoke snaked across the single room in the cottage, spreading an oaky scent. The warmth was a welcoming contrast to the outside winter chill that crept into the small house like icy fingers. Her bones groaned when she moved, and—not for the first time that day—she cursed her old age. Even more, she cursed her mortality. The powers she possessed were no match against the passing of time—she was only human, after all, and her magic had limits—but then again... she was a clever woman, and clever women could often find their way around such constrictions.

Long ago she had built her house in the Shadow Marshes, which were the Borderlands between the human world and the Arallfyd, known as the land beyond the mists. Mortals tended to stay clear of the Borderlands, partially out of instinctual fear, and partially because most were raised with the scary tales that served as a warning. Told from parent to child, these stories were all but fiction. The creatures that inhabited the Shadow Marshes—the Faerisees—were often deadly, and to most humans they were the very representation of everything they feared in the dark.

The old witch grew up with the same tales, but did not frighten as easily, and throughout her unnaturally long life, she had gained knowledge beyond the common mortal man. She knew how most of the faerisees were born with a subservient nature, despite their inherent bloodlust, which made it easy to bond alliances with even the most frightening among them. The magic the old witch possessed was powerful, and that made it easy to manipulate the monsters of the marsh. She could have been even more powerful if it hadn't been for her treacherous human coil. Her mind was still strong, but her bones betrayed her.

It took some effort for her to lower her frail body in the gnarled rocking chair. Her hand shook slightly when she took the long pipe, crafted from nixy bones, and placed it between her yellow teeth. With no more than a whisper, she lit it and inhaled. The earthy taste of the tobacco made her tongue numb and her lungs tingle. For a moment she just mused, letting the old chair rock backward and forward in the same steady rhythm as her heart. Then she closed her eyes, lids fluttering with movement as her thoughts weaved a spell that allowed her to reach out to the world outside her little cottage. It felt as if she emerged from water when the magic took hold, morphing the darkness to an unhuman version of the outside world, colorless and blurry around the edges, while simultaneously sharp in the center, as if she had the sight of a bird of prey. A cacophony of sounds and scents, far clearer than the sight itself, tugged at her senses, trying to pull her in all different directions. When she had first learned to hone this spell, many decades ago, it had been quite overwhelming, tearing at her sanity. Now the old witch knew how to focus and ignore that which was no use to her.

In the distance, squelching sounds of mud sucking at the hooves of horses echoed through the Marshes, and before long the witch became aware of a scent that did not belong. Every part of her focus was drawn to the newcomer, and back in the hut a thin smile curled on the chapped lips. The visitor she had been expecting was nearing.

Soon, she thought, *soon I will be able to conquer age itself.* The rocking chair continued to creak softly as she pushed herself back and forth, her eyelids still closed. Her mind reached out to the night creatures that stood watch, merging her thoughts with theirs, and she used their sight as easily as she could her own. Through the eyes of the frogs and water dwellers, she could barely make out the carriage as it made its way through the rain; a lone rider sat on the perch. The cargo she waited for lay inside, warm and dry.

Her eyes fluttered open only a second before the knock sounded. In response, she waved a finger in the air. The door flew open. A man dressed in a dark blue coat and a tall top hat stood in the entrance. His clothes were expensive, but the downpour had degraded the fineries to a wet, sodden mess; the man was soaked from his fine hat to his even finer boots. His coat—which was the only thing thick enough to withstand the rain—was draped over his shoulders, and underneath he held a sleeping girl in his arms. She was no older than six.

"You... you are the witch? The one who's been haunting my dreams?" His voice trembled as he spoke, and he hovered in the door opening, the rain still streaming down his hat and shoulders.

"I am she." She waved her hand at him. "Come in before that child gets wet and wakes."

The man stepped inside, and an unseen force shut the door behind him, making him jump ever so slightly.

"I... I gave her a brew of poppies and firedragon root," he said, recovering himself, as he moved the coat and held out the child as if he were showing the witch a fine piece of fabric.

"The little one won't wake anytime soon then." The witch nodded with approval. "Put her down there." Her bony finger pointed at one of the two bedsteads of the cottage. The man obeyed with a gloomy expression on his face. Carefully he placed the child on the coarse mattress, but there was no fatherly affection in his caution; he did not even cover her with the woolen blanket that lay at the edge. The man's coldness worked in the witch's favor—there would be fewer bonds to sever from the child's mind. The mother's love would be difficult enough to overcome.

The little girl was the loveliest of creatures, and it was obvious from the features of her delicate, heart-shaped face that she was not human. Her large eyes were closed, and thick feathery lashes twitched from the dreams that ran through her unconscious young mind. The hair, combed in perfect ringlets, was the color between silver and gold that was equal to the beauty of the second moon. The man looked down at her, his lip curled into a sneer.

"I thought it would be easier to keep her asleep. Having her awake can be rather... unpredictable."

"You mean because of her special talent? It has already developed, I assume?" There was an eagerness in the old woman's voice.

The disgust on his face was thinly veiled. "She... she isn't natural."

She looked at him. Her visitor was young, rich, and handsome—the type of man who was used to getting what he wanted, and the girl had been an unpleasant surprise. The witch knew that this human never bargained for a half-breed child that wasn't even of his own blood, and that her very existence was an insult to his ego. Another man's seed had put such a precious specimen as this girl in his wife's womb. This young human would never be able to appreciate the "gift" he and his wife had been granted.

"The things she does..." His words faded in thought.

"This girl is special." The witch brought her pipe to her lips and puffed. The man never looked at her, his gaze remaining on the child.

"I have done my part; the rest is up to you." There was a chill in his voice, and his brown eyes were harsh. "I don't care what you do with her as long as she doesn't come back."

"Do you believe yourself to be less of a monster by bringing her here rather than spilling her blood?"

The man gaped at her, then closed his mouth. He chose to ignore her question, but there was an edge in his voice.

He pointed toward the bedstead where the little girl slept. "You have to promise me that I will never see that *thing* again."

"You won't see your daughter ever again."

"That *thing* is not *my* daughter," he spat, anger flaring in his eyes. "I don't know who or *what* spawned it—my wife refused to tell me—but I know it's not *mine*. I knew from the moment it was born." Then he composed himself. He was a sophisticated man, and the witch guessed he very rarely showed his emotions so vehemently. His eyes glazed over with thought, and his voice sounded thick when he spoke again. "I will tell her mother that we were lost, and that we spent the night in the Shadow Marshes. When I woke, there was nothing left but Alleria's dress, and it was covered in blood." He bowed his head and cleared his throat. "I have one of her dresses covered in pig's blood. I'm convinced the story is credible enough for her to accept it." His chest rose as he took a deep breath. He closed his eyes and bit his lip before he spoke again. "My wife... she... she's very delicate."

He forgave his wife for having her indiscretion, the witch thought, *but he would never forgive the child for being the result of it. The fool has no idea what treasure he holds in his hands.*

The man shifted his weight from one foot to the other. "I assume we are done here?"

"I have the child. There is nothing more I want from you."

"Then I should go. I must bring my wife the terrible news." He turned to walk out the door, but the witch stood from her rocking chair.

"You love your wife, do you not, Master de Nacre?"

He turned to face her, his eyebrows raised in surprise. "Of course I do, what a silly question."

"In fact, you love her so much that her sadness will hurt you." The witch looked at him and blew a ring of smoke from her pipe.

"I don't like to see my wife suffer, that is true."

"She'll be hurt when her only child is presumed dead." Another ring curled in the air and elongated until there was nothing left. The man stared at it, and the old witch could see discomfort in his face. "Do you hate this child more than you love your wife?"

His brow furrowed and his mouth became a thin stripe. "Yes."

"I don't believe you. You may *think* you hate that little girl now, but wait until your wife refuses to stop crying. Because she won't stop, My Lord. In fact, she'll lose weight and become deadly pale... and so terribly ill. The thought of raising this bastard child won't seem so bad compared to losing your lovely young wife to grief. And what will you do then?"

"I won't lose my wife to grief. We will have a child of our own to set her mind from things. She'll be happy then and this... this *thing*," he pointed at the sleeping child, "will be a distant memory."

"You won't have another babe, Master de Nacre... your seed will never grow. You were never meant to have any children, young lord. Any fruit in your wife's belly will not be yours. And when you realize that, the girl that you hate so much now won't seem like such a punishment. After all, only you and your lovely wife know she's not of your blood, so why not keep up the pretense? That's when you'll set up a search party of eager peers. You will feel cheated by our arrangement, and after a few days of searching you'll convince them that maybe I had something to do with the disappearance of your daughter. Then you will lead those men right to my little cottage, where lo and behold you'll find Alleria and demand that child back from me. Of course I couldn't possibly return her, so you will force me to kill you and yours. Not that it will be difficult, but it will bring others to find their way to my home, seeking justice or vengeance, or whatever your kind seeks nowadays... and my peace and quiet will be disturbed for many years to come. The last thing I need is to be constantly vigilant for bumbling humans to try and burn my house down."

"I will not do anything of the sort, I have no love for that child, and I do not wish her back. My wife *will* stop crying, and I *will* give her another child." His cheeks were flushed with anger, and he balled his hands into fists.

"So you give this child willingly to me? In full conviction?"

"I certainly do." To emphasize the words, he stomped on the ground. The witch felt a soft breeze in the warm air of the cottage, and she smiled.

"Good, very good. Though, instead of letting you go, I have a better idea. In about two days' time, some traveler will find the remains of your carriage a hundred miles away from the Shadow Marshes with your mangled and half-eaten corpse and the blood-stained dress of your daughter. They will try and find the girl for several days, but no one will really believe she's still alive. They won't think to look for her here; after all, you had no business in the Shadow Marshes, did you? And your body was found so very far away. After a few weeks, everyone will give up on the search, and no one will know I have the girl." A smoke ring curled in the air, but instead of a circle, the shape of a skull leered at the young visitor. "Thank you for your discretion, by the way. I'm very happy you drove your own carriage here, so I don't have to dispose of servants as well. It makes the whole ordeal so much less... complicated. The fewer people involved, the fewer loose ends to tie up." The old witch shot the young man her most grandmotherly smile, exposing her crooked yellow teeth.

"Old woman, you must be joking." The floor creaked when he took a step back, his chest puffed out and back fully erect. His handsome face was a mixture of incredulity and disgust. She shook her head only slightly, her ancient eyes shining with surprising youth. With a deliberate slowness she raised her arm and snapped her fingers. The door flew open once more, bringing a tornado of dead leaves into the cottage. The air that followed carried the strong scent of petrichor. Shadows trickled inside. They slithered across the floor, the walls, and the ceiling like flat black snakes. Some took on a solid shape, and Master de Nacre looked around with wild eyes. The old witch inhaled the sour scent of his fear and smiled.

Around the two figures, the shadows loomed and grew to the size of men. They were tall and broad, but their shape was not altogether human. Dark gray faces could be seen within the blackness of their form; milky white eyes stared from the darkness and sharp, yellowed teeth were revealed by cruel smiles. The shadows, seven of them, approached the frightened man, fangs bared.

Master de Nacre screamed and turned to run for the door, but the shadows pounced on him like hungry predators. The cries of the young man were faintly muffled by the sounds of the rain and wind in the night. The old witch watched the mass of shadows writhing and fighting for scraps. A pool of blood spread on the floor with a languid ease. She sat back in her rocking chair as the creatures ate their fill.

"Enough," she said before the remains were completely devoured. "I need his loved ones to recognize him still. Bring him to his carriage and drive it into the northern canyons, far away from any of the Borderlands." The creatures hissed softly, and the old witch could feel their resistance, but did as they were bade. As fast as a murder of crows, they flew from the cottage, the remains of their victim in their midst. The old witch looked at the blood stain on the floor. *The girl can clean that up in the morning,* she thought with a hint of satisfaction. She leaned back, closed her eyes, and watched her shadow creatures dispose of the gentleman's body. Gently, her rocking chair moved back and forth, creaking with a soft rhythm. The girl on the bed slept through it all.

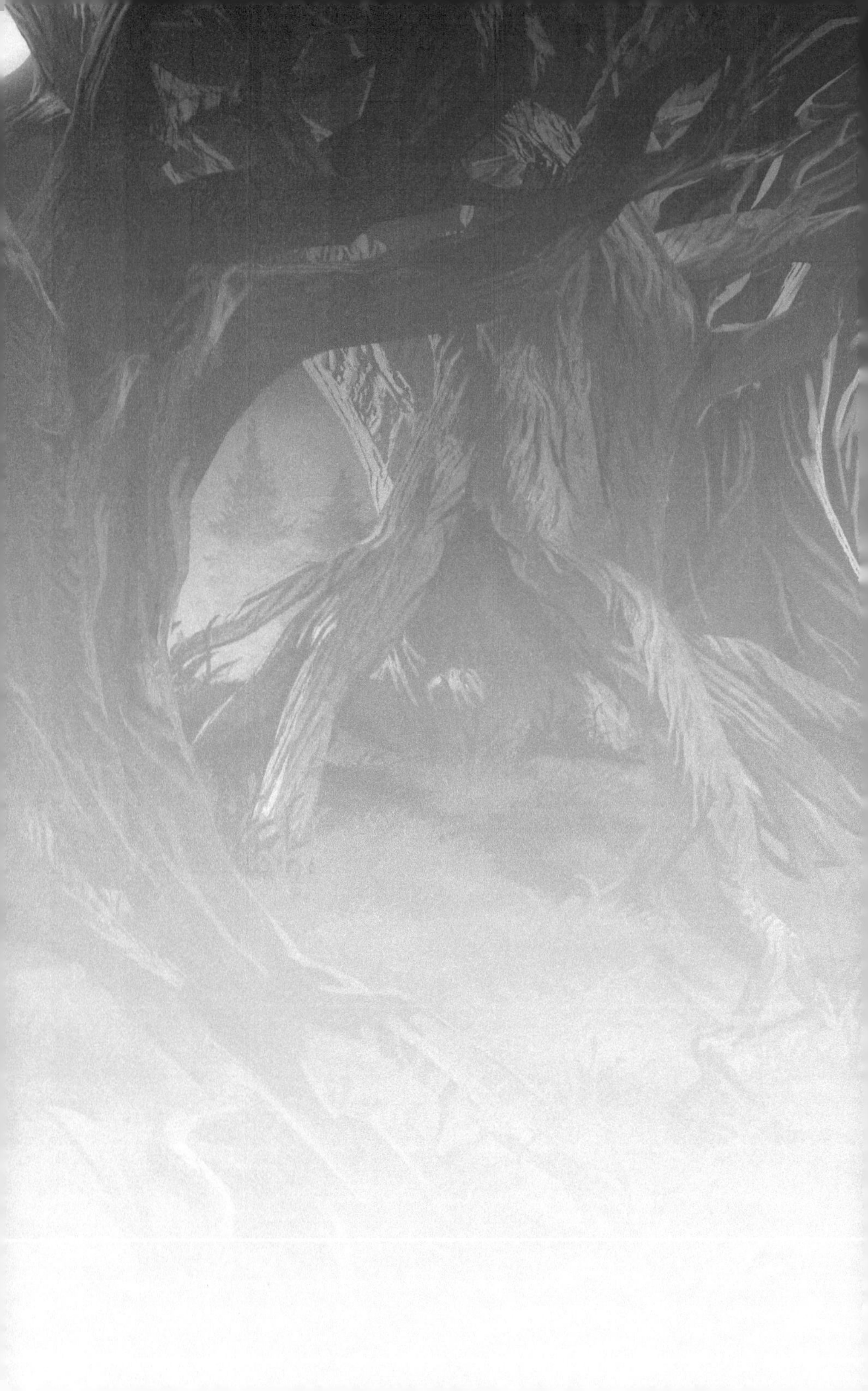

CHAPTER ONE

*C*areful now... gently.

Her fingers wrapped around the snapping lily weed that grew at the edge of the blood swamp, and she took great care not to let the tiny plant bite her with its poisonous teeth. Her inhuman blood would prevent her from instant death, but the poison would still make her sick for several days—as she had found out the hard way, a few times before.

The daylight slowly faded, and with the dying light her time ran short; after dark, the Shadow Marshes became dangerous to Alleria, and even though she'd been a child of the Borderlands for as long as she could remember, she would never truly belong here. Darkness brought with it creatures that were even more deadly than those who lived in the light.

The Borderlands, or "in-between lands," as some named the place at this side of the magical boundary of mist, kept the dangerous fath tywyll locked in the Arallfyd, "the Otherworld." Once every Blood Moon—a rare and unpredictable occurrence in the human world—the fath tywyll could cross through the mists and wander the human lands for as long as the light of the moon touched the earth. Humans feared the Blood Moon, for it heralded terrors that some of them could not even imagine. Aside from the path of death and destruction the fath tywyll left behind, they also left some of their offspring in the bellies of young, worthy women. The seed of men would be stolen too, and many males deemed worthy would bear the mental and physical scars of a dark night with an even darker creature.

Alleria knew all the stories of the Arallfyd, the Blood Moon nights, and of the fath tywyll. The old witch had educated her well, and she had been an eager student. The stories meant more to her, because she wasn't all human; she was a tylwyth teg, a half breed, and blood of the otherworlders coursed through her veins. Alleria was conceived on the night of the Blood Moon. If she wished, she could cross through the mist and travel to the Arallfyd, something full-blooded humans could not do without deadly repercussions. She often dreamt about what the world would be like on the other side of the magic veil, away from the witch who raised her. Sometimes she would imagine just running away and stepping across the border, knowing that the human witch could not follow. But those thoughts were always short-lived. Something stopped her from even exploring these ideas too deeply; it was almost like a small voice in her head, and in the end, she never dared to venture near the mists.

The Shadow Marshes were infested with inhuman creatures; not the fath tywyll or even the tylwyth teg, but a lesser breed of crude monsters called the faerisees. Some said that the faerisees were the offspring of the tylwyth teg, but they were more animal than humanoid, so it was a far-fetched theory. No one knew where they really came from, only that they were as dangerous as they were magical, and they only lived within the Borderlands.

There was much to fear in these marshes, but nothing was as terrifying as the human witch—Tumsa—who held Alleria captive. Tumsa was calculating and cruel, her magic and shadows often tricking faerisees of lesser powers to her cottage where they would fall victim to her potions or rituals. The faerisees were dangerous—without exception—but not all of them were intelligent, which made them easy prey for the witch. Alleria feared the old witch above all else.

With a swift movement, she swept the moonrock dagger across the snapping lily weed and cut the plant in twain before it could sink its little, thorny fangs in to her flesh. Slimy, yellow mucus ran from its cut stem down her hand, the sap tingling on the coarse skin, and she rubbed it off on the hard grass. The mucus was only poisonous when ingested, so she had to be careful not to get any in her mouth. Her hand trembled slightly as she put the plant in her wicker basket, together with all the other herbs and plants she'd gathered. Alleria hoped Tumsa would be pleased with her; she'd found almost everything the old woman sent her out to look for, and her sore back couldn't bear another night of beatings. The shadows elongated, a warning that she had less than an hour to find the last herb and return to the cottage. The nearing of the evening made her rush because if she stayed away too long, Tumsa would reach out with her inner-eye, and she truly hated that invasion into her psyche. The infiltration of the old witch's mind—probing and slithering around her brain like a black mucus eel—felt violating.

Her eyes glanced toward the red sun barely visible above the tips of the marsh trees. The final herb grew near the edge of the bog, and she didn't expect it'd be a challenge to find it—she'd saved the easiest plant till last.

With a sigh, she set her basket on the ground and fell to her knees. Carefully, her fingers pried apart the sharp blades of grass that grew near the water to look for the final herb, the siekalot plant. Her eyes met those of the reflection in the murky surface of the bog water, and for a moment, she held her own gaze. She spent so much time avoiding her own reflection, that when she did come across it, it had a strange hold on her. As if she couldn't look away, not even when she was in a rush. In faraway dreams, she was a pretty little girl with porcelain skin, whose heart-shaped face was framed with curls of silver and gold, but the reflection in the water betrayed no evidence of that child.

I'm a monster, she thought, and touched the rough face covered in coarse, brown hair. The tips of her fingers ran over the crooked bucked teeth that protruded from chapped, thick lips. *There is no beauty here.* In vain, she tried to straighten her back, but the hunch on her shoulder wouldn't allow her. Her right arm dragged across the floor when she walked, and she had to stretch out her neck to see straight. She reminded herself that beauty wasn't everything, a sigh hissing through her lips as she tore her gaze away. The temptation to slap the water's surface and create ripples to distort the image was great, but this was not the kind of water she'd be wise to touch or disturb. Who knew what sort of attention she would attract with her impulsive behavior? The best way to survive the marshes was to stay unnoticed.

The blue of siekalot was a stark contrast as it bloomed between the gray-green grass, and it let itself be picked without much resistance; in all fairness, it was only really dangerous when consumed, and had no strange oozing poisons or acids. Alleria held it up to her face and inspected it while her left hand reached for the basket. There was nothing but grass. She looked up, and to her horror, she saw the basket moving toward the water of the bog.

Oh no.

A long, slime-covered arm, green and black, with nails shaped like the talons of a small owl, clutched the wicker and dragged it slowly toward the edge. As quick as she could move, Alleria grabbed the basket and pulled it. The arm pulled back, and in desperation, the girl put her weight behind her and gave the basket a final jerk. The wicker tore with a loud snap, and several herbs spilled out in a dramatic arc.

Curse the seven Raven gods.

Anger rose in her stomach, but she managed to suppress the emotion. Alleria's temper had always been volatile, and when she let it get the better of her, bad things happened. The old witch kept a sharp eye on her, taught her to manage her emotions, and one of Tumsa's curses kept her in line. When Alleria gave in to anger now, the spell would make her physically ill—so ill, in fact, that if she did not regain control in time, she would lose consciousness. All she could do in a situation such as this was to keep a level head, or whatever was trying to steal her basket would have her at a disadvantage. Luckily, she had eleven years of experience in fighting for her self-control, and most of the time she won the battle.

Another arm emerged from the bog, and long, black hair, the texture of seaweed, slowly rose to the surface of the murky water. It took Alleria a moment to recognize the creature, but when she saw the sharp, gray-green nose peer through the stringy hair, she knew what she was dealing with.

Jenny Green-Teeth. Her breath caught in her throat; this was exactly the type of creature whose attention she did not want. Panic tickled her senses, a haze of silver-blue color clouded her vision, and she felt her emotions spin out of control. The darkness inside her—the malevolent energy she fought to control—sank through her body and reached her soles, where it seeped out of her into the ground. The grass at her feet withered, and a wave of nausea hit her stomach before she managed to compose herself. She took long, deep breaths, her hands still clutched onto the wicker remains, and she sang a rhyme in her head that she always used to calm her senses.

One Raven black, a herald of birth.
Two Ravens black, are of childhood and mirth.
Three Ravens black, make me a woman grown.
Four Ravens black, find a mate for me alone.
Five Ravens black, for the child that I bear.
Six Ravens black, see the gray in my hair.
Seven Ravens black, for the end of my life.
I was child, maiden, mother, and also a wife.

The rhyme was silly, a children's game—but it was one of the few things she remembered of her life before the Shadow Marshes, and it was the only thing that stilled the fury in her veins. The nausea faded, and she felt the dark energy retract. Her chest heaved with slow and deliberate movements. The dead grass under her feet crunched. *If only I knew how to channel this power and use it against creatures like Jenny Green-Teeth,* Alleria thought. But she couldn't, she had no control, and not all faerisees were vulnerable to her innate magic; in fact, most of them weren't.

The creature emerged from the water, her face peeking through the wet strands of hair. Jenny was the ugliest creature Alleria had yet encountered. Puffy eyes of a sickly yellow color looked out through the dark hair, and the long, crooked nose covered in warts twitched as she sniffed the air.

"Faru, fari, what is this treat?" The faerisee's smile revealed jagged, greenish-gray teeth that looked sharp enough to chew through bones. "A little lassie, good to eat." Her movements were sluggish, but Alleria wasn't fooled by this act. If she turned to run, the hag would prove surprisingly fast, and she'd grab her.

"I am a child of the Marshes; you hold no power over me." Her voice shook, but she managed to stand her ground.

"Little bite, little morsel, you speak of power, little frog? Little nibble, little petal knows not she speaks to the Mistress of the bog." Her body was misshapen, like the bark of a gnarled tree, and she swayed softly back and forth. Her legs were invisible in the dark water, but her tall frame hovered over Alleria. Her sharp teeth snapped.

"I am the servant of the witch Tumsa. Her protection cloaks me from your appetite." There was a small chance that Jenny would fear Tumsa, as the witch had some power over the Shadow Marshes, but Alleria knew only a few of the Marsh-dwellers felt any true awe for the human witch. Green-Teeth was a direct descendent of the tylwyth tegs, and though Tumsa was powerful—gaining more power on a daily basis—she was also mortal, and many descendants felt a deep contempt for the mortal world.

"Tumsa mumsa, lora-ley. Witches brew makes green skin burn, and cursed words make Jenny Green-Teeth's stomach churn. Such a shame, a tragedy, a loss. Jenny wanted the little nibble but not the fight with her boss. The little bite would have been most appetizing. The smell of her flesh is most tantalizing." She curled her long, gnarled finger with the impressive nail on the end in a "come hither" manner. "Come again, little morsel, and I might not heed your mistress' warning. I will eat you up, flesh and soul, and leave Tumsa with her mourning." Her words still echoed in the air when she sank back into the muddy water of the bog. Jenny purred before her head lowered in the water, and Alleria kept a breath until the green and black head disappeared from view. Every part of her wanted to run, but the sight of her spilled herbs stopped her in her tracks. If she didn't bring them to Tumsa, the old witch would punish her.

The words of Jenny still rang in her ears. The faerisee could decide to come back and eat her after all, and yet she dashed forward and picked up the herbs. A quick scan told her that her herb collection was still complete, and though the basket was broken, it would suffice to carry her finds as long as she held it with care. She ran back to the cottage while she clutched the broken basket to her chest, her heart pounding with a mix of fear and excitement, the adrenaline from the encounter coursing through her body. Bare feet covered in calluses so hard that they almost felt like hooves to the touch dashed over the forest ground. The thickened skin protected her from the sharp rocks and grass of the marshes, and though they were unsightly, she was grateful to have them.

In a matter of minutes, she saw the little cottage lying snuggly in the shadows of the elder tree ahead of her. It was a quaint house made of black wood, and any passerby would probably think it pretty or at least well-built. To Alleria, the building was more than a house or a home; it had been her prison for the past eleven years. No matter where she ran, the old witch inside that house would find her and bring her back. What the witch wanted with her, other than using her as a servant and a student, remained a mystery. All Alleria knew was that there was something special about her seventeenth and her eighteenth years, and as the time drew near to the former, the old witch had become more mysterious.

When the leaves of the marsh trees turned gold and yellow and red a few weeks ago, she knew her seventeenth autumn was near, and every day, she waited for the witch to tell her another cycle had passed. Alleria slowed her pace and her breathing when she was a few yards away from the cottage.

She inhaled deeply right before she opened the door; she hated going back indoors. The heat of the fire hit her like a stifling damp cloth, and she entered the building on her tippy-toes, trying to be invisible as she eased the door shut. The old witch was sitting by the fire, her eyes closed. To Alleria's relief, a soft snort betrayed that Tumsa was asleep instead of scrying. As softly as she could, Alleria walked around the house and placed her gathered finds in the jars where they belonged, silently hoping she would not wake the snoring woman.

"Alleria?" The sharp voice startled her, and she stopped dead in her tracks. "Is that you, child?"

"Yes, Tumsa." Alleria's voice was monotone and dutiful.

So much for crawling into my bedstead unnoticed.

"Did you bring the plants I asked you?"

"Yes, Tumsa, I found them all."

"Good." A silence filled the room, and Alleria was too afraid to move. The witch slowly rocked back and forth in her chair, the sound of the creaking turning the girl's stomach to stone. The muscles in her legs trembled, but she daren't move a step. Tumsa lit her pipe and closed her eyes again.

"The birds saw something today." The creaking sounded louder as the speed of the rocking increased.

Oh no, those damned birds.

"The birds told me that you ran into Jenny Green-Teeth."

"Yes, Tumsa." The girl's voice was soft and strangled, and fear weakened her knees.

"You didn't find this important to tell me?"

"I... I didn't want to bother you... you were sleeping, I..." A large cane flew in Alleria's direction and connected in a dull thud with her shoulder and her neck. She cried in pain and curled into a little ball as each blow produced stars before her eyes. The side of the cane caught her on the ear, and her skin burned with the impact.

"Please," she begged, "I had no idea that Jenny lived in that bog. I was just looking for your siekalot."

"No excuses." The cane emphasized the words with a another whack across the young woman's back. The witch rose to her feet, and Alleria noticed Tumsa didn't need her walking stick.

I swear the old woman is getting younger and stronger every year.

"You lost your temper, did you not?" The tone in her voice was menacing, and Alleria could feel the old witch's mind press against hers. For a moment, the world seemed to shift, and everything around her changed to a strange purple hue as Tumsa's consciousness merged with her own.

"Yes... I lost my temper, but only briefly. I... I couldn't help it. I did as you taught me." The cane stopped its beating, and Alleria suspected that the witch felt her pain.

"I can't be with you all the time, child. You need to control that temper of yours." The old woman searched around in her mind, prodding and probing, and Alleria showed her almost everything—all but a little hidden part that Tumsa couldn't reach, a secret part that was all hers. The old witch retracted from the girl's mind as fast as she entered and left Alleria feeling empty and disorientated.

"Drink your broth and go to bed. Tomorrow is an important day." The witch didn't elaborate further, and Alleria was too scared to ask. Obediently, she walked to the small, black cauldron that hung over the fire. It was the concoction she made that afternoon, only Tumsa had added some more herbs. She scooped some of the broth with a wooden bowl and took her usual place on the floor near the fire. The heat of the liquid stung her lips, but she drank without complaint. The herbs didn't improve the flavor of the food, and though she ate berries and plants in the marshes, Alleria forced the broth down. She was used to getting only a little food—one of the witch's many punishments was starvation—so she ate what she could find and when she could eat it.

"Time is passing, and plans are coming together." The old witch stared into the fire, and Alleria wasn't sure if she was really speaking to her or just thinking out loud. As a rule, Tumsa hardly spoke a word unless she was asking questions or giving direct orders. The witch turned to her, and her eyes narrowed with such an intense glare it sent a chill down the girl's spine.

"You are a big part of my plans, child. Therefore, I need you to be obedient. Can you be obedient, Alleria?"

"Yes, Tumsa." She nodded and tried to keep her mind as blank as her expression.

"Good, because it's very important that you do exactly as I say. I've waited a long time for this, and I need you to be a good girl." Tumsa looked down at her, to her spot on the floor. Her voice took on a gentler tone. "You're almost a woman grown now. You walk the existence between childhood and that of the adult. You have no one but me, Alleria. Everyone that ever loved you in this world is dead. There is no one who will care for you. Remember that." Her gnarled finger pointed at Alleria, then the old witch sighed. "It's time for you to turn in. We shall talk again tomorrow."

Alleria nodded again, fighting the emotions that raged within her. She blinked and finished her broth as fast as she could, after which she slinked away to her bedstead. The thin, wooden doors creaked when she closed them, and her little hole in the wall was cast in darkness. The gentle rustling of straw was a comfort to her, and although the witch was just the other side of the doors, Alleria felt safer in her dark and meager bedstead. It was the only place in this world that was truly hers. This was where she dreamt of heroes from fairytales coming to rescue her from her prison. Not just dashing, handsome princes, but sometimes it would be the fairfolk her mother used to tell her about. Sometimes she dared to dream about conquering the witch herself, but that always came with a deep-rooted fear of being found out. What if the witch would see any residue of those thoughts in her mind? Dreams of being rescued wouldn't be as bad. And yet, the dreams of conquering the witch herself were the most satisfying.

The older Alleria became, the more the dreams would be about handsome men, and they'd kiss her, and her fur would split open and reveal a beautiful princess. The real stories about princes and princesses, the kind her mother used to read to her when she was small, were almost forgotten—but that didn't matter, Alleria made up her own.

She leaned her head against the wood and exhaled. *Those are just dreams. No one will ever come for me.* With a heavy heart, she snuggled under the coarsely knitted woolen blankets. She didn't know what tomorrow would bring, but she dreaded the arrival of the morning the same way she dreaded each new day.

CHAPTER TWO

Loud rain drummed on the thatched roof of the witch's cottage and woke the girl from her fitful dreams. In her sleep, she had fought off a version of Jenny Green-Teeth who was even taller and more monstrous than real life. The shape of the greenish hag hovered over her, teeth as large as Alleria's arm snapping at her. The wicker basket was all she had to defend herself with, but it was broken, and an unseen force gently strummed on it. Still half asleep, Alleria comprehended that the drumming was not part of the dream, but the sound of rain in the waking world. She opened her eyes—thick with sleep—and pushed the doors to the bedstead with enough delicacy to prevent them from making noise. With a smooth movement, she flung both hairy legs over the wooden rim, and Alleria pushed herself off to land with a near-silent grace onto the floor. She froze, hoping that the little sound she made did not wake the old witch, but the soft snoring in the bedstead across from her affirmed that Tumsa still slept. Any moment in the day without the old woman was a good moment.

She made her way to the hearth to relight the fire. During the night, the cold seeped into the cottage, and the autumn chill tingled on her furry skin. If Tumsa woke and felt the cold on her bones, Alleria would surely suffer for it.

She put some of the logs on the fire and added kindling. From the mantelpiece, she grabbed the flint and steel and struck the one against the other. Her cold hands were numb, and it took her several strokes before the sparks turned into a flame. A few sharp jabs from the cold-iron poker ensured that the fire spread to the rest of the wood, and she stood and stared at the licking flames that curled around wood and metal alike.

The faerisees hated cold-iron, but Alleria felt comfortable holding it, as if it strengthened her in some way. In her mind's eye, she used the poker as a weapon to strike the old witch and run for freedom. The temptation was there, but Alleria knew she probably didn't have it in her to kill another person, and she was far too afraid to even try. If she didn't kill the old woman, it would be her turn to retaliate, and Alleria didn't even want to think what Tumsa might do to her.

She had seen what happened if someone crossed the witch of the Shadow Marshes. Not only had she been witness to several horrifying deaths, but it was her job to clean the blood and remains after the witch grew bored with the victim.

Even though the old woman meant to keep her alive, Alleria had faced her own share of torments. She never spared the rod, but that was only part of the torture that Tumsa inflicted upon her. Once, the old hag had cursed her to have large, black boils all over her body that made her skin feel as if she had been beaten with a flaming branch. The boils grew, burned, and itched for days, until they exploded in painful pops and black liquid dripped from the open wounds. Alleria cried in silence that day, too proud to show how she'd suffered.

Another time, the witch took the skin from the girl's right arm for bringing her the wrong herbs, and it took several months to grow back. The pain was so intense that it made Alleria physically ill, and she suffered from a fever for several days. Of course, that did not excuse her from her chores; there was no love or mercy for the witch's young ward. Tumsa's curses were painful, as a rule, and they were always frightening. The memory of them seeped into the girl's nightmares and kept her docile during the long days of captivity—despite the strong temper she was forever suppressing.

The fire roared, warming the cottage nicely. Alleria stepped away from the flames and made her way to the round window to look at the marsh outside. The downpour came from the clouds with such force, it almost reminded her of liquid mist. She hated the rain, always had. A faint memory—one that she could never quite grasp—hid in the back of her brain, and it was linked to the rainfall. Sometimes she dreamt about a man who carried her through a deluge, his strong arms wrapped around her as if she weighed nothing. Someone she knew in a life past, someone who'd brought her to the little cottage and condemned her to this prison... someone who'd left her behind. Yet, whenever she tried to remember the details, the dream always faded.

Her hatred for the downpour ran deeper than the memory alone. When it rained this hard, she was not allowed to leave the house, which was one of the worst punishments Alleria could imagine. Tumsa found it too difficult to scry when nature was at its most violent, and she kept the girl close on days like these. Alleria wanted to go out more than anything, to leave the house and roam through the marshes, as she did almost every day, but instead, she shrugged her shoulders and grabbed the pail and brush. With a nod of her head, she sank to her knees and dipped the brush in the pail to scrub the floor. The witch would sleep for several hours still, so she had time to clean before seeking out the goat in the small pen behind the house and milking it for breakfast. Alleria would make sure Tumsa had her hot porridge when she woke; she would do her very best to please the old woman as much as she could.

As Alleria expected, the old witch allowed her out of the house to milk the goat and get water from the well, but she wouldn't allow her any further freedom. No matter how hard she wished and prayed to the Raven gods, the downpour never let up. The minutes of the day crawled by, and every hour seemed to last forever. Alleria thought about the old woman's words the night before, and she tried to understand what was so special about this day, but nothing seemed out of the ordinary. Tumsa spent the day looking in her ancient book—which she normally only used twice a day for lessons she wanted the girl to learn—and ordered Alleria around to cook and clean.

Alleria was disheartened that the lessons were lengthier than usual, because each time her pace displeased Tumsa, the old witch summoned the cane to beat her.

Come evening time, more fresh bruises and welts covered her skin than usual, and though they were difficult to detect under the coarse hair that grew on her skin, she felt the aches. The light—already dim from the rain—slowly faded, and Alleria rushed to find more candles for Tumsa to read by. She didn't want the old woman upset again, her body already too sore. She scurried through the house and placed enough beeswax pillars near the rocking chair to light up the area, and when she felt satisfied the old witch could read, she prepared the meal for the evening: prickly vine stew. It was Tumsa's favorite, but Alleria hated cooking it. The thorns were difficult to peel from the vines, and she couldn't use a knife, or she might damage the vine itself and let the precious liquids out. The process was arduous and long, and by the end, Alleria always had bleeding fingers.

A knock on the door startled her and she dropped the vine she'd been wrestling with. Her heart pounded with instant adrenaline. *No one knocks on our door. I wonder if Tumsa invited a visitor, and if that's what she meant by a special day,* Alleria thought. But when she looked at the old witch, she saw Tumsa was as surprised as she was. The visitor was obviously unexpected. A moment of silence passed, both women staring at the door, when the visitor knocked again.

Alleria sat frozen, her eyes wide with fear—she did not know what to do or how to respond to this alien situation. After the third knock, the witch raised her hand and snapped her fingers, and the door swung open. In the doorframe, Alleria saw the silhouette of a man. His shoulders were broad, and he wore a long coat and wide-brimmed hat. The rain poured off him in long streams of water, and Alleria experienced a strong feeling of déjà vu. The stranger stepped inside the house with an air of confidence, and Alleria, who didn't know what to do, sought eye contact with Tumsa. To her surprise, she saw an expression on the old witch's face that she had never seen before. *Fear.*

"Halfway Jack, you are in my house." The words spilled from Tumsa's wrinkled lips and sounded more like a gasp than a statement.

"Tumsa, that I am." The man took off his wet hat, and Alleria watched the water that had collected on the rim spill onto the wooden floor. He shook his head and rubbed his black hair with a gloved hand. When he looked up, Alleria had to catch her breath. She'd not seen many men in her sixteen-and-a-bit years of life, but the ones she had seen were not as handsome as this one. Her eyes glanced over the strong chin and straight nose. His skin was a light fawn, and his eyes were two different colors, one as blue as the summer sky, the other as green as the poisonous frogs that lived in the south marsh. A small, neatly trimmed goatee and mustache graced his chin and upper lip. Thick eyelashes and shapely eyebrows crowned his eyes, and there was a crooked smile on his perfect mouth. Alleria's stomach tickled, and she pictured her rib cage opening like the doors of a pen to let out a large cloud of butterflies.

"Quite some weather we seem to be having." He winked at the old witch and shook the coat from his shoulders, revealing the pair of black trousers and the black shirt he wore underneath. Alleria blinked and thought of the pirates in the fairytales she half remembered, all handsome and dashing, and perhaps a little dangerous.

"Why are you here?" The witch's voice sounded cold, and her rigid body language betrayed her discontent. Tumsa was the most fearless creature Alleria knew, and those who visited the little cottage would grovel in her presence, so this curious shift of power left her feeling uneasy. This man, this stranger, acted as if the old hag were in an inferior position. Halfway Jack pulled up a stool and sat by the fire. Steam rose from his damp clothes like breath in cold air, and he rubbed his hands together near the crackling flame. *He sits so close to me, but he doesn't see me.* Alleria averted her eyes and stared at the floor. She felt embarrassed for being so intrigued by the handsome man. *I must not think of him now, but tonight, when I'm alone in my bedstead, I will make up stories about him, and I will dream of that handsome face and strong arms.*

"Why are you here, tylwyth teg," the witch demanded.

Tylwyth teg... he's like me...

The man stretched his tall body, an amused look on his face, and put his hands behind his head.

"You know why I'm here, hag." He turned to Tumsa and smiled, his eyebrows waggling suggestively. "I come for the gosgeiddig."

The witch paled, and she stood from her rocking chair in one brisk movement. Alleria looked at her. The old woman looked brittle, not strong, not even dangerous. The girl's heart leapt a little, and she felt a small flutter of hope. *Can it be that the witch is not as powerful as I thought?*

"I want you to leave this house." Tumsa's voice croaked with hysterics. "You can't have her. She's mine. She was given to me by her father, so she's mine to keep." The words hit Alleria every bit as hard as the wooden cane had. Her eyes widened and she averted her gaze again, this time to the hands that lay in her lap.

"You lie; the gosgeiddig was fathered by a fath tywyll, and not just any. You know who fathered this child, do you not? Do you expect me to believe that he would ever give his child to a mortal witch?" One side of Jack's mouth curled up in a sardonic smile, and he snorted.

"I've raised her since childhood. She is like a daughter to me." The old witch pleaded now, as if she had any care for the girl besides her own selfish needs.

Alleria looked from the witch to the stranger. *Me! They are talking about me.* She didn't move; she didn't even dare to breathe.

"She's seventeen now, is she not? That's how I could find her. She needs to be baptized. All tylwyth tegs do; you know that, old woman." Alleria glanced at his face, and she thought she saw a glimmer of mockery there.

"Her seventeenth year only starts at the full second moon. I was going to baptize her tonight." Tumsa took a step forward, her hands hovered in the air as if reaching out to the stranger. "Please, Jack, this is no concern of yours, leave us be. There will be no harm to the girl." She shifted from one foot to the other, and though her skin was wrinkled, her demeanor reminded Alleria of someone much younger and childlike, like a little girl pleading with her parents. The sight of this confused her; the witch was such a frightening force in her head, and seeing her reduced to pleading was overwhelming.

"I'm taking her." The tone of Jack's voice made it clear he was in control and wouldn't tolerate arguments. The witch let out a whining moan, and she took a few steps back, her gnarled hand gripping the back of her rocking chair for support. The stranger got to his feet, his gaze locked with hers, and it was Tumsa who looked away first.

"You can't do this to me." Her voice sounded soft, barely above a whisper. "I won't let you." She looked at him through her white, greasy hair, but Jack just laughed, his eyes sparkling. For a moment, Alleria could almost see through her own veil of fright, and the part of her mind that she kept so carefully hidden dared to overtake her thoughts.

He's going to take me away. I will be free. Her mind buzzed. The idea of freedom was almost too much to bear. She couldn't even fathom what it would be like to be away from the old witch's tyranny. The cottage had been Alleria's prison for nigh on eleven years, and part of her accepted the predestation of captivity. At the same time, that small part hidden safely in her mind never truly allowed her to believe this was her fate; Alleria never truly lost herself in the subservient role she played to appease the witch.

Don't be too hopeful, Alleria, the voice of caution told her. *You don't know what will happen yet. Tumsa might look frightened, but the old witch won't give you up without a fight.* She watched the man step toward the witch, his impressive height dwarfing the old woman in comparison. Alleria braced herself for the shadows to come, but somehow, they did not.

"How do you plan to stop me? Your magic? Your minions?" He leaned toward her, his face still smiling, but there was a menacing tone in his voice, and the old woman recoiled a little. He straightened his back and wrapped his arms in front of his chest, his expression suddenly serious. "I didn't think so. Not in this place—not in the Borderlands." He shook his head. "You may live here, mortal, and you may believe this is the realm of the faerisees, but in reality, this is the domain of tylwyth tegs. And you may even have power over your little monsters, but you would be a fool to mistake me for a faerisee. You know quite well what I'm capable of. We have crossed paths before, and it did not end well for you."

Tumsa looked away and bit her lip, but Jack wasn't finished yet.

"Your magic has no effect on me, not here, and your minions fear me more than they fear you. You might stand a chance in the human world, but even there you would have to be very clever." His oddly colored eyes glanced around the room and finally settled on Alleria. She cringed and pulled back in her little corner near the hearth. *What could he possibly want from me?* His stare made her uneasy. She felt exposed, and yet a hint of excitement coursed through her veins. Jack's face was gentle, and he smiled at her in a most reassuring manner. Her heart skipped a beat. *He sees me.*

"Don't be afraid." Jack took a step toward her and knelt down near the cowering girl. "I'm going to take you away from here. Would you like that?" Too afraid to nod, Alleria could only dart her gaze toward the witch—the power Tumsa had over her was not yet broken. The old hag returned the stare with intent, and Alleria felt the witch's mind coil around hers. For a moment, she felt the temptation to give in to it, as she always did. A force of habit, one born from fear... but then she blinked, and a strength within her fought back this time. Her mind closed and she refused to let the old woman in. Tumsa's eyes widened in surprise, and she pushed harder. Alleria moaned, but the witch could not penetrate her will.

"Stop that." Halfway Jack's voice cut through the silence in a sharp bark, and Alleria felt the mind retreat a little, but it lingered at the edges of her consciousness, like a wolf stalking its prey from the tree line. Jack turned to Alleria again and touched her cheek. Her lip trembled a little, and she felt empty and overwhelmed. *I don't know what to do...*

The touch of Jack's warm fingers eased her fright a little, and Alleria couldn't remember the last time anyone touched her out of kindness. Her heart went out to this man who knelt in front of her, and for a moment, she believed all her dreams might come true. She wanted to believe.

"I have something for you." His gloved hand fiddled with a string around his neck, and he pulled out a pouch made from animal skin. Alleria's bright blue eyes followed his every movement. She wanted to speak, to say something to him, but she couldn't find the words. She wasn't used to talking to people; she rarely even talked to the old witch.

Halfway Jack turned the pouch upside down above his left hand, and a little necklace fell out. Alleria had seen necklaces before—most of them magic charms. No symbols or pendants adorned the simple chain, yet it was pretty, woven gold with a little button or bulb in the front.

"Let me put this on. Every girl needs some fine jewelry."

Her heart sang. She raised her long, coarse hair so he could place the piece around her neck. The chain felt warm on her skin, and she marveled at the feel of it.

"Alleria..." Tumsa's cry sounded like a warning, and she felt her muscles stiffen. "Alleria, come to me." The breath caught in Alleria's throat. She wanted to obey; she was too frightened not to. She pulled away from the man and dropped her hair, her eyes wide and filled with terror. *How did I dare to dream such dreams? I belong here, with Tumsa.*

"Alleria, is that your name?" The man looked at her with his odd-colored eyes, his voice soothing as if he spoke to a wild animal. "Listen to me, Alleria, you are safe when you're with me. That silly witch can't harm us, not in this place. Her magic is inferior to my kind."

Alleria nodded, but she didn't move an inch.

Does he speak true? She was tylwyth teg, yet the witch could hurt her with her magic just fine. Why would Jack be different?

"You are tylwyth teg, like me." He echoed her thoughts as if he could hear them. "You don't belong here with a human witch, but with your own kind. This is not your place. You should come with me."

A sudden hope blossomed in her chest, and she let her mind indulge in a brief fantasy of a place where she would be welcomed by others like her. A place where she would no longer feel like a prisoner, and where she wouldn't be lonely anymore. Jack's voice guided her, and she turned around to let him fasten the necklace around her neck.

"Foolish child, don't let him flatter you like that." The witch's voice sounded in her head. *"Halfway Jack is far more dangerous than I am, and don't you think for a second that his intentions are good."* Alleria turned to the witch, their eyes met, and panic rose in her stomach, but she managed to fight it.

"I still fear you," she admitted to the witch inside her mind so that Jack couldn't hear her.

"Then obey me," the voice returned.

Alleria almost pulled away again. Obedience was all she knew and all she could remember, but the tiny bit of strength she guarded for all those years rebelled, and she could almost taste the freedom.

"No." This time she did not respond with her mind but with her mouth. The word sounded loud and clear, breaking the silence of the room. With a grim look of determination, she held up her hair for Jack, and her eyes never left the witch. "I don't want to be your prisoner any longer." Alleria was surprised by the venom in her own words, and she did not want the witch to see how sick and frightened she felt.

"You are a dumb child, and you will regret this decision." The witch spat on the ground.

"Don't be angry at the girl, Tumsa." There was a smile in Jack's voice, and Alleria felt his hot breath tickle her neck. "I would have taken her with me even if she chose you. It's just easier this way."

Something in his words made Alleria feel wary, but she knew she'd made her decision. Halfway Jack placed the gold chain around her neck and fiddled with the clasp. Hairs from her neck caught in the woven gold, and she felt a slight pull. The necklace was tight around her throat, almost constricting, and Alleria felt uncomfortable wearing it, but the chain was a symbol of her new freedom.

The man held out his hand to her, and her hands trembled as she took it. He tugged her up and led her toward the door. The witch took a step to block their path, balled fists rested on her hips, and Alleria pulled back, but Halfway Jack held on to her. "It's okay," he whispered, and he glared at the witch. "Step aside, Tumsa. I will bring you to harm if you don't." The old woman was afraid; Alleria could see her wilt a little.

"Remember, Jack, you have the power in the Shadow Marshes and the Borderlands, but when you venture out of them—and I know you will—you *will* lose the upper hand. Perhaps my magic isn't as strong as yours, but your kind has a lot of enemies, and they might be willing to be my allies. I will find a way to harm you, and I will avenge myself because you took that which belongs to me."

Jack sighed and grabbed his wet coat from the table. "We shall see when that day is upon us," he said while he dressed, his face twisted in a wicked smile, and he winked at Alleria. "Don't you worry, old hag, you may get your day yet. But it won't be this day." He put his hat on his head and waggled his dark eyebrows at the young girl. "Are you ready?"

Alleria wasn't as confident, and though she nodded, she cast a fearful glance at Tumsa, whose nostrils were wide with fury.

"Good." Halfway Jack touched the necklace around Alleria's neck, and the little button on the front grew. The gold spilled out in a long trail that expanded until the end of it fell to the ground. Alleria's mouth opened as she gazed in surprise at the strange elongation of the necklace, and at that moment, she realized she wasn't wearing a piece of jewelry... the thing around her neck was a chain. When she looked up, she could see the old witch's wicked and triumphant smile.

"Did you think you were free, child? Did you think you would escape this life of captivity? You know nothing of the world, little girl." Her voice was a harsh croak. "You will never be free; you were not meant for freedom. All you have done is found yourself a new master, and I can promise you that the life he offers will be far worse than the life you had here. You will wish for your old existence in this cottage soon enough."

Tears welled up in Alleria's eyes. If she hadn't been so disillusioned, she would have probably been angry, but now she just felt broken and empty.

The witch turned to the man and pointed a gnarled finger at him.

"And you, Halfway Jack, you don't know what sort of prize you have just claimed. This is no ordinary girl, even for a tylwyth teg—and her temper is dangerous. I *do* know who fathered her, and I know how to handle her, because I studied her sort for a long time. You don't know what you are getting yourself into, vain creature, and I promise you it'll be me who has the last laugh."

Halfway Jack tipped his hat at the old woman with a smile. Her words obviously didn't impress him, and he bent down to pick up the end of the chain.

"Come on, Alleria, we have a long way to go." Alleria stood frozen, but tugs at her chain forced her to walk. With a snap of his fingers, Jack opened the door, revealing the dark Shadow Marsh outside. When they stepped into the darkness, the rain fell heavily on her head, and she felt cold and afraid.

Now that the initial shock had worn off, anger lingered on the surface of her emotions, but she suppressed it. The last thing she needed now was to faint. Halfway Jack set a brisk pace, and Alleria followed, her head bowed with defeat. The little cottage disappeared from view as they walked on in the rain. A mixture of emotions whirled through her mind, and though she felt sad for the chain she wore, a little part of her also felt relief that she got to leave her old prison behind. She refused to believe what was out there could be worse than the horrors she had witnessed within those four walls.

CHAPTER THREE

The rains didn't let up, and the two travelers walked for hours while darkness crept over the land. Every part of Alleria's instinct screamed to run back to the cottage—there were too many dangers in the Shadow Marshes when the sun had set—but her captor walked ahead of her with big strides, giving her no choice but to follow. She struggled to keep up with the tall man. Half walking, half stumbling, she kept her arms wrapped around her, partially to keep the cold at bay, but also to prevent the knuckles of her hand from dragging across the ground.

Halfway Jack proved nimbler than Alleria expected. The way he moved and weaved a path through all the dangerous plants and around the small, hidden bogs made her suspect the tylwyth teg had a form of second sight. No one was this familiar in the Shadow Marshes without some form of taught or innate magic. After several hours, Alleria's feet hurt despite her thick callouses, and her bones were chilled. The fur on her skin gave her some comfort against the autumn wind, but the clothes she wore were not suited for the weather. Determined to be strong, she pushed through her fatigue and followed the rapid pace. The words of Tumsa rung in her memory: *"You will never be free; you were not meant for freedom. All you have done is found yourself a new master, and I can promise you that the life he offers will be far worse than the life you had here. You will wish for your old existence in this cottage soon enough."*

Her thoughts went to the cottage, and she wanted nothing more than to crawl into her familiar little bedstead, not because she longed for the life she left behind, but out of fear for the unknown life that lay ahead of her. Here, in the rain and the darkness, she felt exposed. Who knew what this Halfway Jack would do to her? When he'd knelt before her and offered her the chain as a piece of jewelry, he'd seemed so friendly, which made his betrayal sting even more. Alleria cursed her own naivety, and she hated herself for believing a stranger would come to her rescue.

Halfway Jack stopped in his tracks and turned to the exhausted young woman. She could barely make out his shape through the rain. All she saw was the shadow of the heavy, wide-brimmed hat and dark coat. Jack shouted at her, his voice a low rumble over the sound of the downpour. She leaned in to hear him better.

"Yonder is a cave where we can rest for the night." He waved in a direction ahead of them.

She nodded and put her hands over her eyes to protect them from the rain. Everything on her body was soaked, and the coarse fur felt heavy with the water. Halfway Jack turned on his heel and walked in the direction where he'd just pointed, and Alleria quickened her step once more to keep up with him. Unlike her, the man obviously did not suffer from any fatigue. A few times she almost fell, barely keeping her balance. Her guide did not seem to notice and he drove her on without mercy.

Just when Alleria was about to reach her limit and fall to the ground in exhaustion, she saw the outline of something black through the gloom. It was difficult to make out through the relentless rain and the dark, but she assumed it was the cave Halfway Jack mentioned. The sight of it filled her with new hope that drove away a little of the weariness. Jack fell back a little and offered her his hand. For a moment, she considered not taking it, but then she obediently grabbed hold and allowed him to guide her into the rocky crevice. The shelter was cold, even colder than outside in the rain, and even more than before, Alleria was aware of how thoroughly soaked her clothes and skin were. Her teeth chattered and her body shivered uncontrollably.

"Sit on one of those rocks," he said. The cave was very dark, so Alleria had to feel her way around in the gloom to find the rocks he mentioned. Jack, on the other hand, moved around with far more ease. The whooshing outside was somewhat muted by the stone walls, and she could hear Jack throw several items on the ground near her. Minutes later, a small spark appeared, which bloomed into a fire.

Their surroundings lit up, and Alleria held her breath. Though the cave was not very big in size, it reached so high, making it impossible to see the ceiling. The smoke from the fire rose into the darkness, and she was pleasantly surprised that the air below stayed clear. In the small cottage, the smoke was always obtrusive on cold and rainy days and would get into her lungs and clothing.

"I came a little prepared." Jack spoke to her from across the fire, his mouth twisted in a crooked grin that made him look young and impish. He couldn't have been a more than a few years her senior.

The fire warmed her a little, but not enough to chase away the bone-numbing chill. Jack turned his back and took several steps away from her. He rummaged around at the back of the cave, and when he returned, he carried a large backpack.

"This will hold us over for two days." He opened the flap to the pack and pulled out a rough knitted blanket, which he threw at her. She caught it with clumsy hands and wrapped it around her shivering shoulders. The blanket was actually softer than she expected, and it stroked the areas where the hair on her body was thin or absent.

Jack opened the sack a little wider and pulled out some oddly shaped parcels.

"I don't have a lot of food, but tomorrow we can hunt, and the day after we'll be in Gwahanol, where we can stay in a proper inn." He looked at her with unspoken expectation, as if he wanted her to respond. She gaped at him, unsure how to proceed. The old witch had only allowed her to speak when she was asked a question, so Alleria was a little rusty when it came to the art of spontaneous conversation. At a loss for words, she instead nodded. Halfway Jack pursed his lips together and shook his head.

"Quiet type, huh?" He shrugged and opened the parcels one by one. If the insides contained food, it was the kind that Alleria had never seen before. Or at least, she couldn't remember if she ever came across food like that. Jack handed her a fist-size chunk of one of the morsels, which was dark green and felt grainy in her hand, like a lump of compact sand.

She looked at him quizzically.

"It's food. You can eat it. It's safe," he said with an encouraging smile.

She studied the food, sniffing it. It smelled a little bit of sweet mushrooms. When she squeezed it between her fingers, the whole thing came apart, and she quickly stuffed the crumbling bits in her mouth before they could slip from her grasp. It wasn't unpleasant, a little bitter, but better than some of the things the witch had made her eat. Across the fire, Jack smiled at her again, his face illuminated by the flames. His stare made her uncomfortable.

"You were not at all what I expected." Jack put a bit of food in his mouth, his eyes lingering on her, and Alleria's head sank between her shoulders. "Then again, I'm not sure what I was expecting really. There are only a few tylwyth tegs in this world, and I haven't met many myself." Halfway Jack scratched the back of his neck when he spoke and pursed his lips. "Only pure bloods and faerisees, and there are plenty of those." He bit into his food and shot Alleria a glance. "You're seventeen, so you're too young to have seen a Blood Moon. I can confidently guess that the fath tywyll are probably still unknown to you, am I right? I don't assume that Tumsa would let you cross through the mists?" The flood of words overwhelmed her, and she nodded again. For some reason, she just couldn't find words, and to hide her embarrassment, she stuffed the last of the green food in her mouth.

"You've probably seen a lot of faerisees in that swamp of yours." He leaned back a little and cocked his head at her, his eyebrows raised with curiosity. Alleria swallowed her last bite and struggled to find her voice.

"Yes, there were many... where I lived, I mean." Her cheeks flushed, but the red blush wasn't visible under the thin layer of hair on her face, especially not in the darkness of the cave. Alleria cursed herself for her lack of eloquence.

"Your voice... it's very different from the way you look." His smile revealed a flash of white teeth. "It's very sweet and feminine. It's a funny contrast, because you look pretty fearsome." He chuckled, and Alleria felt her heart sink in her stomach.

Is that how I look? Fearsome? Tumsa never spoke of her appearance, though she had seen the looks the visitors—Tumsa's clients—gave her, if they noticed her at all. There was always a look of shock on their faces, often mingled with disgust. Alleria's appearance bothered her, but because she rarely came in contact with others, she had the luxury of forgetting about it most days. Now she traveled with this man, this beautiful man, and for the first time, she was painfully reminded of how different she was. Her ugliness reflected back at her from his eyes, his smile, and the way he treated her.

Alleria bit her lip and fought the sadness that clung to her chest like a silver swampspider.

"Can you tell me more about the tylwyth teg?" The question slipped from her lips before she realized she spoke, and she clamped her hands over her mouth. Halfway Jack laughed, a low but genuine sound, and he stood.

"I mean..." she tried to explain. "You're tylwyth teg, so you must know more about your kind... our kind, than Tumsa did." She covered her mouth again, afraid that behind his smile lay a cruelness equal to that of the witch. Perhaps he would beat her for her insolence.

Jack sat on a stone next to Alleria and looked at her with his odd-colored eyes. She felt his warm hand around her wrists, and he pulled her hands away from her mouth.

"You don't have to be afraid to speak to me, Alleria. I won't hurt you." Behind the kind smile she saw a graveness in his expression. "That witch wasn't very kind to you, was she?" He searched her face, as if he could find an answer in her expression, but when she failed to respond, he shrugged and let go of her hands.

"To answer your question..." He stretched his arms and arched his back, the bones in his body cracking. "You and I are both tylwyth teg, the mixture of human and fath tywyll blood. But we're not the same, you and I. You are different, and your kind is extremely rare. The fath tywyll aren't the same as humans, where their only difference is culture and variations in pigment. In the Arallfyd, there are thousands of different breeds of creatures, all called the fath tywyll, who often look very different from each other. Most don't even share a similar genetic code, so breeding among different species isn't always possible. Your bloodline is rare, and your father... has mixed his bloodline with that of a human. The only tylwyth teg sired by him that I know of is you. That makes you a very desired commodity."

His words stirred something in her chest, and she lowered her eyes. *Desired.*

"Who is my father?"

"That's a secret I would rather keep a little longer, if you don't mind," Jack said. "And I'll even keep it if you *do* mind."

Part of her wanted to argue, to push the question and make him tell her, but she didn't know how to ask. Instead, she remembered something he had said to Tumsa.

"You spoke of me needing to be baptized?"

He let out another laugh. She noticed how his eyes sparkled.

"Oh… right, I almost forgot about that, good thing you reminded me. It's not such a big deal, really. We lead humans to believe that it's very important, because it works in our favor if they don't quite understand it. It's a ritual we perform to celebrate the passing of time. There are rituals for all four phases, and this one would represent you stepping out of childhood, so to speak."

"Does that mean I'm a woman?"

"I would say so." He looked at her, and Alleria was glad he didn't have any disgust on his face when he did.

"If it's important to you, I can do it now if you want." His hand rubbed his forehead, and he raised his eyebrows. "This is normally the sort of thing your parents should do with you; it has more meaning then."

"What parents? Tumsa told me they were both dead. I barely remember them. Alleria frowned, and she scraped her naked foot across the floor. "I don't know what I want."

The wind played with Jack's hair, and she could feel it tickle the hairs on her shoulder and neck. He shrugged and grabbed the pack, opened it, and pulled out a knife. The blade slid across his thumb, and red blood welled up from the cut. Without much ceremony, he smeared it across Alleria's lips, making her start, and she nearly slid off the rock she was sitting on.

"By the blood of mortal, and the blood of the immortal, you are now entering the circle of new life. May the earth be under your feet and the sky above your head. May your body be fertile and your mind be keen." His fingers weaved a sign in the air, leaving a slight luminescent imprint in the dark before it disappeared, and Jack sat back to wrap a cloth over his bleeding thumb.

"That's all?" Alleria couldn't hide her surprise and mild disappointment. Rituals with Tumsa were more elaborate than this.

"Well, that's the important part of it. I'm sure Tumsa would have dressed you in a white robe and cleansed your body with Elson water, but it's really not necessary." The whole ritual felt rather empty, and Alleria wondered what it was really for and what good it did her, but she was partially relieved. She wiped the blood from her mouth and sat back down on her rock, her eyes fixed on her feet.

Halfway Jack watched her, his expression curious, and Alleria took a deep breath making the most of the situation.

"What are your plans for me?" Her heart felt heavy as soon as she spoke the words, and it didn't help that Jack looked away, his attention focused on the backpack.

He rubbed his neck and stood. He paced a few steps and then sat again. It was obvious to her that he struggled to find the words, and when he finally spoke, she saw a mixture of sincerity and torment on his face. "I won't insult you by lying to you. You deserve better. I plan to take you to Mtumwa, to the slave market." He shook his head. "I'm going to sell you... into slavery. I need..." He hesitated, and Alleria saw his expression harden. "A creature like yourself will fetch me a handsome price, that's all."

Alleria's emotions were muted as she took in his words, digesting them.

I'm a slave. She wondered if this was any different from her life up till now, and yet the thought angered her. The sudden rush of indignation took her by surprise and she had to struggle with the unexpected, overwhelming agitation. There was something unnatural about the way she felt, as if something were urging her anger on. She wasn't sure where the feeling came from exactly, and why it spun out of control, but the emotion was fierce. A voice from the hidden part of her consciousness spoke—no, *screamed*—out. She barely recognized it.

"You don't have to accept this, Alleria." At once she became aware that the inner voice was not her own. Something crossed the barriers of her

consciousness, something dark and familiar. *Tumsa. Oh please, not now! Not when I'm this fragile.* The old witch waited on the border of her mind for a moment of weakness, and this was the perfect time.

"Give into your anger child, embrace it." Her words sang through Alleria's head, and the old witch nudged at the upset in her heart, willing it to grow. Alleria fought, but Tumsa was strong. *How did I not notice she was with me all this time? Am I so used to her being a part of me?*

"One Raven black, a herald of birth.

"Two Ravens black, are of childhood and mirth.

"Three Ravens black, make me a woman grown—" Her voice shook as she muttered the rhyme under her breath, but Tumsa pushed against the anger in her mind. Her head throbbed and she felt the beginning stages of the queasiness. Halfway Jack's face filled with alarm, aware that something was wrong.

"Alleria? Are you okay?" His voice was soft but urgent.

She shook her head, the nausea of anger overwhelming, and she felt the rock she sat on crumble slightly. Thankfully, there were few living things in the cave; the rocks were less affected by "that thing that she did" than plants or animals would be. It proved more difficult to seep the energy from inanimate objects.

"Alleria?"

"Tumsa." The only word that crossed her lips as she felt the curse pull at her consciousness. Jack got to his feet, looking around the cave to see if something else was in there with them. It only took him a few seconds to realize it was the old witch in Alleria's mind. The edges of her vision were spotted with black, and for once she was glad for the curse of the witch. Instead of giving in to her anger, Alleria gave in to the darkness.

"Stay awake, Alleria," Tumsa's voice screamed in her head. But her own curse was too strong, and Alleria slowly sank into the silent oblivion.

CHAPTER FOUR

Warm arms held Alleria when she woke up. The rain had stopped, and the early morning light peered through the opening of the cave. For a moment, a strong sense of disorientation mastered her senses, and she struggled against the arms around her to get to her feet. The figure that held her stirred, and Alleria jumped away as soon as he released her.

"Good morning." On top of a pile of blankets, Halfway Jack leaned on his elbow and grinned at her. "I see you're doing better."

She bit her lip and lowered her head, the memories of the night before flooding back to her. Tumsa had been in her head, which meant she still knew where Alleria was. Not that it mattered anyway, because she wasn't free. She pondered if it really mattered who her master was. Jack had treated her better than Tumsa ever had, so in that regard, there was a difference in who 'owned' her. Alleria didn't know what the future had in store for her. Perhaps she would be enslaved by someone who was fair and kind, but it was just as likely that her new owner would be cruel and vicious, as the old witch had been. Alleria hoped it was the former, but she didn't fear the latter. Aside from dreaming about freedom, she had never actually expected to ever be free. In a way, she had resigned herself to a life of abuse, and it was a mindset that easily numbed any thoughts of hope or rebellion. No matter where she would eventually end up, Alleria would do what she did best: she would survive.

"What happened to you last night?" Halfway Jack rubbed his hands through his hair and gave her a quizzical look, his face fresh from sleep. "You screamed bloody murder and then you fainted. You mentioned the old witch."

Alleria considered telling him about how Tumsa could enter her mind at will, but something deep within decided to keep her secret.

"I... I... have fits sometimes. It's in my head... something isn't... ehm, right. Tumsa makes me broths against these spells," she lied, forcing a smile. He scrutinized her face with squinted eyes. Alleria willed herself not to hold her breath, and after long, agonizing seconds Jack shrugged.

"Is there anything that sets off these fits, or are they random?"

"I-I don't know."

"Well, if you feel anything, let me know, okay?" Agile as a cat, he stood and kicked apart the smoldering pieces of wood, covering them with the cave's dirt. Alleria rushed to help him by clearing up the blankets. Work made her feel more at ease; she enjoyed being useful. Within minutes, they were all packed, and the only evidence of their night in the cave were a few scattered remains of the campfire.

"We have a long trip ahead of us, you and I. The market is at the other side of the Arallfyd and at least the most part of a year's travel away." Jack grabbed the chain around her neck. "So we might as well make the best of it." The chain tugged at her throat, and Alleria felt a bitter taste in her mouth. The cord of the chain was so thin that it looked rather useless, but she was not fooled by appearances. She had seen magical items before, and none of them were what they first appeared. She was convinced that there would be no chance in breaking that chain.

"Come on, then." Jack held out his hand and helped her across the jagged stones of the cave entrance.

To Alleria's relief, the sky looked clear, so the chances of more rain were slim. The smell of wet wood and fresh mud hung in the morning air. Deep pools of rainwater glimmered on the marshy grounds, waiting to be soaked up by the earth. The mud was cold to her feet and stuck to her skin, but Alleria moved on as if she didn't notice.

They walked for hours and never stopped once—not even to eat or drink. Jack simply handed her food or a flask of liquid while they continued their hike. After a few hours, Alleria's feet and back hurt; she was unused to both the pace and the length of their journey, and her body protested. Jack carried the backpack as he walked through the rough terrain of the Marsh with the same ease that a normal man would walk on even roads, while she struggled to maintain her steps, and her rough clothing kept getting ensnared by thorny bushes.

When the third sun was starting to lower in the sky, a sure sign of evening falling, Halfway Jack finally slowed.

"There is a shelter near here where we shall stay for the night." He looked at the sky. "We could've had a few hours traveling yet, but then we would have to sleep with no shelter, and I would rather not sleep out in the open. Not in the Shadow Marshes."

Alleria nodded, and he beckoned her to follow. She was hesitant when he turned north, and her heart picked up a faster beat. After a few more steps, she came to an abrupt stop, the chain strained between them. When he felt the chain go taut, Jack stopped too and turned to his companion.

"Why did you stop?" His voice sounded out with puzzled amusement.

"We can't go that way." The blood drained from her face. Jack raised his eyebrows at her. "That's north," she explained in slow, careful words. Her eyes were round and her lip quivered.

"I know it's north; the shelter is north."

"We're too near the boundary. We can't go further north." Alleria dug her heels into the mud, and her chain remained a tight cord between them.

"The shelter is at the edge of the boundary. We have no other choice, Alleria." His expression betrayed his impatience. "Trust me, it's safer to stay in a shelter, especially around these parts. It's worse here than your part of the marsh."

"Near the boundary are the mists." She refused to listen to him, not wanting to stay near the boundary. Behind that border lived the fath tywyll, and she didn't care if Halfway Jack had met them before; Tumsa had warned Alleria about the creatures from beyond the border, instilling a healthy fear in the girl. Even if they couldn't cross the border except on a Blood Moon, the mists were supposedly dangerous enough.

"We don't have time for this. I want to get to this shelter before dark so I can hunt for our food." Jack pulled gently on the chain to urge her on.

Alleria shook her head and folded her arms, her lips a thin line of determination. As much as she feared being defiant, she feared the mists more.

"I don't want to go there."

A shadow cast over his face, and Halfway Jack didn't hide his annoyance. "Don't be silly, girl." In two large strides, he stood before her, picked her up as if she weighed nothing, and then threw her over his shoulder. She struggled under his grip, but her resistance was in vain; Jack was far too strong, his grip was like iron.

"No, please—" Alleria wanted to say more, but the words were lost to her. The bones in Jack's shoulders pressed hard against her stomach, which winded her, and it was enough to silence her. Her muscles relaxed and she slumped over his shoulder. Tears welled up in her eyes and caught in the little hairs of her cheeks.

A slave—you are nothing more, Alleria; you best remember that.

Between the branches of a Caretree—one of the few allies to man in the marshes—Alleria could spot the dark wood of the shelter Jack had mentioned. It wasn't the kind she had expected; it wasn't so much a hut or a cave, but a platform which lay partially under a natural roof of wood and foliage. She'd heard of these trees but had never actually encountered a living one. The Caretree was supposed to provide safety for those who resided in its branches, but how exactly they worked was a mystery to her. She recognized the purple hue of the bark—Tumsa's rocking chair was made from the same wood. If she squinted her eyes, it looked like a giant, dark purple hand with three fingers and a thumb, which held the platform in its palm. The Caretree stood proudly only a few hundred feet from the barrier of mist. Halfway Jack put Alleria on her feet, turned her around, rested his hands on her shoulders, and bent down to look her in the eye.

"I need you to listen to me, girl."

Alleria nodded and looked away, but Jack put a finger under her chin and forced her to look at him.

"It's important that you follow my lead while we travel. I know you're not used to this—that witch probably didn't let you wander off so far—but I need you to trust me. I know all the places where we will travel, and they are dangerous. Every single one of them. So if you don't listen to what I say, you could get hurt. The last thing I want is for something to happen to you." The words were almost kind, and Alleria's heart fluttered; no one was ever kind to her.

"You are a very important investment for me," Jack added, and the lightness of her heart sank to the bottom of her stomach. *An investment.* Alleria feigned a smile, but she wasn't sure if she managed to look genuine, or if Jack would even know the difference.

He helped her to climb the tree to the platform. The construction was only eight feet off the ground, but the bark was so smooth her feet slipped off when she attempted to climb. Jack lifted her up and allowed her to climb directly onto the platform. When she scrambled to her feet, Jack followed her. With little effort, he pulled himself onto the platform, and Alleria watched his movements in awe. *He moves with such grace.*

"It's best for us to stay off the ground in this part of the marsh. There are a lot of subsurface dwellers around, and they are always hungry for meat." The thought of these creatures made her shiver, and she wrapped her arms around herself.

With a dreamy expression on her face, she looked out over the marshlands. The view was incredible. Alleria could see over the thick, dark gray underbrush that was splattered all over the ground. Trees in all shapes and sizes surrounded them on all sides, and a smattering of brightly colored flowers clustered near their trunks. Far off was a hint of the mists that indicated the border of the marsh. The sight of them struck fear in her heart, and she prayed that the mists would not come closer. They were known to wander, which made them unpredictable, though the Caretree seemed situated at a safe-enough distance.

Jack walked up to a large knothole in the thickest of the three branches and put his hand in.

"*Edrychwch droson ni,*" he said reverently, asking the tree to please look over them in his native tongue. He beckoned Alleria to come over. She obeyed, startling a little when he grabbed her wrist and forced her hand in the hole.

"Say the words."

"*Edrychwch droson ni,*" she repeated, her voice meek and hesitant. Her fingers stroked the inside of the hole, which was as soft as velvet. A soft, purple-white light appeared in the veins of the bark, illuminating the entire tree. It shimmered for a few seconds and then faded again.

"The tree has accepted us at its wards for the night. We've been deemed worthy," he said with noticeable relief. "Sit," he ordered, and she lowered herself onto the wooden platform. Jack took her chain and bound it to one of the branches. "I'm sorry to tie you up, but I need to hunt, and

I don't want you to get any funny ideas. Even though you came along with me willingly, I don't want you running back to Tumsa, or simply escaping and getting yourself killed."

Alleria looked away and refused to respond; she wouldn't give Jack the satisfaction. It wasn't as if she were planning to go anywhere, not here in this unfamiliar place in the marshes. That would just lead to certain death—and she was no fool.

"I will start a fire so you won't be too cold, and then I'll hunt for our dinner."

Alleria pulled her knees up to her chin and wrapped her arms around them, then she buried her face in her soft fur. Jack hesitated for a moment before he jumped off the platform. After a few minutes, he returned with an armful of wood. Carefully, he built a stack at the edge of the platform and lit a small fire.

"Isn't building a fire in a tree dangerous?"

"Not if that tree is a Caretree. These trees have a substantial bit of a magic to them, and I promise you that it will not catch fire." He winked at her and patted her head. She cringed when he reached out to her, as if he were about to strike her with force, and she saw that her reaction made him sad.

"I'm not going to hurt you. I know I'm a stranger to you, and I understand that I'm not exactly your friend, but I promise you that I don't intend to abuse you." She still shied away from his touch, and he threw up his hands and rolled his eyes. "Think of it this way: Would I damage my wares?" Her eyes blinked, and she lifted her head slightly and shook it. He sighed and let his shoulders slump. "Then find comfort in that."

Comfort wasn't exactly what she found, but perhaps a modicum of reassurance.

Jack picked up his backpack. From it he pulled a long, sharp knife then weighed the balance in his hand.

"The tree will protect you while I hunt. I'll be back in an hour, so try to entertain yourself without me." He leapt from the side of the platform, disappearing once again to leave Alleria alone by the fire. The forest was cast in an eerie silence except for the low-moaning wind that rustled along the leaves and brushes. On the platform, the fire crackled, and little specks of flame danced into the air that glittered like fireflies. Alleria stared at their twinkling ballet, but they were hardly a distraction for the tug-of-war of feelings that raged in her head and heart. The fatigue she had been suppressing all day was dragging her down, and part of her was grateful for the alone time. Yet, simultaneously, she felt exposed in this strange place all by herself.

With heavy limbs, she pulled the backpack Jack had left behind toward her and began to unpack the blankets. She picked the blanket she had claimed as her own and wrapped it around her before she found a comfortable place to sit against one of the thick branches. There was something peaceful about this tree; she might not know all it could do to protect her, but she felt safer here than she had on the ground. With a sigh, she nestled closer against the bark, her tired mind running free with thoughts. She wondered why Jack and the old witch were so interested in her. She couldn't imagine her getting a high price on a slave market at all. She didn't possess any talents, wasn't particularly strong or fast or beautiful. She had a decent set of brains, and she was a good student, but her knowledge was limited to what she had learned from Tumsa and the Shadow Marshes, which wouldn't really be of use to most people. There was some magic to her, sure, but she couldn't control it and she couldn't see how it would be of any use to anyone else. They could have her magic for all she cared.

Alleria just longed to be a normal girl. She wondered who her father was, if perhaps it was because of him that she was so coveted. Thinking of her father led her mind to meander to the image of her mother, and Alleria wondered if she was still alive. There were a few very vague memories that she held, but she didn't know what parts of those were true and what she had made up.

She rubbed her nose with a long, furred finger and inhaled the scent of the burning wood. The sparks that fell on the platform quenched instantly with a hiss, as if they had fallen into water.

A noise like a *woosh* followed by a *thump* grabbed her attention, and she swallowed a scream when a horned firetegu landed on the platform.

So much for the protection of the Caretree.

Alleria clumsily jumped to her feet and instinctively wanted to run. She knew some about the firetegu, though she had always managed to stay clear of them; they were known to breathe fire on their victims and eat the charred corpses. Before she leapt off the platform, she remembered the chain around her neck and came to an abrupt stop. With a fearful glance at the lizard, which was the size of a wolf, she made a cautious way to the branch where the chain was tied. The knot looked simple, but her fingers couldn't pry it open.

"What are you doing?" The voice of Halfway Jack sounded across the platform, and Alleria turned around to face him, her expressions a mask of panic.

"Firetegu!" she cried. "We have to run. Please help me; I can't get away if I'm tied up." To Alleria's mild annoyance, her captor didn't spring into action. Instead, he laughed at her.

"You mean this guy?" Jack kicked a heap of lizard flesh at his feet. It was dead.

I feel so stupid.

"These guys are great to eat." He pulled the creature toward the fire and sat on the floor. He cut a big chunk off the dead animal, then he pulled a thin stick from the stack of unburned wood and sharpened the end into a point. Nimble fingers pushed the meat onto the stick and handed it to the baffled girl.

"Do you know how to cook with a stick?"

Alleria nodded, her cheeks still warm with the flush of embarrassment. She took the meat and held it above the fire, slowly rotating the stick to cook everything evenly. Within minutes, a tantalizing smell tickled her nostrils, and Alleria's stomach growled in approval. The tension of the incident slowly ebbed away, and she found she could relax again.

"Tell me about your life, Alleria, so that I can get a better sense of who you are and who I'll be traveling with."

"There's not much to tell," she confessed. The conversation made her uncomfortable. She wasn't used to banter, but she had to admit it was pleasant to be noticed by someone else.

"I grew up with Tumsa at the cottage. It wasn't a very exciting life. She taught me about herbs, potions, and faerisees. Most of my days just comprised of going through the Marshes, finding herbs. I would bring them back to the cottage and do my chores like cooking and cleaning. Nothing more. Tumsa did not like me to speak to her customers, and they never really wanted to speak to me. I don't know many people, and I've never done anything of note."

The way his eyebrows lightly arched betrayed his curiosity. "What about your life before the witch?"

She plucked a piece of floating ash from the fur on her knee and sniffed. His questions were more difficult to answer than the man must have realized.

"I barely remember that time. I have this image of my mother in my head, but to be honest, I don't know if she really looked like that, because I don't remember her face. My father is even more of a blur. I can't remember him hardly at all. The things I do remember are mostly just feelings I had or situations I was in. Like, I don't remember my mother clearly, but I do remember her telling me stories. It's something I've held on to because I would tell those stories to myself at night when I lay in bed. I've always loved stories." Her chest expanded as she took a deep breath, and she stared at the stick she still rotated. Her hand was so near the fire that the heat was only just bearable; it licked at her skin.

"Do you remember how you got to the witch's cottage?" Jack pushed another piece of wood between the flames and turned his own stick—which he wasn't holding but had propped up between several large stones—to roast the raw side.

"No, all I remember is rain, a lot of rain. I think my father drove me to the witch, but I'm not sure. The witch told me both my parents are dead." She bit her lip again and curled the fingers of her free hand around some of the thick hair on her leg.

"Do you believe her?"

"I don't know. I don't want to believe her, but part of me does. Not that it matters, does it? If I'm going to be sold at a slave market, I'll never see my parents again even if they are still alive."

Halfway Jack frowned but said nothing. There was an uncomfortable silence, and Alleria couldn't stand it. She prattled on.

"My memories are probably false as they are. I don't remember having fur when I was little, so there's probably some wishful thinking inter-mingled with reality."

I remember blood, but I'm not sure that's accurate either, she thought, but kept it to herself.

Jack nodded slowly, but she wasn't sure he heard her by the way his eyes were glazed over with a distant look. He snapped out of it with a shake of his head and then turned to her, his odd eyes narrowed.

"You said you didn't really talk to any of Tumsa's clients, but did you have any friends in the marsh itself? faerisees, maybe?" He waved his hand with an air of nonchalance and then leaned in with an impish smile on his lips. "A boyfriend perhaps?" Jack winked his blue eye as he said the word boyfriend, and Alleria's mouth fell open. She opened and closed her lips several times, as if she were a fish gasping for air, and then she wrinkled her nose at him.

"Do you mock me?" As soon as the words left her, she regretted her impertinence, and per habit, she clapped her hands before her mouth. Fear circled her stomach like black smoke. *He will surely beat me now.*

Jack just shook his head. "I'm not mocking you." He took her hands from her mouth. "Why would you think that?"

Alleria lowered her hands and pulled at the hairs on her arm, her eyes averted.

"Are you blind?" Tears threatened to well up in her eyes, but she repressed them. "I'm a monster."

Jack cocked his head at her, his eyes narrowed as if he were trying to see something that he hadn't noticed.

He shrugged. "You don't look like a monster to me. Beauty is in the eye of the beholder, Alleria. We are tylwyth tegs, and some of us will look very inhuman. To a human, you may be revolting—in all fairness, my particular kind of tylwyth teg doesn't find you particularly attractive either—but to one of your own, you could be the most alluring creature to walk this world. Don't sell yourself short."

His words took her by surprise.

There could be others like me.

The thought of this made her heart flutter again. The idea of not being alone was strangely hopeful.

Would I find creatures like myself alluring, though? I think not.

Alleria looked up at Jack and feigned another smile.

"Perhaps you are right," she lied.

He pursed his lips, still staring at her. "I'll tell you one thing, you may not be much to look at for me, but you have the most beautiful eyes I've ever seen." His smile was warm and genuine, and he pulled his gaze away from her too soon. Alleria touched her cheeks, which felt hot and flustered.

"I think we can eat that now." He pointed at the stick. One side of her meat was a little scorched because she had forgotten to keep turning her stick during that last part of the conversation, but the flesh was still soft and tender to eat. It tasted delicious, and Alleria was surprised by the rich, gamy flavor of the deadly creature. Halfway Jack cut another piece of meat off the carcass and held it over the fire.

For a moment, Alleria forgot she was a captive, and for that brief time, she was a companion on the road to a distant land. The prospect of the slave market worried her, but for now, she was content to be away from the old witch. She hadn't felt the beating of the stick for several days, and her bruises and wounds were starting to heal. For the first time in eleven years, she relaxed.

CHAPTER FIVE

Something woke Alleria from a deep sleep, and she rubbed her eyes and sat up. Halfway Jack was perched on the edge of the platform, crouched like a cat, his body tense as if he were about to leap. Alleria pushed the covers off her warm body—the contrast of the cool air giving her goose bumps under the thin fur—and walked toward him.

"Go back to sleep." His voice sounded brusque and had none of the friendliness it had only a few hours ago.

"What's going on?" She tried to peer over the edge of the platform, but Jack's arm shot out and pushed her back. She stumbled backward a few steps, an expression of confused hurt on her face.

"Trust me, you don't want to see this. You're safe here; just go back to sleep. I'll protect you." Then he half turned. "Please." Resigned to his order, Alleria was about to turn around and go back to bed when a shadow appeared behind Halfway Jack. The girl's reaction was fast.

"Behind you!" she cried, the adrenaline in her body pumping instantly. Jack swirled around with a speed that she'd never encountered before; his movements were just a blur of motion. The knife he held in his hand reflected the light of the second moon. Something yelped, and the platform shuddered.

"Alleria, move to the middle of the platform," Jack barked and she obeyed. He slowly took a few steps back. "They've touched the tree now." Alleria had no idea who "they" were. Her body trembled with cold and fear.

The platform shuddered a second time and she heard a loud creaking. All around Alleria there was movement. The tree came to life, the branches swaying and folding into each other, surrounding the platform until they turned it into what looked like a cage. But the movement didn't stop there. The branches expanded and twigs shot out the sides and hooked into each other. A roof and walls covered the platform and the whole construction reminded Alleria of a wicker basket.

"Jack... what's going on?" Her voice squeaked with terror.

"It's the Caretree, it's aware that we're under attack. We are the target, and it can sense the malice in the creatures below, so it reacts." He ran his hand along the wood in a manner as one might stroke a horse.

"Will it harm us?" She grew up around magic—human magic that involved rituals and spell casting—but she had never witnessed the natural magic of a Caretree before.

The only magic I know ends in blood and death.

"No, this is a pretty safe place. There are only a few types of magic that can penetrate the shield the tree makes. No natural phenomena can harm it, not even fire."

"What about those things outside?"

"Those were woodland wargs. We're safe from them here, but I worry about how long they will persist in their hunt. The tree provides a little food and liquid for its occupants, so we'll survive, but I don't want to be stuck in a tree for several days." His face was shrouded in semidarkness, and Alleria squinted to see his features. She didn't mind staying in this tree for longer—after all, there was no rush for her to end up at the slave market—but the idea of being trapped while they were under attack unsettled her. Her instinct told her to run.

Alleria knew of woodland wargs—large wolf-like creatures with matted, black fur and gleaming, red eyes that walked on either two or four legs. Troupes of them occasionally passed through the Shadow Marsh during their mating season. They were aggressive and certainly dangerous, but they were more territorial toward males than they were to females, so Tumsa and Alleria never really suffered from their presence. The wargs ignored the women, and because of that, the old witch never felt the need to teach Alleria how to defend herself against them.

"Can we get out of here?"

"There is always a way," he said, stepping into the light of the fire that miraculously was still smoldering. His face brightened, and in the gloom, she could see him wiggle his eyebrows at her. Alleria was amazed that, despite their situation, Jack could still smile.

"Stay here. I'll come back for you." He put the knife between his teeth and fell to his knees, searching for something that Alleria couldn't see. After a few seconds, Jack found what he wanted, and he took the dagger from his teeth and pushed it between two planks. The dagger stood upright, and Halfway Jack hit the hilt with the palm of his hand. A piece of wood came away, revealing a dark opening. He stuck his hand in the tree, and near him a hatch popped open.

"Stay here," he repeated and slid down the darkness of the hatch.

It's not like I have a choice, she thought, exasperated, and she tugged on her chain that was—despite all the morphing of the tree—still stuck to a branch. She didn't even know how she was ever going to get loose now, since part of the bark seemed to have swallowed the end of the chain.

The noises outside grew louder—deep, hollow barks and low grunts echoing through the quiet of night. The gods only knew what would happen to her if the woodland wargs got the better of Jack.

Would I remain here in this tree until I die? Or would the magic of the tree release me? Alleria rested her head against the wood and sucked her bottom lip between her teeth. *My death would take only a few days.* Jack mentioned the tree would produce the necessities to survive, but she could not detect any indication of where this nourishment would come from or how to demand anything from this magical sanctuary.

Alleria stamped her foot and sat back against the stem. After a few minutes, restlessness settled over her and she sprang back onto her feet. With large steps, she paced through the confined space, her hand touching the woven walls and her head shaking in thought.

What if this would be a good opportunity for her to escape?

As if in response to her thoughts of freedom, Alleria felt something slither across her consciousness. *Tumsa.* The alien mind nudged at her own, but she noticed it wasn't as strong as it had been the day before.

The old witch tries to see through my eyes, but she can't. Perhaps it's the distance between us after all. Maybe if I get far enough away from her, she'll lose her hold over me.

The mere thought filled Alleria with hope, though she was cautious with her excitement. There could be a multitude of reasons why Tumsa wasn't in control of her mind yet. Maybe the old witch didn't try hard enough, or maybe she was still worn out from the previous attempt. The tree could be another cause of the weakness, and perhaps the magic of the shelter prevented Tumsa from a proper attempt.

Alleria only had basic knowledge of magic, so the only certainty she had was that it was unpredictable. Overwhelmed by hope and fear, she succumbed to an urge to run, and her gaze settled on the end of the chain again. She exhaled and moved toward it to see if there was any chance to unfasten it. Her fingers pulled and twisted the chain, but the tree held fast. Alleria's cheeks were flushed and she felt the blood rush in throbbing beats through her ears. A mixture of emotions blossomed in her chest, and she pulled a little harder on the small, metal links, her heart pounding louder with each beat.

"Please, before he comes back..." Alleria begged no one in particular as she fiddled with the chain. The tree responded with a shudder. The branch that held the chain retracted into the wicker of the walls, and the metal fell to the floor. She needed a moment to catch her breath, the excitement making her dizzy, but she steeled herself and grabbed the chain. With round eyes and open mouth, she examined the end of it, her brain working rapidly. It was long and thin, so she wrapped it around her waist to keep it out of her way.

Unsure of what to do next, she hesitated for a brief moment, and then she ran for the hatch. Before she opened it, a memory blossomed in her mind's eye, painful and vivid.

I ran away before.

The memory was enough to falter her determination. Alleria took a step back and considered sitting again, but she didn't. Instead, she hovered near the hatch.

This is different. I'm not a child anymore. And I'm already almost free.

With a dramatic gesture, she opened the hatch and squatted near the hole where Halfway Jack had disappeared, her face betraying the conflict she struggled with.

What if it's the tree blocking Tumsa, and outside of it her magic works fine? What if she finds me? She stood once more and walked back to the wall. Her paces to the hole were slow, her mind racing as she tried to make sense of her mixture of elation and fear. *Where will you go, Alleria? Where will you hide from the witch?*

Then she stood as straight as her disfigured body would allow. Without giving herself more time to think about it, Alleria jumped through the hole. She had expected to be in a free fall, but instead she landed on something hard, and she found herself on a large, steep slide. Gravity pulled her down the chute; the rises and falls of her stomach were something she'd never experienced before, and she wanted to either sing or vomit—she was unsure of which. The woodland wargs crossed her mind, but she felt little fear for the creatures. They were dangerous, yes, but usually only when provoked or really hungry. Unless you were male, and then your scent automatically provoked them. They had bad eyesight and seemed to struggle with picking up female pheromones, so Alleria believed she had a real chance.

Her slide ended roughly at the bottom of the tree; the grass and dirt impacted with her skin when she landed. A slight hint of gray in the sky and the waning light of the second moon betrayed that it was nearly dawn. There were no movements around the tree, but in the distance, she heard sounds of fighting.

Overwhelmed by a mad sense of recklessness, she ran with a song in her heart. Her legs moved faster than she could ever remember them moving, and she barely felt the rough terrain under the thick soles of her feet. The sounds of struggle faded into the background as Alleria darted between bushes and trees, and a gentle, cold breeze played with the hairs that covered her body.

At first, she busied herself with thoughts of her escape, but slowly, the dangers in the Borderlands overwhelmed her mind. Doubt cast a black shadow on hope, and her pace slowed. She had no plan, did not know what to do or where to go. There was no one out here for her, nothing to fall back on.

A wonderful, sweet scent lay thickly in the air, and the mere smell of it made her mind relax almost involuntarily.

It's still pretty dark, but daylight will be upon me soon, and I—Alleria's thought was cut off when the world around her tilted at a nauseating speed. Her head and back hit the muddy earth before something pulled her upside down, dangling her by the legs. The impact made her skull and bones ache, and she was too dazed to struggle against the bonds around her feet. The world faded in and out of blackness, and Alleria struggled to stay focused on her surroundings.

Only when something wet and cold closed around her body did her eyes flutter open and her brain snap back into consciousness. She didn't know what was happening; all she knew was that something had her, and her instinct kicked in. That sweet scent tickled her nostrils once more, even more pungent now, but Alleria was no fool; she could smell the rot and death hidden underneath. She struggled. Her hands reached out and felt the strange structure that enfolded her.

Rubbery and sticky...

She inhaled deeply.

I know this smell.

It dawned on her what held her in its grip: a marsh trap—which was a large plant that lured creatures with its intoxicating, sweet scent and grabbed them with a lasso-type construction hidden on the ground. *Pretty stupid to fall for that, Alleria,* she scolded herself inwardly. She stayed calm; the old witch had taught her what to do in the unlikely case she were ever trapped by one of these things. She knew she had time, as the digestion process of this plant was slow, and if she kept her head cool and managed to free herself within the next seven hours, she would be fine. It took a while for the digestive juices to kick in.

Lack of oxygen would be a more immediate danger. The plant's skin was porous, which would at least give her a modicum of oxygen for the next few hours, but it was creating a coating on the inside to protect itself from the digestive fluids. Once that process was complete, there would be no more oxygen, and that would cause her to pass out and slowly choke to death. This dreaded shrub would devour her corpse over the next few weeks. The unfortunate thing about the plant was that the material it was made of was strong, and difficult to destroy, without a good weapon.

Now think back to your lessons: These plants are very sensitive, but to what? Alleria took a deep breath and tried to recollect what Tumsa told her.

Salt, they're sensitive to salt. It dries up their digestive liquid. This knowledge would have been extremely helpful if she'd had any salt on her person. Alleria carried nothing, just the clothing on her back and the chain around her neck. No weapons, no salt... she needed to be more creative.

She still dangled upside down and was still a little stunned from the blows to her head, which made thinking difficult. The first things she would need to tackle were the cable vines around her ankles. If she could get them to loosen somehow, she could free her feet and set herself the right way up. The plant had left her some wiggle room, only fully enclosing her feet and ankles, but it gave her enough space to stick out her hands. Pulling herself up by her stomach muscles proved to be too great a feat, so she tried to push herself off. Her fingers gripped the slimy sides of the plant, and the sticky beginnings of the digestive layer tingled her skin.

The plant's slippery structure made it almost impossible for her to get a proper grip, and each time she made progress, she would lose her grip and end up dangling—blood rushing to her head. Alleria refused to give up, so she repeated her movements. Her tendons burned with the effort and her head spun. Fatigue and discomfort turned to panic, and Alleria felt her calm and her lessons slip from her mind.

I don't want to die in this plant.

She took a deep breath, sickened by the smell of her prison, but she needed to get her anxiety to subside, and she needed to rest her muscles. When she felt she was once again in control of her body and mind, she tried again. Calmer this time, less frantic.

After several efforts and what felt like an eternity, she managed to pull herself toward her feet. With strength born from desperation, she held onto her ankles with both hands, her body trembling. Alleria propped herself up against the wall of the plant—the slight sting tingling at her back this time—and there was a lot less room for her to move around up here, but at least it took some of the tension away from her stomach muscles. She bent her knees, which made her legs ache with the force. There was no way she could hold this position for a long time.

The vine that held her was thick and sturdy, and the coarse texture imprinted in the naked skin of her palms. She attempted to break the vine, but it was too strong. She was not discouraged, though; she'd stripped vines like this before, and knew it just took time and effort. Her nails were thick and strong. Frantically, she peeled at the outer layer, her body shaking with the effort to stay upright. After a while, she managed to tear a miniscule strip from the vine. Her body ached with the strain of her awkward position and the digestive goo was definitely getting stronger; it made her skin burn under her rough-spun clothes. Alleria fought the temptation to let go and dangle, to give up the struggle.

This takes too long; at this rate I'll pass out before I'm halfway. Her chest heaved with deep breaths, and she continued to peel. The task proved slow and arduous, and she had to change her body position often, redistributing her weight, or she would just slip and fall again. With each moment that passed, it became a little harder to breathe.

Maybe I have less time than I thought.

Concentration made way for panic, but Alleria fought it this time. Hysterics would do her no good—she needed to stay focused—and with determination, she dug into the vine and pulled away a new layer.

"That's quite a mess you are in, Alleria," a familiar voice echoed through her head. *"If you promise you'll come back to me, I'll save you."* Alleria almost fell when she heard it, but she gripped the vine tightly enough to keep her balance.

"Tumsa?" she muttered. The mere sound of the old woman's voice caused her head to bow in obedience for a brief second, but then she furrowed her brow with determination. "No." Alleria's nails peeled at the vine again, her heart pounding but her resolve made of steel. Suddenly, she thought of something.

Bad things happen when I get angry. It's worth a try.

The voice of Tumsa cackled in her head, but she didn't listen to her words; instead, she used the old woman's image to fuel her anger.

Now, if I can only stay conscious long enough to get out of here.

The anger started in her stomach and rose, like a kettle filled with black, bubbling water. It was such a release to let out the pent-up emotion that she'd been repressing; the wrath flowed out of her pores like a flood. The plant around her shuddered, and a strange, stale scent wafted through the organism. Nausea welled up in her stomach and drowned out the anger with sharp pains, but she pushed through it.

She thought of Tumsa and of her evil cane. Alleria pictured the reflection in the water, her sad, bucktoothed face covered in hair. And when that wasn't enough anymore, she thought about how she was abandoned by her parents. How her father gave her to a witch before he died.

The anger surpassed the feeling of nausea, but instead of letting go, the plant struggled against her power. The pod around her loosened a little, but the grip on her ankles tightened even more.

Fresh air poured into the plant, enough to distract Alleria from her determination. Her loss of concentration was enough for the familiar black spots to develop in the corners of her eyes. *Please, Alleria, focus.* She tried to stay conscious, but the darkness won. The last thing she remembered as her body slackened was a sense of falling.

CHAPTER SIX

The sunlight woke her, or perhaps it was the presence of the figure standing only a few feet away from her dangling body. She blinked against the bright sun, her head throbbing as if an iron mallet were beating against the soft tissue of her brain, and to her dismay, she understood that she was still upside down. The blood tingled in her cheeks as gravity pulled at her insides.

At least she wasn't dead.

"You know how long it took me to locate you?" The voice belonged to Halfway Jack, and Alleria could hear from his tone that he was genuinely displeased with her. "I almost didn't find you at all. If the awful stench this plant makes hadn't caught my attention, who knows what would have happened." Jack pulled away one of the large leaves of the plant's maw. "What did you do to this thing, anyway? It looks rotten." She saw his eyes glance over the plant. "No, not rotten... something else. I can't quite put my finger on it."

"Please cut me down. My head hurts, and I can't feel my legs." Alleria's voice sounded hoarse, her throat thick and tongue dry. Jack cocked his head so he was almost face-to-face with her. His features were pinched with a mixture of amusement and annoyance, and the dangling girl couldn't tell how he felt.

"I'm rather upset with you for running away."

"I'm sorry. I won't do it again."

"I won't give you the chance to try again, you can be sure of that." Jack straightened up and produced a knife from the folds of his clothing. A few cuts, and the plant released Alleria from its grip. She braced herself for the fall, but Jack moved with uncanny speed and caught her in his strong arms.

"I thought if I treated you in a good way, you would stay near me, and I wouldn't have to chase you or keep you trapped. Just because you are a slave, that doesn't mean I feel comfortable treating you as such, but if you give me no other choice... then I will treat you accordingly." He bit his lip and shook his head slowly. "Your life with the witch was worse than your life with me, Alleria." His odd-colored eyes seemed to bore into hers, and she felt the skin of her cheeks burn.

He did not save you from the old witch, he just stole you, she thought defiantly.

His hand slid past Alleria's dress to her waist, and he pulled at the chain wrapped around her midsection. With a sigh, he wrapped the end of the chain around his right wrist. He puckered his lips and blew gently on the metal. The chain immediately formed a band around the joint, and he held it up for her to see.

"Now we are bound. I didn't want to do it this way, but you will stay close to me, at all times. I will not take my eyes off you, understand?"

"Yes, I understand." Alleria bowed her head. Jack sighed again, and he walked in the southern direction, toward the borderland town of Gwahanol.

The orange and pink colors of dawn were making place for the bright light of morning when the two travelers arrived at the borderland town. When Alleria was a young girl, she lived in a city, or at least she thought she had. Memories of that time came to her in shards over the years, and she always wondered which parts of those recollections were true and which were constructed by her imagination. She often pondered if her paternal home was really the castle she remembered, and if the pet fairy dragon that slept at the foot of her bed at night was an actual living creature or just a stuffed toy. Childhood memories were tricky, especially if there was no one to remind you of what really happened.

For eleven years, she lived in a tiny world that consisted of a cottage and a limited part of a marsh, so when she walked into the town of Gwahanol, which was one of the greater merchant towns in the land, the grandeur overwhelmed her. There must have been a hundred or more houses that circled the large, neatly cobbled town square. The buildings that stood in the center were partially made of stone—an indication of the wealth of the citizens. Gwahanol was a lively place where people bustled through the streets carrying baskets with food or wares. Mothers shooed their offspring through the crowds to get them to the local school in time.

As much as Alleria enjoyed seeing the people, she wasn't used to so many stimuli, and all the movement around her felt intimidating. The sounds that echoed through the streets were louder here than those in the marsh, where all you heard were the songs of birds and insects, and the occasional calls of other beasts.

Alleria followed Jack closely, her hand resting on his coat, and when a sight or sound startled her, she dug her fingers into the fabric. Halfway Jack led them to a large building decorated with ornately carved purple signs.

Tumsa had taught Alleria how to read, so she could make out the words "The Sultry Scullery Maid" painted in curly, gold letters.

"Tonight I'm sleeping in a real bed." Halfway Jack smiled and stretched out his arms as if he wanted to hug the very building itself.

The door opened before Jack even had a chance to knock, and a plump woman in a revealing, red dress stood in the opening, her chubby hands resting on ample hips that spilled out under diaphanous fabric. A strong, honeysweet scent surrounded the short frame.

"My word, if it ain't Halfway Jack come to grace us with his presence." The woman slapped the side of her thigh, causing her large hips to wobble, and laughed. To Alleria, this female was the strangest creature she had ever seen. The woman's provocative dress and darkly applied makeup were completely alien to her.

Bright green colors accentuated the woman's small eyes, and the prominent lips were painted like plums. Flaming red curls, almost the same color as her dress, were adorned with purple and yellow feathers. Joy spread on the round face, but Alleria saw something else in the features too—something keen, and perhaps even cunning. The way the woman licked her lips made her uncomfortable.

"Madame Lubrique, it's always a pleasure to see your shining face." Halfway Jack grabbed the chubby hand and kissed it, his gaze never leaving the colorful lady's small, painted eyes. In response, the woman covered her mouth and cheek as if she were blushing, only she was not. Then she stretched out her hand and let her painted crimson nails run across Jack's face with a teasing gentility.

"You're a good boy, Jack. I'll tell the girls you're here." The woman produced a fan from her ample bosom and opened it with a flick of her wrist. "I expect you'll be wanting to see Lola again?" Jack tipped his hat in reply. The woman nodded and turned on her heel. Halfway Jack followed her inside, dragging Alleria along.

The inside of the building appeared even more impressive than outside. Fabric adorned everything—the floor, the walls, even the ceiling—all colored in warm red, pink, and gold hues. On plush sofas loitered gentlemen with their shirts open, accompanied by scantily clad women or young men.

Blood rushed to Alleria's cheeks; she knew enough of reproduction to get a vague sense of what was going on, but not enough to fully understand what sort of place this was. Alleria had pieced together her knowledge of human courtship with the way animals and faerisees would mate. In the marsh, there had been plenty of creatures for her to learn from—some were similar to humans—and it was part of the lessons that she received from the old witch, who taught her the magic properties of intercourse as well as the natural ones. But she'd never been this close to any humanoid form of sexuality, and despite her naivety, Alleria could not deny picking up on the erotic tension in the room.

Madame Lubrique clapped her hands, and girls fluttered toward her from all sides. Dressed in the same diaphanous fabrics as the Madame, the girls looked like colorful birds to Alleria. Their bosoms peeked out from above tight corsets, skin light like cream or dark like the deepest marsh pools. The girls came in all shapes and sizes, but the one thing they had in common was that they were each lovely and gracious, which made Alleria feel like a monster in comparison.

A full-figured girl with golden curls and large, hazel eyes stepped forward, and she wiggled her fingers at Halfway Jack as a form of greeting. Her face was pretty, and she wore the same striking colors as Madame Lubrique on her eyes and lips.

"I've missed you," she said with a coquette tone of voice, and Jack leaned forward to kiss her on the cheek.

"It's always nice to see you again, Lola." There was an expression in his eyes that Alleria had never seen before, which both frightened and excited her.

Madame Lubrique looked over Jack's shoulder, and for the first time, she noticed his young companion.

"What did you bring us, Jack?" Her voice was not unkind, and her expression betrayed her curiosity.

"This is Alleria. I'm taking her to the Mtumwa slave market."

The girls tittered a little, and one or two shot Jack a reproaching look. Lola looked at the girl with open disgust, and Alleria wanted to hide under a rock.

"What is it?" Her voice was sharp and high-pitched, and her perfect little button nose wrinkled. Alleria felt an instant dislike for the girl, but she contained her humble stance and turned her eyes to the ground. She had been treated worse in her young life.

"It's a girl. Now you leave her alone." Jack looked at the girls and shook his finger at them, a scolding smile on his face. "I'm not here to get your opinions about my profession, ladies. I'm here for other things." He shot them a confident smile, and from the pocket of his black coat, he produced a gold coin, which he flipped at Madame Lubrique. The plump woman grabbed the coin from midair with the speed of a marsh cobra, and the coin disappeared, together with her fan, in her décolleté.

"Do you want me to take care of your... possession, Jack?" the woman asked him, and she pointed at Alleria, who tried to ignore the word "possession."

"No, Alleria stays with me. She's a runner."

"I can look after her." The woman placed her hands on her hips again.

"I'm sure you can, but I will see to this myself."

"Even when you..." She didn't finish her sentence, but wiggled her thinly plucked eyebrows meaningfully. Jack smiled and nodded.

"We'll be fine. Come Lola..." Halfway Jack put his arm around the blonde. "This has been a long journey and I need a bit of fun." She giggled, and something in Alleria decided she hated the blonde woman even more.

To her horror, they led Alleria to a small room that contained even more fabric than the entrée room downstairs. It was divided into two sections, and thin curtains created a meager sense of segregation. One side was taken over by a large bed covered in pillows, cushions, and throw blankets. On the other side stood a large, red sofa that was so bright in color it hurt Alleria's eyes.

"Does that thing have to come with us, Jacky?" Lola pouted, sticking out her full bottom lip, and batted her long eyelashes. She pushed her body up against Jack and ran her finger across his chest in a slow back-and-forth pattern. "I might get distracted."

Jack flashed her a bright smile.

"No, you won't." He pulled her closer to him and pressed his lips against hers. It was the first time Alleria saw people kiss in real life, and she felt a pang of jealousy.

The kiss also made her uncomfortable, even voyeuristic, and she tried to stand as far away from them as the chain around her neck would allow. Her hairy arms wrapped around her thin shoulders, and she hung her head while she turned her back toward the couple.

Halfway Jack pulled on the chain when he was done, and Alleria responded to the movement. He led her to the large sofa in the adjoining room and made a hand gesture for Alleria to stand still. Jack held up his bound wrist and tapped on the chain twice, then he blew on the metal, and the bond opened up to become a chain again. He bent down and put the chain around the leg of the sofa; after another breath, the material closed again, and Alleria was bound to the furniture.

"Please, not here…" There were tears in her eyes when she begged, but she wondered if Jack even noticed.

"You shouldn't have run, Alleria. This is your punishment."

Her bottom lip quivered and she turned her face away. If only her pain meant something to Halfway Jack, but it didn't. When he turned his back to her, she slumped to the ground next to the sofa and pulled her knees up to her chin. Hands wrapped around bony legs, she hid her face in the little space between arms and knees. Only once did she look up and she saw Lola peel Halfway Jack's black shirt off his chiseled chest through the see-through curtain. His body was beautiful, strong muscles lining his torso, which was broad at the shoulders but narrow around the waist. Alleria's face flushed and she quickly looked away.

It's not fair. Why does someone who is so wicked, who would sell innocent people for money, look so beautiful, while I—who never harmed a soul—look like a monster?

From the other side of the room, Lola giggled, and Alleria felt her temper rise despite herself. Her emotions were a confusing mixture at all times now, and she clung on to her slipping sense of control.

"Foolish girl." Tumsa's voice was strong in her head and caught her off guard. The presence had done a good job of remaining hidden from her up to this point. *"You wonder why you've been battling with your emotions?"* The old witch's voice was filled with malevolent glee. *"Did you really think you were strong enough to withstand me? You are mine, Alleria, and you will always be mine. I've got a claim on you. I would rather see you dead than belong to someone else."* The words were filled with venom, and the witch's anger ran through the girl's body like a parasite. A wave of utter dominance swooped over her, and she felt Tumsa's mind drive her consciousness back. Everything the old woman thought and felt echoed through her head, as if she were a spectator in her own mind. The desire for power, the anger, and the intelligence all swirled through her. Lined within the thoughts, Alleria could see madness.

The old woman is crazy.

She always knew that Tumsa was a little insane, but when her head was filled with the entirety of the old hag's mind, she was suddenly aware of the extent of her fanaticism. Tumsa's presence violated the girl.

"You are under my spell, Alleria. I will always find you. I have all the time in the world to conjure up a spell that will bring you to me again. Sooner or later, I will succeed."

Screams from the world outside her mind tugged at her consciousness and she opened her eyes. To her surprise, she found herself sprawled across the floor, her body twitching. The sofa she was tied to was nothing more than a heap of kindling, and the soft material that once lined it was shriveled and no longer red but a faded, weathered brown. The whole thing stank of a stale, rotten smell.

Halfway Jack stood bent over her, dressed in only his breeches, worry clearly painted across his face. Alleria wanted to beg him for help; her arm stretched out, but no words came from her lips, only a soft moan. Tumsa was still in control, and whatever spell the old hag had cast was painful. Foam ran from the young woman's mouth, tears poured in slick streams from the eyes that rolled back in her head, and the tendons in her neck burned with strain.

"Alleria..." Jack knelt next to her. She felt his hand on her shoulder, and her body shook with spasms. Once, twice, her back arched, and without warning, she sat up straight. The oddly colored eyes of Halfway Jack narrowed, and he repeated her name. "Alleria?"

"No, Jack... not Alleria." The girl's mouth moved, but the voice that came from her lips was not her own. The young body still twitched, but not with the same violent jerks of before. Alleria's eyes were wide open and she looked a fright. The woman—Lola—stood behind Jack, her pretty face filled with horror.

Alleria's hand raised, not by her own choice but by Tumsa's. The movements were rough, like a crippled spider. The voice of Tumsa swirled like a whirlwind in Alleria's head, loud and thunderous. She could see what the old witch was seeing, and it confused her. Not only did she see through her own eyes, but she could see herself from outside of her own body too, as if part of her were somewhere else in the room looking down at her. Alleria realized that Tumsa was watching her through the eyes of some creature, perhaps a spider or a fly, as well as through Alleria's own mind.

Why is she here now? she wondered desperately. *If she could take control of my body, why didn't she just do so sooner when Jack and I were alone?*

"What is wrong with your beast?" Lola screamed. "What is it doing?" The voluptuous woman held her cheeks and her voice rang with shrill panic.

Jack didn't respond to her cries. His eyes flashed with anger, and he held the gaze of Tumsa in Alleria's body as her distorted frame scrambled to her feet. Halfway Jack took a few steps back. The limbs flailed around when she took clumsy steps through the room, giving her the look of a puppet on strings.

"Tumsa."

"Yes, Jack, because I may not have any power over you, but I still have power over Alleria. And I will show you what she can do. You may be immune, but your precious lady friend isn't. Allow me to show you some of Alleria's wonderful talents."

That's why Tumsa hadn't revealed herself before... She needed a victim, Alleria thought, misery filling her heart. When she understood what Tumsa was about to do, she wanted to cry out and warn Lola, but she did not have enough control to speak.

Jack and Lola, too stunned to move, just gaped at her. Without warning, Alleria's hand lashed out and grabbed the chubby prostitute by the arm.

"This is what you are carrying with you, Halfway Jack." Tumsa cackled, and Alleria could feel the old witch's laugh burn in her throat. The hairy arm forced Lola's limb up for everyone to see, and the woman's skin changed under the touch. The soft, smooth flesh lost its firmness and, as by magic, wrinkles and liver spots appeared. The veins in her hand became more prominent, small blue cables pushing upward from the once-young hand, while folds of lined skin drooped over muscle and bone.

Jack moved forward and ripped Lola's limb free; the woman, in turn, fell to the floor and clutched her arm as she yowled.

"Try to sell her now, half breed," the voice of Tumsa screeched. "Everything you care for, Alleria will turn to dust if you don't return her to me, Jack. I will suck the youth, the life, and the spirit out of every single thing, using her body. She's mine, Jack... mine. And don't you forget it." With a dramatic exit, Tumsa withdrew from Alleria's body as fast as she had arrived, and Alleria slumped to the floor like a sack of potatoes. A dull thud broke the shocked silence, and then Lola screamed.

"My arm, what did that thing do to my arm?" Lola wouldn't stop screeching; her pain filled Alleria's head. All Alleria could do was cry.

"Lola, go downstairs." Halfway Jack spoke sternly to the girl, his voice cutting through her screams, and Lola's panic visibly lessened from the sound. Alleria could feel a hint of natural magic in the air, and she wondered if Jack had hidden talents that he used to calm the woman. "Get someone to look at that."

Lola blinked at him, tears welling up in her eyes.

"My arm looks so old. How can this be?" For a moment, Lola was subdued, and she looked terribly young and fragile, but it didn't last long, and a look of pure rage formed on her pretty face. Without warning, the woman turned and flung herself forward, her feet kicking and her nails digging into Alleria's hairy skin.

"You did this to me, you monster! Turn my arm back—make it young and beautiful again. Turn it back!"

Alleria wanted to tell Lola that she couldn't, but she just didn't have the words to speak. Instead, she curled up in a little ball and accepted the blows dealt to her.

Halfway Jack picked up Lola around the waist before she could do any real damage and pulled her away from Alleria.

"Lola, it's not the girl's fault. Stop hurting her, she's more of a victim than you are."

"*She's* more of a victim?" The woman's face was ugly with indignation. "She ruined my arm." She pushed him with her good arm. "She scarred me for life. And you don't even care. You don't care what that beast did to me. It's your fault too." The heavy makeup ran down her face with the tears, and there was nothing left of the once-polished appearance. "You brought that thing here, and look what it did to me." She held out the offending arm, which looked alien on her young body. "Look, damn you." It could have been the arm of an old hag. Alleria averted her eyes, the sight of it too much for her to stand.

Did I cause that?

Alleria felt the magic again, but this time, it didn't seem to calm Lola as much as it did before. Jack's arms still around the screaming girl, he led her outside.

"Let's find someone to look at that," he repeated, and then he closed the door behind him, leaving Alleria alone in the room.

Alleria raised her head and closed her eyes, probing her own consciousness. The thought of the old witch still lurking made her sick.

She's been manipulating my emotions, Alleria thought, and she remembered how strange she'd felt the day before. *Could Tumsa have anything to do with my running away? If so, why didn't she help me when I was caught in the plant? Perhaps she did want me dead?*

She could see Lola's old, wrinkled arm in her mind's eye and remembered something from many years ago. Her head filled with sounds and voices, the echoes of memories. A female voice—not Tumsa, someone else, perhaps her mother—screamed at her.

"Alleria, what have you done? What happened to the dog?"

She couldn't remember the rest, but the words repeated themselves over and over in her head. Lola's panic reminded her of those words, of those voices from her past.

What am I?

By the time Halfway Jack returned, the floor under Alleria's face was damp from her tears. Warm arms wrapped around her and lifted her from the ground. She refused to look at Jack, so she buried her face against his chest. He was dressed now, and the fabric of his shirt rubbed softly against her skin.

"Lola..." Alleria's words came out in a sob; she wanted to ask if the woman would be okay, but she couldn't form the sentence.

"Don't worry about Lola, little one. I will see that she's compensated for the incident." His arms squeezed her tight, and for a brief moment, she almost felt safe.

"I don't know how anyone can ever compensate for what I did."

"Trust me, girls like Lola would gladly give up their arm for the arrangement I offered her. Plus, there are plenty of clients who would pay a little extra for a girl with an oddity. Girls like her have been through worse. I know some clients who like to beat their companions to a bloody pulp, so having a withered arm is child's play by comparison."

Alleria blinked the tears from her eyes. "People beat them?"

"Some do far worse. It's not uncommon for a madam to lose her girls to certain clients. This is a harsh world, Alleria. Your witch isn't the only evil creature."

"I didn't say..."

"I know you didn't." Jack shook his head. "Come on, no point in staying here." His fingers squeezed her shoulders, and he peeled her off him and put her on her feet. "Let's go before we provoke more trouble."

She nodded in response and followed him out of the room and down the stairs, where people parted the way for them as if they carried something poisonous. No one spoke a word, but several dozen eyes followed their every move. Jack gripped her hand and pushed open the door. Relief washed over Alleria when she felt the cold outside air. It took her several minutes before she dared to speak.

"Jack, I'm so sorry, I didn't know Tumsa could do that."

"That makes two of us, Alleria. I had no idea."

"Will you bring me back to the witch now?" For the first time, Alleria found the courage to look up at him, and to her surprise, he smiled and shook his head.

"No, I have something entirely different in mind. We're going to get rid that witch for once and for all."

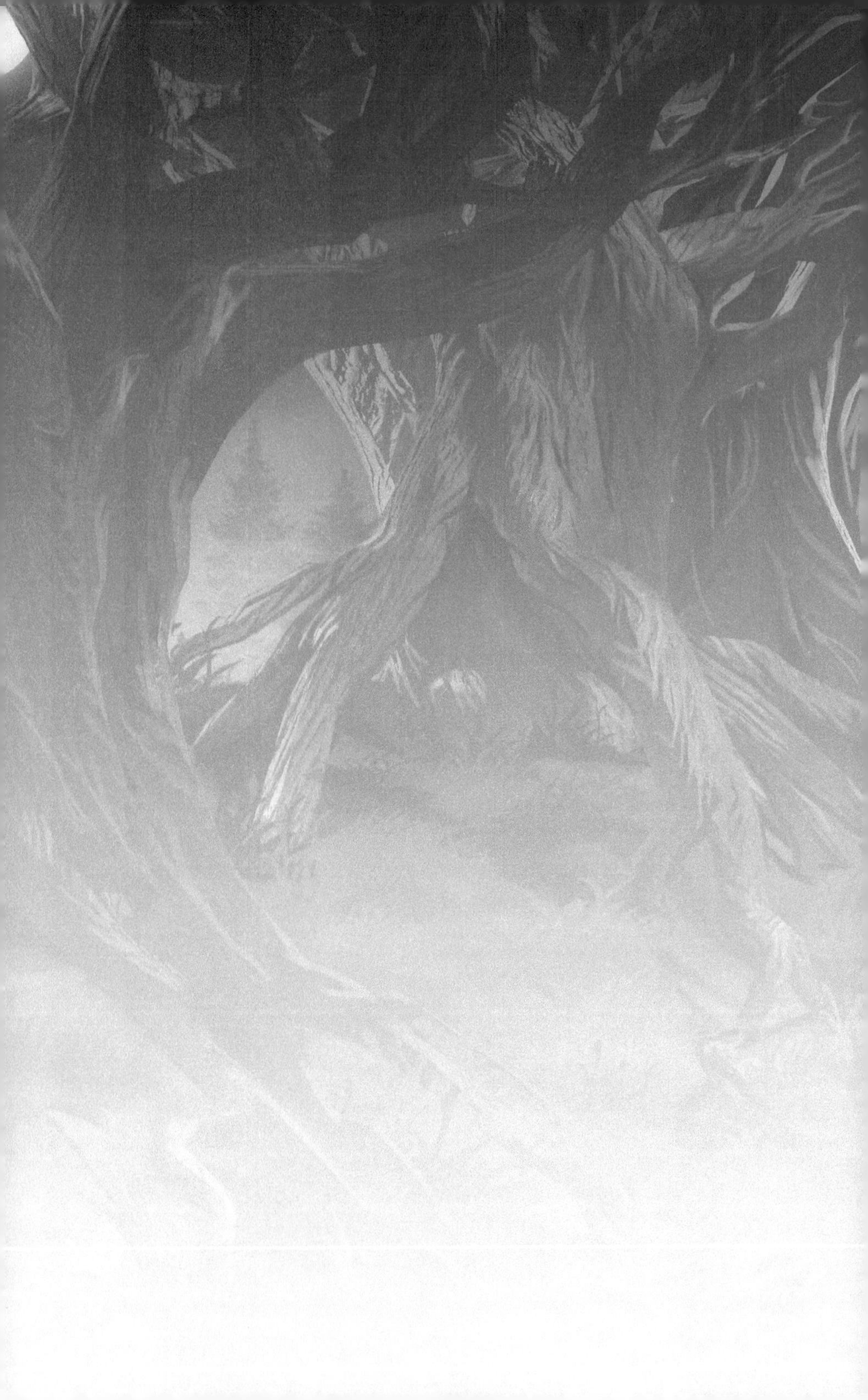

CHAPTER SEVEN

The red sun set hours before they reached their destination, leaving only the dim light of the waning moons to guide them. The silver of the second moon was the brightest as always, while the black of the third moon was only a dim, dark circle in the sky, and the soft golden color of the first moon barely illuminated anything. Jack had tied the end of the chain to his wrist once more, but instead of walking in front of Alleria, he led her by the arm like a companion. His night vision was much sharper than hers, which was clear from the way he maneuvered her around obstacles with relative ease.

They had walked in silence during their hike. Alleria's thoughts were held by the events at the Sultry Scullery Maid. No harsh words or angry looks were exchanged, of which she was grateful, but the pensiveness that had seemed to overtake her captor was unsettling nonetheless. He was quiet and distant in a way he had not been before.

Alleria wasn't sure where they were going, but Jack had led them from the city, back to the marshes, instead of moving toward the human world. Right before the last of the suns had set, the marshland had faded into woodlands, and to her relief, there were fewer lethal creatures as they walked on. The woods seemed friendlier, but Alleria was still wary. These were still the Borderlands after all, and nothing was truly safe within the Borderlands.

They moved north, toward the mists. Alleria felt too empty to make a scene about the destination. After her experience with Tumsa, the thought of dying didn't hold the same sway over her. Part of her was fooled into thinking she welcomed death.

"We're almost there, Alleria." For the first time in hours, Jack spoke. His voice startled her. "We'll be going very close to the mist. You will be able to see it, and I don't want you to be frightened, okay?"

"Okay." Her voice sounded flat, but the mention of the mist—despite her melancholy—still made her heart pound with a painfully heavy thud.

Her small hand found Jack's, and she weaved her fingers through his. The tall tylwyth teg reciprocated her touch and clutched her grip tight. Together, they walked toward the faint clouds that formed in the distance. The mist was a ghostly white color, undeterred by the low lighting; the clouds themselves glowed soft in the dark. It was beautiful, but the sight made the young woman's blood run cold.

"I'm afraid, Jack." Alleria's whisper sounded hoarse, and the wind carried away the words. Jack gave no response, and she wondered if he heard her. The temperature dropped more the closer they got to the mists, and her entire body trembled with cold. Her old clothes did little to protect her from this weather; the layer of hair on her skin warmed her, but not enough. Wisps of mist slithered across the ground and surrounded them in elegant swirls, moving as if they were living crea-tures—and perhaps they were. One never knew in the Borderlands. They were more than just air and water alone, that much was sure, because Alleria felt a tingling as the swirls licked at her skin. It was as if they were made of velvet lined with tiny shards of glass. She wondered what it would be like to enter the actual wall of fog.

"It's here somewhere..." Jack let go of her hand, and Alleria shook with an involuntary shudder; the absence of his warm skin left her cold and bare.

The tylwyth teg turned from side to side, his eyes scanning the earth, searching for something, and then he took two steps forward and stomped on a specific spot on the forest floor. Without any warning,0 the ground shuddered, and a hatch door popped open from a pile of soft mulch. A warm light beamed out in an eerie glow, and Alleria saw the silhouette of a head popping out from the opening.

"Halfway Jack, I knew you were coming." The voice sounded nasal.

"Thank you, Merwig, I have a favor to ask you."

"Don't you always?" The man laughed and opened the hatch door wide enough for the two travelers to enter. Jack picked up Alleria and lifted her into the hole. Gnarled hands caught her from below and gently helped her to her feet.

The girl blinked and took in her surroundings. Hollowed out in the earth was a round room, spacious and surprisingly neat for a hole in the ground. The walls were made of brushed earth and the carpet was made of moss, yet it looked as solid as a house of wood. A thump behind her heralded Jack's entrance into the underground home, and he brushed at his arms and ruffled his hair to rid himself of some of the sand he had acquired on his way down.

There was a kitchen with a black stove. A metal pipe led from the stove through the ceiling, and Alleria wondered where the smoke would come out, and if passersby would see it or mistake it as part of the mists. Wooden countertops and cupboards were carved with images of woodland creatures and painted in a soft yellow color, which made the area look light and cheerful. Next to the kitchen, she saw a living area with a hearth built into the earthen wall and wooden chairs covered in furs. A roaring fire illuminated the room, and here and there stood pixie lamps to brighten the darker areas.

"Come in, come in," the man called Merwig said. "Take a seat by the fire, child. You look cold."

Alleria glanced at him. He was an odd-looking fellow, old, but not as old as Tumsa. His body was thin as a rake, and he had a disproportionately long head. His skull was thin, like the rest of his body, and the long chin and protruding forehead reminded her a little of a crescent moon. Brown hair peppered with gray shot out in unruly strands on the bottom, while the top was bare except for a few random wisps that he had attempted to slick down over his shiny cranium.

Thick, round goggles framed his pale gray eyes and made them look bigger than they actually were. The lanky body bore a cotton white robe; thin, bare feet peeked out from underneath, with toes that were covered in tufts of brown hair.

"Thank you, sir." Alleria spoke softly and followed the stranger to the living area. He indicated for her to sit on a chair with a high back, as ornately carved as the kitchen counters, which was covered in furs that looked like they once belonged on the backs of strever beasts—dangerous creatures that looked like long-haired bison with the head of a fox. Alleria sat and pulled her legs up against her chest, allowing the warmth of the fire to chase the chill from her bones.

"Merwig, I need a favor." Jack sat on the chair next to Alleria and leaned toward the man, who took the seat to her other side.

"So you said. Yes, yes." The man took off his goggles—revealing that his eyes were actually very small and round—and wiped them on his robe. "What can I help you with?"

"Are you familiar with the witch, Tumsa?"

The man stopped rubbing the glass of his goggles and shot Halfway Jack an irritated glance.

"Of course I'm *familiar* with her," he snapped. "Anyone who knows anything of Marsh Magic is *familiar* with her. Lives in the Shadow Marshes. Despicable woman." The man spat on his goggles and fervently continued to polish them.

"I took Alleria from her house."

Merwig looked at her with renewed interest, his owlish eyebrows shooting up in a furry arc.

"Is that a fact?" He inclined toward her, and his small eyes blinked a few times. "That must have angered that evil hag." A smile appeared on his thin mouth, and the corners of his lips reached up too far, creating a comical look.

"Yes, it made her so angry that she won't stop bothering me." Jack leaned back. "She cursed the girl, and now she has power over her. I don't like it."

"Oh yes, I can see right away that this girl is cursed." Long, thin fingers twirled around the hair on her face. "Not just a single curse, either. There are so many curses on this child, it's a wonder that she's still standing." The fingers pointed at random parts of her physique.

"Really?" Jack studied Alleria as if he could discern what sort of curses she was put under just by sight.

"Oh yes." Merwig clapped his hands together. "This one girl has enough curses to accommodate an entire village."

"Can you uncurse her?"

"Most likely." The old man replaced the goggles on his nose and blinked at Alleria. "It won't be easy though; in fact... removing some of these curses might be rather dangerous. I can do it, but I can't guarantee the girl will live." His tone was matter-of-fact, but when he looked at her, the little round eyes drooped with concern. His gaze never left hers.

Jack sighed and sat back. "I don't know if..."

Alleria coughed, and when she spoke, her voice was strong. "Do it."

Both men looked at her in surprise.

"I would rather die than live like this."

Jack furrowed his eyebrows and looked as if he were about to speak, but he didn't say a word.

"I know you consider me your property," she continued, "but we both know I'm no use to you in this state. Tumsa will make good on her threats." She took a deep breath. "Besides, I have no intention of dying."

"The witch will fight. She has her claws in you pretty deep, I can tell. I have an eye for that sort of thing, you see?" Compassion shone through on the old man's face.

"I know. She took over my body. It was the worst thing I ever had to live through, and I've been through a lot. I never want something like that to happen to me again."

"It will take several days. Do you understand what that means?" There was a new expression on his face, one of eagerness, as if he wanted to take on this challenge.

Alleria shook her head. She didn't know, but she didn't care either.

"It will hurt—not just a little bit, but a lot. You *will* want to stop, I promise you that you will, but as soon as I start, there will be no way back. This will take every little bit of strength you have."

"I understand."

"Eh…" Jack stood. "I'd rather not lose her. I need this girl… I mean… this girl will make me a lot of money."

"The child is right, Jack. She'll be no use to most people, her being cursed like this. That witch is over there in her marsh, looking up new spells and new ways to make your life a misery. Best let me do my thing." The man rose to his feet and offered his hand to Alleria. "I'll need your help, Jack. You will have to hold her down during some of these rituals. The procedure won't be pretty. Earth spells seldom are."

"So much for turning coals into fire fairies then," Jack muttered.

"If you want beauty, tylwyth teg, you should find yourself an illusionist, not a sorcerer." Merwig locked his arm into Alleria's and pinched her cheek. "Let's see who we can find under all these curses, shall we?"

Alleria had thought the little burrow was merely one room, but she had been mistaken. Beneath the old man's living area was another space.

This one was much darker and certainly less cozy, the walls lined with gray stones, and wood covering the floor. Across the ceiling hung hundreds of different herbs; Alleria recognized most of them, but some were too exotic for her teachings.

"What do you know of spells, Alleria, my girl?" Merwig eyed her as she glanced at the herbs. The old man rubbed his thumb and forefinger across his head and rested them on the bridge of his nose, where he squeezed lightly. "I assume you have seen your fair share of magic living with Tumsa?"

"I know that most magic is performed with rituals, and spells need a physical component."

"Yes, for mortal magic this is the case. However, fath tywyll, tylwyth tegs, and even a few faerisees often have the special talent to perform magic without components." He wiggled his bushy eyebrows and smiled. "It's called source magic or blood magic, depending upon whom you ask." He led Alleria to a large, wooden table and began to remove the bottles, vials, and other items that were scattered across the surface. Alleria helped Merwig relocate the delicate objects and he offered her a grateful smile.

"I'm a faerisee, Alleria… as you might have guessed from my appearance." He waved his hands at his form. "I know a little source magic, but your witch Tumsa is human, which means we're dealing with base magic."

With care, Alleria picked up a vial that contained a dark brown liquid, the center of which glowed with a soft light. It was pretty, the substance reminding her of a maroon sky with a thousand miniscule stars.

"Will it be easier or more difficult to break Tumsa's curses… considering they're base magic, I mean?" She turned to Merwig, and the expression on the old man's face tightened her stomach with concern.

"Easier for *me*, in many respects. Base magic is very physical, and thus it's easier to pinpoint the spells… but harder for you, my dear. Base magic is very dirty, very visceral." His long fingers rubbed the bald spot on his head. "It will be more painful for you when I dispel your curses. Most of these curses placed on you—or sometimes even *in* you—will have to be retracted corporeally. Do you understand what that means?"

Alleria shook her head, her knees wobbling. "No, I really don't."

"It means that over the time Tumsa had you in her captivity... how many years is that?"

"Eleven..." Her voice was barely above a whisper.

"Over those eleven years, the old witch had been preparing you for whatever devious plan she had in mind. She probably rubbed things on you, involved you in rituals, and even fed you certain things."

The blood drained from Alleria's face and she felt faint. Her mind raced across all the weird soups and broths she ate over the years. She thought of the pungent soap the witch used to clean her skin...

She planned everything.

"The old witch dug her claws deep into the core of your being, dear child." Merwig's long, bony fingers scratched the tip of his pointed chin and he wrinkled his nose. "But I'm very good at what I do, so there's hope." He winked and flashed a sparkling smile. "But it'll be messy."

"What do you mean by messy?" Halfway Jack asked. He looked as worried as Alleria felt.

"I mean messy in the quite literal sense of the word, I'm afraid. Some of these curses will be easy to dispel with counter magic, but I'm sorry to say I'll have to cut some of these curses out of her."

"C... cut?" Alleria's legs threatened to buckle, but Jack's strong hands grabbed her waist and held her up.

"Yes, cut. And I might have to burn some of them out with magical flame." Merwig pinched his chin and turned to Alleria. "It shouldn't scar you, but it will hurt just the same. Are you ready for that?"

Can anyone be ready for that?

Alleria nodded her head. She wanted these curses out of her. She wanted to be free from Tumsa, even if it would hurt beyond all belief.

"Lie on the table, child, on your stomach first. Like so..." He spread his arms to show her what he wanted, and Alleria obeyed. Her breath was shallow and rapid from fear. With gentle hands, Merwig bound her wrists to the table.

"These might not be enough, Jack. If she breaks out of them, I need you to constrain her." Jack nodded, his mouth a thin line and his eyes grim. He pulled up a stool and placed it in front of Alleria at the table. "Can we sedate her somehow?"

"I will use some spells to take away the pain where I can, but I'm afraid that there are certain things I simply can't protect her from. Magic is a cruel mistress. It asks for sacrifices, and one of such sacrifices is pain."

Jack ran a finger across her forehead, his face a mask of sympathy. "I'm here, little one. Just look at me while Merwig does his mojo, okay?"

"What if... what if I do that thing again... that I did to Lola's arm?" Alleria felt the tears well up in her eyes. "I could hurt Merwig."

Jack laughed.

"Don't worry, Alleria, there are few people more resistant to magic than I am. Merwig happens to be one of them. I would have never brought you here if I thought you could endanger him." His words eased her conscience, and she put her head on the table. Merwig pottered around and he rubbed a cool ointment on her skin.

"This will take some of the pain away. But as I mentioned before, I can't fully sedate you."

The old man put candles on the floor around the girl, lighting them with a magical fire, and with a blue piece of chalk he drew symbols in a circle on the wood.

"Those should take away some of the old witch's control. Or so I hope."

The light of the candle reflected in the strange blue chalk symbols, and for a moment, they looked animated. Alleria was mesmerized. She turned her head to look at Merwig and regretted it immediately.

In his gnarled hands, the old man held a large, sharp knife. He pushed the blade into a flame and glanced at her with an apologetic smile. Then he turned his attention back to the knife and muttered something about disinfection. Alleria's eyes grew large at the sight of the blade, and she quickly squeezed them shut. Jack's hands slid into her own, and he gripped her fingers.

"You can do this, little one. I know you can. You survived eleven years with that evil, old witch, so this should be a piece of cake for you."

Alleria didn't open her eyes, but she nodded in response.

I can do this.

Behind her, she heard Merwig chant in old Fenuine, one of the magical languages of the human world. She could make out some of the words, and understood they were said to form a protection spell.

"Place this between her teeth, Jack," Merwig instructed. "We don't want her biting off her own tongue."

"Open your mouth, Alleria." There was a quiver in Jack's voice.

She kept her eyes closed but opened her mouth. Something that felt and tasted like a wooden stick was placed between her teeth, and Alleria clenched down.

Please don't tell me when you start. Just do it; don't make me wait.

As if he heard her thoughts, Merwig gave no warning when the knife cut into that dreaded hunchback, which had been her bane for many years. Searing pain shot into Alleria's flesh, and her teeth bit down hard into the wood. A scream escaped from her throat, guttural and animalistic. The pain was worse than any beating she'd ever received.

To her horror, Alleria felt something move inside her skin, a writhing that she couldn't quite place. Her flesh ached as if someone tore it off her back, and she screamed again. Jack muttered soothing words, but she could barely make out what he said until he pulled back abruptly and screamed: "By the old gods, what are those?"

The stool fell to the ground as he got to his feet. She peered up at him, her face covered in cold sweat, and saw how he stared at her back in horror.

"There are spiders crawling from the wound, Merwig—do something." Jack pointed at her back.

"They need to come out, Jack. Those spiders *are* one of the curses."

"You mean she had spiders inside her body this whole time?"

"There will be plenty more inside her, Jack. Some things will be worse than spiders."

Arachnids scuttled everywhere, all over her body, the table, and even the floor. When some crawled on her face, Alleria screamed. Jack brushed the offending creatures from her skin, pulled the stool back up, and sat, then he continued to tell her everything would be okay.

"Alleria..." The voice in her head was sharp and hysterical. *"What are you doing, Alleria? You will stop this immediately."* The wound on her back throbbed even harder now, and Alleria's limbs struggled against the bonds, though it was not she who controlled them.

"Tumsa." The girl's voice was muffled because of the wood, but Jack understood. There was a scent as the straps and the wood underneath her started to wither under her touch. The old hag pulled up Alleria's right arm and managed to free it from the half-rotten bond, but Halfway Jack jumped on it with the speed of lightning. The tylwyth teg held it down while the old witch in Alleria's body fought with him. Tumsa screamed in the girl's ear, but her voice got weaker, and Alleria could feel herself regaining control over her magic as the spiders crawled away from her young form, scattering everywhere.

While he still held down her arm, Jack stomped on the creatures that crossed his path. Alleria saw them more clearly now. They looked like swamp spiders, with their tiny bodies and long, hairy legs, but there were subtle differences. Their abdomens carried a little red symbol of magic. It was the symbol for restraint, and though she was utterly disgusted and upset, Alleria experienced a strange freeing sense in expelling these monsters from her body.

"There are no more spiders," Merwig announced after a while, and Jack let go of her hand. The old man bound her wrist back to the table immediately, and he uttered some words that seemed to heal the rotting wood.

"We're not done yet, Alleria, not even close. This was just the first layer. I will have to dig even deeper."

She nodded, sweat drenching the hair on her face and head.

Several times during the extraction of the curse, Alleria lost consciousness. The night dragged on, every minute filled with torment, passing with the slowness of an hour.

Jack made up the girl's whole world during the extraction of the curses; she tried to focus on him, on his beautiful face and his strange eyes. He, in turn, talked to her, repeated over and over that Alleria would be okay, that she was stronger than this, and she believed him.

She listened to him from far away, from a deep well somewhere in her mind—his voice soft and faint—and it was the only thing she could still hear through the pain.

Several times, she wanted to give up, to just let the pain win so that she could slip away quietly into the darkness of death. But there was a voice inside of her that ordered her to listen to Jack, that ordered her to fight for a life she hadn't quite lived yet.

And so, she fought with all the willpower that remained hers. After what seemed like an eternity, a sweat-soaked Merwig squatted in front of her. His enlarged eyes gazed at her from behind the thick glass. His breath was ragged.

"I have removed five of the curses. We still have quite a few to go. Do you need a break, or do you want to keep going?"

"Keep going." The girl's voice was hoarse and barely audible.

"Are you sure? This is quite a strain for you, and I'm afraid it's not going to get any better."

"Keep going," she repeated.

"Jack, you better leave. I've come to the discovery that for one of the bigger curses, I need to strip her from her entire skin. I would rather not have anyone around but me, as it might be dangerous for her. She'll be very vulnerable—very prone to infection, and I want to keep the contamination risk to its minimum."

Alleria heard the words, but she could barely register them. It felt as if the old man were talking about someone else, not her.

"You're going to strip her from her skin?" Jack's mouth opened and his eyes were round. "Are you insane?"

"No, this witch worked some very dirty magic on her. I had a suspicion it would be bad, but I had no idea what kind of hot mess I would come across in that poor child."

Alleria saw Merwig's face through her tear-encrusted eyelashes.

He shook his head. "I need to rid her of that foul skin and burn it. The good news is that the other remaining curses are quite minor and won't take up much time to dispel, but the bad news is that this last major curse will be the most laborious of all the tasks, and the most dangerous."

"She'll have no skin." Jack pulled his stool closer as if he wanted to protect her.

"I have a remedy for that. Remember that the skin she has on now isn't her true skin; it is one made for her. With the aid of magic, I can give the girl her original skin back. Within a few days, she'll be right as rain. In fact, I believe she'll look like her true self again, and you won't even see a scar. The skin will just grow back on the whole."

"I don't know if this is right, Merwig... look at the poor creature." Halfway Jack's breath tickled her cheek when he leaned over her. A soft hand brushed some of the soaked locks from her cheeks.

"Jack." Alleria's voice was weak. He looked at her, obviously surprised that she still had the strength to speak up.

"You don't have to do this, Alleria. The witch doesn't have a hold over you anymore." He brushed more hair aside and she moved her head a little to face him. Every movement caused her pain, making her wince.

"Jack, go upstairs."

"Alleria, he wants to take off your skin." The tylwyth teg cocked his head at her, his eyes pleading for sanity.

"I've had skin taken from me before." She managed a weak smile, but only a brief one, which was instantly replaced with a more determinate expression. "I *want* to do this, Jack. You say she doesn't have a hold over me anymore, but as long as her curses are inside of me, she will always own me. I may never be a free woman, but at least I can be free of Tumsa. Give me that much at least."

His brow furrowed, but he stood and kissed her on a cheek that was wet with tears and sweat.

"You must be the bravest girl I've ever met," he muttered in her ear, "or the most insane one."

Then he left, and Alleria rested her head on the wood again.

He can't talk me through this part, I need to do this alone.

When the knife sank into Alleria's skin and she could feel Merwig pull at her flesh, she fainted—thankfully.

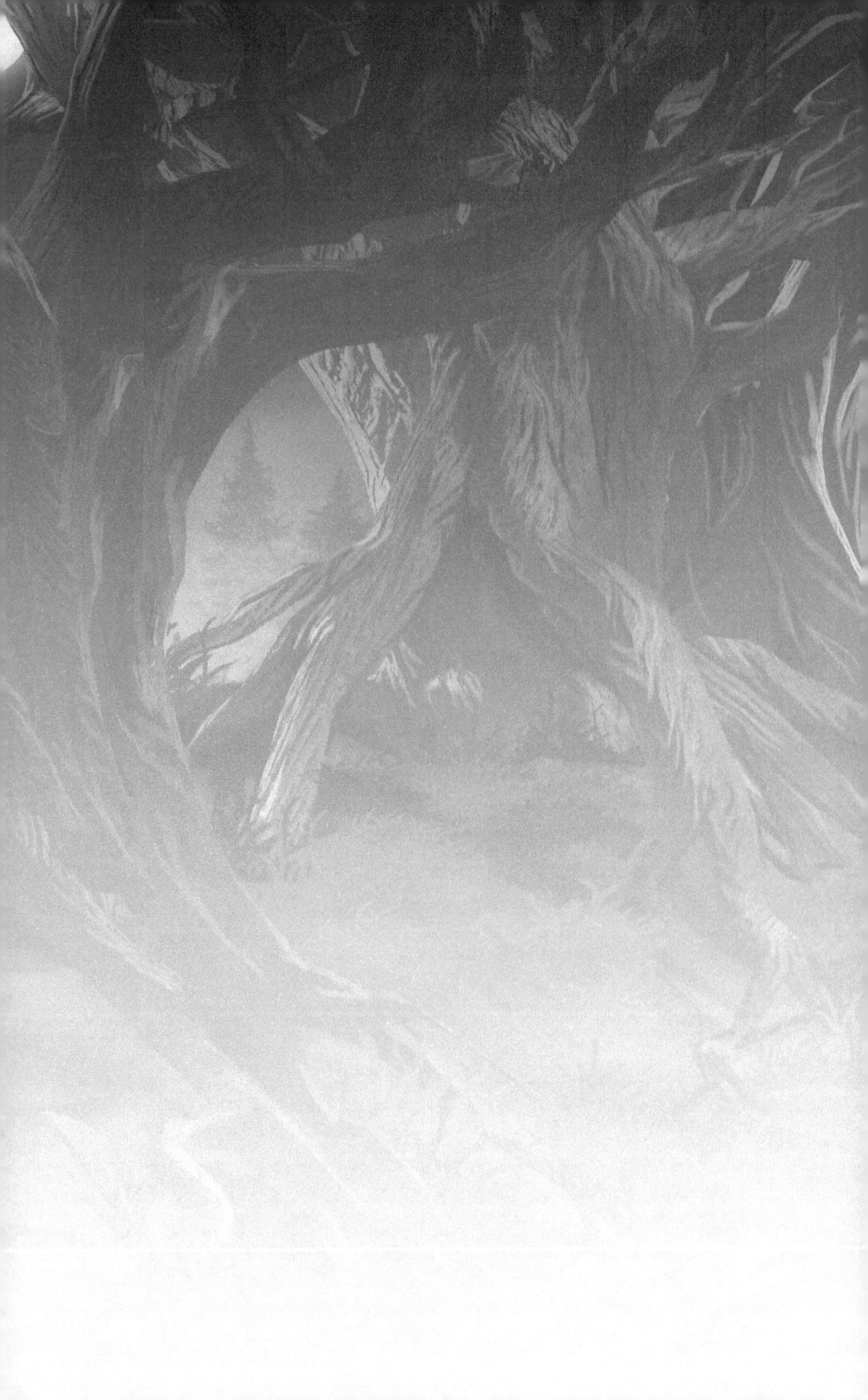

CHAPTER EIGHT

During the next few days, Alleria drifted in and out of consciousness. Merwig wrapped soft, wet plants around her body and assured her that her skin was growing nicely. The old man wouldn't let Jack near his patient. He explained that it was too dangerous; Jack's mere presence could cause infection that might kill her. The bed she slept in was comfortable, and though the pain was still intense, it lessened every day. Merwig fed her a brew of poppies and firedragon root to sedate the discomfort as much as he could, and Alleria tried to recall the last time someone cared for her.

When she lived with Tumsa, she was seldom ill, and even on the rare occasions that she felt under the weather, the old hag never looked after her or even acknowledged Alleria's need for rest and healing. She was still expected to do her tasks.

The lifting of the curses changed something deep inside her. Her mind was clear and open, and she realized she was in control of it for the first time since she could remember. No one was peering into her consciousness; no one controlled her. It was as if she were born anew.

Now that she no longer suffered from the many curses, Alleria discovered an inner strength she did not know she had. Her whole body was lighter, as if someone lifted a physical weight from her. The relief was exhilarating, but the pain and the medicine Merwig gave her kept her drowsy.

On the third day, Alleria woke up without pain, and Merwig informed her that it was time to take off the plant bandages.

The old man worked fast and with delicate fingers. The skin was still sore, but it was surprising how much healthier she was feeling. The cold air nipped at her damp epidermis, the sensation entirely alien to her. After he removed all the plants, Merwig washed her body with lukewarm water, and there was an expression in his eyes that Alleria had never seen before. She couldn't place it; it didn't look like worry or disgust... it was something else. Alleria thought it was wonderment that she saw in the round eyes.

The old man took a step back to admire his handiwork, and he clapped one of his thin hands in front of his mouth.

"Oh my... oh *my*." The top of his bald head gleamed with sweat. Then he snapped out of whatever he was thinking and handed Alleria her clothing. She grabbed them and put them on.

Her hands glided over her arms.

The hair... it's gone, just pink skin.

Alleria touched her arms, her neck, her face... all the hair was gone, and in its place was soft, naked skin. For a moment, she feared *all* her hair would be missing, but when her hands reached for her scalp, she felt thick locks under her fingers. The hair was so different, long and soft, not coarse or knotted like only days before. With a fresh sense of curiosity, Alleria pulled on a strand and held it in front of her face. The locks were the color between silver and gold, the color of the second moon... not brown and rough.

Am I dreaming?

"It seems, Alleria, my dear, that the witch's curses had quite the physical effect on you."

"How is it possible that I made such a transformation in only a few days?" she asked, her voice stronger than she had heard it in a while. "You stripped off my skin, and yet I look perfectly fine as far as I can tell?" She held up an arm, twisting it as she let her gaze glide across the perfect skin to prove her point.

Merwig chuckled and hid a grin behind his hand.

"Magic can do wondrous things. As soon as I burned your skin... well, not really *your* skin, but the skin you have worn for the past eleven years... let's just say your old form started to reappear. It needed some time to grow and heal, but it restored you in such a way that your body became that what it should have been if magic hadn't intervened. Even your hair has reverted to the length that suits a girl your age," the old man said. "You now look as you were supposed to look. It's quite complicated and at the same time rather simple. You could say that my magic completely negated anything that Tumsa ever did to you."

"Does that mean she has no more power over me?" Alleria's eyes stung with tears.

"She shouldn't have. No more than she has power over other things. She's still a dangerous old woman, so please just stay away from her if you can. She can get a hold over you once more if you give her a chance."

Alleria nodded; she would avoid the old witch at all costs if she could. Her hand rubbed against her arm, and the soft skin was alien to her touch, as if it didn't belong to her. A little part of her almost missed the familiar feel of her fur.

"Come upstairs and let us see what Jack will make of you." Merwig held out his hand and Alleria put her small, pale fingers on his palm. The nails were short but pink and exquisite, not like the thick, ugly, claw-like ones she had before, and the hand was so delicate.

Merwig led her up the stairs into the spacious living area. Jack stood by the hearth, his back turned toward them as they entered. He leaned with one hand on the mantelpiece, and with the other he prodded at the fire with a metal poker.

"I think I might have a bit of a surprise for you, Halfway Jack."

Jack turned around, and Merwig pulled Alleria forward. She jumped when Jack dropped the poker. It landed on the floor with a loud thud. Jack's mouth fell open, but surprise turned to rage within a fraction of a second.

"What is this?" he barked. "Where's Alleria?"

She screwed up her face and folded her arms. "I *am* Alleria."

"No..." Halfway Jack struggled to find the words. "You can't be Alleria, you're... you can't be her." He turned toward Merwig, his face flushed with anger. "I want *my* Alleria back, not this creature. Whatever this is."

She gawked at him.

"I am the only Alleria there is, *me*. So take it or leave it. In fact, I would rather you leave it. I'll just be on my way."

"Jack, be reasonable." Merwig held up his hands, but Jack paced across the floor.

"How am I going to take *that* across the human lands to the market?" He pointed at Alleria as if he were pointing out some foul beast, disgust clear on his face.

Oh by the gods, what do I look like? Am I so hideous that even Jack, who accepted me as a hairy monster, does not want to be seen with me?

Alleria's hand went up to her face, which was as smooth as her arms.

"Jack, she'll probably fetch you a steeper price at the market looking the way she does now," Merwig pleaded, but the handsome tylwyth teg would not let him finish.

"I won't be able to get her there. People will ask questions. No one was going to care when she looked like some hairy beast or faerisee, but if she looks like this... I can't guide her with a chain around her neck. Those stupid humans will probably have me hanged or something."

Halfway Jack sank down in one of the chairs near the hearth and put his hands in front of his eyes.

"I don't understand..." Alleria looked from Merwig to Halfway Jack, too confused and drained to feel emotion. "What do I look like?" Merwig turned to her, and he slapped his hand against his shiny forehead.

"Oh, dear child, I forgot to show you." He grabbed her shoulders and led Alleria to a silver mirror that stood behind a little table filled with knickknacks. "That's what you really look like, my dear."

She stared at the mirror, but instead of seeing the reflection she knew to be her own, a stranger gaped back. The girl in the mirror was obviously not human, her features too delicate.

Large blue eyes—similar yet completely different to Alleria's own eyes—blinked at her. The heart-shaped face had a small button nose and full and shapely lips. Alleria felt a pang of jealousy when she studied the beautiful girl in the mirror.

I don't look like that.

The girl in the mirror would never have sore knuckles because her hand dragged on the floor, she wouldn't have to pick tangled plants from the fur of her legs, and people would see her—really see her—when she walked by. Alleria reached out her hand to touch the girl who looked back at her.

There was shock in mirror girl's face, the same shock Alleria had seen on the faces of the humans who looked at her. For a moment, she thought the mirror girl was afraid of her, but then she realized that she was being ridiculous.

I am this girl.

Tears poured from her eyes and she forced herself to look away. The sight of her reflection was too much for her to bear; it broke her heart.

Why can't I be happy? I don't look like a monster anymore. I've always dreamt of this.

"Well, this isn't quite the reaction I was expecting." Merwig scratched his gleaming skull and shrugged. "I don't know what exactly I was expecting, but I'm sure it wasn't this. I wasn't prepared for tears from you, girl. Nor was I prepared for your anger, Jack." He threw his hands up in the air and left Alleria to stand in front of the mirror by herself.

"I'm sorry... it's just—" she said, but the old man waved his hand in dismissal at her.

"Tea anyone?" His voice sounded light and casual, and Alleria was overcome with a wave of gratitude.

"Can I help?" She turned and walked toward him, and her eyes connected with Jack's as she moved past her captor. He scowled at her from behind steepled fingers.

Merwig waved her over, and together they brewed some tea.

The little house was quiet, like Tumsa's house had been, but friendlier, and Merwig was a jolly soul. They poured the tea in wooden mugs and Alleria put one down in front of Jack. Everyone took their place around the table and they all sat in silence; each brooded on their own thoughts.

"So, about payment." Jack was the first to speak, his eyes fixed on the mug in front of him. "How can I repay you for this?"

"I'm guessing you won't allow me to keep the girl?" Merwig smiled with impish delight.

"Obviously. What would you want with her anyway?" Halfway Jack raised his eyebrows.

"I could use a companion to help me around here. I'm getting on in age, and she seems like a lovely creature. If she's as bright as she is pretty, I could teach her a thing or two." Merwig put his lips to the mug and muttered over the rim, "I could use an apprentice, and I've always wanted a daughter. She could be that to me. Her mere presence would make me a little younger." From behind the cup Alleria saw his lips curl into a smirk. "You tylwyth tegs don't know the burden of aging, but this old faerisee suffers greatly." The old man nipped of his mug again. The comment about aging confused Alleria.

"I age…"

"Yes and no. Granted, you mature, just like humans do, but the aging process is different for you. Your bones don't grow brittle, and time doesn't make you wither in the same way it does us. Age only strengthens the tylwyth teg." Merwig pointed a gnarled finger at her. "After our intimate few days, I'm pretty sure I know what you are. Your kind is quite a mystery to us, because you are rare, especially females, but I suspect you mature as fast as a human being. When you reach a certain age, say twenty-five or so, your body won't change very much. It's all part of the glamour, you see? Beauty is part of your race's strength. You are bound to look young and beautiful for many centuries. You will never look old the way we do. And while not all tylwyth teg are blessed with beauty, they are all blessed with a certain everlasting youth."

"What am I?" The steam of the tea clashed against Alleria's skin, and she felt so naked without the hair covering her face. It felt wonderful and embarrassing at the same time.

"You're a tylwyth teg, that's all that's important." Jack's hand slid over her mug, and he pushed it down, his voice sharp. "Don't let Merwig fill your head with funny stories."

Alleria's eyes darted from Jack to the old man, and she noticed that Merwig looked sad.

"Jack, would you mind if I had a word with you in private?"

"Fine." The two men got up from their seats and walked toward the stairs. Alleria stayed behind and stared at the cup.

I want to stay here.

Near the kitchen, the sound of muffled voices became clear, and Alleria quickly got to her feet to see where the sound came from: an air grate nestled in the floor, and she could hear the faint echoing sounds of the conversation.

"If the wrong guy buys her, he will kill her, Jack. Do you know what the heart of a gosgeiddig can do? It will make a very powerful spell, or even a youth elixir. You put that girl in danger if you sell her on the market."

My heart? Someone may want my heart?

Alleria swallowed a lump in her throat but stayed quiet.

"I won't sell her to a wizard."

"Jack, be reasonable. I can pay you in some gems. It may not be as much as you would fetch on the market, but at least it'll be something. You don't want to see this girl hurt any more than I do. I know you better than this, my boy. You have a good soul."

"How will I know that you won't cut her up once I'm gone?"

Merwig snorted.

"You insult me, Jack. You don't mean what you say. You know very well I wouldn't kill that lovely young woman." The man sighed, and there was no response from Jack, so Merwig continued. "I like the girl. She's been through so much. Don't forget that I know the old witch that held her captive. Her life can't have been easy." There was a moment of silence, and Alleria heard footsteps.

Someone is pacing.

"I wish I could sell her to you, Merwig," Jack said after a while, "but I can't. I need far more than you can offer, and I'm running out of time. There are few things in this world that are as valuable as a gosgeiddig. I'd be a fool to let this one go."

"But the girl..."

"I don't want to see her hurt, I really don't. But I want to see *me* hurt even less. If I didn't need... if I didn't need the money the way I do, I would give her to you. Free of charge. But such is life, and we all need to make choices." There was a sigh, and Alleria couldn't quite make out if it was Jack or Merwig who made the sound.

"I choose me." Jack's voice sounded morose.

"Is this about Enarina? Still?"

Who is Enarina?

"If you mention her name again, old man, I will slit your throat." The venom in Jack's voice startled her.

"I'm sorry, it's none of my business." Merwig didn't sound frightened.

"We're going to go upstairs, and I'm going to take Alleria with me. I don't want you filling her head with your nonsense about staying. And I don't want you to scare her about the slave market either, do you understand? That would just be cruel."

"Yes, Jack."

"When I come back from Mtumwa, I shall compensate you handsomely for the work you have done here. I'm very grateful, despite the inconveniences it will pose."

"She does look lovely, doesn't she?"

Jack didn't respond, and seconds later, Alleria heard footsteps on the stairs. As fast as she could, she ran back to the chair, praying her heavy breathing or flushed cheeks would go unnoticed.

"Alleria, drink your tea. We're going to leave today." Alleria didn't respond; she just drank her tea in silence.

"Wait, Jack." Merwig held up his old hand and Jack shot him a warning glance. "The girl's clothing won't be appropriate for this weather. I have some things that can help." He opened another latch in his floor and jumped through. Moments later, he reemerged holding a beautiful sky-blue dress—the color of Alleria's eyes—and a dark blue cloak.

"It's not much, and it won't do for winter, but it'll keep you warm enough this autumn. Better than that sack of a dress you're wearing now." She looked down at the burlap garment that hung loosely over her slender frame. Merwig handed her the clothes.

"That's very beautiful."

"It belonged to my wife. After she died, I parted with most of her clothing... but this..." He struggled to find the words, and Alleria saw his eyes grow moist. "It was her wedding dress, you see?"

Alleria covered her mouth with her hand. "I can't take this."

"Yes, you can, my dear. It would make me a happy man to know that Fiorna's gown was out in the world again, bringing another girl happiness." An impulse hit her, and Alleria wrapped her arms around Merwig, who accepted the hug and squeezed her with his bony frame.

"You're a strong girl, Alleria. Not many could have survived what you did. Now you need to find yourself." He brought his mouth near her ear and whispered: "The slave market need only be another port in your life. It doesn't have to be the last one."

She nodded in response, her lips pressed together. Merwig opened the hatch and she stepped down into a small bedroom. A comfortable bed with a straw mattress was the only furniture in the little room, and there was not a lot of space for her to stand or move. The dress proved difficult to put on, with ribbons and hooks and buttons that made no sense to her. The last time she wore fine clothes, someone else had put them on her. After a while, she just gave up; the dress covered her bare skin, which was good enough for her. She almost tripped when she made her way back up the stairs, as the hem of the dress was longer than what she was used to, and she held it up to avoid further stumbling.

"You look beautiful." Merwig clasped his hands together and beamed like a proud father who was about to send his daughter off to the ball.

"You put that dress on wrong." Jack glowered at her. "Come here, I'll fix it." He pulled Alleria toward him and fiddled with the hooks and ribbons. When he yanked on the strings on the back of the corset, Alleria held her breath. The dress hugged her tight—to the point of becoming uncomfortable. Next to her was the silver mirror, and she glanced at her reflection. The image made her blush. Her milk-white bosom was quite ample, and the dress pushed it up to show the soft curves. Ashamed of her uncovered state, she placed her hand on her chest, avoiding eye contact with either man.

"I... I feel a bit... exposed."

"Don't be silly, all women wear dresses like this," Jack snapped. "That horrible dress you were wearing earlier won't keep you warm, and it would have fallen apart in a matter of months." He jerked at the strings again, tightening the corset even more, and fiddled to tie a bow. "This is better. I agree with Merwig, though I would have preferred something that made you stand out a little less. If that's even possible." He handed her the dark blue cloak and turned to Merwig.

"I'll reimburse you for the clothes too."

"Don't bother, Jack." The old man pursed his lips in a grim expression. "Those clothes are invaluable. They are my gift to Alleria, not to you."

Merwig stalked toward the top latch and pulled out a rope ladder. One by one they climbed to the surface. Both men helped Alleria to her feet; she was still getting used to walking around in a dress and corset. Once on top, the old man folded his thin arms around her again and when he released her from the hug, he squeezed her cheek. Then he embraced Jack.

"Remember my offer, Halfway Jack. In case you change your mind."

Alleria feigned confusion, looking from one man to the other with her eyebrows raised.

"I shall keep it in mind." Jack waved at the old man and turned to the girl.

"I'm going to put your chain back on."

Alleria touched her neck with her fingertips. *I hadn't noticed it was gone.*

"You ran before, and maybe that's because of the old witch, but I can't trust you not to do it again. Without the witch's curses on you, the chance of you wanting to escape is bigger." He took the chain from the pouch and dangled it in front of her. "I wish things could be different, Alleria... but they're not. I don't ask for forgiveness from you."

"Good, then you shan't have it." Her voice was cold, but she couldn't be angry at him, not after the past few days. Not after the way he sat by her in her hour of need. Not after he had allowed her to take the risks that she had taken.

Jack nodded and put the chain around her neck. Immediately, the cord grew, and he fastened it around his wrist.

Together they walked away from Merwig's house. The walk was painful to the girl, as her feet no longer had the thick skin under their soles, and every little pebble, every twig, every bump hurt her when she walked. Jack noticed her clumsy steps and stopped walking.

"What's the matter with you?"

"My skin... it's different. My feet hurt." Alleria sat and pulled a sharp pine needle from her sole. A drop of blood welled up from a small wound. Halfway Jack bent down and grabbed her right foot in his hands. With a furrowed brow, he studied it and then pulled something from his backpack that appeared to be a piece of skin from a blue-green reptile. Alleria had never seen anything like it.

"I can't make you proper shoes right now—I don't have the skill or the tools—but this will hold you over until we can find some actual footwear. Equor skin is very thin and flexible, but it will protect your feet from almost anything, even fire. I was going to have a tunic made with it the next time I was in the Arallfyd, but your need is greater than mine."

"Thank you."

With rapid movements, Jack bound the material around the sore feet, and Alleria found it surprisingly soft to the touch. To her surprise, she felt nothing of the ground beneath her when she stood; her feet were perfectly comfortable as if she were walking on clouds. Without another word, Jack got to his feet and turned on his heel. He tugged on the chain ever so gently as he walked, and Alleria followed him in silence, the corners of her mouth curled up in a half smile. Nothing had changed and yet everything had.

CHAPTER NINE

The mists twirled all around them once more, caressing the hairless skin of Alleria's face and sending chills down her back that caused goose pimples to break out all over. The girl's step quickened and she moved up to walk alongside Halfway Jack rather than behind him.

"We should have been out of the mists by now, Jack. They seem to thicken, and this worries me. The way toward Merwig's house was far less misty."

"We're not going back the way we came. We're going further into the mists."

Alleria stopped dead in her tracks. "We're what?"

"We're heading into the mists."

"But the mists are the border to the... the..." Her mind raced to find the words, but she just went blank.

"To the Arallfyd? That's exactly where we are going." There was not a spark of humor on his stolid face, and his eyes warned her not to cross him, but Alleria ignored the warning.

"We can't go there... it's not allowed."

"That's the point. *We* can go there, you and I, and we will." He pulled at the chain, though gently, but she refused to budge.

"Don't start this again, Alleria." Jack sighed. "Don't make me carry you, I will make you sorry."

"It's dangerous in there." She folded her arms and frowned at her captor.

"It's dangerous out here, it's dangerous out there..." He pointed south. "We can't go into the human worlds. Not with you looking like this. It'll get us into all sorts of trouble. It will get *me* in all sorts of trouble." He stomped his feet with frustration and swung his arms as he spoke.

"Why are you so angry with me?" she asked. "What have I done to deserve this?"

"I'm angry because you weren't the creature I thought you were. This was supposed to be an easy job. Easy and well paid. You were supposed to be this quiet, unnoticeable little thing. I could just bring you to Mtumwa and get what I needed." His hands moved with each word. "That was it, that is what I was told. But no... things just turned out different. Instead, I have a cursed beauty on my hands that tries to run away." He turned his back to her and slumped his shoulders. "It was never my plan to take this detour. Or to go to Merwig. What happened there... I can't put it from my mind. I had to watch you being cut open, and horrible things came out of your body. You might have witnessed the spiders, but were you aware actual shadow beasts lived under your skin?"

Jack put his arm in front of her and pulled down the sleeve of his coat, where underneath lay a nasty wound. Jagged teeth marks, embedded deeply in the flesh, glowed in an angry red semicircle, the skin around it almost black and covered in pustules. It had healed for the most part, but Alleria could see it must have been painful.

"One of those things actually bit me. The bite was so deep that not even Merwig could fully heal it. And that's not the worst. The way you look now... I can't take you into the human lands. I can't even imagine how those mortals would respond to something like you. So now I have a whole heap of trouble on my hands." He kicked a rock from the ground and it skidded across the earth. "Yes, I'm a little upset about that."

Alleria stuck out one of her hips and rested her hands on her side, her head held high with a pride she hadn't felt before.

"Excuse me for inconveniencing you, while you bring me to your slave market." She stomped her foot, and the black magic inside her started to ooze from her pores. "I'm so sorry I was taken by a horrible hag when I was a child. My apologies for being abused and misused, for being cursed. If only I knew how upsetting it was for you when *my* body was cut open to release the spiders and shadow beasts, and whatever else I've been carrying with me for eleven years… I would have never done it. My deepest regret is that Tumsa invaded not only my body, but my mind and soul to inconvenience *your* little trip. I'm sorry that I'm not an easier *slave* to transport. I'll try and watch my manners from now on, shall I? Get myself more involved with the etiquette of being enslaved?" Alleria shot Jack a dark look, barely aware that the grass under her feet was turning brown.

"Are you sure I got the same girl back from Merwig? You don't sound like the same girl. I like the hairy one better. That one knew when to shut up and obey."

"No, I'm not the same girl. Someone ripped a bunch of curses out of my body; I would say that would make me pretty different." The brown stain spread and there was a slight smell of old age. Jack looked down.

"Mind your temper. You're doing that thing again." He pointed at the forest floor and immediately Alleria calmed down. "That's another reason why I can't take you into the human lands for a longer period of time, Alleria. That insane power of yours. Do you have any idea what that could do to humans? We need to find a way to get you to control that, or you will be a danger to yourself as well as others. And if we can't find a way, we must find you an owner who could help."

She eyed the withering grass with a cold lump in her stomach.

I wish that was just a curse too, one that Merwig could cut out of me. Her anger deflated so rapidly that she felt empty and docile.

"Oh," is all she managed to say.

"Yes, oh," Jack parroted. "I am sorry for your life, Alleria. And I'm sorry I can't make it better for you. Perhaps one day you'll meet someone who is kind, but I'm not that someone. You could do worse than me, though, believe me." His voice was gentler and he rubbed the back of his neck.

"So, for now, we're just going to have to live with each other. I will have to live with the fact that you are a bloody nuisance, and you will have to live with the fact that I'm the bastard that's holding you captive. And you *will* follow me into Arallfyd because there is no other way. If I have to carry you the whole way, so be it. But I would prefer it if you walked yourself."

"There is no need to carry me."

"Good. Now come along, and we'll not speak of this again until it is absolutely necessary."

He turned abruptly and continued to walk deeper into the mist. With a heavy heart, Alleria followed him.

The deeper they ventured into the mist, the thicker the substance became. Around them was the soft howl of a wind they couldn't feel and the whole place was so eerie it filled the young woman with nerves. The farther they ventured into the fog the less she could see. Even Jack, who walked but a few feet in front of her, was obscured by the thick, white clouds.

She wrapped the blue cloak around her body, it protecting her a little against the chill in the air. Dark shapes cast silhouettes and Alleria couldn't make out if they were figures or just shadows caused by the swirling movements of the thick condense. On occasion, she believed that she could make out a pale, white face near her own, but the vision was gone as soon as she tried to concentrate. The chain around her throat glowed in the mists and it was warm to the touch. The light spread in a thin line, and though Alleria couldn't see Jack, she could see where the chain wrapped around his wrist.

Magic light.

"The mists are thicker than I'm used to." Jack's voice sounded distant. "We need to press on; we're almost out."

From the corner of her eye, just outside of the hood she wore, Alleria saw a pale figure move. The motion startled her and she stopped walking.

"Jack, there's something in here with us." The girl's whisper was harsh and Jack did not appear to hear her. "Jack?" she called his name and she felt the pull of the chain between them slacken a bit. Carefully, she stepped forward.

"What is it, Alleria?" He was close to her now, his face a little obscured by the white, but she saw his features and felt the warmth of his sweet-smelling breath on her face.

"There's something in the mist." Her voice rang with the alarm she felt, and Jack's expression changed from laconic to cautious. His body language changed too and he appeared more tense.

"Where?"

"I saw something there."

"That's not good." His hand reached out for hers.

He's not wearing gloves.

The warm touch of his skin gave her a jolt. "We'll need to move faster."

Something behind them made a noise. *A giggle?* The tiny hairs on the back of Alleria's neck stood up straight. They ran, with Jack holding her hand and leading her through the mists.

"What are these things, Jack?" Alleria panted.

"I don't know, and that's what worries me. The mists are a barrier; there should be nothing in here but the tylwyth tegs that cross it." He picked up speed, but his legs were longer than hers, and Alleria struggled to keep up. There was movement all around her. The white figures were fast and they were bigger than she first thought. Because of the speed they were moving at, she couldn't really make out any features, but she saw faces, and they frightened her.

"Damn it, I don't understand this. There is too much mist. We should be on the other side by now. Why are we still in the barrier?" Jack ran even faster, and this time, Alleria fell. Strong hands caught her and lifted her off the ground.

"I'll carry you. It'll be faster." He hooked his hands under her legs and held her like a child, while she in turn wrapped her hands around his neck. Alleria peered over his shoulder. There were hundreds of shapes in the mist. She saw them more clearly. Tall and gaunt figures, a shade whiter than the mist, advanced on them. A face without a body appeared right above Jack's shoulders, only inches away from Alleria's own face, and it moved along at the same speed that he ran.

"Oh Jack... it's right upon us. Can you see it?"

"No, I can't see anything, but I feel there is something here... something bad." He picked up speed and Alleria felt the impact every time one of his feet hit the ground. The face moved with the travelers no matter how hard Jack ran.

The features were feminine and horrifying. Slanted, red, bloodshot eyes looked out of the deathly white face and the lips of the hideous mouth were dry and cracked. The creature smiled at Alleria, revealing rows of pointed, overlapping teeth.

The thing leered at her; it looked as if it were about to pounce. The chain around the girl's wrist flared up, the heat stinging her skin, and the creature grimaced and drew away, only to come back seconds later. Alleria pulled the chain and dangled it in front of the creature. It flinched and drew back again.

I don't know what sort of magic this chain holds, but I'm grateful for it.

Jack ran, and the creature followed, but not as close as it had been. Its kin followed the duo at a distance, like ghosts in a line, approaching them with caution. As they ran, Alleria noticed the mist gradually fade, and the creatures fell back more and more the thinner the fog became. Eventually, the mists around them disappeared, but Jack didn't stop running until the specters were far behind. When he stopped, he let Alleria slide to the ground. Her body glided past his and she felt the pounding of his heart through his clothes.

Jack bent over and supported his weight by putting his hands on his knees, panting, his face a bright crimson.

"What was that?" he gasped.

"You're asking me? I've never been in the mists. How would I know?"

"Because you saw something. Did you get a good look at what was there?"

"I saw figures, and a face. A very scary face." Alleria shuddered and wrapped the cloak tighter around her shoulders. The image would haunt her as much as the thought of the spiders crawling from her hunchback.

"Whatever it was, I hope we won't come across it again."

Jack straightened himself, but his face was still flushed with the effort.

"Best to move as far away from the border as we can before we make camp."

I'm in the Arallfyd. Alleria held her breath in tense wonder. All the excitement with the monsters in the mist had distracted her from that realization. She looked around and found herself in the middle of a forest. It was different from the forests in the human world; everything about this place was new. The grass and the moss had a different hue—still green, but the tones were far more vibrant. The trees were smoother and looked painted rather than real, as if someone tried to make a fairy story come to life. Their bark was more purple than brown, and big, pink flowers peeked between the bright green leaves. But the forest lacked the lightness of a fairytale; it was a dark beauty that surrounded the two travelers.

The trees, the grass, the way the sun shone through the leaves above—spreading its light in golden rays—it looked too perfect. There was none of the wildness of nature. The grass didn't grow up in straight blades, but instead curled elegantly at the tips. The birdsongs around her were beautiful and harmonious, far more intricate than anything Alleria ever heard in the Shadow Marshes.

Perfection, but none of it is comforting.

"You'll get used to it." Jack patted her on the back as if he could read her mind and tugged the chain around her neck. "Now come on, we have a long way to go before we're near a suitable place to set up camp, and I would like to get there before dark."

The terrain proved easier for her to walk on. The ground was even and flat, no hidden holes to step in, no sharp plants to snag her clothes. Alleria was wary of her surroundings; the Arallfyd seemed to be too good to be true, and she didn't trust it one bit.

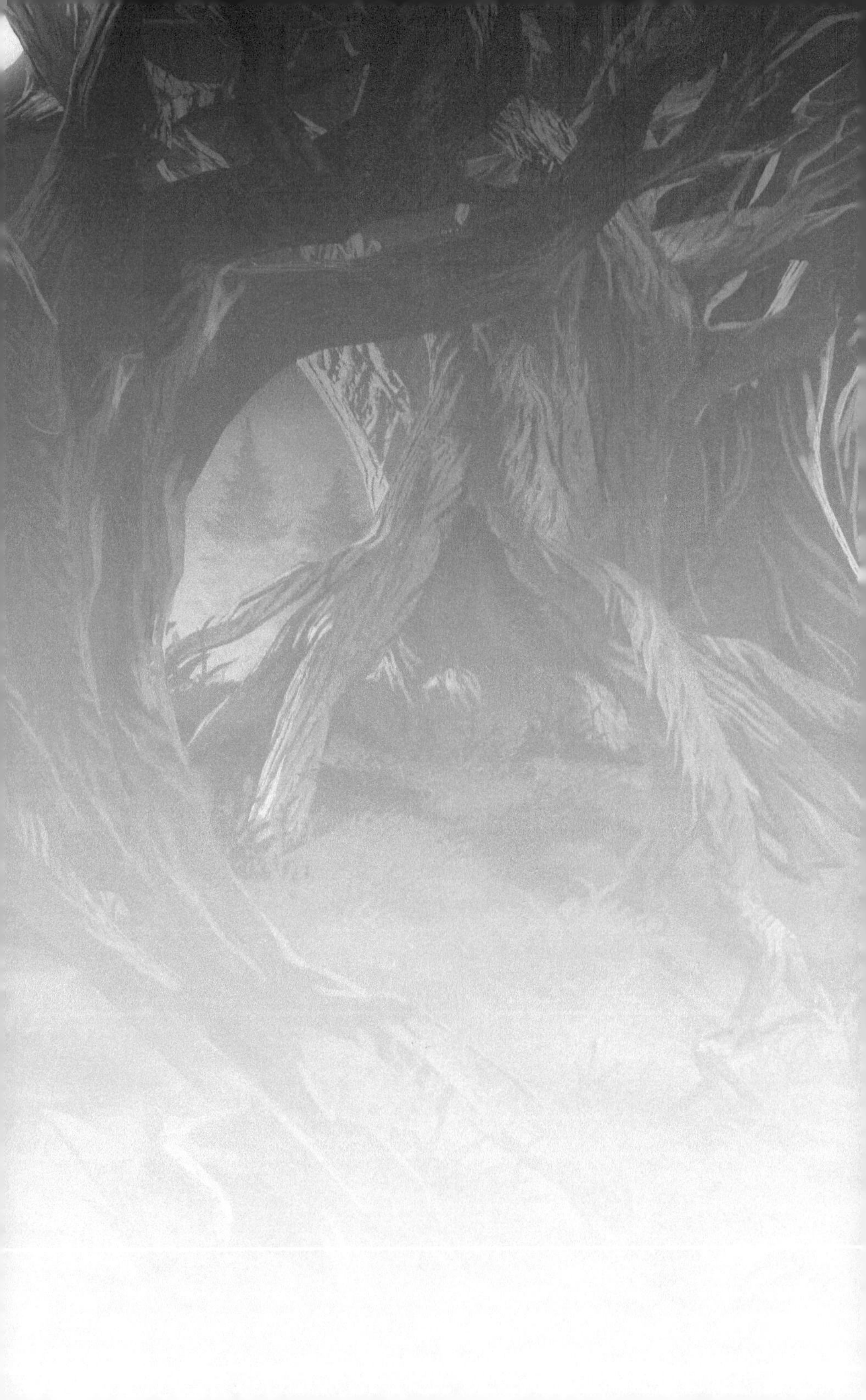

CHAPTER TEN

Her feet were sore from walking when they finally stopped for the night. Little blisters had formed between her toes, causing her to limp a little. The soreness did not stop at her feet alone. Her new shape required her to walk differently, and this wasn't as easy as Alleria had first thought. Over the years, she had grown used to letting her arm droop to the floor, but now she was forced to walk upright. Everything about her took some getting used to. Her body, her mind, nothing was the same.

Part of her still expected Tumsa to pry into her consciousness, see through her eyes, or manipulate her thoughts. She had never realized how invasive the constant presence of the old witch had been, but the absence of the second mind was all too obvious now. Her thoughts were free and unhindered, and Alleria could finally think for herself without having to be cautious.

Jack made camp near a small brook, which to Alleria's surprise, didn't run. It was completely still. He slipped the magic chain from his wrist and he pulled a silver spike from his backpack. Alleria watched in silence as he placed the chain on the ground and rammed the spike through it. Both flashed with light, and Jack shot her a satisfied look. Then he slid his fingers across the delicate links and the strange metal elongated under his touch.

"This way, it'll allow you to wander about a little. You can get water from the brook, and if you need to do… feminine stuff… it will reach to those bushes over there. Don't think this spike will let you go as easily as the Caretree did. That was a little of a mistake on my part, one I don't intend to repeat."

Alleria's fingertips played with the silver cable as she gazed at Jack. His odd-colored eyes squinted and he wrinkled his nose.

"Don't look so innocent; it makes me suspicious. I'm going to hunt for our dinner. *Stay. Here.*" He uttered the last two words with deliberate slowness.

When he moved from sight, Alleria pulled on the spike as an experiment, but it was as immobile as she expected it to be.

I hope I don't get attacked by Arallfyd monsters, she thought with some bitterness, but she knew that Jack wouldn't leave her here unless he thought it was safe. So far, the Arallfyd had been kind to her. No poisonous plants, no hungry creatures; she almost wondered why everyone was so afraid of this place. Her throat was dry, so she made her way over to the brook for a drink of water.

The reflection on the still surface caught her by surprise again and she stared at herself.

You're so vain, Alleria.

It proved difficult to peel her gaze away from the mirror image. The transformation was overwhelming and Alleria needed time to get used to this new face. She had to admit the reflection pleased her. At first, she hadn't been happy, but the more she thought about her change, the more she came to terms with it.

Suddenly, the fairytales she made up in her head weren't so unrealistic. Alleria nestled the grass—which was as soft and smooth as velvet—and put her hands under her chin as she studied the still water.

Her mind went back to the memory of Jenny Green-Teeth, and if she hadn't been able to see the bottom, perhaps she would have been more wary. Instead, she fantasized of a handsome prince who would find her at the slave market amidst a large group of other girls. The prince would fall instantly in love with the sight of her. She couldn't quite picture his face, but he was dressed in a crème-colored suit with gold stitching, and his cap had the feather of a pili bird. In her fantasy, she stood on a podium, surrounded by hundreds of people. All were bidding for her because she was the most exquisite creature they had ever seen and they had simply lost their hearts to her. She flushed from the mere thought that anyone could find her attractive.

The prince, of course, would be one of the bidders, and one by one, the others would drop out, until it was only he and one more contender left. The other man, obviously dark and evil—though equally handsome—would leer at her kind prince, concocting evil plans to make Alleria his. But her prince would be no fool, and a harsh battle of wits would see him victorious. He'd take her in his arms and break the chain from her neck with one hand.

"Alleria, I've loved you from the moment I saw you. I could never keep you as a slave. You are free to go, but I hope beyond all hope that you would do me the honor of becoming my bride." The imaginary prince's eyes would be filled with desire, his lips close to hers. "Oh, Alleria, I want to..."

Water splashed in her face and she jolted upright.

Jack laughed. "Looking at yourself in the water?" She wiped the water from her cheeks in cold indignation and refused to meet his eye. His mockery was an insult. She crawled away from the water and sat with her back toward him, wrapping her arms around her legs.

"Don't sulk." He winked. "I'd look at myself in the water, too, if I looked like you."

A laugh escaped his lips and Alleria rolled her eyes.

"I brought us some food. Are you hungry?"

She grunted, but her stomach informed her that she was famished. They hadn't eaten anything since they left Merwig's house many hours ago.

"Why don't you get us some twigs to make a fire and I'll clean the meat." He put two rather ordinary looking rabbits on one of the flat stones near the brook and waved her away with one hand.

"Yes, master." Alleria curtsied, and he shot her an annoyed look.

"Don't call me that."

"Why not, that's what you are, aren't you? My master. And I'm your slave."

Jack turned from her and focused on the rabbits. "It's not like that."

"What is it like then?"

"Just collect the wood, okay? I want some dinner."

Alleria shrugged and walked to the trees. Behind her, she heard Jack mutter, "I liked you better when you were cursed. You weren't so angry."

There were several branches that were useful to make a fire, and Alleria collected them in the crook of her arm. Something moved between the branches and she dropped the twigs on the ground. Her foot caught on her chain, making her fall backward. She landed quite hard on her backside and was still scrambling away when Halfway Jack crouched near her.

"What frightened you?"

A shaky finger pointed at the green creature that crawled from between the branches and Jack laughed. He picked it up. It was about the size of his thumb and slightly fatter, with spiky tufts of hair protruding from its body.

"Don't touch that," Alleria squeaked, her eyes round with terror. "It looks poisonous."

"It's a woolly caterpillar. They are harmless."

Halfway Jack held up the caterpillar for her to inspect, chuckling. He put it back down on the moss and both their eyes followed the creature as it crawled away.

"I didn't realize you were afraid of such a little thing."

Alleria crossed her arms and wrinkled her nose.

"Where I come from the little things are the deadliest."

"Fair point, the Shadow Marshes must have been a pretty dreadful place to live."

He offered Alleria his hand and pulled her up from the ground, then he bent down to pick up the fallen twigs.

"These should be enough to get a fire started. Why don't you sit down while I get dinner on?" She patted her dress and straightened herself, then moved to find a good space to sit.

Within the hour, Jack produced a rather fine meal of roast rabbit and some cooked vegetables that Alleria had never seen before. The food was delicious, better than anything she remembered ever eating. Even the vegetables, which looked like black turnips, were soft and juicy.

"Why do people say the Arallfyd is so frightening? It seems more pleasant than the Shadow Marshes."

Jack wiped his mouth with his sleeve and thought about her question.

"It is more pleasant. Nature is far more docile here than in the human world. If you are one of the fath tywyll, life can be pretty good here, with few things to worry about other than... well, different clans. Sometimes you have to worry about your own clan too." He poked the fire, his eyes dreamy and distant. "There are monsters here, though. And the monsters that dwell here are unlike any you have seen in either the human world or the Borderlands. Not all the fath tywyll are humanoid. Beyond the mists, only the ones that flood the human lands for the time of the Blood Moon are known. I suppose those are enough to strike terror in the human hearts, as they tend to spread chaos when they travel to those lands. Some will leave a trail of dead behind them. But I can tell you that there are far worse fath tywyll on this side of the mists."

"Why do they cross the border at all?"

"Well, I can't be sure—I'm not fath tywyll—but I believe that they find power in the human world. The same way humans need components for base magic, the fath tywyll seek certain things in the other world to further their positions in the Arallfyd. A lot of them just want to spread their seed, to make sure that they have allies on all sides. We are products of such ambitions."

He bit another piece of rabbit and chewed in contemplation.

"Of course, some of them just rampage for fun. The humans are lesser beings, and they make excellent hunting trophies. But I do believe that the fath tywyll try to find a way to break down the border. There are many treasures to be found in the other world, and I know some species of the fath tywyll would like to rule humanity."

Alleria shifted on her spot and clutched her bowl of food, a cold chill running down her spine.

"But they can't though, right? There is no way to destroy the border?"

"None that I know of, but I'm sure there is some loophole somewhere. There is always counter magic. The answer probably lies with the tylwyth teg. I mean, look at how we can cross with such ease. No one knows why that is. There was a time the tylwyth tegs weren't safe to go to the Arallfyd, because the fath tywyll would take them and perform tests on them to establish what made them able to cross the border. They would even go as far as dissecting us. Some even used their own offspring to conduct these experiments on. None of the research proved valuable, and in the end, the Council of the Hierophants decided to make a law against it. There are rules about our traveling here now, but we pretty much have a free pass through the realm. Though, it never stops being dangerous, for not every fath tywyll sticks to the laws of the council."

Alleria ran her finger across her empty food bowl and licked the juices from the tip with her tongue.

"I've heard of the Council of Hierophants. It was mentioned in several of the lessons that Tumsa taught me, though she knew very little about them aside from their particular talents for joint conjuration. They are able to combine their spells to create new ones, but only if all of them partake of the ritual of AO. I never quite understood what their actual function was aside from being powerful sorcerers. Are they the rulers of the Arallfyd?"

"Yes and no. No one force or council is the sole ruler of all of the Arallfyd; the way the hierarchy works is far more complicated. The Arallfyd has a great many who believe that they rule their own lands. There are fourteen kingdoms in total—twelve small and two very large and powerful ones. The twelve small ones are, in turn, split into several duchies. The dukes and duchesses have a lot of power over their own domains, though there is a monarch who technically reigns the entire kingdom. But the duchies all have their own rules, and some even have different currencies. As long as all the fealties are paid, most monarchs care little for what happens in the different parts of their domains, until the moments of the great rituals and festivals, when the Arallfyd comes together. Suddenly all rules change and the monarchs become rather possessive and often boastful of their territories. Then there are the two large kingdoms, which hold far too much power in comparison to the small ones. One is reigned by the Moonlords, the other by the Lord of Ravens. In order to keep some constraint on the chaos that would naturally occur from the different domains, and to make sure the two large kingdoms won't try to take over the smaller ones, the hierophants are the ruling government that bring all the kingdoms together. They rarely intervene for fear of rebellion, but they have the means to make sure that there is peace and equality between the kingdoms."

"Are the hierophants born to their role, or are they chosen?"

"It's a lifetime position, but they aren't born to it. It's the monarch's choice to put forth someone who can fill the position of hierophant. This is a mere formality to keep the monarchs appeased with the council because before they are even allowed to bring them forth, the chosen one must first be approved by the Parliament of Seers, who are the only neutral fath tywyll in the land. Once each monarch who wishes to bring someone forward has done so with the Parliament's blessing, the common folk get to vote. It's a bit of a farce because the common people rarely deal with the Council of Hierophants, and it's usually the candidate that has the Parliament's preference that wins."

"It sounds unnecessarily complicated." Alleria scratched her nose, struggling to keep her attention on the story Jack was telling her.

"It's complicated, but it's not unnecessary. This is politics, my dear. And part of politics is to keep everyone feeling important. This way, there is less chance of disgruntled individuals who feel overlooked. It's not a foolproof plan, but the fath tywyll are proud and often vain. They're also creatures that are prone to chaos, so keeping the lands from warring with each other is a great feat. Both the Council and the Parliament play an important role in this." Jack ran his fingers through his hair and let out a sigh that almost sounded like a whistle. "I don't envy them having to deal with this many different types of fath tywyll."

"Will we run across the fath tywyll while we are here?" Alleria perked up with the idea. She was part frightened and part excited by the prospect.

"Yes, plenty. We have a long way to travel, so we can't avoid them. But with any luck, we'll avoid the kind that you've heard those scary stories about. At least, I'll try to stay far away from them. They don't always uphold the council's rules. Like I said... they're prone to chaos." He leaned forward and gave Alleria a hard stare. "You are a valuable girl. Even in these lands, and there are those who will do you harm to get what they want from you. That's why it's important that you stay close to me and listen to what I say."

She countered his stare with a hard glare of her own.

"So you can bring me to a slave market, where people want to buy me to cut out my heart?" Alleria sucked on her lips, clenching them between her teeth. Jack's shoulders jerked at her words and he rubbed his hands through his hair.

"You heard that, huh?"

"I did."

Jack shifted his weight a little and held his head between his hands.

"Listen, Alleria… I won't lie to you. I'm not a good man and I don't have your best interest at heart, so don't expect that of me. But I promise you I will not sell you to someone who will only want you for your heart. There is more to your magic than that, which is why Tumsa kept you alive too. There are others like her that will just require your company."

"That's comforting."

"You know what you can do, right? You know what your power is?"

"You mean what I do when I'm angry?" She put down her bowl and rubbed her arms.

"No, the other thing. The reverse thing."

"No?"

"When you're angry, you age things. You suck the youth and the life out of things. But that's only a part of your magic, and it's uncontrolled. Your kind… you can do so much more. The way you take away youth, you can also give it. In a way, you stop or slow the aging system. When you are a little bit older, you should be able do so much more with this talent too. You'll not only be able to restore youth but also grant beauty. Do you know how valuable that is to most people? You don't have to die to extend people's lives. I can imagine a rich, old woman would like to keep you as her companion. Your life as a slave doesn't need to be a horrible one. I'm allowed to refuse a sale and I will make sure you don't go to anyone I don't trust."

He looked at her through his hands.

"It's still slavery, I realize that, but I really think you'll have a better life with these people than you did with the witch. I know some of them, and they're not bad people. This way, we all win."

"Yeah… slavery, it sounds like a real win to me." Alleria rolled her eyes and Jack shook his head and sighed.

"Nothing I can say will make this better. It's the situation that we're in right now. Sorry, little one, but it's not going to change."

There was a moment of awkward silence, and then Jack got to his feet and took the empty food bowls to the brook where he rinsed them out. Alleria swallowed. The prospect of slavery still made her sad, but Jack had managed to quell her fears ever so slightly. The idea of being a companion to a rich, old lady didn't seem so bad. Perhaps her new owner didn't have to be cruel. And there was always the prospect of freeing herself one day.

Halfway Jack glanced over his shoulder at her, a shadow of an emotion crossing his face. Alleria wanted to ask him about the woman Merwig mentioned, but she struggled to remember her name, and she was afraid that this would cause upset. Jack set the bowls out to dry. When he was finished, he grabbed his backpack and produced a blanket that he threw at Alleria.

"I had planned to travel from one warm and comfortable inn to another. Unfortunately, I'm not prepared for a long camping trip. We'll need to get some supplies in the next village unless we can make it to the shelter first."

"There are villages in the Arallfyd?" Alleria couldn't hide her surprise.

A smile bloomed on his face and Jack laughed at her. "Villages, towns, even great big cities. I don't know what you've been told about the Arallfyd, but it's more like the human world than you would think. It's not all just woods with monsters in them. Now get some sleep; there will be a long walk in the morning. I'll mind the fire for a bit. I need less rest than you."

The grass made a comfortable bed for the girl. She pulled the blanket around her slender frame. From across the campfire, she watched Jack, and he returned her stare with an expression she hadn't seen before. The sight of him brought butterflies to her stomach and she had to remind herself that she hated him very much.

The fatigue of traveling overwhelmed her now that she was lying down. She surrendered to sleep and horrible dreams, where pale women who lived in the mist tore open the skin of her face to reveal even more spiders. The dream creatures pulled Alleria's heart out of her chest with blood-drenched claws, only to reveal that her heart was actually Tumsa.

The nightmares woke her up several times, and she found Jack by her side. His hands stroked her hair and his soothing voice told her all would be fine. Before she fell asleep, once more, she felt less convinced of her hatred for him.

CHAPTER ELEVEN

As the days went on, the nightmares seemed to fade, though Alleria still jumped at every moving shadow around them, afraid one of the mist women would jump out at her. Jack navigated by the way the trees grew. He told her about the nature in the Arallfyd, and Alleria was an eager student. She learned which plants were edible and which could heal aches and pains.

Inwardly, she hated herself for enjoying Jack's company, but it proved hard not to. He was lively, and he was the first person to make jokes in her presence. Alleria kept her face a stolid mask when he quipped, determined not to give him the satisfaction of her smile. Her amusement would stay secret. To her regret, he never took her into the town where he got his supplies. Instead, he forced her to wait on the border of the woods. But when he came back, he carried a large backpack with him, filled to the top. One of the things he had brought her was new shoes. They were the strangest pair Alleria had ever seen, looking more like socks made from spun silver than shoes, but when she put them on, she felt how strong they were. They fit perfectly as if they shaped to the size of her feet—and perhaps that was exactly what they did.

Each evening they set up camp and each day the travelers packed up their belongings again and walked for many miles. Alleria was grateful for the new shoes. Not only did they protect her feet and keep them warm, but she also noticed she had fewer blisters now that she was wearing a decent pair.

Their journey through the Arallfyd was quiet and uneventful, but never boring. There were too many things to see and too many things to learn about this strange new world. The woods were so beautiful, with their elegant trees and colorful plants, and Halfway Jack was filled with endless knowledge and stories. Each of the areas had its own charisma, and she was stunned by all the colors that set them apart. There were creatures too, and to her relief, most of them were harmless, some even friendly. Alleria met her first unicorn when they made camp under a lavender-colored waterfall one night. The beast was the most beautiful thing she had ever seen. Its coat gleamed like the silver of the second moon and its mane and tail were white—but viewed from certain angles, you could see the rainbow in them. It wouldn't let Jack near it, but Alleria was allowed to pet its regal head. It was an experience she wouldn't soon forget and it pained her when she had to leave it behind the next day.

The weather changed more noticeably the farther they traveled, and the clothes that Merwig gave her didn't provide much warmth anymore.

"We have to walk a bit faster, Alleria," Jack announced after nine days. "We need to make it to the shelter before the winter is upon us, or we'll freeze to death."

"You will too?"

"Oh, yes. I'm not immune to the harsh cold of the Arallfyd winter either. Even the fath tywyll respect the Arallfyd seasons. Once we get to the shelter, we'll spend all winter there."

The idea of winter in the Arallfyd frightened Alleria. The marshes never got truly cold, just nippy at best—the temperature was always moderate, and she'd never experienced real frosty weather, not even by human standards.

"What if there are already people in the shelter?"

"I doubt there will be. It's only for tylwyth tegs, and there aren't that many of us. Few would be daft enough to venture here for winter."

"We were."

"The other choice was worse in our case." He pinched her cheek and winked. "We'll be okay. It'll be a little cramped, but we can survive the winter."

She flinched at his touch. "If you say so."

When the first snowflakes began to fall, Jack informed her they were two days away from the shelter if they kept up this pace. He smiled and told jokes, but he couldn't hide the panic in his eyes. Alleria saw right through him. He didn't want to scare her with facts, but she felt quite confident that winter in the Arallfyd was nothing like she had ever seen.

The temperature had dropped several days ago and was still dropping by the hour. The cold made her skin tingle unpleasantly. At night, her blanket barely gave her the warmth she needed, and Jack kept the fires lit high. But the cold, damp weather caused some of the branches they found to be too wet to light, and though he was all smiles, Alleria saw he was struggling.

Jack urged her on during the day, and she walked until her feet bled and she felt half insane with fatigue.

"Come on, we can't be too far from the shelter when the snow really starts, which will be anytime soon. Every step is one step closer to safety. Come on, Alleria. We don't have two days."

Feet torn, despite the new shoes, Alleria stumbled on. It was getting harder to put one step in front of the other, but she let Jack's voice guide her through the cold. The snow fell, pretty and light at first. Alleria marveled at the loveliness—this was the first time she had seen snow—and caught the sparkling flakes on her outspread hands. However, the flakes lost their appeal when they grew bigger and bigger as the day progressed. Thick lumps of snow landed on her face, hair, and clothes. They melted on her cloak and soaked the material. The snow was soft as powder, making it impossible to walk on top of, and so they had to wade through, which made them even colder and wetter.

Jack moved with the same grace as he always had, but Alleria struggled. The chill seeped into her skin and bones and her movements were stiff. The snow came up to her ankles, finding its way into her shoes, freezing her toes, and for the first time, Alleria missed the layer of fur she used to have.

Jack bound her feet with cloth to keep as much of the cold out as he could, and it helped a little—enough to keep her going.

Within an hour, the snow was up to her calves, and half an hour later, up to her knees. Both the cloak and dress were soaked. She shivered so violently it hurt, her teeth chattering in a melodic rhythm. Each movement was a struggle and she lost her balance every other step.

When the darkness fell, Alleria gave in to the weariness and fell flat on her face. The snow cushioned some of the blow and she barely registered that she'd lost the battle with gravity. Strong hands grabbed her and pulled her up.

"I'm too tired. Just leave me here. I don't want to move again." Her words were barely audible from her shivering lips.

"You need to keep moving, Alleria. If you stop now, you'll die." Jack pressed her against him and she could feel his warmth.

"I don't care. My life isn't that good anyway. Death might be nice. It might be less cold."

"If you die now, this is all your life will ever be." His words were harsh and the warmth of his skin brought some life back into her. "I can carry you, but it's better if you walk yourself. That keeps your blood flowing and will keep you warm."

She didn't listen to his words. Alleria didn't want to move again. She slumped against Jack.

"You're so warm... so nice and warm." The hands lifted her up and pulled her against him tighter. Alleria rested her head against his chest and tried to feel as much heat as she could.

CHAPTER TWELVE

She must have dozed off for a moment. When she woke, Jack still carried her. The warmth of his skin heated up her fragile, cold frame, but her body felt rigid from the lack of movement. She blinked her eyes and wiped the heavy snow from her eyelashes. Jack was covered too, his coat appearing almost completely white.

"Nice to see you're awake." He tried to smile at her, but it looked forced. "We're almost there, little one. Just hold on a tad longer, okay?"

Shame flushed her cheeks. "I can walk again, Jack."

"No, it's better if I carry you. We move faster that way."

"No, it's okay, I can move now. No need for you to carry me." She struggled, but Jack held on.

"Listen, I forgot that you weren't as well equipped for the cold as I am. My body... it works differently. Cold can make you slow, and it will take longer for me to get to that point. Just accept my help, okay? I feel bad enough for bringing you here, dressed as you are. I just assumed we would have more time before the snows. The winter came early this year."

She sighed but gave in and nestled against him. The snow picked up even more and Jack struggled to move forward. He held her up high because he was up to his waist in the white material. All Alleria thought about was to keep warm, and to warm Jack in the process, so she pressed her body against his and rubbed his chest and his back with her arms to keep the blood flowing. Whatever advantage his warm-blooded body had, it was cooling rapidly now, and his movements were becoming as lethargic and stiff as hers had been.

If he can't walk anymore, we'll probably die.

They moved on with slow determination for another hour while Alleria tried to warm her companion and herself as best she could. She used her warm breath to bring back some heat in the man's cheeks. Then, without warning, Jack shouted. She almost jumped out of his arms with shock.

"I found it. We're here, Alleria... we're safe."

Whatever Jack claimed they had found was hard to make out; all she could see was a large mound of snow, but Jack assured her it was a shelter. He put her down and she sank deep into the snow, the frost a shock to her semi-warmed system.

Jack dug in the snow with his hands and Alleria—eager to help and to keep moving—pulled clumps of ice from what looked to be a door. She was so exhilarated by the sight of the wood under the white powder that, for a moment, she forgot the cold. There was warmth and safety within. It only took twenty minutes of digging for them to reach the door, and a wave of disappointment hit her as she opened it. The inside was as chilly as the outside—but at least it was empty.

"We'll have to clear a path several times a day, and even at night; otherwise, we'll get snowed in. Luckily, the snow in these parts is pretty loose and the door opens to the inside. It should take us only an hour or so each time to do the entire path." Jack eyed the door and the route in the snow. "It's different from the snow in the human world. The consistency works in our favor, but the temperature won't. And don't worry about the weight. It's also lighter than human world snow. Plus, this shelter was especially made to withstand it, so it won't collapse." He shrugged and closed the door.

Jack lit a few candles and the sight of the room made Alleria's heart sink. The wood in the house was a dull gray color. The living area was a square room that branched off to a small kitchen with a robust stove. In the middle of the room was a large hearth, which was open on both sides. There was a door on the south side of the living room, but it was closed, so Alleria couldn't see inside. Thick animal pelts lined the floor, brown, black, and white fur overlapping, but nothing could cheer up the destitution that this room embodied. Sturdy wooden shutters lined the walls on all sides. Alleria couldn't pinpoint what was so upsetting about the place, but the thought of staying in that house for several months depressed her. Although she had never stopped being a prisoner, the days on the open road had given her more freedom than she'd ever had before, and she wasn't ready to give that up. She wrapped her hands around herself in an attempt to fight off the cold... and the sadness.

"Don't worry, little one, we'll get this house warmed up in no time." Jack pointed at a large hearth. "See, someone left us logs. Now, you hold that bucket while I open up the chimney; we don't want snow in the hearth. It'll make it harder to light the fire."

They worked together laboriously, and within an hour a fire roared, spreading a new heat through the little house.

"The good thing about this shelter being covered in snow is that it will keep the warmth in." Jack smiled at her and he poked at the wood that crackled in the hearth. Red and gold flames chased away the gloom of the house somewhat and bright shadows danced on the skeletal chairs and table. She still felt stiff, and the heat of the fire hurt her skin, especially her fingers, which burned with the warmth. Jack—on the other hand—seemed absolutely fine, as if he'd never experienced any cold at all. He turned to Alleria, his gaze gliding over her clothes, and shook his head.

"You need to take those off. Just keep your underclothing on. I can't have you walking around with wet clothes on; it'll kill you." His movements looked wild while he unbuttoned his coat and pulled it off, as if he were making a point. Alleria flushed and pulled at the clasp of her cloak.

"I... I..."

"This is important, Alleria, no time to be bashful." He sounded impatient with her as he stripped away more of his own clothing. Alleria stared at Jack's lightly bronzed skin, the ripples of the muscles on his chest, and his shapely legs. Her face turned an uncomfortable shade of pink.

With a heavy heart, she peeled the damp clothing from her thin frame, every muscle in her body aching and spasms shooting throughout. Her teeth chattered again. Jack helped her with the ribbons on the dress because her fingers were too frozen. When she dropped the heavy, wet material around her feet, she was left with nothing but the diaphanous undergarments she wore beneath, which would have been rather embarrassing if Jack hadn't stripped down to his breeches, which were very short, very tight, and left little to the imagination.

Jack opened the doors to a bedstead and took out thick blankets, which he shook to rid them of dust. A musty smell tickled her nostrils.

"Come here. We need to get you warmed up as fast as we can. I've kept the fire low up till now because you are still too cold. You shouldn't be exposed to too much heat in one go. There is a better way of warming you up."

The floor felt like ice to the soles of her feet as she tippy-toed toward Jack who was seated on the skin rug by the fire. He wrapped the blanket around him and held one end open for her to crawl under.

It'll be warm, Alleria; stop being such a child.

His naked skin was so warm that for a second, it, too, felt a little painful. He wrapped one arm around her when she crawled under the blanket and she soon got used to his temperature. He held her tight and she placed her head on his chest and listened.

His skin was soft against hers. She felt his hand move on her back, rubbing the heat into her, as only hours ago she had done to him. Her body protested, but slowly she felt the warmth return.

"I'm glad we made it in here when we did. I don't think we would have survived too long out there," she whispered.

Jack leaned back on the furs, and Alleria—who didn't want to lose the warmth of the blanket or his body—moved to lean back with him.

"Winter will be long, Alleria, and it'll be hard to be cooped up here together, so we need to make the best of it, okay?"

She refused to respond. The warmth made her drowsy, and not just her; minutes later, Alleria heard Jack snore lightly and she realized it was the first time she'd seen him sleep.

Hunger gnawed at her stomach, but the longing for sleep won. The journey had proved too draining. Sleep came easily.

Jack was up before her, as usual, and when Alleria woke up huddled in the blankets near the fire, he was busy cleaning the room. It was day, though the thick layer of snow didn't let in much light. The tantalizing scent of meat broth tickled her nostrils and she turned to see that a cauldron hung above the fire.

"Where did you get the food from?"

"Good morning, sleepyhead." Joy rang through in Jack's voice. "You slept like a log. I cleared the path to the door twice without even rousing you."

"Oh… I must have slept soundly. I was very tired." Alleria rubbed her eyes and graced Jack with a crooked smile. "Where did you get the food from?" she repeated.

"The storage room." Jack looked pleased as he pointed at a hatch in the floor. "The guardians of these woods stock up the food supply in the shelter every autumn so that the tylwyth tegs can pass through during the winter." There was something different about Jack; Alleria couldn't quite make out what it was.

"That sounds strangely considerate."

She pulled the blankets up to her bosom and raised her eyebrows at him.

"Well, yes... but we have to pay for our stay. This is not for free. Everyone benefits from this." He put his dishrag in a wooden bucket, wrang out the excess water, and rubbed it across the table and the chairs. Alleria watched him work. It was odd to see another person doing what was usually reserved for her, but she had to admit she didn't hate it. For once, she didn't jump up to help.

"What do you have to pay? Gold?"

"No, here in the Arallfyd, gold doesn't hold the same value. I can leave all sorts of things, as long as they are valuable to me. Or I can leave a favor, which I must make good on before next winter."

"How will these guardians know you'll pay though? You could just leave and they'll never know it was you."

Jack laughed, his hands pressing against his shaking stomach. Alleria didn't understand what was so funny and his reaction annoyed her.

"You really don't know the Arallfyd, do you? They'll know who stayed here. And it's bad for business to anger the guardians. No one will take the risk. We need these shelters to be here, so we all play by the rules. You compare us to humans, Alleria, and you must remember that we're not. Our way of life might be similar, but we're not the same. We are bound to rules, and we don't just break them like the human world does. In most cases, we can't break them."

"Did you not say yourself that a lot of the fath tywyll didn't stick to the council rules?"

"Well, yeah, but that's different. Those are rules of law, and not the rules of nature or magic. Rules imposed by a society are more like what we know of the human world. But there is a whole other dimension in the Arallfyd. You can't compare the two."

"So the guardians are magical?"

"Of a sort, yes. Nature and magic lie very close together in this place."

"I have much to learn."

She rolled her eyes at him, but he didn't notice. Then, out of the blue, it hit her what was different about him. It was his clothes. Instead of his coat, black shirt, and trousers, he now wore what looked like a long, woolen tunic with dark breeches underneath. These were definitely not made in the human world. She couldn't put her finger on it, but the fabric looked different, almost alive somehow, and the cut was nothing like she had ever seen. Jack looked like a creature from another world.

"Where did you get the clothing from?"

"I brought them here last time I came to visit. They're very warm, made of gnotig fur." He pulled at the fabric and smiled at her.

"You've been here before?"

"I've been known to hide out in the Arallfyd during the winter, yes." He winked at her. "Mainly because most tylwyth teg won't. I have some more warm clothes, though I don't think any of them will be in your size, so we might have to adjust them a little."

Alleria's cheeks flushed.

"You have other clothes, and you tell me this *now*? You let me sleep in my undergarments while you had other clothes for me to wear?"

She struggled to get to her feet. The blanket had wrapped itself around her right ankle and she accidentally stood on it with her left foot, which made it difficult for her to move. She was unwilling to let it go and lose her only cover. Instead of showing remorse, Jack laughed at her.

"Don't be so silly. I don't have a hidden agenda."

He shook his head and let his fingers glide over the rim of the bucket. An amused smile played around his lips.

"It's better to warm up skin against skin, Alleria. I should have demanded you be naked." The dishcloth dropped in the soapy water with a loud splash and Jack picked up the wooden bucket.

"You have no manners." She pulled her lips in a thin line and shook her head almost imperceptibly.

She still didn't manage to untangle herself from the blanket, so Alleria let out an exasperated breath as she sat with force.

"I didn't realize I had insulted your delicate sensibilities, my lady." Jack laughed and put the bucket in the corner of the kitchen. She ignored his comment.

"Are my clothes dry? I need something to wear for—"

Before she finished the sentence, a tunic and something that looked like breeches with the feet still on landed in front of her. They were all made of the same strange wool. Alleria rubbed her thumbs over the material; it was soft as goose down. She looked at Jack and he pointed at the door at the end of the room.

"Change there."

The room revealed a rather spacious area that she could only describe as an outhouse. There was a wooden seat with a hole in the floor and an empty bucket next to it. Alleria had never seen an outhouse attached to a house before, and this was usually with good reason, because the smell could get pretty horrible. She was the one who was in charge of digging the new holes for the privy back at Tumsa's cottage. Every few months, she would have to move the little wooden building, fill up the stinking hole, and create a new one. It was the worst job. She wondered how they would fare with this outhouse. Would they have to move it too?

Carefully, she lifted the lid and peered into the darkness. To her surprise, she didn't just see earth underneath, but what looked like some sort of well... only, not quite. There was no water at the bottom, and instead of stone, she was looking at wood that didn't only go down, but also veered off to the side. It was impossible to see where it ended up, but

Alleria understood that she needed the bucket to flush everything away. She hoped this was a good method against the stench.

This shelter truly is prepared for winter, she thought with a smile. It had to be, because in the weather they were having, it would be impossible to go outside for those specific needs. An indoor outhouse was the only option and this one seemed to be well thought out by whoever created it.

Aside from it being a practical place to wash and do those other things one might prefer to keep private, it also provided enough room for her to get dressed. She pulled the tunic over her head. The material of the garments tickled her skin, but it was very warm. It sure felt nice to have warm feet again.

Alleria thought back to the journey in the snow and she was surprised she'd arrived at the shelter without any real damage to her body. She'd never had any experience with the cold, but she'd read about the effects of frost and wondered if she owed any gratitude to the fact that—like Halfway Jack—she was not fully human. Alleria's inhuman genes had helped her against poisons too. She would have died many times over in the Shadow Marshes if not for that.

The tunic clung tightly against her curves—she still felt uncomfortable with the idea that she had curves—and when she exited the indoor outhouse, Jack shot her a strange look.

"It's a bit snug," she admitted.

"You actually look very nice," he said, then turned away from her, his head bowed. Curiosity tickled the girl, and if there had been a mirror, she would have sneaked a peek. Jack didn't look at her directly again, but he handed her a broom and asked her to aid him with the housework.

They spent the day cleaning the shelter, and Alleria tried to make it look homier by rearranging the furniture. In the cellar, she discovered the pantry, though perhaps storage room was a more accurate description, considering it held more than just consumables. She was stunned by the amount of food stacked across the shelves. The storage room was cold, as if the heat of the room above would not penetrate the underground space.

There were meats suspended from the ceiling, ready to dry, and cured vegetables floating in large glass jars that lined the many shelves. One side of the room was filled with fresh vegetables, most Alleria had never seen before, though she did spot some familiar ones like potatoes and cabbages. Fish wrapped in salt to make them last longer were stacked in boxes and the whole room smelled of dried spices. Big bags of wheat, oats, rye, and something that Alleria didn't recognize but looked like some sort of reddish clumpy flower stood in one of the corners. There were strange foods wrapped in cloth that were slathered in something similar to beeswax.

The sound of footsteps coming down the stairs made her look up.

"Don't let the sight of all this food fool you; we should be lucky if this gets us through the winter." Jack moved behind her and she felt his warm breath on her neck. Alleria's skin reacted involuntarily to his closeness.

"Even though it's just the two of us, we need to eat sparingly. Start with the fresh produce because that won't last. The cold should keep everything fresh longer, and since we're in the Arallfyd, it takes more time for them to wither, but by the end of next month, we'll be forced to eat nothing but the dried meats and the food in the jars." His finger tapped against a jar with dried tomatoes.

"When the worst of it is over, I can hunt some of the winter beasts to nourish us."

She turned around to face him and regretted it instantly; they were too close, and she felt uncomfortable. "Can't we leave when the worst of the winter is over?"

"No, it will still be too cold to survive the night. We can't leave here until the snow melts in spring." He brushed a hair from Alleria's cheek and she turned her eyes away.

"How long will that be? Until spring, I mean?"

"It depends. Winter doesn't work the same here as it does in the human world. It doesn't have a set time. It could last anywhere between two and six months."

"Six?"

Jack nodded, his eyebrows raised with mirth and his lips curled in a smirk.

"We'll be fine, don't you worry. I've done this before. Though I must admit, I do tend to get a bit of cabin fever now and then. But you can help me get past that."

A warm hand patted her on the shoulder. His eyes fell on the chain around her neck.

"I can take this off. We won't need it. There is nowhere to run except to your death in this place."

His hands glowed hot against her cold skin when he took off the chain; he slipped it back into the pouch around his waist.

"Thank you."

Jack pinched her cheek, but Alleria pulled away.

"Let me show you the well. It's a rather important part of the house," he said, as if taking the chain off was not an important moment.

To Alleria's surprise—much like the outhouse—the well was *in* the house, in a separate little alcove in the kitchen, inside what looked like a cupboard from the outside. Jack picked up a long stick with a heavy metal ball welded onto the bottom. Swinging his legs over, he climbed on the side of the well.

"What are you doing?"

"Breaking the ice. It'll be frozen. We'll probably have to do this every time we use the well, but once we've broken it, the new layer will be thin, so it won't need this much force. The water underneath should be fine; the earth never freezes all the way down."

With the might of a warrior, Jack brought the stick down on the ice and it shattered with a loud crack after only one blow.

"If you can't break the ice, ask me. Don't start fiddling around with flames or anything like that. We don't want to pollute our only water source because then we'll be forced to start melting the snow."

Jack jumped off the side of the well.

"I can break the ice; don't you worry about me." His lips curled in a crooked smile. "Let's go eat and see how the broth I prepared tastes. I have to admit I can't take all of the credit for making it, as I found the broth itself in one of the jars downstairs."

Whoever had made it, they knew how to cook, because it tasted delicious. The hot liquid, salty and meaty, tingled on her tongue. They ate in silence, each lost in thoughts of their own. After the hot breakfast, Alleria continued to clean the house while Jack went outside to shovel the snow again. Opening the door allowed some of the flakes to drift inside the shelter and Alleria took care to mop up after Jack.

After a quick look around the house, she found a wardrobe filled with blankets and even a few colorful throws, which she draped across the table and chairs. The orange, purple, and green hues brightened up the small room.

When darkness fell, the little house looked more cheerful, almost homely. Behind two of the larger shutters, she found two gigantic bedsteads, big enough to hold at least four people each. Alleria made to claim one for herself, but Jack shook his head.

"We can't leave the fire on when we sleep, so we'll need to share a bed. The nights are especially cold, and we will have to share body heat."

The thought made her uncomfortable, but deep in her heart, Alleria found the idea of sleeping next to Jack strangely alluring.

It won't be as lonely, and I'll feel safer having him near, she told herself, but she knew that was not the true appeal.

From the remnants of broth he made in the morning, Jack cooked a lovely stew with some of the dried meats and fresh vegetables. Alleria marveled at his cooking skills, which were far superior to hers. They sat on the skins by the fire and stared at the flames while they ate their meal. Afterward, Jack placed a bed warmer between the flames. He winked at Alleria and made his way to the kitchen.

"I found something in the storage room," he told her when he cleared up the plates. He handed her a stone flask.

"What is it?"

"Fire wine." He wriggled his eyebrows at her and smiled.

"What's fire wine?" Alleria looked at the flask dumbfounded, to the great amusement of Jack, who chuckled in response. "No, really, I don't know what it is."

"Alcohol."

She blinked at him.

What's so funny about alcohol?

"For cleaning wounds?"

"No, you silly goose, for drinking."

He slid next to her on the skin rug and glanced at her, his eyes filled with expectation.

"Don't tell me you've never drank alcohol before."

Alleria shook her head.

"Of course not. Tumsa and I only drank fresh water or milk. We used alcohol for some of her rituals and spells, and for cleaning wounds—never for drinking."

"Try some."

He nudged her elbow and she pulled her arm away irritably.

"It's a form of poison. Why would I want to put that in my body?"

"Don't be such a stick in the mud. It's not the same as poison... not really, anyway."

"Is it safe?"

Jack fell back, shaking with laughter. There was something about him that reminded her of a child, the way he was so easily filled with glee.

"Is it safe?" he repeated, his voice breaking. "No, it's not safe. That's the point of alcohol." He sat up and looked at her, still chuckling. "You need to lighten up a little, Alleria. You're far too serious. I think having a little drink might actually bring a smile to your face."

With nimble fingers, Alleria took the stopper from the flask and smelled the contents. It had a sharp, tangy odor, with a hint of sweet mixed in, but it immediately reminded her of open sores, and the idea of drinking it was unappealing.

"Stop making faces and just take a swig."

She shrugged and put her mouth on the flask. Something was bound to happen, she saw it by the openly expectant expression on Jack's face, so she closed her eyes and ignored him.

The alcohol touched her lips and the first taste she got was sticky sweet.

Quite lovely, actually... until she tasted the alcohol. Alleria's eyes popped open and the heat wave that passed through her larynx and into her stomach made her cough loudly. She almost dropped the bottle, but Jack took it from her grasp with lightning-fast motion.

Her throat still burned and she leaned on her knees while she coughed. Jack laughed at her. She wanted to hit him over the head, and at the same time, she couldn't help but chuckle.

"That stuff is terrible." Alleria sat again, still coughing slightly. "Why would you drink that?"

"To stay warm." The bottle pressed to his lips, he took a swig to demonstrate. "Because once you're used to it, it'll taste nice." Another sip. "Because it relaxes your muscles. Because it makes you smile and forget how horrible this world can be... even if it's just for a few moments."

Alleria wiped her mouth with the back of her sleeve and held out her hand.

"In that case, give me some more."

She pulled the bottle from him and took a smaller sip this time. The alcohol still burned, but she could taste the sweetness better now and had to agree that it was actually quite nice.

"Don't drink too much; that's never good. A light buzz is pleasant, but drunkenness leads to new troubles."

His body leaned into hers, his face close to her own, and he fumbled to steal the bottle from her grip. He placed it to his mouth, the stone bottleneck hiding his smirk. "Also, there isn't a lot of this stuff, so it'll have to last us all winter."

They drank for a while, each taking a little sip and passing the bottle back and forth, until Jack put it away. Alleria hiccupped, her head light and giddy.

"You know, when we walked through the snow, I actually missed being covered in fur."

A giggle bubbled up in her stomach and escaped through her nose and mouth. Jack rolled over and examined her, his gaze a little unsteady.

"I've never heard you laugh. In fact, I don't remember if I've ever seen you smile." He squinted and looked up in thought. "Hmmm, maybe I have..."

"I don't remember if I have ever laughed before. Not a real laugh, anyway." The giggle exploded into fits of laughter, though Alleria couldn't decide what she found so funny. "It's nice to laugh, I like it. Very liberating."

"I agree, I like to laugh." Jack slurred his words and put his hands under his chin.

"But you have a lot more to laugh about. For me, life isn't exactly funny," she scolded, a smile still welded on her face. When she glanced at him, she saw an expression of pain cross his features, but it was gone as soon as it came.

"Yeah, a lot…" His voice trailed off. Alleria frowned, displeased that she upset him.

"Where do you live, Jack? Do you have a house?" She turned her head as his eyes glanced over her face, and he moved a little closer to her, their bodies near, yet they didn't touch.

"No, I used to have a house, but I sold it. Now I just roam the lands and do business. I don't like to be tied down."

"It must be nice to travel. I don't remember much about my parents' house, but I know I didn't like being cooped up in Tumsa's cottage. The marshes were wonderful and I loved to roam there, despite their danger."

Her pink tongue ran across her lips and she tasted the lingering sweetness of the fire wine. The warmth of Jack's hand as it touched her cheek startled her. When their eyes met, she saw a funny expression on his face. The lightheadedness cushioned the awkwardness she would have felt and she smiled at him, her eyes heavily lidded and dreamy. There was a shift in his movement when Jack brought his face close to hers, his lips brushing against the skin of her ear as he talked.

"You've never been with a man, have you, Alleria?"

Her big, blue eyes widened and her mouth dropped open. The look was obviously comical because Jack laughed at her again. When he pulled back, her face felt cold and hot at the same time. Jack rolled to his back with his hands under his head, looking up at the ceiling.

"It will be very difficult for me to restrain myself around you all these months, Alleria." The odd-colored eyes never looked at her as he spoke. "You're a very attractive girl, and we'll be here for a long time together, cooped up with no one around. It will take every bit of my restraint not to try and seduce you." He rolled to his side and studied her. "Did you know that people will pay more for a virgin at the market?"

He rubbed the back of his neck.

"That's not the only reason why I won't try to make you mine, but it's a damned good one. In truth, I can't take advantage of one so innocent."

His fingers stroked her ankle. "You sure are a temptation—" A sigh, and he rolled onto his back once more, right arm covering his face.

"I don't understand..."

"No, I don't suppose you do. You've never experienced that specific kind of affection, have you?"

He sat up suddenly and leaned toward her again, the tip of his nose resting against her cheek.

"Do you know what it's like to be kissed, Alleria? Do you know how it feels to have someone's lips pressed against yours?"

Hot breath, scented with sweet fire wine, swept over her skin, and it warmed her more than the alcohol did. Butterflies escaped invisible prisons in the depths of her stomach, and her body responded to his proximity.

"No."

She wanted to say more, but her thoughts were jumbled, and the image of Jack took over her mind: his face, his hair, his mouth...

Oh, his mouth.

Ripples ran up and down her skin and she closed her eyes, her lips slightly open to receive his kiss... her first kiss.

"Such a pity too; I hope whoever I sell you to will appreciate my restraint." He pulled back and touched her on the chin. Alleria's eyes grew wide and her mouth dropped again. A hot flash of indignation coursed through her.

"And if they don't, they can always cut out my heart."

The alcohol had made her brazen. Jack turned and shot her a sharp look.

"We talked about this, Alleria."

"No... *we* didn't. You talked about this, and I listened. Because that's what slaves do."

The words—filled with venom—rolled off her tongue, the cold pang of rejection still sharp in her chest and the anger and frustration of her lifetime bubbled to the surface.

Control your temper, Alleria.

"You're not my slave." The room was cold despite the heat of the fire and the warmth of the alcohol that ran through her.

"Yes, I am. I am here to do as you please. If you wish me to go to the slave market, I must follow you. But fine... you say I'm not your slave, and yet you talk about your buyers appreciating some restraint? Who says you need restraint? If I truly am not your slave, then my body is my own, and I will not allow you to touch me. You disgust me."

I've said too much, I can see it in his face.

Jack's eyes narrowed and his mouth widened into a sneer. Without warning, he pounced on her, pinning her to the floor. The weight of his body was heavy and warm and the hairs of the fur rug tickled Alleria's exposed neck. With his knee, he pried her legs apart and he put his face directly above hers.

"Do you think you wouldn't give me your permission?" he hissed at her, the alcohol still slurring his words. He pressed his chest down on her, his knee resting painfully between her legs. "If I really wanted to, do you think you would be able to withstand me?" Anger and fear mixed into a bubbling darkness, and the fur rug underneath Alleria grew rigid and stale, the tangy scent of old age wafting upward.

"You would hurt me in such a way? Are you that cruel?"

"Hurt you? Do you think I would force myself on you? Me?" He moved his head to flick the hair from his eyes. "I am far crueler than that, little girl. I would make you beg me for my touch." The smile on his face was cold as ice and Alleria shivered.

"You have far too much confidence..." But she didn't finish her sentence. A wave of emotion hit her, her body trembling with desire.

He's doing something to me.

The darkness retracted immediately and Alleria didn't have the faintest idea what was happening to her, but she felt the effect on the rug reverse. Instead of growing staler and older, it was getting supple once more, and it was as fresh as the day it was first made.

It's not Jack who's reversing it, it's me... this emotion... it's so strong, and it wraps around me like a comforter.

There was a certain freedom in this desire. Alleria wanted to press her lips against Jack, to offer herself to him, all of her. She spread her legs a little, not fighting his weight but allowing him to rest on her. Above her were the eyes, one green and one blue, staring into her soul, and there was an expression in them that she had seen before, only now intensified.

Hunger.

His hand touched her jaw and part of her neck and he moved in closer. She awaited his kiss with much anticipation, her stomach making little somersaults. The moment before his lips pressed against hers, he pulled away.

"I can have you whenever I want, Alleria, and you will let me." The smile on his face was harsh and his eyes mocked her. They remained in that position for the longest minute of Alleria's life, then the ruthless expression melted from his face and Jack shook his head. He pushed himself away from her, leaving her cold and exposed, the shame flushing her cheeks pink.

"That's not the same as consent, Jack... and you know it," she said softly.

"I can't make you do anything that you don't secretly want, Alleria. I can only break free lust that is already there. If you truly felt nothing for me, my power would have no effect on you."

The words hit her like a slap in the face and Jack ignored her shocked expression. He jumped to his feet and poked the remaining logs in the fire before he put the grate in front of the hearth. After a few seconds of doubt, he turned to Alleria, his face a mask of innocence.

"These will burn out nicely. We should go to bed. I've put something that will be suitable for you as a nightdress over there." He pointed at a long chemise draped over the chair. "Put that on."

The floor felt cold against her soles when she walked, even through the woolen feet of the breeches, a contrast to the heat of her body. The warm feeling she had was gone and lust mingled with a sense of disgust. Alleria plucked the chemise from the chair and made her way to the outhouse. Closing the door behind her, she leaned against the wood and took a few deep breaths. The room, and everything in it, felt unstable.

Is this what alcohol does to you? Makes the world spin? It was so pleasant before, but now...

She peeled off her clothing—fingers shaking—and slipped the garment over her head. Alleria pictured Jack's handsome face and the smell of his breath as he leaned on top of her. The thought made her blush again and she waved her hand near her cheek to cool her face. Then she thought about the sleeping arrangements.

How am I going to sleep in the same bedstead as Jack after this?

Her mind would be more at ease if she could sleep in the other bed, and perhaps in light of their strange conversation, he would allow her the space. She took a deep breath and pushed at the door. At the same time, Jack opened shutters to the bedstead. Alleria crossed his path and made her way to the other bed, but Jack pulled her arm.

"You've had more to drink than I thought. It's in here." He pulled the bed warmer away and put it near the hearth. "I made the bed nice and warm for you. Just crawl in."

Her stomach twisted as she crawled into the bedstead on her hands and knees. The blankets were so warm they were almost hot to the touch. Alleria nestled herself in.

Jack stripped off his clothes, except for his breeches, and crawled in the bed with her. The skin of his chest looked soft in the light of the candle.

She felt grateful when he blew out the flame. There was a soft sound as he placed the stub on the shelf above their heads.

The dark provided her with a false sense of safety until she felt his warm body slide in next to her under the covers. A heavy arm rested across her stomach, and for the briefest of seconds, she was afraid to breathe.

Her muscles were stiff, her body rigid with tension, and Jack must have noticed because she could feel his hot breath on her skin when he whispered: "No need to be afraid, little one, your honor will be intact after this night. The only reason we share a bed is to share the heat. I will be a perfect gentleman. Even if my behavior before left a lot to be desired. I do apologize."

His fingers lightly touched her hair in a conciliatory pat; then he nuzzled his nose into her hair, and she heard his soft, rhythmic breathing. Within minutes, Jack's light snoring hummed in her ear, and she felt relief. She could breathe again, and most importantly, the desire to kiss Jack was almost gone... almost. Eventually, she, too, fell asleep.

CHAPTER THIRTEEN

The difference between day and night was subtle due to the lack of daylight, and the two companions lived in a relative darkness. Alleria longed for the light and even more for the outside world. The day after the shared bottle of fire wine, Jack acted standoffish and irritable. Alleria couldn't do anything right in his eyes. Whatever she did, he corrected her and took over. There was not a lot of work to be done in the house, and there was even less distraction from their cooped-up situation. Jack had more chores to keep his mind off things. Six times a day and twice a night, he shoveled the snow away from their door. He assured Alleria that once the snows stopped, he wouldn't have to shovel quite so frequently, but she could see in his eyes that he enjoyed it. Shoveling was one of the few tasks that required him to be out of the dwelling, and though Alleria offered to help, he would always mutter some excuse.

Once again, she was imprisoned, and this time she didn't have marsh lands to wander about in.

At dinner, Jack poked at his food, but he didn't eat, and Alleria ignored the way he chased a vegetable around his plate.

"I owe you an apology." His eyes were still on his food and he refused to look at her. The spoon that was halfway toward her lips hovered in the air. "A real one this time."

"I don't understand."

"Last night... when we drank... I..." He rubbed his hand through his hair and over his face.

"Oh... that." Alleria shrugged. "Nothing happened. I'm worth more as a virgin, so I was perfectly safe."

"No, you weren't." He looked at her through the strands of dark hair that fell over his forehead and across his eyes. "You weren't safe, Alleria, because I was playing a nasty game with you. I can't touch you, because... because, well, just because. But I would have let you touch me." He looked away and sighed. "And I played a dirty game to make that happen."

"The alcohol?"

I really don't understand, and it makes me feel dumb.

"What I did to you last night, it was unfair, and I stepped way out of line. You hurt my pride, and I was a little drunk. It's no excuse, and I feel like a heel because of it. It won't happen again."

"You mean what you did with that power of yours?"

"Yes."

"What exactly does your power do?"

"I can find someone's desire and amplify it to the point where they can't resist it anymore."

"Oh..." She put her hands to her cheeks to hide her blush, but Jack noticed it and laughed again.

"I promise, I won't do that to you again." His hand crossed his heart and he kissed the fingertips. "You're a lovely girl... perhaps a little too lovely for your own good. But I need to show a little constraint." His face showed a hint of alarm. "I mean for your sake, not for the clients... I should never have said that. That was a low blow. It doesn't help that I can feel your reluctant desire for me. I can tell you that it's difficult to be good."

"I should be very angry at you for what you did. You know what Tumsa did to me; how is this different?" She tried to keep her face strict, but her relief was impossible to hide.

He's a freak too, just like me.

"I would like to say it's different because I only tamper with emotions that you already have. But you are right, it's just as despicable, and I truly am sorry." He sighed. "Can we please not be enemies? It will be a long winter if we are." A cold gust of wind swept in from under the door—a disadvantage of keeping it snow free, and Jack rushed to put a blanket in front of the gap. When he came back, his face was solemn, but a twinkle shimmered in his eye.

"Come on, Alleria, let us not fight. You can rest at ease because I can't control your mind. Your actions are your own. I can't force you to actually kiss me or... or more. So even if I use my power on you, the choice will always be yours to make. My power just lowers boundaries a bit."

Jack held out his hand for her to shake, and she accepted it.

You are a dangerous man for me, Halfway Jack, a very dangerous man. Because even now, in the light of day, when you don't put your strange power on me, I still dream of kissing you. And I hate that you can sense this.

Alleria graced him with an awkward smile and squeezed his hand.

"This would have been easier on me if you hadn't transformed."

He winked and Alleria felt her smile falter. Her eyes lowered for a brief second. Jack didn't notice as he spooned the food from his plate into his mouth, his appetite obviously refreshed.

"We need to find a way to keep ourselves busy because there won't be enough chores around the house until the worst of the winter is over."

Jack took their plates to the kitchen where he washed them with water and a rag.

"If we don't find things to do, we'll go mad. I know I will. We need a schedule."

After a bit of exploring, Alleria stumbled upon clothes in one of the wardrobes. Much of the fabric was still good, though the garments were mostly old and torn.

"People leave stuff they can't use here. What's garbage for one person may be treasure for the next," Jack explained. There were skirts and tunics in different faded colors, and when Alleria tried them on, she found none of them fitted her form. Jack found some needle and thread and taught her to sew proper stitches so that she could adjust the costumes to her size.

"I'm surprised Tumsa didn't teach you how to sew." He tapped on her fingers when she made a wrong turn with her needle. "Underneath, like I told you," he scolded.

"There was no need. People would bring her old clothes and there was always something there for me to wear. She even made me wear a burlap sack on several occasions. Tumsa would just cut out holes for my arms and my head." Alleria frowned as she pushed the needle through faded red fabric. "It didn't matter what I looked like."

While she sewed, Jack was cutting little figures out of one of the logs they used for the fire. He told her he would make a game for them to play at night.

"Is there anything you can't do?"

"I'm a wandering spirit, so I need to be a Jack of all trades." He laughed at his own pun and Alleria rolled her eyes but chuckled along.

"I know a little bit about everything, Alleria. And I know a lot about nothing."

She raised an eyebrow and rested the sewing on her lap.

"Do you know about love, Jack?" The words were out of her mouth before she realized she'd said them, and Alleria was surprised at herself for asking the question. Jack's face darkened and there was a sadness in his eyes.

"I... I'm sorry, I didn't mean to pry."

"I know about love. It broke my heart once—"

The knife in Jack's hand slowed to a stop and he put the figure—which looked like it was shaping into a small cat with an arched back—down.

"It's only fair that I tell you the story of why we are here right now, why I want to sell you on the market. It's not your fault that you are in this situation. I don't exactly consider myself a slave driver, and I had never expected to sell anyone on the market, but here we are."

"Is this about the girl that Merwig mentioned?"

"Enarina?"

"I think that was her name—"

The silence in the house was accentuated by the winds howling outside. Jack stared at his work, but he was silent. She wanted to say something, perhaps comment on the storm, but she felt deflated.

"Almost seven years ago, I was a different man—well, more of a boy, really—than I am today. My mother was a human woman, like yours, and like you, I was raised in the human world. We were very poor. No one wanted to marry a woman who had given herself to one of the fath tywyll, voluntarily or not. That sort of thing taints a woman in the eyes of common men. My mother suffered, but she never showed it, she was so strong." A small smile played on his lips and Alleria could see a genuine affection on his face when he recalled the memory of the woman who gave birth to him.

"Mother raised me all on her own, and she did small jobs for rich ladies and gentlemen. She'd cook and clean, mend clothing... I can't remember a day where that woman wasn't working. We lived in a small room in a boarding house belonging to this sour old woman called Miss Pritchett. The old bat used to frighten me when I was little, and she had plenty of chores for my mother too, who rented the room for a few coppers a month. When I grew older, my mother taught me how to help her. At first, I only kept our room clean, then I took on chores like cooking, mending broken things, and even sewing. I would help Miss Pritchett out with the work around the boarding house. The house itself was rather large and made of real stone. It even had two stories, and I was always fixing the stairs and the shingles on the roof or cleaning the chimneys. I hated working for Miss Pritchett, she was so unkind. She looked like an old vulture, the way her neck stuck out, and her nose was like a beak. To a young boy, that's terrifying. Gray hair like steel... you know the thought of her still frightens me a little?" Jack laughed and he mimicked Miss Pritchett's body language. He pushed out his neck and hunched his shoulders, walking around the room like a bird. Alleria thought he looked more silly than he did scary.

"She would turn to me and say: 'You are not worth the salt of this earth, tylwyth teg. Instead of calling you Halfway, your mother should have called you Halfwit.'" Jack let out a loud cackle and Alleria hid a smile behind her hand. With an annoyed shake of his head, Jack sat again, his face more serious than it was moments ago.

"I told my mother that I disliked the old woman, and Mother decided I was old enough to help her with the chores she did around the rich houses instead. There was one house she was particularly eager to take me to, and that was of Old Man Metisse. It turned out that this old man was a faerisee, and he showed a particular interest in me."

Alleria put her sewing to the side and hung on to his every word. She pictured the people he talked about, and in her head, they looked like the characters from her fairytales—caricatures with colorful clothing.

"Old Man Metisse was as wealthy as a man could be. Well... is, he's still alive, and he's even richer now than he was then. The reason why he is rich is because Old Man Metisse—or Boss Metisse as he liked to be called—has very little scruples and is a dangerous person. I didn't know that when I started working for him. All I knew was that he offered me a handsome sum to bring parcels around the western provinces. I took the job gladly, and within a year I had made enough money to get my mother out of that boarding house. I was only thirteen at the time, but I looked like a grown man. The old man really liked me; he took me in his confidence from time to time, and when he discovered some of my half-blood talents, I became his bodyguard."

His talents?

A pang of curiosity went through Alleria and she yearned to know what his talents were besides the one he demonstrated, but she didn't want to interrupt his story.

"Boss Metisse liked to collect magic items, especially from the Arallfyd. His house was (and probably still is) lined with them. But the old man had a dream, and he wanted to possess one of the hearts of Odalyn, a magical diamond that has minor healing powers. There are more powerful healing items, but the heart of Odalyn is rare and very beautiful, so the boss had his own heart set on one. Later I learned that the diamond was the key ingredient for certain magic spells, and that was the real reason why the boss wanted one. And, as you may have guessed, I was the person who would get it for him. To make a long story short, I found the diamond in the Arallfyd, and I traded it for something equally precious that Metisse gave me before I left."

Jack's expression changed and his Adam's apple bobbed as he swallowed. The difference was subtle, but it intrigued Alleria; she cocked her head slightly and squinted her eyes.

"On my travels—while I searched for the diamond—I met Enarina. She was a beautiful creature with warm, light brown skin and hair the color of flames. I was young and I didn't realize that there was more to life than beauty. The time I met her I was merely fifteen, two years younger than you are, Alleria, and I believed it was true love. I would have killed for her. We only spent three months together, but they were the best months of my life. Then one night, after we retrieved the diamond, Enarina lay in my arms. We had just made love and she looked at me with her beautiful hazel eyes.

"'It's good that you managed to get the heart of Odalyn for your boss,' she said, her face near mine and she kissed my cheeks, lips, and chest with tiny feather kisses.

"'I am so relieved that I found it. It took me a lot longer than I thought it would. I'm sure Metisse is impatient by now, and he's not the kind of man you want to be impatient with you.'

"'Is he very dangerous?'

"'Yes. When I first started working for him, I had no idea how dangerous he was. But I stood by his side for a few years and I have seen things. Let's just say that man has a nasty temper. I'm glad he likes me. He'll like me even more when I bring him this diamond. Perhaps he'll reward me generously, and you and I can make a life together, away from him.' I turned to her, my eyes filled with excitement, the thought of being with her was so exhilarating. 'I know we only just met, but I know I love you. I want to spend the rest of my life with you.'

"She kissed me and gave me the most perfect smile. 'Silly Boy, I don't want to spend my life with you. You've been fun, that's for sure... but this thing between you and me... that was just business.' Before I had a chance to react, she pushed an onyx dagger into my heart. The pain blossomed through my chest and I stared at her in shocked confusion. My whole world shattered at that moment."

A gasp escaped Alleria's lips and she held up her hand to cover her open mouth. Her eyebrows were furrowed and her heart beat fast against her chest.

"I'm so sorry, Jack."

"She betrayed me. After she stabbed me in the chest, she took the heart of Odalyn and left me to die. She looked me right in the eyes when she did it."

The memory was visible through the pain in his expression, and Jack shook his head, his mouth thin with anger.

"You should have seen how she laughed at me, when I fell backward, my hand clutched around the weapon. If Merwig hadn't found me, I would have not survived the night. She probably expected me to die instantly, but I'm a tylwyth teg, and we are tough creatures to kill."

His hands fumbled with the shirt he wore and he ran his fingers across a fair scar line on his chest. It was so faint Alleria hadn't noticed it before. It looked almost like a blond hair lying across his skin.

"The worst was yet to come because I had to go home empty-handed to the boss. I thought I knew what a vindictive man he was, but really, I had no idea. I learned though... I learned soon enough when he called me to him.

"'I've been thinking how I'm going to punish you for losing my diamond,' he told me. The old bastard leaned back in his chair and looked at me. 'You lost me something, and I need to show you how serious this is. How angry I am with you for letting some girl rob you. I trusted you, Halfway Jack, and that trust is gone. How do I know that you didn't just screw me over? How do I know there really was a thief? Maybe you wanted to keep my diamond for yourself. There is no way of knowing these things. So, you need to be punished, and then you need to make amends.' Beneath the table stood a large box and he clicked his fingers for one of his guards to pick it up. 'Normally I would kill you and everyone you love, because I don't tolerate this kind of failure. But that won't get me my diamond back. And I need that diamond, Jacky boy. I need it before the next Blood Moon, because if I don't have it by then, I will be in serious trouble when the fath tywyll cross the border. Do you see where I'm going with this?' I nodded, but I really had no idea. 'Lucky for you it'll be another six years before the Blood Moon rises again, so that'll give you some time. So you get me a heart of Odalyn by then, and I won't have to kill you too.' His words made my heart skip a beat, and I thought

'Who did he kill?' Then he pointed at the box and told me to open it..." Jack buried his face in his hands and sighed. For a moment, it appeared he might cry, but he composed himself. "When I did, it was the still face of my mother who stared back up at me. Her eyes were terrifying, still filled with fear and yet so dull at the same time. They cleaned the face up, so there was no blood, but she didn't really look like my mother anymore. I didn't want to give Metisse the satisfaction of seeing my tears, so I swallowed my emotions."

For the first time since Alleria met Jack, he looked fragile, and she rested her hand on his arm for comfort. He patted the back of her hand. "The boss wasn't done with me yet. The sight of my mother wasn't enough.

"'In case you consider running, my boy... don't. I have a little trick for that too.' He snapped his fingers again and the door opened. A wizard—human by the look of him—entered the room and he was holding a mortar, on top of which lay a long, needle-shaped dagger. The two bodyguards held onto me, even though I wasn't going anywhere, and the wizard stepped closer.

"'Hold his head; I need him to be very still.' The man's voice was nasal and whiny, and I hated him instantly. Strong hands held my head and hair and I didn't struggle. Whatever the wizard meant to do to me, there was no use fighting it. I've always known when to pick my battles. To my horror, he dipped the needle dagger in the mortar and brought it to my eye. Thumbs held up my eyelids, I don't even know whose thumbs, because I was too busy struggling inwardly against my rising panic. The wizard pushed the point of the weapon into my eye and I felt a slight burning sensation. The penetration of metal in my cornea was less painful than I thought it would be, but something entered my body, and I felt it crawl deeper into my eye."

He rubbed his eye at the memory of it and Alleria shuddered.

I had my skin removed, she reminded herself. *I've seen my own share of horror.*

"When the wizard did his thing, he chanted some sort of spell and left the room. Whatever magic he cast, it went straight through any natural resistance I had; this was a powerful man, and he worked for Metisse.

"'Now you can't go anywhere without me knowing where you are, Jack. You are mine, and if you even consider running away, I will find you, and I will torture you to death.' Needless to say, I believed him. I haven't seen him in all this time, but I still fear that man. I've been looking for a heart of Odalyn for six years now, and I finally found one a year and a half ago. There are only three in the whole world, I found out, and they are not cheap. The owner of the heart wants a Servantian dagger. Lucky for me, those are less uncommon; unlucky for me, they cost more coin than I can just come up with. This time, I didn't have anything to trade with, so I had to find something."

"And you found me?"

"It was a lucky stroke on my part. I happened upon one of Tumsa's more knowledgeable customers, a faerisee who sat in a tavern at the edge of the Shadow Marshes with three companions.

"'That old witch has a gosgeiddig living with her, I'm sure of it,' I heard him tell his friends. The man was clearly drunk. 'Don't want to mess with that nasty hag, or I would grab that gosgeiddig for my own. They are very valuable. I know people at Mtumwa who would pay almost anything for a creature like that. I think it might be the only one in existence right now. I wonder if the old witch knows what she has in her hands.' The men discussed how they would steal you from Tumsa, but I knew they were all talk. I, on the other hand, had nothing to fear from a human witch. Her magic could only harm me in the mortal world, and even then, she would need to cast some powerful spells to penetrate my natural resistance."

"So you came, and you claimed me." Alleria closed her eyes for a second and saw the image of Jack standing in the doorway.

"I did, and the rest is history."

"So, if you don't sell me on this market, you will die?"

"Yes." Jack picked up the wooden figure again and he chipped away at a small piece to create a tail for the cat.

"It's nothing personal, Alleria. You are the first person, and the last, I will sell into slavery. I honestly wish I didn't have to, but time runs short and so do my options. At the market, you will raise enough coin to buy me my dagger, and probably even a lot more."

Alleria shrugged and picked up her own sewing. "It's the story of my life, I guess. I serve a purpose for someone."

She bit her lip and didn't look Jack in the eye.

"That's not true. You are worth a lot more than serving a purpose for someone else. It's just... I'm selfish."

All she could do was nod. They worked in silence, each deep in thought about the story Jack just shared.

Their routine helped a little to pass those seemingly endless dark days, but the winter was long and dull, and both inhabitants of the shelter felt restless. After a few weeks, the captivity wore Jack down. He paced back and forth like a trapped animal. Both he and Alleria kept looking for things to keep them busy. When he finished carving the little figures for his game, they spent most nights playing it in a variety of ways. Alleria learned that she loved playing games and it helped Jack act more relaxed. There was something joyful about that time of day.

Though they spent a lot of time in each other's presence, they found a way to have some privacy too. Alleria used the bedstead as her private place, while Jack would spend long periods of time in the outhouse. She wasn't sure what he did in there, but he always gave her a funny look before he excused himself.

To keep the shared time pleasant, Jack told Alleria stories about his many travels. In one of the drawers, he found a deck of cards, which added variety to the games they played. At first, they followed the actual rules, but after a while, they would make up their own variants.

They often laughed, and Alleria became more comfortable with each day that passed. It took a long time for her to feel less uncomfortable when he snuggled up to her at night. His touches were never inappropriate, but there was a look in his eyes that she caught from time to time that put her on edge. Alleria would never tell Jack how she dreamt of that night when they drank the fire wine. In her fantasy, Jack used his power on her again, so that she had a lame excuse to kiss him and give herself to him without having to bear the consequences. In those daydreams, he kissed her with passion and hunger. She daren't think of anything more than that, not even in her fantasies, and her thoughts came to an abrupt stop as soon as the dreams pushed further than her comfort zone. When the imaginary hands of Jack ventured further south, Alleria would sit up, her face flushed. She would wipe all thoughts from her mind, her heart pounding with excitement.

The winter was at its worst now, but the heavy snows had stopped, and they only had to shovel twice a day. The snow still kept in some of the heat, but if they forgot to put the blankets in front of the door, the wind would blow inside to cool down the house and play with the ash in the hearth. Sometimes the wind was so fierce that bits of snow—frozen so deeply they'd turned to chunks of ice—fell off the house, and the two people inside could hear them slide across the roof. Alleria dreaded opening the door on those windy days, but Jack insisted on clearing the snow.

"There should always be an escape route, even if it's impossible for us to make it far in the snow. If something should happen, I'd rather die with a chance of escape."

"What could happen in here, though?" she asked him, her nose wrinkled and her mouth twisted in a grin. The look on his face melted her smile like ice on fire.

"Never forget that this is the Arallfyd, Alleria. Walls and locked doors don't always keep things out. In the human world, I am convinced of my strength and powers, but here, the rules are different. Even for me."

The thought of something coming in through the walls frightened her and she felt out of sorts when she crawled into the bedstead that night. The wind was loud and she listened to it howl all around them. Finally, she started to drift off to sleep, but only for a moment, because a loud pounding woke her up.

"Jack?"

Alleria looked at him, but he was already up and climbing out of the bed. The knocking came once more, echoing with a hint of menace through the silent house.

"Stay in there, Alleria." Jack grabbed the axe that stood next to the hearth. Then he muttered as an afterthought: "This must be my punishment for scaring you earlier."

"Who could that be, Jack?"

"I don't know. No one should be able to survive the winter in this weather." The door trembled with the impact of the pounding. Whoever was out there wasn't going away and Alleria couldn't blame them. Not with this weather. Jack hovered in front of the entrance, the axe hanging loosely in his right hand, and with his left, he opened the door. Cold wind burst into the warm house and blew snowflakes all around Jack's half-naked body.

In the door opening stood a tall man, even taller than Jack, and his shoulders were broader than any Alleria had ever seen. The figure, clad in layers upon layers of furs, took a bold step inside. The wind still blew through the house and Alleria hid behind the shutter of the bedstead, shivering.

Jack pushed against the front door to close it and the newcomer offered to help, but Jack needed little effort to close it by himself.

The figure beat the snow from his many furs and pushed back the hood that covered his features. Underneath, he wore a woolen hat and a scarf that covered the entirety of his face with the exception for his eyes. With rough motions, he pulled everything from his head and neck, revealing a reddish face with a thick, blond beard.

"Thank you, stranger." The voice was deep and boomed through the house. "If you hadn't let me in, I would have frozen to death out there."

A gloved hand pointed at the door of the house and Jack's grip tightened on his axe.

"Your presence surprises me. How did you make your way through this weather?"

The man pulled heavy gloves from his big hands and looked at Jack with a shrug.

"A magic spell went awry and I landed up about a day's walk from here. I knew about the shelter, and thought it was my only hope. I don't mean to intrude, but I'm afraid I have no other choice." The stranger and Jack stared at each other, and Alleria tried to understand their hostile body language.

"I hope I entered a friendly house."

"According to the rules of the guardians, I can't turn you away unless your actions warrant me to do so. You are welcome in this shelter for the rest of winter."

The man smiled with visible relief and offered Jack his hand. Jack looked at the hand for a moment, and then—much to Alleria's relief—reached out and grabbed it.

"The name is Brand, Brand the Traveler."

"Halfway Jack."

A sharp whistle blew through the man's teeth.

"I've heard that name spoken with awe."

"I've never heard yours spoken at all."

Brand laughed. He was different from Jack—louder somehow—and his presence filled the room. The stranger peeled off his many layers of clothing, leaving only a tunic and breeches to keep his modesty, and he splayed out the rest by the hearth to dry. The fire was out, only smoldering ashes, but it was still the warmest place in the shelter.

Under the layers of fur, Brand was a muscular man. He had the build of a warrior with thick shoulders and a narrow waist. Jack wasn't a slender man himself, but Brand was different. The newcomer's arms looked like small tree trunks and Alleria was fascinated by the sight of him.

"Are you a lone traveler?" Brand's eyes rested on Alleria's woolen garb that hung over the chair.

"I travel with a companion." Jack took a step back, placing himself between Brand and Alleria.

"She's resting now, and it's best if we don't disturb her."

I want to be disturbed; this is the most exciting thing that has happened to us since the night we drank fire wine.

The door to the bedstead opened under the light pressure from her fingertips, and before giving Jack the chance to protest, she stepped out, a blanket clutched firmly around her shoulders.

"I'm awake." Her face was a mask of innocence, but Jack's eyebrows furrowed at the sight of her. "You're not disturbing me."

The large newcomer bowed his head slightly, too modest to look directly at Alleria in her current state of dress.

"A pleasure to make your acquaintance, Madame."

Alleria extended her hand for him to shake. He took it in his own large palm and brought the fingers to his lips. The hairs of his beard prickled against her skin.

"Nice to make your acquaintance, Mister Brand. My name is Alleria."

"Please, just call me Brand, Miss... or Mistress?" He looked at Jack, his eyebrows raised.

"Then I must insist you call me Alleria," she said, ignoring his comment.

She turned her attention to Jack, her shoulders straight and her head held aloft, as if she were the lady of a manor house rather than a lost traveler in a shelter.

"Can you build us a fire, Jack? I'm sure Brand is very cold after his travels."

Discontent beamed from Jack's face, but he didn't argue, and pulled the fire screen away from the hearth. Within minutes, a fire roared and lit up the house.

Alleria's eyes tingled with fatigue, so she assumed it was very late at night, or very early morning. A smile crept up on her face as she busied herself with lighting candles, the arrival of Brand making her blood run faster.

A memory surfaced from the back of her mind and she saw her mother fuss over the house, getting ready for visitors. The scent of the perfume her mother wore came back to her, but the woman's face was still obscured from her mind. Through the murkiness of memory, Alleria saw the living room of her old house, but the recollection was fleeting and she lost the image as soon as she had it. She shook her head, physically ridding herself of the image, and continued to light the candles.

The room of the shelter brightened with each candle that burned. The two men sat at the table, each silent for different reasons.

"You must be hungry," Alleria said, and grabbed the furs in front of the fire to hang them over one of the empty chairs. "I can heat up some of our supper." Her voice was chipper. "It's not much, I'm afraid; we are trying to make our supplies last as long as we can."

"Something that will be more challenging with a third mouth to feed." Jack shot Brand a critical look.

"The shelters are built for eight, if necessary," Brand countered. The two men locked eyes and the tension was almost tangible.

Eight people? In here? That wouldn't be possible. It's too small and... Alleria wrinkled her nose at the thought.

"The pantry isn't stocked for eight. Maybe eight children, but not eight hungry men." Jack's voice was harsh and he leaned back. "The winter could be over in two months, or it could last another three after that. We won't know."

"I've brought some food along with me. It might not last us very long, but I'm a great hunter. Once the weather outside will permit us to leave, I will provide food."

If Brand was affected by the sneer on Jack's face, or the sharpness of his tongue, he didn't show it. Instead, he reached under the table and pulled out a large sack that Alleria hadn't noticed before. The man got to his feet and stretched to his full height before holding the sack upside down and emptying the contents on the table.

Vegetables, sausages, a ham, a plucked chicken, fresh herbs, grains, and all sorts of other foods spilled out. Foods that were fresh and that Alleria and Jack hadn't tasted in weeks—or with some foods in Alleria's case, at all. A tomato, round and plump, rolled across the table, and she caught it before it fell and bruised itself. The sight of the food made Alleria's stomach growl, and she suppressed an urge to hug the newcomer. She held up the tomato to Jack, her face open and bright like that of a small child, and noticed Jack narrow his eyes at their guest.

"You said you ended up here because a spell went awry... yet you bring a sack of food?"

"I was supposed to be further north, toward the Rinko mountains. My companion is there, and I brought the food for him as a gift."

The pale eyes of the newcomer never strayed from Jack when he talked, but Alleria saw something in his face, only briefly, and she thought: *He's lying.* From the dark expression, it was obvious that Jack wasn't fooled, but he never said a word. Jack grabbed the food from the table and pushed it back in the sack.

"We'll put this with the rest of the food."

"Let me…" Alleria grabbed the sack—which proved heavier than she expected—and opened the hatch. With a grunt, she lowered the food down first, and then followed, holding a candle to ward off the darkness of the storage room. Alleria put the candle on one of the empty shelves then squatted near the sack. Her stomach growled again as she grabbed a handful of fruit. Saliva welled up in her mouth and she couldn't resist plucking one of the pink berries that hung from an intricate stalk. The berry burst in her mouth and tasted of summer and sweet things.

How can there still be fresh fruit in winter? Perhaps not all parts of the Arallfyd are covered in snow, she mused. She expressed her good mood with a soft, melodic whistle as she worked to tidy up the food, but as she reached up to place the precious fruit on one of the shelves, a movement in her peripheral vision stopped her short.

A translucent figure of a woman walked through the storage room, her mouth moving as if she talked to someone, but no words could be heard. Behind her, Alleria saw a vague image of a beautiful room lit with a thousand candles, and then the woman disappeared. The girl's mind raced and she thought of Jack's earlier words… perhaps something got in after all. Her hands shook with nerves, and she didn't want to unpack the sack anymore, so fleeing the basement was the only thing she could think to do. The light of her candle extinguished, and when she turned around, she found herself staring into the face of a man—equally ethereal as the woman, only this man wasn't just a phantom image; he stared straight back at her.

It was a wicked face, and two eyes filled with darkness glared at Alleria. Her scream sounded through the storage room and she stumbled backward. The face disappeared, and moments later it was replaced by the worried features of Jack.

"Alleria?" He wrapped his arms around her shaking shoulders, leaning her against his warm chest. "What made you scream?"

Every muscle in her body trembled as she pushed Jack away and scrambled to her feet.

"Something was in here... someone. People, I mean. I saw a woman, and then when I turned around, I saw a man with black eyes. I didn't even see all of him... just his face. Like the woman in the mist, only darker."

Alleria's mind struggled to recollect that moment.

"You saw them here?"

"I don't know if they were actually here, or if they were in my head. Perhaps the fatigue from a short night is playing tricks on me."

One of Jack's eyebrows lifted and Alleria knew he wasn't buying it.

"We have a guest," she argued without much conviction.

"That guest will be here for the rest of winter. He can wait."

She waved away his words with an expression of mild annoyance.

"No, that's not what I meant. Perhaps it's the presence of the guest that has me seeing things. I can't get used to a stranger's presence as easily as you do."

"We shouldn't take this lightly, Alleria. You haven't seen anything before, so there could be a reason for what you saw, and I aim to find out what it is and if there is a threat. And if that has something to do with the newcomer, then I must find out why."

"Can we at least speak of it upstairs? I feel a bit shaken by the experience."

He took her hand and led her in front of him, his body still so close that she felt his heat radiate against her back.

"Is everything all right?"

Brand extended his hand to Alleria and helped her from the stairs. The muscles in his hand and wrist rippled under her touch.

"Yes," she said, and a forced smile sat rigidly on her lips.

"No," Jack argued. "Alleria is about to explain what happened down there."

Warm, familiar hands pressed down on her shoulders and guided her to one of the chairs.

Jack stayed near her, and Alleria wondered if he really cared about how upset she was or if he was more protective because he felt threatened somehow by Brand's presence.

"It was nothing. I was unpacking the food that Brand brought with him and I saw the image of a woman. I thought it was a ghost at first, but it wasn't just her. There was a background too, as if I were looking into a different room. It had to be a lady, because she was dressed in fine clothing, with pearls in her hair. I think she was laughing and talking, though I couldn't hear any sound. Then I turned around and I saw a man with black eyes. He frightened me, and I screamed. I promise there was nothing more to it." It was only partially a lie, because she left out that the man was looking straight at her. She might have imagined it, but Alleria was convinced he had seen her.

Jack took one of the seats next to her and Brand sat across the table.

"Do you think it was a vision, or did you feel a presence?" Jack asked. He leaned forward and touched her face. With his thumbs, he pulled up her eyelids and inspected her eyes.

"I didn't feel anything, I just saw it." She pulled her head away from his grip.

"Alleria, did the woman have blonde hair and a dimple in her cheek?" Brand didn't look at her when he talked. Alleria closed her eyes to recapture the face. It was hard at first, but suddenly she was overwhelmed by a clear image of the female.

"Yes, she did. A pretty girl."

"I believe you saw my sister." Brand glanced up, but instead of looking in her eyes, his gaze settled on her chin. His large hands pulled at a chain around his neck and he brought out a small locket. The little clasp on the locket made it difficult for his thick fingers to open, but he managed after a few silent moments. Then he handed over the locket and Alleria looked at the tiny portrait of a young woman.

"That's the girl I saw."

"Is your sister dead?" It was Jack who asked the question that was on Alleria's mind.

"No, no. It's nothing like that. She isn't dead, and you're not seeing her ghost, so don't worry. The problem is—that's what you're picking up on—I worry about her."

Brand's eyes met Alleria's. His face was handsome, not perfect like Jack's, but pleasant and attractive. The blue-gray eyes were kind, and when he pressed his lips together, the same dimple appeared as she had seen on the girl in her vision.

"Alleria, could it be that you are a 'sensitive?'"

Alleria shrugged and shook her head.

"This is the first time this has ever happened to me. I doubt it's more than a coincidence."

"Were you born in the Arallfyd?"

"No, but I've been here a few months now, and it's still the first time this has ever happened to me." An apologetic smile curled around her lips. "So I really don't think I'm a sensitive, as you say."

"I'm probably projecting my grief, and you're picking up on it."

"What of the man with the black eyes?"

"I don't know, lass. I don't know who he is or why you saw him." Brand cast down his eyes and a chill ran through her spine. She sensed it again; *He's lying.* Instead of asking him more questions, she let it go and looked at her fingers.

"It doesn't make sense that I suddenly started seeing things."

"My presence could very well be the thing that sparked your talent."

"Could be," she muttered while she kept her face as straight as she could.

There is more, and he knows, but he won't tell. Can I blame him? We didn't exactly welcome him with open arms.

Alleria looked at Halfway Jack, but he struggled with his own thoughts, the dark look on his face telling her all she needed to know. Then his expression changed and he smacked his hand on the table. The noise startled her and she jumped a little.

"We best show our new lodger where he can stay, shan't we?"

Alleria opened her mouth, but she decided against speaking.

"Alleria, would you mind putting some food on? I'm quite hungry myself."

She nodded and ran to the hearth where she put the kettle on the chain.

I could add some of the fresh tomatoes to the stew. Perhaps some of the herbs.

Then she remembered she would have to go down into the pantry again and decided against it.

Jack gave Brand a little tour of the house and showed him the other bedstead.

So much for keeping each other warm at night, Alleria thought with a hint of a smile.

"There are some extra garments downstairs. I don't think Alleria has destroyed all of them yet with her sewing."

Jack winked at her and she rewarded him a look of mock outrage.

"Something suitable for night clothing will surely fit you."

He handed Brand a candle, and when the large man walked downstairs, Jack quickly approached Alleria and spoke in a low voice.

"I don't trust him. He brought something in here with him, I can sense it, but I'm not quite sure what. This is no lost man, Alleria, don't let him fool you. He came here for a reason. No one could be out there in mid-winter unless they are either fath tywyll or sent by fath tywyll."

"Is he dangerous?"

"I'm not sure yet, but we'll find out soon enough."

"I'm not sure yet, but we'll find out soon enough."

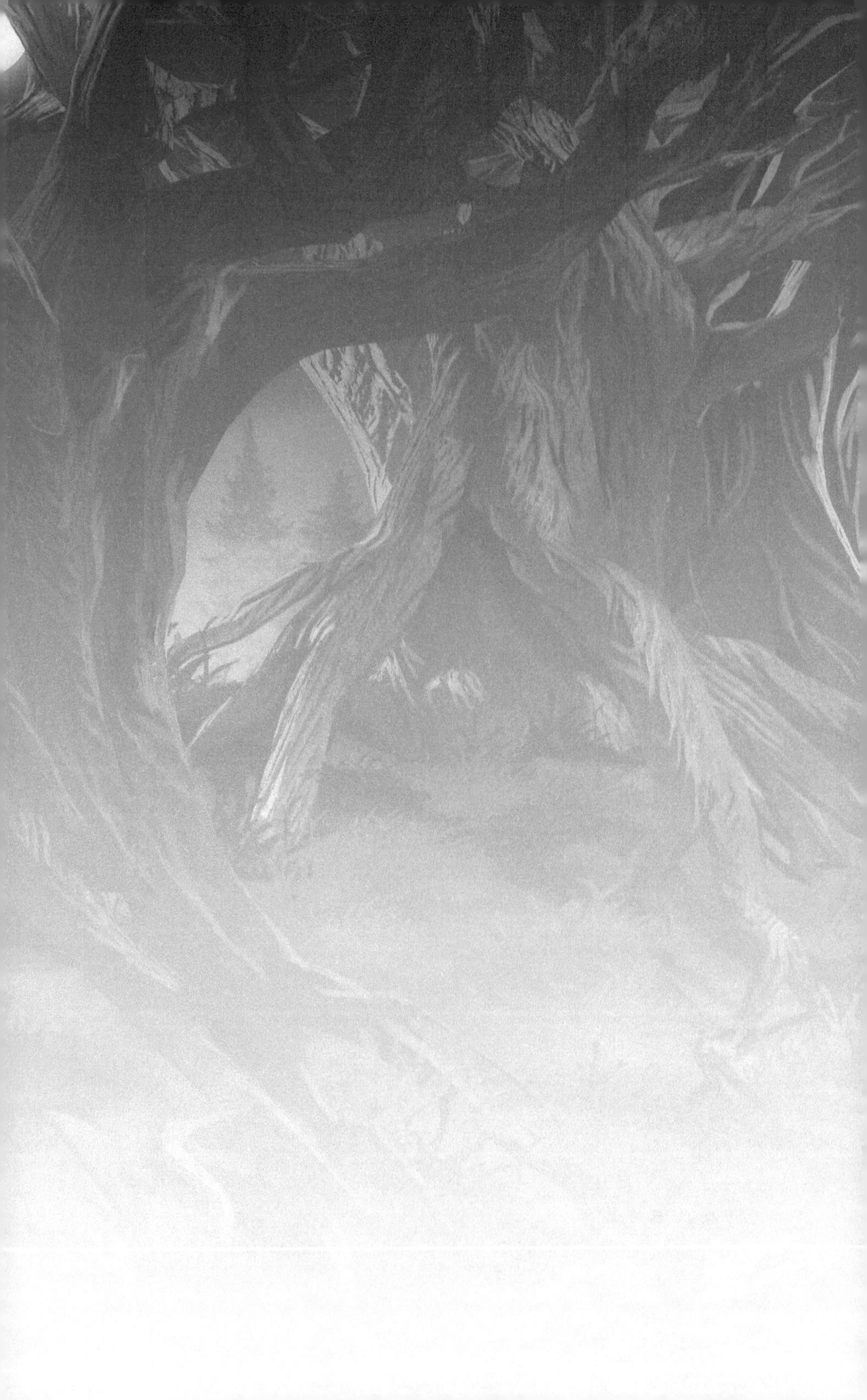

CHAPTER FOURTEEN

The new tenant turned out to be a kind and charming man, in Alleria's opinion. He helped around with the little chores, though she really didn't want any more help. The work kept them sane. Jack and Alleria had found their flow in passing the time together, but only after the arrival of the new person, with fresh new stories and perspectives, did they realize how much value there was in novelty.

Brand couldn't cook, so Jack and Alleria took turns in preparing the meals. Jack was the superior cook, but Alleria had picked up a few things from him in the months on the road together.

Brand did his fair share for entertainment. Not only was he filled with stories, but he also knew a lot of games and was eager to teach his two new companions. Despite the broad man's good nature, Alleria was on her guard around him. She had to admit she was happy for his presence, but there was something that didn't feel entirely right about the man.

One night, she sat next to the hearth, fabric on her lap, listening to the sound of Jack shoveling snow outside. She motioned for Brand to join her by the warmth of the fire and he pulled his chair closer. "Where are you from?" she asked. Her needlework was improving, though she doubted she had a future as a seamstress.

"I'm a wandering soul, Alleria. I'm not really from anywhere."

"Like Jack."

Brand nodded. His hands weren't idle; he whittled one of the wood logs into a shape Alleria couldn't quite make out yet.

"Most of us tylwyth tegs are wanderers. We feel the pull between the human world and the Arallfyd. Neither can be truly our home, and yet we long for both."

"I'm a tylwyth teg." The words escaped her before she thought about them, and she wondered if she had said too much. Brand's knife stopped and he stared at her in interest.

"I know, remember? You told me you weren't born here the first day I arrived." He leaned forward and inspected her face. "You're so beautiful that when I first saw you, I had expected you to be a fath tywyll."

The words took her aback and she flinched. Brand lifted up his hands to apologize. "I didn't mean any offense..."

"No, no, I don't take offense, I... I'm just not used to compliments."

"I find it hard to believe that a beautiful girl like you isn't used to compliments." He looked at her in a way that made her feel as if she were lying.

"I... I'm not... I mean, I wasn't..." She stumbled to find the words. "Let's just say it's a long and painful story."

"So no suitors aside from Jack?"

"Jack?"

"Yes. Neither of you ever elaborated about your relationship. Are you wed?"

Alleria took a deep breath. She and Jack had ever explained about their situation. She had instinctively felt that it might put more strain on the already complicated dynamic with the two men.

"We're not married, and our relationship is somewhat complicated and very private." Her voice was stern. She wondered if she would have told him more if she had trusted him. Brand seemed satisfied with the answer. He was quiet for a few minutes when he gave her the most bizarre look.

"Tell me, Alleria... have you ever danced?" His question came out of nowhere, stunning the poor girl.

Brand got to his feet and offered her his hand. She shook her head and waved her hands in a dismissive manner.

"I... I don't... I never..."

The thought of dancing made her uncomfortable, but the smile on Brand's face was genuine, and she couldn't help but return it with a smile of her own. Her delicate, pale hand slid into his ruddy palm, and he pulled her up, placing his other hand on her waist.

"All you have to do is step forward twice, bend through your knees, step forward again, then step back and twirl. Can you do that?"

He showed her the steps, and after a few tries, she was less wooden in her movements.

"If only we had music!" Brand exclaimed. "I play the lute, and a little bit of the flute, but I have neither instrument on my person. I guess we'll just have to make our own."

Brand cleared his throat and sang a fast and cheerful song. The voice of the large man was clear and deep, and it filled the little house with joy. The melody made her heart light.

Maid come dance and hold my hand,
We'll twirl until the morning.
If you will take my hand and dance,
I'll kiss you without warning.
"No," she said, don't kiss me, Lad.
My father won't be pleased, you hear?
He'll beat me black, he'll beat me blue,
If you ever come too near.
An innocent dance is all I ask,
now come and don't be dour.

I won't try kissing you, this I swear,
(Well maybe in an hour.)
And so I danced with maiden fair.
We twirled across the room,
And laugh we did, and kiss we did,
Which led us to our doom.
When father came, cudgel in hand.
He beat us till we bled.
And after all the bruises healed,
He saw that we were wed.
So sing with us and dance with us.
We dance the dance of life.
I'm sick of taking these same steps,
As husband and as wife.

When the song was over, they both fell to the ground in exhaustion and laughed until their sides ached.

"That poor man and maid in the song. And all for stealing a kiss."

The tears welled up in Alleria's eyes, not from sadness but from laughter, and her body tingled with adrenaline. It was the first time she ever danced with another, and it was exhilarating.

"You are a good dancer, Alleria. Are you sure you haven't done this before?"

Brand turned toward her and leaned on his elbow, his eyes shining in the firelight. Alleria felt that treacherous blush stroke her cheeks again.

"The outside is shoveled. It's unsettling how much snow fell last night. Usually the snows are mild this time of winter."

Jack's figure loomed over them as they lay on the floor. His face was cast in shadows, but Alleria heard from the tone of his voice that he was aggravated.

"What were you two doing? You made a lot of ruckus."

"Brand taught me how to dance."

She rolled onto her stomach and looked up at him. Jack squatted and she could see his face in the firelight. His brow knotted above his nose and the corners of his mouth twitched down.

"I could have taught you how to dance."

"But you didn't," Brand said, a light mocking tone in his voice, "so I did." He jumped to his feet and arched his back with a pleased groan. The tension between the two men was palpable. Alleria turned away to ignore it and stared at the fire. In the flames, she saw movement, and to her horror, the face of the man with the black eyes stared back at her. Her hand shot up to cover her mouth and she swallowed a yelp. She remembered the last time she mentioned the man to Jack and decided this time to keep her mouth shut. It was only a mirage, after all, so no need to create more stress in the house. The dark face stared transfixed at her and she closed her eyes.

It's not real; he's not really here.

The joy of the dancing was replaced with a cold sense of dread, and Alleria excused herself to go to bed early, leaving the two men to glower at each other.

After the incident with the fire, Alleria saw the figure more frequently. The face appeared everywhere, especially in the moments when she was alone. It hid behind the shelves in the storage room, leered from under the table when she cleaned the floors, and stared at her from the flames or the liquid in the cauldron. Its presence affected her mood. She wondered if she should talk to Jack about it, or perhaps to Brand. The figure didn't seem to do anything, just watch her, and only her. She wasn't sure if he was anything more than an image, and she felt a little embarrassed that only she seemed to notice him. Once she saw Brand looking straight at it and he didn't seem to notice at all.

One night, as she lay awake in the bedstead, with Jack snoring gently next to her, she lit a candle to keep her company. A shadow crossed the wall. From the wood, a figure emerged and detached itself slowly from the dark. Hands pushed out of the wall, followed by arms, and they leaned on the edge of the bed. A head came out next, the dark eyes looking straight at her.

"I am Death."

The voice was a little more than a hiss, and the dark eyes held hers. It was the first time the thing had spoken and Alleria felt panic build inside her.

"I come for your heart, gosgeiddig." The lips on his thin mouth never moved, but she could hear each word clearly.

"Jack."

Her voice shook and was barely above a whisper, but Jack woke in an instant. When he sat up, the shadow crept back into the wall. He turned to Alleria.

"What is it?"

"Do you see it too?"

"No, but I can sense something."

She felt a strange sense of relief mixed with worry. *This thing can't just be in my imagination.*

"It's the man with the black eyes. I've seen a lot of him lately."

Jack's eyebrows furrowed and he rubbed his neck with his hand.

"And you chose not to tell me?"

"I didn't want you to think I was mad. No one else seems able to see him except for me."

Jack sat on his knees and grabbed her hands.

"Alleria, I won't think you are mad. This is the Arallfyd, and there are different rules here than the human world or the Borderlands. You must always tell me everything." Alleria nodded, but Jack wasn't satisfied, and he pushed his hand under her chin. "I'm serious, Alleria, no secrets. Not while we're here."

"Yes, Jack, I understand. I promise, I will tell you everything from now on."

He wrapped his arms around her and settled back under the blanket.

"I'm starting to suspect you might have the third sight, Alleria."

"I've heard of second sight, but never of third. What is it?"

She pushed her nose into the folds of his nightshirt.

"Third sight is when people can see thoughts and feelings that others project. For example, when someone feels very strongly about something, you might pick up on that."

Alleria slapped his chest and pulled away from him.

"You mean like Brand's sister?"

"Yes, like that. If it was his sister."

"Who else would she be? They looked alike."

Jack shook his head but didn't respond. Alleria shrugged, pursing her lips.

"People with third sight can often see spells too. For all we know, someone is scrying on you and you picked up on that. Or we just have ghosts."

Alleria gnawed on her thumbnail and thought about what Jack said.

"Tumsa used her birds to scry on me. I don't think I ever saw anything weird then. Why would I suddenly start seeing... oh..." She slapped the palm of her hand against her forehead. "Because I'm in the Arallfyd. That changed everything."

"Magic becomes more tangible here, so where before you might have just merely felt it, now you can actually see it. It's just a theory, but it's not a crazy one. I've known others that could see spells." Jack scratched his chin. "It started with those things in the mist, didn't it?"

"Yes, you didn't see them either, but you felt them... didn't you?"

"I feel things. I'm sensitive toward magic too. Different from you, but the concept is the same. That is why I need you to start trusting me, okay?"

Jack put his arm around her again and pulled her close to him.

"Okay," she muttered softly.

Why do I feel so safe with him? I feel like I am a part of his life, and he is a part of mine. I know he doesn't have my best interest at heart, and yet...

The thoughts spun in her head until they became incoherent, and she fell into a deep sleep.

"Tell me about the man with the black eyes, Brand." Jack cocked his head at the large man across from him at the breakfast table. Alleria held her breath. "You know more about him; he came exactly the same day you did. So tell me about him."

"I don't know what you're talking about." Brand shrugged and spooned some porridge into his mouth.

"Don't play dumb with me. You know very well what I'm talking about. Alleria picked up on this thing and *you* know more about it. I'm sure whatever it is, you're linked to it."

"Nothing is linked to me, only memories and emotions. I think Alleria picked up on those. If she turned them into a man, then I'm very sorry. There is nothing I can do."

"I saw him too," Jack lied.

Brand's face paled a little and Alleria bit her lip.

He does know.

"I... I didn't bring him."

"But you know who he is."

"I have a suspicion." Brand looked at the food in front of him. "If I'm right, he's harmless."

"What is he?"

"They call him the 'Calling Man.' He comes and warns people of a terrible fate."

I am Death. I come for your heart, gosgeiddig. The words echoed through Alleria's mind.

"Why is he here now, when you are here? Why not sooner?" Jack's eyes narrowed to suspicious slits.

"I... I don't know."

"Stop lying to me, or I will cast you out in the snow."

"As if you could." Brand puffed up his chest, but Jack made no effort to change his body language.

Panic played at Alleria's heartstrings, and she wanted to cry out and tell them to stop, but her desire to learn more about the man with the black eyes compelled her to stay quiet.

Brand sighed and ran his fingers through his thick blond beard.

"I might have brought it in here. I have a tendency to attract spirits as I travel. It's in my blood. Normally, they only show themselves to me. It's not just spirits; it's strong emotions or memories too. I can project them, and sensitive people will pick it up. I'm not in control of this... gift."

I understand what that is like. Alleria bit her lip.

"Why didn't you tell us this that first night?"

"I didn't think anything would happen, and I was afraid I would make you wary of me."

"So you lied and let us find out for ourselves. Clever plan. We're not at all wary now."

"I didn't know you were sensitive, did I? It's not like you came out with that on day one either." Brand pushed away his bowl of porridge. "I wanted a place to stay and I didn't want people to be scared of me or accuse me of bringing in ghosts. So I stayed silent. I had a suspicion Alleria might be a sensitive when she saw my sister that first night, and if she had seen anything else, I would have eventually come forward. I just didn't want to risk being thrown out in the cold." He folded his arms and glowered at Jack.

Jack sat back, and Alleria could tell by the way he scratched his chin and neck that he was not all together pleased with Brand's answer. He looked like he was about to say more, but instead, he closed his mouth to a thin line.

He wants to keep the peace, Alleria thought. *The house is too small for arguments.*

"Your affairs are not my business, but if they affect me and mine, they are. So is there anything else you wish to share with us?" Jack's tone was businesslike, but there was a hint of menace under the surface.

"Nothing that would affect either of you, but feel free to ask me any questions. Apart from my 'gift,' I have no secrets."

Alleria fidgeted with the brightly colored tablecloth, her eyes fixed on her plate.

"I have no questions."

With meticulous care, Jack put his cutlery on the plate and placed his hands behind his head. His eyes never broke contact with Brand's, and the large man never once looked away.

"And what of you? Are there things I need to know about you? After all, the Calling Man is seeking young Alleria out. Is there any danger I should be aware of? I don't know anything about you two, save your names. I don't even know what you are to each other. At first, I thought you were husband and wife, but I understand from Alleria that you are not wed. I can't imagine any man capable of staying away from a creature this lovely, yet there is no intimacy between you. I know you want there to be. I've seen the way you look at her, Halfway Jack. I recognize the lust in your eyes."

Alleria looked from one man to the other. There was no change in Jack's expression, but she felt a shift in the tension just the same.

"Our relationship is nothing you need concern yourself with."

Jack's voice was light, but from Brand's expression, Alleria could tell he felt the threat behind the words as well as she did.

"There are no dangers that haunt us at the moment, so you can rest assured that there is no threat upon your person. We are just here to sit out the rest of winter. Judging by the snowfall, it will be a short winter this year, which will work to all our benefit. Come melting day, we can be on our separate ways."

"These are your sentiments. Does your companion feel the same way?" Brand raised his eyebrows at Alleria and his eyes pleaded with her to say more.

"Alleria feels the same."

"She has her own mouth; you don't own her."

"Yes, he does." Alleria cringed at her own words. The loyalty she felt for Jack was overshadowed by aggravated temper. The moment she said it, she regretted it. Brand looked eager to continue the conversation.

"What does she mean?"

"She doesn't mean anything."

Jack got to his feet and put more logs on the fire.

"I'll start dinner," he announced. "We will end this conversation now, before it gets out of hand."

Brand looked as if he wanted to argue but he thought wiser of it. Again, his glance lingered on Alleria, but she turned her back to him, picked up her sewing, and made her way to the bedstead, the only place where she could be alone during the day.

She sat in the bedstead with the doors closed and held the half-finished shirt in her lap. She had forgotten to take a candle inside, and it was too dark, so she couldn't sew. Instead, she just sighed with a heavy heart. The slave market lingered in her mind and she swallowed a sour lump that hung thick in her throat.

I want a real life now, one where people like me. I want to dance again, and I want to be loved. But I don't want Jack to die.

Tears welled up in her eyes and she sobbed softly.

The winter would soon be over and then they would be on their way. She would be sold as a slave and never see Jack again. And she'd be outside of the Arallfyd, where she'd be without her newly discovered talent.

She thought about the Calling Man. The myth was not one she ever heard tell before. Tumsa had shared a great many tales with her, but nothing that even resembled this one. There was much she didn't know about the Arallfyd, and she had no reason to doubt Brand's word. The question was, then, what did the Calling Man want to warn her about? The slave market? Or was there some other danger?

The atmosphere in the house changed after the confrontation and Jack was more distant than usual. The days were long, and though Brand did his best to fill them with his jokes and singing, the tension remained evident. Every now and then, the big man would ask Alleria sharp questions to determine her and Jack's affiliation, but she daren't talk to him about any private matter, afraid of Jack's reaction.

She liked the large man, and despite her reservations about him, she warmed to his personality. He made her laugh, even more than Jack, and she loved to dance and sing. She found she had quite a talent for music, and the big man taught her various songs that suited her clear soprano. He was such a joy to be around, Alleria started to wonder if she had ever really caught him lying, or if she'd just picked up on Jack's paranoia and went along with it.

And yet the laughs were accompanied by a hint of darkness, because the man with the sinister eyes always watched her from the shadows. Brand never saw him. Jack couldn't make out the shape, but still could sense the creature, and his worry was obvious to Alleria.

Relief came when the temperature rose. Jack woke her one morning, handing her some furs and a cloak, which she donned before following him outside.

The snow was bright, and her eyes were not used to full daylight. She squeezed them shut. It took her a while before she could fully open them and make out her surroundings.

Around her was a sea of white that sparkled in the sunlight. The beauty of it was breathtaking, with almost everything covered in a fine, powdery layer. The thin tree branches showed hints of browns and black that offered some contrast against the white.

"It's still too cold to travel," Jack announced, "but I can hunt some of the winter creatures now. That should get us some fresh meat for our stew."

"It's so lovely out here."

Her bare hands sank in the soft snow; the biting cold nipped at her skin. The snow was different from when they first journeyed to the shelter; the top was still soft, but the bottom was more compact, and Alleria didn't sink all the way down anymore.

"I encourage you to go outside every day. Just don't go too far. The weather is still too cold, and you're not dressed for the temperature—not even with the clothes you made. Make sure you can see the house at all times when you go out."

"You're not dressed for the cold either," Alleria retorted, and she threw a handful of loose snow in his direction.

"I don't need to be. I won't get as cold as you do."

He winked and threw snow back.

"You didn't feel that then?" Alleria laughed, and this time she packed a real snowball and hurled it in his direction. "Or that?"

Jack laughed and defended himself with his arms, but she didn't stop, and after her fourth snowball, he retaliated with some of his own. Brand, who was still asleep when they left the house, poked his head around the door.

"Excellent, the worst is over, the thaw is setting in. The end of winter is upon us."

Alleria chuckled and flung a snowball at him too, which landed on the large man's cheek. The confounded expression on his face caused her to hiccup with laughter. Brand joined them in their snow battle. Both Jack and Brand targeted Alleria with their icy projectiles, but then Brand shifted aim and threw a snowball at Jack. Before Alleria could register what was happening, the happy mood had changed to something else. She watched how the two men threw snowballs at each other with such force, the impact of the snow left angry, red marks on the exposed skin of their faces. Contrived smiles were plastered on their faces, but she sensed the anger between them.

This'll end badly.

Every fiber in her body screamed at her to do something, and in a sudden bout of inspiration, she ran past them.

"The first to catch me will get the most meat in his stew tonight," she cried as she ran as fast as her legs could carry her, faster than she ever thought she could.

It was Jack who caught up with her first. He grabbed her around her waist, but the momentum caused her to trip and they both fell into the snow.

"Got you."

There was laughter in his face again as he wrestled to sit on top of her. He held her wrists to either side of her head and leaned forward.

"What did I win again?"

His breath felt hot on her face.

There is that look again.

"Meat," she muttered. The cold of the snow seeped into her clothes, leaving her wet and chilled. Her lips trembled and her body shivered. Jack noticed and scrambled to stand. He pulled her to her feet and rubbed her arms, forcing the blood to flow through her limbs.

"Go inside and take off those wet clothes. You'll catch something."

He leaned forward and kissed her lightly on the nose. Alleria felt a jolt run through her body. Without a word, she turned and ran toward the house. Brand followed her lead and they were both out of breath when they got inside. The cloak hung heavy and moist on Alleria's shoulders, and Brand put more wood on the fire as she pulled off the material to hang it to dry in front of the hearth. She slipped into the indoor outhouse and changed her shift for a clean one. When she returned, she became aware that Jack had entered the house. Alleria moved toward the fire and kept her focus on the cloak, which she smoothed with her hand. From the corner of her eye, she saw he picked up a knife and the axe.

"I will get some wood to make a bow and arrow. I'll be back. You two start breakfast."

The door slammed behind him, leaving Alleria all alone with Brand. The two worked together in silence, her making porridge from the remaining grain that he had brought along with him, and him cleaning the bowls from the night before.

"Now that Jack's not around, will you tell me what you are doing here?"

"Does it matter?"

"I think it does. I think you are in danger, Alleria. The Calling Man visits you, and everyone acts as if that isn't a terrible thing, but it is. If you won't tell me what's going on, I won't be able to help you."

"You can't help me, Brand. It will just build more tension in the house and we still have weeks to go before we can each go our different ways."

Brand hovered right behind her and his large hands forced her to turn around. He pushed Alleria's face up toward him with his finger.

"Alleria, let me help you, please. Something is wrong, and you won't tell me what it is."

I want to tell him; I want to cry on his shoulder and scream that the world is so unfair. I want someone to care about me, to protect me. But if I tell him... Jack...

"It's complicated, Jack and I..."

What do I owe Jack?

"We... ehm."

"Are you lovers? You don't seem like lovers."

His eyes bored into hers, and Alleria felt a little uncomfortable with the expression on his face.

"No... Jack and I aren't intimate in any way. He's my... ehm, I'm his—"

"You're not family."

"No..."

"Friends?"

"Not exactly."

Just say it, Alleria, you want to say it.

"He's going to sell me at the slave market."

She watched Brand's limbs stiffen as he struggled to respond, his face twisted.

"He what? Alleria, tell me you are joking."

His large fist slammed down on the counter.

Is this an act?

"Please don't make a big deal. It doesn't matter."

"Doesn't matter? How can you say that? He wants to sell you into slavery. That's not a little thing. This is your freedom."

"I haven't been free since I was six. Halfway Jack took me from a horrible situation. I lived with this mean, old witch... my life actually improved when he found me."

"That doesn't justify it, Alleria. You need to get away from him. The snow will start melting soon. You can come with me. You don't have to stay here. We can sneak out at night, and I will take you somewhere safe, somewhere Jack won't find you."

"I'm not afraid of Jack. I know it's not right for him to sell me as a slave, but I can't blame him. I know why he's doing it. Besides... I owe him."

Brand's eyes flashed with anger, and his cheeks were crimson. "You don't owe him your life."

"I do, actually. He saved my life. I would have died in some plant if it wasn't for him. And I was in a horrible position before he took me away from the old witch that owned me before him. It's a long story, and not one I wish to share. Let's just say… it's not as bad as you think. Please, please don't talk to him about it. It will only create more tension in the house. I don't want that." She looked at him. His face was a mask of anger, she could see his jaw muscles standing out just above the line of his blond beard.

"Brand, Please? I should have never told you."

"Yes, you should, and you should have told me sooner."

"Please, don't create problems. I have good reasons for going along with Jack," she said, and Brand lowered his gaze.

After a brief moment of silence, he answered, his reluctance clear in his voice. "I promise."

He kept his promise, but not with much grace, and when Jack came back carrying long, flexible branches, suitable to make a bow, Brand glowered at him. Jack raised an eyebrow, but he didn't say anything. Alleria pushed the bowls filled with porridge across the table in the hope that the food would lighten the mood. It didn't. They ate in silence.

The whole day was awkward, and when they stepped into the bedstead that night, Jack turned his back to Alleria.

"I told Brand what I am to you."

"I know."

Jack pulled the covers further over his shoulder, his back still turned toward the girl. He let out a deep sigh.

"Does it make you feel better?"

"That someone is sympathetic to my plight?" Her voice was sharp. "A little."

"It must be nice to have someone to help you vilify me."

"You're being a child." She pushed against his shoulder. "Don't turn this around on me. I'm not forcing you to sell me at the market. I've never asked for any of this. *You* are doing this to *me*, not the other way around."

Jack sat up and his eyes blazed in the light of the candle, the rest of his face cast in shadow.

"I'm not the one who stole from you, Jack. I've never harmed a soul in my life. But I've been hurt, and you are one of the people who've hurt me."

"I'm so sorry, Alleria... I can't... I won't..."

His hands grabbed her and pulled her close. The anger that threatened to rise in her chest melted into sadness. Tears spilled from her eyes and ran in warm streams across her cheeks. Jack put his face in the nape of her neck, his arms around the back of her head. They sat for a few minutes, engulfed in a world of warmth and darkness, when she felt his head move a few inches. His breath was hot on her cheek.

Every muscle in her body froze and she concentrated on the softness of his lips brushing her skin. Jack pulled her a little closer and she allowed him, not daring to move a muscle.

"Don't hate me," he whispered against the corner of her mouth, and she felt his lips exploring hers. He kissed her cheek, her bottom lip, and finally all of her mouth. Alleria's body sang at his touch. The sensation was so different than the last time. She was in control of her body. His lips pressed against hers for a second time, and she responded to the movement. With a languid motion, his tongue slipped into her mouth and curled around hers, soft and rough at the same time. This was the most pleasurable feeling she had ever experienced. With a simple movement of his arm, Jack pulled her even closer and entangled her limbs with his own as if they were one organism. Strong hands played with her hair, rubbed her back, and tickled the skin of her legs as he kissed her. There was so much power and passion in the gesture that she forgot all the bad memories in an instant. His hand moved up her leg and under the off-white chemise. She panicked, and with a grace she didn't know she possessed, she pulled away from him and jumped up out of the bedstead. On bare feet, she made her way to the smoldering fire.

What is wrong with you? Why did you let him touch you?

But she already knew the answer. Jack was the first person she had been with for a long period of time after her life with Tumsa. She had enjoyed her time with him, but more importantly, her transformation from monster to girl had been in his presence. To Alleria, that meant something. Despite everything he had done to her, she cared deeply for him.

The kiss sat on her lips and Alleria could taste his mouth on hers still.

I need to go for a walk.

She struggled to get on her clothing, and when her head peeked above her jumper, she saw Jack standing by the fire. He pushed the metal poker into the ashes, his back toward her.

"I owe you an apology." His voice sounded hushed in the quiet room. "Again."

The scent of ash and wood tickled her nostrils, and Alleria inhaled deeply.

"No, you really don't."

"I didn't mean to make you uncomfortable."

"You didn't. It wasn't discomfort, it was... I just feel very confused, that's all."

On the floor were the shoes he bought her and Alleria rushed to put them on her feet.

"Would you mind if I go for a walk? Just around the house; I'm not going far. I just need some fresh air."

"It's nighttime... I don't think it's safe."

"I won't go far, I promise." She wrapped the cloak around her shoulders, determined to get out of the stifling house and away from Jack, who took up every bit of space in her mind.

"Alleria." Jack's voice pleaded with her.

Behind her, the bedstead creaked, and Alleria could hear the door open. *Not now, Brand, please not now.*

"If she wants to go, who are you to stand in her way?" Brand's voice was deep and filled with anger. "I don't care what she says, she's not your slave."

"Go back to bed." Jack's voice sounded icy and his body language was stiff and menacing. "Let's not do this now, when emotions are high. We might say or do things we regret."

"Don't you tell me what to do. *I* am not your slave, Halfway Jack." Brand puffed out his chest and took a step forward.

"Can we not do this?" Alleria pleaded. "Please? Brand, just go to bed. Nothing happened."

"You plan to sell her on the slave market? Do you know what they do with gosgeiddig? They cut them open for their hearts."

How does he know this? How does he know what I am? Jack wouldn't have told him, and I know for sure I didn't.

"You're suspiciously well-informed..." Halfway Jack stepped toward Brand. "Tell us, who are you really? What are you doing here? Are you here for Alleria?"

The corner of Brand's mouth twitched, but he didn't respond to Jack's question. Instead, he turned to her.

"Alleria, we're not putting up with this any longer. I don't know what he did to you, but it stops here tonight. You're coming with me as soon as the roads are clear. I'll protect you from this maniac. We can be happy together, you and I. Perhaps you would even consider staying with me..."

"We?" Jack shook his head, an angry smile playing on his lips.

"Brand, no..." A flush heated her cheeks.

"In fact, I think I should teach this guy a lesson right now..." Brand and Jack exchanged a hateful glare.

Before Alleria had any time to react, Brand stormed toward Jack. Jack was prepared and punched his right temple.

Crack.

The horrible sound echoed through the shelter and Alleria saw every movement as if time had slowed. Brand's eyes widened with the impact but then sank to a half-lidded position, and his mouth opened in a crooked sneer. A pink tongue drooped from his lips and he fell down; a tremor vibrated through the wooden planks of the floor with the impact.

Oh, by the gods, look at his neck.

Brand's head was turned at an awkward angle, one that shouldn't be physically possible for anyone to twist their neck. Jack hovered over the fallen man, his face ashen and his mouth thin with determination. Alleria ventured forward and looked at the face of the man who only moments ago was defending her freedom. The side of his temple was dented and covered in blood, bits of splintered bone protruding through the flesh. One eye was open and the other still half lidded. The way his tongue lolled from his mouth made Alleria gag. She checked for a pulse but could find none.

"You killed him..." Her voice was no more than a gasp. Jack stared at the corpse. Then, Brand's body twitched and Alleria screamed. The mass of flesh convulsed and Brand's already open mouth spread even wider. From it, long, black fingers poked out, four on each lip, and they pushed the mouth open wider until the skin tore with a sickly rip. Horrified, Alleria looked at the exposed jaws and the black, misshapen head that pushed its way through. The head faced up, staring at her with its black eyes.

"No..."

"Alleria..." the creature hissed, its lips once again not moving. "My master wants you... You will be sssafe."

The black shape pushed itself from the body of Brand and slithered toward her. She grabbed the nearest thing—a chair—and flung it at the monster, but it just passed through it as if the body were made of smoke. Alleria froze, unable to move from fear. Jack cursed.

"It's an ulubieniec, one of the minions of a fath tywyll lord. Damnit, why didn't I see it before? I knew there was something wrong with him."

Jack's voice pierced the haze of panic that clouded Alleria's thoughts. She couldn't take her eyes off the creature as it advanced on her. Jack moved in her peripheral vision.

"Run, Alleria. These things can be dangerous."

The word "run" broke her spell and she moved toward the door. The creature turned to follow, but Jack stabbed one of the smoky trails that Alleria assumed were the thing's legs with his knife and nailed the creature to the ground.

That knife can hurt it?

At the door, she stopped running. Her heart pounded so fast she felt stabs of pain in her chest.

"What about you?"

"I'm in less danger if you're not here, trust me. Just run."

"But the cold?"

The creature howled and hissed and writhed under Jack's knife. He shot her a desperate look.

He doesn't know either.

Beneath him, the creature grew in size, the darkness that made up its body spreading out in slippery tentacles. The monster's eyes watched Alleria, and it opened its mouth, revealing a hypnotic black void.

"Don't look at it." Jack pulled out the knife and swung at the creature again.

She turned and grabbed at the door. Cold air hit her in the face as she pulled her cloak around her arms and ran. The door banged and bounced off the frame a few times, a roar escaping through the gap before it finally shut. Alleria darted across the snow, afraid of the thing inside, afraid of the cold outside, but most of all, afraid to be alone.

CHAPTER FIFTEEN

In the dark, the little warmth of the sun was just a memory, and the snow wasn't as pretty as it had been during daylight. *Menacing* was the word that came to mind. Alleria's hot breath stung against her frozen lips. She fought back the tears that threatened to spill, worried that her fear might somehow to turn to anger, as it sometimes did. The outcome of letting her emotions get the best of her would be rather unpredictable at the best of times, let alone what could happen in a place like this that was known for its capricious magic.

I'm lost.

It had never been her intention to run away so far, but panic drove her with great speed deeper into the forest before common sense could catch up with her. Any attempt to turn around and find the shelter proved fruitless; everything looked alike in the dim of night. Swallowed by the darkness, she trudged on, finding it impossible to navigate her way through the trees with any clarity. Every gust of wind was a torment as the cold bit into her flesh, penetrating to her very core. The trees were a deeper shade of black against the night sky and the snow was a soft gray contrast against the gloom.

I'm going to die here.

The farther she walked, the more overwhelming her sense of disorientation became. She even slowed her step, as if she could regain control by taking in her surroundings more deliberately, hoping it would temper the anxiety that was blossoming like a sickly flower in her chest. The trees around her seemed to thin, and to her surprise, Alleria found she had wandered into a clearing. She halted for a moment, taking a deep breath. Being in the open felt less oppressive, and yet she felt infinitely more vulnerable at the same time. The sky above was a blue-black canvas splattered with sparkling stars that looked like precious gems. It was a different sight from the human world or the Borderlands. The colors were hues she had never encountered before in nature, and the bright silver second moon shone clearest on the dark backdrop above. There was a very faint glow of the first moon, but no matter how hard she looked, she couldn't find any hint of the black of the third moon. It was far bigger than she had ever seen; it seemed closer to the Arallfyd than to any other place in the world. It made the area come to life with its glow, as if someone sprinkled millions of diamonds in the soft white snow. For a moment, the beauty of her surroundings lulled her fear and a sense of true freedom welled up in her heart. But it was fleeting.

The sound of flapping startled her, snapping her from her short reverie, and a large figure swooped down from above. The size and shape indicated that it wasn't a bird. A swish near her warned Alleria that there were more, and she saw a similar creature flying in her direction. Her blue eyes scanned the skies and she spotted at least five of those things.

A being larger than a man, with an impressive wingspan, descended down on her. The second moon illuminated the back of the creature, revealing two gigantic batwings flapping from powerful shoulder muscles. Between the wings was a human-looking torso attached to a long, insectile abdomen, which ended in a stinger the size of a grown man's arm. Before Alleria could react, it was upon her. Large faceted eyes reflected her pale face, and sharp mandibles snapped at her.

Alleria froze on the spot, horrified by its appearance. A fraction of a second later, she screamed. She never had a chance to run because the creature spat some sort of sticky stuff at her. The substance covered her cheek, neck, and shoulder. The impact stung, and it was as strong as a swamp spider's web. The arm she'd raised to protect herself was completely tangled in the strange strings that appeared to be in a state between liquid and solid. Alleria's feet were still free, and she turned to run while struggling with the creature's snare.

A second shape swooped in, and a blast of webbing hit her in the side, her cloak catching most of the burst. Behind Alleria, another creature spat at her, this time engulfing her feet and toppling her over. Her hands were stuck, preventing her from stopping the oncoming blow of her fall, and so her face connected with the snow-covered ground. Bursts of white and red light danced around her vision and she twitched as more of the strange tissue engulfed her. Her breathing became labored and Alleria fought against her rising panic. Talons pierced through webbing and clothes alike, scraping her skin. A jerk ran through her whole body as she was snatched up into the air with such a speed her stomach lurched. She couldn't see a thing.

Stiff with fear, she held her body as still as she could, worried the beast would release her from a high altitude, and all the while she tried to control her own innate magic. It would not benefit her to make her prison rot, not while she didn't know how high in the air she was already. The fall could kill her.

The temperature dropped significantly during their high-speed journey, but the webbing served well to contain most of her body heat, so she was cold, but not freezing.

The journey felt endless to the cocooned girl, and despite the stress of flying, Alleria was overcome by emotion and lack of sleep. She slumbered a little now and again.

The unexpected impact with the earth rudely awoke her. She didn't hit the ground hard, but her landing was rough enough to startle her. Hands grabbed her wrapped body, and once again she was lifted, but this time in the arms of someone. The heat of the body on the other side of the wrapping reminded her of Jack, and Alleria hoped that, somehow, he had found her. From the rough manner she was carried, she quickly deduced that he hadn't.

She was at least sure that the person or creature who carried her wasn't one of the winged monsters, for they'd had no legs, and she could very definitely hear footsteps. Whoever her new captor was, they put her down on something soft and pulled at the webbing near her hand. A soft ripping sound was followed by more room to move. Fingers touched hers and they pressed something in her hand.

A blade?

The touch of the object was cold and sharp to her fingers. Whoever loosened her hand had left the rest of Alleria wrapped up. For several seconds, she awaited further actions by the other party with a healthy dose of anxiety. None came and all she heard was a door slam.

For a moment, Alleria held her breath, trying to hear if someone was in the room with her, but all was quiet, and after some hesitation, she decided to make good use of the shank provided. The webbing was tough and very firm, but the object in her hand was sharp enough to cut through if she held the blade at just the right angle. The tension of the cocoon eased, and within minutes, Alleria struggled out, plucking some of the more tenacious residue from her skin and clothes. The worst part was removing the webbing from her face and hair, which was a painful process, and she winced and hissed each time she pulled several hairs from her scalp. She only removed enough to uncover her face fully, leaving large clumps of webbing in her hair.

Maybe I need to stop being everyone's captive, she thought with a hint of bitterness.

Only when her eyes were properly cleared could she fully make out her surroundings. She was in a bare room, no furniture other than the bed upon which she had been placed. The walls were made of stone, and the only light that shone in was from a little metal-barred window in a heavy oak door. Alleria peered through the opening, but all she saw was a stone corridor. She inspected the door but could find neither handle nor hinges on her side. In an attempt to see if it would budge, she wrapped her hands around the bars and pulled. No such luck; it was solid. Once again, Alleria was trapped. With a sigh, she sat on the bed and tried to look at the bright side of things. She was still alive, and the room was at least a pleasant temperature.

Alleria walked through her little prison and ran her hands across the masonry. No loose stones. She tried the floor, hoping perhaps there was a loose nail that she could use to pry open the lock. There was nothing for her to work with. Not that she could have opened a lock with a nail, but she could have at least tried.

She took the knife and tried to disengage the lock, but the blade was too big to fit. The bars were too solid, and the wood of the door was not impressed by the sharpness of the knife; she only managed to carve a few superficial lines.

A thought occurred to her as she was struggling to make progress cutting through the wood. Alleria looked at her hands.

What if?

Gingerly, she touched the lock on the door, willing herself to get angry. She closed her eyes and pictured Tumsa's stick. She could recall the blows it had dealt her with such vivid clarity that she could almost feel the pain and the humiliation all over again. Her temper flared. The darkness poured from her fingertips and licked at the wood of the door, pushing the time into it, aging the wood and the metal. A musty smell entered the room and the lock loosened underneath her fingertips. Before it was slackened enough for her to attempt to push it out, a shadow blocked out the light from the other side of the door. The shock made her heart skip a beat and her power fizzled out like a doused flame. With stealth she didn't know she possessed, she grabbed the knife, crawled onto the bed, and pulled her cloak over her head. A key turned in the lock and the door opened.

Her heart pounded against her chest. Alleria closed her eyes and pretended to be asleep. With the knife clutched tightly, she was ready to spring out at whoever entered the room.

Rough hands pulled the cloak from her and Alleria stared with wide eyes at a tall, thin woman with a strict countenance and a black, austere hairstyle. The breath stuck in her throat as she looked at the woman's face. Deep scars held together by black stitches crossed the skin where her eyes were supposed to be. The rest of the woman's face appeared normal, pretty even, and her expression was stoic. Though her motions were a little jerky, as if she weren't fully in control of her own muscles, she didn't move like a blind person. Her step was confident and effortless and she responded to movement, which made Alleria suspect the woman could see her. The knife lay forgotten on the girl's chest; the sight of this strange creature was enough to keep her mesmerized.

The eyeless figure didn't speak, but her long, slender hands grabbed Alleria with an unexpected force and the woman pulled her to her feet. The knife slid from her torso to the ground. Strong fingers tugged at Alleria's clothes. When the girl pulled back from her in protest, the woman slapped her in the face. The impact stung Alleria's cheek and she was stunned to obedience. The woman's expression never changed, the lack of emotions making her appear more like an animated doll than a person.

Every time the girl resisted any part of the undressing, the female slapped her hard enough to make her teeth rattle, and Alleria quickly fell back into the obedient behavior she had shown the old witch. The knife lay on the floor and her powers were far from her mind.

When she was naked, her hands covering those parts that should not be seen by eyes other than a husband or mother, the woman left the room. Cold pinched Alleria's nude skin and little goosebumps lined every inch of her flesh. The room was the same, yet it felt bigger now that she was naked. She didn't dare sit on the bed, so she stood, hands still covering her delicate parts, and shivered.

After a few minutes—that passed with the lethargic pace of hours—the door opened once more, and the woman reentered.

Not the same woman, she noted, though the similarities were striking. This lady had the same scars where her eyes were supposed to be and the same sober face, but her hair was dirty blonde instead of black. A silver dress was draped across the new woman's arm, the material glowing with dim luminescence.

Magic.

The fabric of the dress rippled when the woman shook it into its full shape. Next to Alleria, the woman was at least a head and shoulders taller, and as thin as a rake. The garb looked small in her hands.

Alleria extended one hand to receive the dress in favor of covering her bosom with the other. Instead of acknowledging the outstretched hand, the woman grabbed her roughly, like a mother would to dress an obstinate child, and pulled the shining silver fabric over Alleria's head. The thin fingers held her arm with a grip that made her wonder if her skin would be bruised come morning. Alleria helped her along as much as she could and was overwhelmed with a familiar sense of humiliation.

Just get angry... that will teach her.

But instead of anger, she felt dull and sad as she ran her hands over the fabric of her new garment. The dress was soft and smooth and fitted like a glove, as if it were made for her. The perfection of the cut surprised her, but she didn't get too much time to think about it because the woman grabbed her by the arm again and pulled her along.

The sharp pain in her arm finally snapped her from her submissive mode and Alleria felt anger grow in her stomach, taking over from her confusion and fear.

No more. Eleven years was enough.

"Whoever you are, I demand you let me go. I will not be responsible for the consequences if you refuse. I have terrible powers..."

Alleria jerked loose from the woman's grip and took on a threatening stance, her hands held a little way from her hips, fingers spread.

I don't have to accept this anymore.

Darkness rose inside of her, but as it pushed to spill from her skin, the dress flared up and she felt an instant release, as if something just sucked up her power. The anger was immediately replaced by confusion. The woman grabbed her again, still not uttering a single word, and held up Alleria's arm. She was half dragged, half led out of the room; the woman wouldn't give her time to catch her footing and she struggled to stand up straight.

The corridor was made from dark obsidian stones and it looked beautiful in a spooky way. Beneath the girl was a smooth floor made from a black marble that contained thousands of small mirror fragments, which were so cold to her bare feet. Fireless lights in the ceiling illuminated the whole corridor with a soft, white glow that reflected gently off the mirror shards in the marble. None of the splendor was natural, and Alleria marveled at the blatant amount of magic use; she had never seen the likes of it. For the first time, she saw the Arallfyd for what it really was and how it differed from the world beyond the border, where magic was sparse and needed to be conserved rather than squandered.

The corridor twisted and turned as the eyeless woman pulled her along relentlessly, finally stopping at the end, where a large door stood tall in the obsidian wall. The lips of the eyeless woman parted and a note that sounded like the shrill tweet of a songbird rang from her mouth. The door creaked open.

Inside was the largest room Alleria had ever seen. It looked like a great hall. A silver-black carpet spread out over the floor like a costly ribbon, just wide enough for the two of them to walk across. Large stained-glass windows lined the walls on either side, casting colorful shadows on the floor. The ceiling was draped with black and silver fabrics. The ground—like the one in the corridor—was a strange black marble covered in tiny shards of mirror. Due to the size of the room, the ground mimicked the night sky spattered with thousands of little stars. On both sides of the carpet stood brightly dressed people—though perhaps "people" wasn't the most accurate description for what Alleria saw. Most looked almost human, but between them some of the strangest creatures stared at her from behind colorful fans and underneath ornate hats. The ladies donned the most beautiful gowns, all decorated with intricate stitching and gems; their partners dressed in outfits to match. Alleria was stunned by the gold, yellow, orange, red, purple, blue, and green of the clothing that brightened up the austere surroundings.

Some of the faces had animalistic qualities to their features. There were those who looked similar to some of the faerisee creatures one might find in the Shadow Marshes, but more delicate and elegant somehow. The faerisees were like crude copies.

Alleria heard very soft whispers behind the ladies' fans, and all eyes followed her every move. The eyeless woman who guided Alleria pulled her along the carpet, and without warning, pushed her forward so that she fell onto her hands and knees. The long, silver-gold locks slid past her face and she pushed the hair aside to look up.

In front of her, on a silver throne, sat a tall gentleman. Most would consider the man breathtakingly handsome; his face was angular and very symmetrical. Dark, slanted eyes looked down on her and a simple silver crown rested on his long hair, which was the color of crows' feathers. On top of a dark robe he wore an opulent black-silver suit of armor. Large, ornate spikes protruded from the metal sleeves and the chest of his breastplate was inlaid with midnight gems in a dragon pattern. Alleria swallowed at the sight of the man, but she did not lower her eyes.

"Stand, My Lady."

The voice was rich and deep, and the man beckoned Alleria with his long fingers.

Lady?

"My apologies for the rough behavior of my servants. I wish no insult to your person."

With slow deliberation, Alleria rose to her feet, her eyes focused on the man on the throne. In her peripheral vision, she saw the strange people lean forward; they obviously wanted to see as much as they could of this spectacle. The man stood from his throne and walked toward Alleria. His movements were elegant and he looked as if he glided on air rather than walked. In a moment of doubt, she turned to look away, but a finger rested under her chin and he pulled up her head, forcing her to look at him. Disproportionately dark irises hid the whites of his eyes and his sinister gaze pierced into hers.

"I am aware that your treatment in my palace has not been gregarious, and I wish to make amends, My Lady."

"I'm uncertain why I am in your castle." There was a hint of fire in her voice and Alleria tried to keep her expression as neutral as she could.

"Why, Lady Nezmysly... you are my guest."

His perfect eyebrows arched and a faint look of surprise appeared on his placid face.

"I don't know who Lady Nezmysly is..." Alleria said, her voice hesitant. "I think you mistake me for someone else. My name is Alleria."

"You are the child of the Lord Nezmysly, are you not?"

His fingers ran through her hair and he held a lock on the palm of his hand, as if presenting her with evidence. His head cocked and Alleria noticed that his eyes never once blinked.

"I have never seen anyone else with hair the color of the second moon."

"I don't know who my father is. I just know that he's one of the fath tywyll." Her jaw set and she squinted her eyes at him.

"May I call you Alleria?" His tone was soft and soothing, and he stepped a little closer, close enough to invade Alleria's personal space.

"If you... you wish," she stammered and the determined look on her face faltered.

"You must call me Gwae. Don't call me Lord Vynorto; you are too special a guest to address me by my formal title."

"Yes, Lord... ehm... Gwae."

"Your father and I are of the same kind. We are rare even in the Arallfyd. When I heard he had a tylwyth teg daughter, I was intrigued. I was aware of your presence as soon as you stepped across the boundary. Unfortunately, I lost sight of you soon after you left the mists."

The mere mention of the mists reminded Alleria of the faces and shapes she saw within, and her body shivered involuntary.

"I was raised in the Shadow Marshes by a witch named Tumsa. My mother died many years ago." *I don't know if my mother is dead,* she thought, but it seemed the easiest story. "I can barely remember her, and until recently, I didn't know about my birth father. The color of my hair could mean anything, and I'm sure I would make an unworthy guest."

The lips of the man curled, but the smile did not reach his eyes. There was something cold about the way he stared at her. His thumb rubbed the lock of Alleria's hair that lay in his hand and he looked at it for a moment, his face impassive.

"You say you know nothing of your father, or of your heritage? Then it is a blessing for you to have come to my castle, for I can tell you all you need to know about your bloodline."

The hair fell between his fingers like liquid and he held out his hand to her.

"Let me show you my castle, Alleria, and let me tell you about the gosgeiddig; the children of the moons."

Alleria slipped her hand in his and he led her over the carpet past all the colorful people. Their eyes burned into the back of her head.

Only when they passed through the large doors and into the corridor did Alleria feel free to speak again.

"Who are the children of the moons?"

"We are a special race of descendants from the three moons, and there are very few of us. There are only three full-blooded descendants, one for each moon, and all of them are male. I am a direct descendent. I was not born to a mother, but created by the third moon himself."

She stared at him, her eyes blinked, and she shook her head.

"You have no mother?"

"No, unless you count the moon as a mother. I don't have any natural parents, and neither does your father. Perhaps the term 'children of the moons' does not apply to us, only to our offspring. We are more servitors of the moons, perhaps even avatars, because we are given certain direct traits of our creators."

"What is your purpose here?"

"We were sent to reign over a certain part of the Arallfyd. Only one of us may reign at one time, so we each live in the Arallfyd for a hundred years before we are returned to our creator's side to sleep until it is our time to reign again. Your father, who is the descendent of the second moon, reigned before me. And he found your mother during the time of the Blood Moon."

"The Blood Moon isn't a separate moon, right? It's more an event? It's the occurrence when the moons are all aligned, and the light of the red sun reflects of them in such a way that it looks like they are covered in blood?"

"Yes."

He rubbed his thumb against her cheek and Alleria felt shivers run down her spine.

"So there would be no descendent for the Blood Moon?"

"No."

When he laughed, his voice sounded ethereal, as if something chimed within the deepness of his tones.

"There are only three. The Gold Moon, the Silver Moon, and the Black Moon, as they were known before they were numbered."

"What happens when you go back to... ehm... your moon?"

"We are in a state between sleep and wakefulness."

"Oh." Alleria looked at her feet. "Isn't two hundred years a long time?"

"It is. That is why, when I found that the descendent of the second moon had a daughter, I was very pleased. I planned to have one of my servants fetch you, but to my surprise you were already claimed."

Alleria pulled away from him and gave him a suspicious look. Gwae held her gaze and the blackness of his eyes seemed to deepen in color.

"How did you know that I was female? No one knew who I was..."

"Not until you were baptized."

"Baptized? Jack just put some blood on my lips. It wasn't as if there was any magical ritual involved."

"The blood was ritual enough, and the time of your seventeenth year, therein lies the magic. It means that you are almost of age, and you are ready for a mate."

A mate? Alleria felt a hot flush rise to her cheeks.

"I don't understand..."

Gwae stopped at a door and pushed it open with his fingertips as if it weighed nothing.

"After you," he said, and Alleria stared into what appeared to be a tower with a long, winding stairwell that led to the top. The same obsidian made up the walls of the tower, only there were little specks of light everywhere. The way the glow reflected off the volcanic glass was breathtaking. It was as if Gwae had made his castle into the night sky itself.

Does the sky remind him of where he comes from? Does it make him feel that he's home?

Gwae guided Alleria to the stairs and she could feel his presence behind her as she ascended. The higher they climbed, the colder the temperature became, and though the strange silver dress she wore kept her warm, her face, neck, and most of all, bare feet, felt the sting of frost. The wind howled through the belfry, and when Alleria looked up, she saw that there was no roof above them. After a long climb, they reached the top and stepped onto what could only be described as a platform.

Above her, Alleria saw the pale shape of the sun, and she realized for the first time it was already morning. Beneath were stretches of forest. The scenery resembled a magnificent sea of dark greens and purples.

"I don't like going back to my creator, Alleria. But each moon must have the same chance to reign in the Arallfyd. Only then can there be balance." He turned, and there was something in his eyes that worried her, an intense look that meant something, only she didn't know what.

"Most of the gosgeiddig are male. That is why they are so rare. Only twice in the whole of existence has a gosgeiddig been female, and the last one never lived beyond infancy."

"Oh..."

Very eloquent, Alleria, pride yourself on your conversational skills.

"That makes you very special."

"I was supposed to be sold at a slave market because of who I am and what I can do. I'm ashamed to admit that I really don't know what I am, and despite a few uncontrolled demonstrations of my power, I don't know exactly what I can do either."

She lowered her eyes and sighed. Mentioning the slave market felt like a betrayal to Jack somehow. Yet, Alleria wondered if she wasn't better off being with her own kind.

"At a human slave market?"

"Yes."

"Those fools wouldn't know what they had on their hands."

"A witch raised me. I think she knew more about me. She never shared the information she had."

"She didn't have any idea either, or she would have traded you with one of the fath tywyll when she had the chance. Many of us would offer great things in return for a female gosgeiddig." The spark returned to his eyes and Alleria attributed it to a strange sense of hunger.

"And now you have me."

"I do indeed."

"Am I your prisoner?"

"You are my guest."

"Then I am free to leave?"

His right cheek twitched a little, but he kept a calm face. Alleria looked away from him and over the lands beneath them. Here and there she saw flecks of snow on the green and purple, but the white spots were melting fast.

"You would be in a lot of danger if you left." He spoke in low, menacing tones. "You are safe in my castle; why would you want to leave?"

The dark eyes challenged her and Alleria understood she was indeed a prisoner, and that Gwae only called her a guest as a formality.

"What are your intentions for life? What are your goals?"

"My goals?"

The question caught her by surprise and she blinked at him. No one had ever wondered what she wanted to do with her life, not even Alleria herself.

"Do you have a beau in your life? Someone you wish to marry?"

His question brought a red flush to her cheeks, and without knowing why, Alleria pictured Jack's smiling face. She pushed the thought aside.

"No, I was... I haven't met too many men. Tumsa, the witch, kept me mostly to herself. I never had the luxury of falling in love."

"Finding a suitable husband is the most important quest in a young lady's life."

Gwae licked his lips and stepped toward her. The wind tugged at Alleria's hair, yet Gwae's long, black locks stayed perfectly still.

"Is it?" Alleria asked, a sharpness in her hollow voice. "I was never raised as a lady. I was raised with herbs and rituals. All I know is how to avoid dangerous creatures in the Shadow Marshes and how to aid with magic spells. I know how to read, and I've read stories about love and romance, but I never believed I would be someone's wife."

She wanted to add that she'd never even considered married life, and that right now she was more eager to find out who she really was than to be someone's wife. Marriage just sounded like another bond, and she'd barely had time to discover herself.

"It is. It is the sole purpose of a female. You must be taught how to be a dedicated wife."

Gwae smiled, but the smile didn't reach his eyes again.

I don't like him.

"You would make a wonderful wife, Alleria, if you were taught how. And I would make a suitable husband for one like you. We are, after all, of the same species."

"I... I... am hardly worthy," she stammered. The idea of marrying this man was off-putting at best.

"You would be a most charming wife. There are few as lovely as you, Alleria. And together we could represent the second and the third moon."

That's why being a female makes me so valuable; with me by his side, he can reign for two centuries rather than one.

"You could bear me sons, Alleria."

Gwae took another step toward her and grabbed her hand. His touch was not exactly cold, but it wasn't warm either—not like Jack's hot skin. His fingers curled around hers and he brought her hand up to his mouth to plant a soft kiss on it.

"Surely being a queen in the Arallfyd is better than being a slave in the human world?"

I wonder if there is really a difference.

"I don't know what to say..." *Do I really have a choice?*

"Excellent."

He smiled at her as if she'd just accepted his proposal.

"Arrangements shall be made for this union. By the next full moon, there will be a wedding ceremony."

"But..."

"Please, Alleria, it is best for both of us if we have this union. I am sure you agree. There is nowhere else for you to go, I'm afraid. The world is not a kind place for the gosgeiddig. I am after your hand, but there are many who are after your heart. And I don't mean your love, dear girl. I mean they intend to rip it out."

"I do not get a choice?"

"I have made the choice for you. A dutiful husband should always choose the right thing for his devoted wife."

At that moment, Alleria decided to play along with the game and act the perfect bride. If he believed that she was willing, she would stand more of a chance of finding her way out of the castle. The next full moon would be the second moon, which gave her a few weeks to escape.

"I would be honored to be your wife."

Alleria hoped the smile on her face looked more genuine than it felt. He squeezed her hand a little and mirrored her smile with one of his own.

"Excellent."

A tug on Alleria's hand forced her to step forward and Gwae leaned in and kissed her on the lips. Unlike his placid face, his kiss was passionate, and despite her hatred, Alleria reciprocated. His tongue pushed his way into her mouth and he pulled her against him with the same hunger she'd experienced when she'd kissed Jack. When she finally broke free, her knees were weak. Gwae shot a predatory glance at her.

"I look forward to our wedding night."

Alleria returned his smile with a watery one of her own.

By the gods, give me a chance to escape this castle before the full moon, or this man will eat me alive.

CHAPTER SIXTEEN

The handmaidens Gwae assigned to Alleria were far gentler than the eyeless women she'd met on the first day. There were five in total, and she honestly didn't know what to do with them. Each wore a dress of the same cut and style, but all had different colors—their braided hair matching the hue of their dress. Alleria wondered if they were sisters, because they were all the same height and equally petite, their pinched and pointed facial features so similar they could have been copies of each other. The girls were unlike the others she had met. Their short postures and unremarkable features made Alleria doubt that they were truly fath tywyll, but if there was another species that lived in the Arallfyd, she had never heard of them. All five girls were named after flowers. Poppy was a redheaded creature in a red dress, while Lily wore white to match her white hair. Lilac dressed in soft purple, Primrose was donned in pink, and Daffodil looked a sunny yellow all over. When they got close to Alleria, she realized that their eyes also matched the color of their hair.

They were silly girls, and Alleria didn't quite know what to make of them. She had never met women her own age before.

The handmaidens moved and talked fast, and they made her feel tall and awkward, yet their cheerfulness was infectious. Alleria, being very young herself, wanted to join along in their jokes and giggly behavior, but she didn't know how to freely behave like a maiden. Alleria had never had the chance to even discover who she was, what she enjoyed in life. She couldn't remember ever laughing the eleven years she lived with Tumsa. Only when she met Jack had she discovered humor and any sense of joy. These girls were so different from her and Alleria was suddenly painfully aware of how serious she was.

Their chatter always surrounded her, and the girls could talk about anything. Gossip was their favorite pastime; they talked about the people at court, about the servants and life in the kingdom. Alleria learned so much from listening to them. Her new room—or rooms—were in one of the south wings of the castle. She stayed away from the court most of the time; only during the evening meals did she join her future husband and grace the courtiers with her presence. Dinner proved a distressing affair; it was unsettling to eat under the staring eyes of the fath tywyll. A beautifully set table, decorated with magical flowers and fairy lights, was set on a large podium, where she and Gwae would take place while all the courtiers stood and looked on from behind a red velvet rope that separated them from the royal couple, each fascinated with every move they made. Servants with large silver platters would present course after course, offering an assortment of unusual fruits and animals. Alleria was reminded of the puppet shows she vaguely remembered from her childhood. The way they sat in silence and ate demure bites from their silver plates with their silver cutlery looked contrived. The length of the dinners was torturous. Alleria's new dresses were uncomfortable, to say the least. The corsets were so tight that her waist looked unnaturally small, making it difficult to breathe, let alone eat, whilst wearing them. She only ever picked at her food. Gwae didn't eat that much more, but he was extremely fastidious about his meals, and he would drag out each course by taking forever to choose the morsels that he wanted to eat. Food was often not to his liking and he would then send it away and demand a clean plate. All the while Alleria tried to keep her dignity and not show how much her corsets were making her suffer.

When they were finally finished, the remaining food would be served to the courtiers. Alleria had never witnessed this, as this would only happen after she and Gwae had retreated for the night. When the hand-maidens had first spoken of the courtiers' dinner, Alleria had wondered out loud if the food was still edible after so many hours. The girls had laughed at her and explained that it wasn't about the food, but about the status. If you were invited to eat the food of the lord of the third moon, it did much credit to your reputation.

"They pay good gems, Lady, to eat your leftovers," Lilac confided in Alleria, obviously delighting in the gossip from the way she lowered her voice and the smile that sparkled in her eyes. "They'll eat anything that Lord Gwae or the future queen touched. Those courtiers are like hungry vultures."

"Not that they eat a lot of it, of course. They ain't that hungry," Poppy added. "Whatever they leave goes to the servants and the poor. We pick out the edible bits and the rest we bring outside to them what needs it most. That way everyone is happy."

Back in the days with Tumsa, Alleria would occasionally dream of being a princess, but now that she was so close to being one, she'd rather just live in the Shadow Marshes instead—though as a free woman, not a slave to the old witch.

Each night, one of the eyeless women would come to bathe and dress her. The nightgowns had the same magical properties as the dresses and Alleria noticed she was never long without dress. Once she had tried to take off her clothing herself, but it proved an impossible task.

During the day, while she attended lessons with a tutor who instructed her not only of the ways of court, but also of the powers of the gosgeid-dig, Alleria was allowed to wear more comfortable garments of the same silver material.

"To be gosgeiddig means to be eternal," the prune-faced tutor said with a sharp voice. She was tall, like most of the fath tywyll women she had met so far.

"Your gift is a gift of time. You can either grant time or you can take it away."

"It works on both living and nonliving things?"

"Naturally. Time affects everything, alive or dead, and those things that were never alive in the first place. Even rocks are touched by time, and your power mimics the passing of it. Your magic recreates all the elements that would affect the objects that you target, and if used to its full extent, it will wear everything down until there is nothing left. Yet you have a counter magic to this, for you are also able to restore time. Give it back, so to speak."

"Are there other things I can do?" Alleria asked with an eager expression on her face.

"You have the makings of a powerful magic user. All gosgeiddig have a natural affinity."

"Will you teach me this?"

"No, the Master does not want you to dabble in magic. It is not becoming of a lady. I will, however, teach you how to be in control of your power. Until then, you must wear gowns made from the absorption material, because we would rather not have any... accidents."

"The silver fabric? What exactly does it do? How does it work?"

"As the name betrays, it absorbs magic. The material is very powerful and rare, and how it works is a bit of a mystery, since the fabric has a natural ability. It's created with silk from crafspiders, creatures that only live in the west of the Arallfyd."

Alleria stroked the material, curled it around the tips of her fingers, and squeezed. Whoever had woven it was a true master. It was soft and comfortable, and it always seemed to keep the part of the skin that it covered at the right temperature.

"If it is so rare, why do I have so many different dresses with the same material?"

The tutor had an expression on her face that Alleria couldn't quite place.

"Lady, you underestimate the wealth of Lord Vynorto. He is the wealthiest of all the rulers, and some say the most powerful. The only one who would challenge his wealth and power is the Lord of the Ravens. It is only fitting that a ruler display his wealth in this manner. Such are our ways."

The tutor glanced at the material, and for a moment, Alleria thought the woman would touch it, but she folded her hands in her lap instead.

"Who is the Lord of the Ravens? I think I have heard speak of him before," Alleria said.

A wrinkled finger was placed against the tutor's lips. The old eyes darted from side to side and the tutor shook her head.

"We do not speak of him. He lives in the north of the Arallfyd, where he reigns. Lord Vynorto holds no love for him."

"What about my father; where does he reign?"

"In this castle. The Moonlords are always here, the place closest to their moon."

The tutor pointed up as if the moons were right above them.

"As long as Lord Vynorto sits on the throne, the dark moon holds the power."

"I haven't been able to see the third moon in the sky at all since I have come here."

"That is because the lord sits on the throne."

Alleria frowned. "I still saw the third moon back in the Borderlands and in the human world."

"Because in the human worlds, the moons are physical, and in the Arallfyd, they are only a magical representation. The lords use the human moons to channel their magic, but here we only have an illusion of those same moons, for we cannot really see them."

"I find it hard to imagine."

"The moons in the other world change too. Right now, we all live in the age of the dark moon, or third moon as you know it. That means that the winters are longer and the crops struggle to grow. There is more poverty and more disease in your world. When the first moon reigns, this will change, and when your father reigns, the human world will be at its most prosperous. Such is the way. Each moon will influence more than the Arallfyd alone."

"Why would the second moon allow him to marry me then?"

"Because then the two moons can reign together and turn upon the third moon. Alliances through blood are the most powerful of all, child. Has no one ever taught you anything?"

Alleria wrinkled her nose and plucked a piece of fluff from her study dress. She didn't answer the woman but shrugged her shoulders. The tutor cleared her throat and was obviously uncomfortable.

Perhaps she is afraid she said too much?

Alleria forced a smile and shifted her weight and she saw the relief blossom on the older woman's face.

"So that is the plan? I'm to be the alliance between the two moons?"

The tutor waved her hand at Alleria with a dismissive gesture; the woman's face was cautious now and her body language was rigid.

"I am not as presumptuous as to say I know what the politics of the Moonlords are. But yes, that is what the plan could be."

"Wouldn't my father be upset if he didn't get to come back to the Arallfyd? If I'm down here, there will be no need for him."

"I don't know. For all I know, the moon will release your father because of your marriage. I am but a lowly tutor, child. I don't know the ways of the gods."

"Gods?"

The woman just nodded in response. Alleria didn't know if she spoke the truth or not, but she decided not to grill the tutor about it any further at that point. The woman knew so much, and Alleria wanted to learn more about the Arallfyd, but if she asked too many questions now, she had a suspicion she would put both herself and the tutor in danger.

"The place I come from knows very little about this land. The Arallfyd is a mystery to most humans and faerisees. The witch who raised me knew a little bit, but not enough to give answers. Why is the Arallfyd separated from the human world?"

The tutor's shoulders relaxed visibly and the woman exhaled. She shifted her weight and patted Alleria on the knee.

"Once, many millennia ago, there was just one world, and the fath tywyll reigned with an iron hand. But the lords of the fath tywyll were vain and they insulted the gods and misused the lands, so the gods banished them to the Arallfyd. To connect the two worlds, they agreed to let the barrier drop for the lasting of one Blood Moon. That way, the humans and the fath tywyll could breed and create children who could walk both planes. The Blood Moon is unpredictable; it can last a week or it can last a decade. The fath tywyll eagerly await it. The Blood Moon of your birth lasted almost four years, which created quite a bit of chaos in both the human world and the Arallfyd, if I remember correctly."

That could explain why Jack is older than me, yet still created under the same Blood Moon, Alleria thought. She had wondered about Jack's age before, but always assumed that he was much older than he looked. *Maybe he is young like I am, after all?*

She enjoyed listening to the melodic tones of the tutor, who was a captivating storyteller. Alleria leaned back on her chair and curled her feet under her legs.

"What of the mists that separate the two worlds?"

Her blue eyes bored into those of the tutor and the old woman sighed.

"The mists are an entity of their own. Both human and fath tywyll fear them, as well they should. The mists have been getting thicker over the last few generations. We know them as the guardians, but they are slowly swallowing up more of our domain. The human world does not suffer from them much yet, but as soon as it is the Blood Moon, the mists will be as free as the fath tywyll. Who knows what will happen then? The council discusses the mists, but we underlings don't know what they plan to do, or if there is anything to be done. All we know is to stay clear of them, but we have done so throughout their existence anyway."

"When we passed through the mists I... I saw something."

"What did you see?"

"There were creatures. They looked like women, and though they did not harm us, I believe they had a mind to."

The tutor leaned toward Alleria, her face a perfect balance between shock and pleasure.

She must have forgotten that I am her Lady, for she now gossips like my flowery handmaidens.

"Women, you say? I have heard tales of the mistwives. They are believed to be spouses of the Lost God, and they dwell on the border somewhere between life and death, seeking warmth. All that pass through the mist without protection stand a chance of being torn apart by them. I hear tales that their numbers have been growing as the mists expand. No one knows why, or if the Lost God is the influence behind their multiplying."

"The Lost God? Why is he called that? Is he lost?"

"He is the most mysterious of all the gods, and he was cast from the Divine Pantheon, but he was called the Lost God millennia before that occurrence."

"There are different gods in the Arallfyd than there are in the human world?"

"Not really, but they do have different names in the other world, and different powers. All magic is more powerful in the Arallfyd, even that of gods. The three moons and two suns are the most obvious examples, because they can be seen. But your goddess of nature, I believe you call her Gaia, is called Ephione here, and she is the goddess of life. Her powers are similar but they work by different rules in both worlds."

"I had no idea," Alleria said. "I thought everything was different. I didn't realize the gods were the same. I never even considered that the mists were a potential threat to the Arallfyd as well; the humans speak of the mists as if they are a part of it. But of course they're not, because the mists are as much a border to you as they are to us. How do the fath tywyll react to the mists? Are they as frightened as the humans?

"Fear works different here. The fath tywyll are calmer and more calculating than humans. You were born in the mortal world where time moves quickly and actions are impetuous and ill-considered. On this side of the border, the passing of time is slow, and our lives are long enough to be cautious with our decisions. The lives of the nobility are ruled by political intrigues and they treat the mists in the same manner. They are aware of the threat, but often act to the world as if there is nothing to fear. No one wants to show any form of weakness."

"This sounds insane. The human world and the Arallfyd should join forces if these mists really do pose a threat."

The tutor shrugged, her bony shoulders pushing against the gray fabric of her dress.

"They're not completely ambivalent. The mists are covertly studied in the same way as the nobility studies their enemies, behind a veil of secrecy. Some even seek ways to take advantage of the magic of the mists. I know there are those who want to control the mists and make the world beyond it accessible for them to conquer. There is power there and the mists that could make a fath tywyll king or lord influential beyond belief." The woman whispered the last words conspiratorially.

"Power in the human world?"

"Yes…" Her mouth opened as if she was about to say something else, but closed again, her attention fixed on the study door. Alleria turned to find Primrose staring back, her face lacking its usual bright smile. The tutor faced Alleria, her features straight, a hint of a blush in her cheeks.

"As for your lessons, My Lady…"

That was the first and the last time Alleria saw that tutor, and the next day, she was presented with another woman who was younger and offered a more austere expression. She never dared to ask questions again.

Alleria's days were filled with lessons; her evenings were filled with meals. There was little time to herself and she was constantly surrounded by teachers, handmaidens, or her fiancé. She had been raised as a solitary creature and the constant companionship was exhausting. She thought back on her time with Jack, who had been by her side every minute of the day as well, yet somehow his presence hadn't irked her as much. There had been moments of quiet between them, and Alleria always felt she had room for her own thoughts. Here, there was always someone demanding her attention.

Gwae was courteous and very romantic. He would lavish her with jewels, flowers, and little gifts, and whenever there were no eyes upon them, he would kiss her with a hungry desire. Though his kisses were all but unpleasant, Alleria couldn't help but wish that it was Jack who kissed her instead.

After the incident with the first tutor, Alleria didn't trust her handmaidens anymore. Their laughs and chatter sounded false. There was a sharpness to the young women, and their tongues were much sharper when backs were turned. Alleria treated them with a polite courtesy, but she was wary of the girls.

At night, when she was finally alone, she was most at ease. Her bedroom was large and beautiful; like everything else in the castle, it looked like the night sky, black and silver. The furnishings were plush and comfortable and servants kept her surroundings spotless.

Sometimes, she would think of the bedstead that had belonged to her in the witch's cottage and realize how far those two worlds were apart. And yet... she still felt as trapped as she did then. Gwae treated her with more warmth than the old witch had, but she feared him just as much. There was a darkness in him that lay under the surface, which she recognized.

Despite Gwae's lust for her, and his assurance that she was special, Alleria felt more worthless now than she had when she knew she would be a slave. Gwae never seemed to treat her as a person, but as a possession. Jack had done so in the beginning too, but near the end...

A sound distracted Alleria from her thoughts and she peered into the gloom. The only light in the room glowed from a moon-shaped symbol on the top of the four-poster bed. She squinted her eyes but could not make out anything other than shadows.

"Hello? Is anyone there?"

No answer came. Alleria sat in silence while clutching the blankets up to her chin. Another noise—this time directly above her—made her blood run cold. Afraid to look up, but knowing she had to, Alleria raised her head. Her movements were slow and deliberate. When her view finally reached the spot where the noise had come from, she swallowed a scream.

Overhead, at the foot of the bed's canopy, illuminated by the light of the crescent moon, hung the upside-down figure of a woman.

To Alleria's horror, she could make out that the figure had four arms, each shifting separately with a calculated motion. The stranger's movements were so fast and spiderlike that Alleria moaned with fright. When the female stopped, her head turned 180 degrees, like the head of a Motley owl, until it faced the young woman below.

Fear and fascination kept Alleria paralyzed, and by the time her brain finally allowed her any thoughts of fleeing, the female had scuttled down from the canopy and landed at the foot of the bed. All four arms rested on the mattress and her legs were crouched in such a way that Alleria was afraid she might leap toward her. Oddly enough, there was no weight or pressure on the bed where the figure sat. Upon closer inspection, it became apparent that the woman was translucent; Alleria noticed the shadow of one of the four posters was visible through her skin. Long, black hair fell over the figure's face. Large, slanted eyes made up from many facets, like those of a fly, peered out from between the dark strands—inhuman, but strangely alluring.

"You must come." The voice was soft and sounded like that of a girl much younger than the figure looked. "I must show you, before it's too late."

She raised her chin and Alleria saw her whole face now. It was narrow and long, with a thin, elegant nose. Small, pink lips and porcelain skin gave her the appearance of a doll.

"Where do you want me to go?" Alleria whispered.

"To the dormant room."

The female moved backward with those same spidery movements and made her way off the bed. Alleria got up and followed her.

The figure—who now stood upright, which made her even more ghostly—walked toward the wardrobe and pointed.

"It will be cold where we go."

Alleria took out the warmest-looking pair of slippers and the hooded robe made from the absorption fabric, which would give her a little extra protection from the cold. She dressed as fast as she could then allowed the female to lead her out of the room and down the endless corridors.

An eerie quiet overtook the castle at night, and Alleria's soft steps sounded hollow on the dark floor.

She shivered and quickened her pace. The ghostly figure led her to the south tower and they descended a set of long stairs. Instead of stopping at the ground floor, as was usually the case, the female opened another door to stairs that led further down. A biting cold hit Alleria in the face when she entered. The temperature made her teeth chatter and she put up her hood to keep her head and neck protected from the chill. The new stairwell led deeper into the darkness. Her translucid guide moved a few steps ahead, unaffected by the cold, and as she descended, a pale glow surrounded her. A moment's hesitation crossed Alleria's mind, but then she bit her lip and followed the female down. In the dark, the material of her cloak and nightgown lit up with a similar dim glow as that of the spirit, making it easier to see where she was going.

The sting of cold in her cheeks reminded Alleria of her journey with Jack. She pulled the soft material of the hood against her cheeks, mouth, and nose, so that only her eyes peered out.

At the bottom of the stairs was another corridor, which ended at a large, ornately carved door. The spirit passed through the solid wood as if there were no barrier at all. The sight baffled Alleria and she gingerly touched the door to see if it was really there. Solid as a rock, and no matter how hard she pushed, it would not budge. There was no handle, just dark wood. For a long moment she stood still, waiting for anything to happen, but when it didn't, she turned and started climbing the stairs feeling utterly confused.

A slight groan broke the silence and Alleria turned to see the door open a crack. Quickly, she ran down the stairs, her curiosity overtaking all sense of caution, and she pulled open the door.

The other side held a cavernous room. Light spilled in from glass-like pillars, illuminating everything in a silver-blue glow. The ghostly shape of the woman appeared by her side.

"You must see."

The female beckoned Alleria to follow and moved toward the pillars. There were seven of them in total. Within the glow of the light floated dark shadows in the depths of their cores.

Alleria moved closer and peered through the glass. To her horror, she saw that the shadows were the bodies of women. Each of them wore a beautiful silver gown made of the absorption fabric, which floated around them as if they were suspended in water. Their eyes were closed and their faces serene.

"I don't understand. Who are these women?"

"They are the wives of Gwae."

Alleria took an involuntary step back, her hand resting on her heart. She could feel the blood drain from her face.

"Are they dead?"

"They are neither dead nor are they alive. They are between two worlds. Gwae holds them here until he needs them."

"What does he need them for?"

"The Moonlord is a man of many vices, but lust is his strongest passion. He awakens one of his wives each night with the sole purpose of having her please him."

Alleria's slender hand cupped her open mouth as she stared at the still figures of the floating women.

"Will he do this to me?"

The figure shook her ethereal head and looked at Alleria with her dark, faceted eyes, half lidded by sadness.

"Not at first. You are new to him still, and as long as you are obedient, he will allow you to move around by his side. But after a while... he... he will ask things of you, things that you will not want to do, and when you refuse him, you will be here... with us. Eternal."

"Us?" Alleria studied the figure. "Are you...?"

The female nodded and pointed at one of the still figures in the glass pillar. Four arms rested by the side of the floating body. The woman looked tragically beautiful in this magical stasis. "How can you stand here and talk to me when you are in there?"

"I am not. What you see is a projection of myself. It is one of the powers I have. And it only works when someone is sensitive enough to see me."

"But you wear a dress of absorption material. How can you use magic?"

"This is telepathy, which works differently from physical magic, and the material is powerless to stop it. My power is only weak; I can't venture too far from my body or I would have called out to my people. No one knows I'm here. It is the lord's right to have multiple wives and he makes sure that he keeps his spouses away from prying eyes. The only time anyone ever gets to see us is during the meals. His Lordship will always dine with his favored wife to keep his people appeased. The countrymen like to see their king dine with a queen. It is tradition."

"He dines with me now."

"Yes; you are the newest and thus the favored."

"There must be something I can do to help you. How can I free you?"

"Do not marry him. Thwart his plans against the other Moonlords. The only way we can be released is if the other lords release us during their reign."

"But Gwae's reign only started a decade ago. That will be a long time."

"Long is not the same as eternity."

"I don't know how to escape. Even if I manage to get away from the castle, I know nothing of the Arallfyd." Alleria fought the rising panic that threatened to overcome her. "I'm not much of a hero. If you had seen my life, you would know that."

"Hero or not, you must run, or join our fate."

The beautiful women looked strangely peaceful behind the glass. Each was different; most of them looked humanoid, though one of them seemed more feline than anything else. The sight of them brought tears to Alleria's eyes.

"It's not fair that he can do this to these women... to any woman."

The bitter taste of anger surfaced in her throat. The gown she wore flared up, a warning that it had absorbed her power.

"If I somehow manage to take off these clothes, perhaps I can age the pillars enough to release the women."

The figure shook her head.

"Even if you could harm these magical pillars, you would only trigger alarms. The Moonlord is very powerful. I do not think you can save us."

"I don't think I could manage to take off the clothes anyway. But what can I do if not that? There has to be something."

The woman opened her mouth to respond, but an unseen force caught her attention and she cocked her head. The dark eyes widened with a look of panic.

"You must go back to your room *now*. Time is running out. *He* moves to your room as we speak. Go! Flee!"

The image of the woman blinked out of existence and Alleria was left with a sense of dread and anger that threatened to turn into panic. The absorption material lit up again as an indicator of her stress. She ran as fast as her legs could carry her while she tried to move with as little noise as possible. The fabric of the cloak and dress flapped behind her—not as noiseless as she would have liked—and her breath stung in her chest as she weaved her way up the many stairs and down the corridors. When she sprinted into the wing of her room, she spotted Gwae standing at her door. Alleria quickly and quietly slipped into one of the adjoining rooms that she used as a reading room for her studies.

Please don't let him have seen me.

Pangs of pain shot through her pounding heart and a wave of nausea came over her. On her tippy-toes, Alleria made her way to the door that joined the two rooms together and put her ear against it, willing her breathing to calm down.

"Lily—"

The voice of Gwae traveled, and Alleria heard the anger it contained.

"Where is she?" A door opened on the other side of the room—the door to the quarters of her handmaidens.

"Lord?" The voice sounded drowsy. "What do you mean?"

"Where is my bride, Lily? She's not in her bed."

Alleria squeezed her eyes shut and inhaled.

"We put her to bed hours ago, Lord. She was sleeping when last Primrose checked."

"She is not here now. Lilac, check the dungeons to make sure that she hasn't discovered that her tylwyth teg friend is here."

Jack?

The realization made her cheeks flush. Who else could he be speaking of?

"I thought you were going to kill the son of the Ravenlord, Master. And send his father the head."

Lilac's voice sounded shrill.

Oh please, if it is Jack, don't let them kill him.

"I will, but I need some more information out of the bastard of Havran first. It would be highly inconvenient if Alleria saw him."

Inconvenient indeed.

"I will find out, Lord."

Footsteps ran from the room and past the study.

"She could still be in this wing, Lord, have you checked the adjoining rooms?"

This was Alleria's moment to move. If Gwae opened the door, he would find her in her cloak, and she couldn't explain why she stood there, but if...

Alleria ripped the cloak from her shoulders and pulled a book off one of the shelves. Stealthily, she jumped on one of the large sofas, lay down, and pulled the cloak over her like a blanket. She feigned sleep; her hand draped toward the floor, the book open underneath her fingers as if she'd dropped it during her slumber.

It took every ounce of the girl's self-control to keep her face calm and her breathing deep and regular when she heard the door open, and footsteps walk in her direction.

"There you are."

Gwae barely spoke above a whisper and Alleria pretended to wake up when his weight pressed next to her. He ran his hands over her face.

"I was worried you had gone. What are you doing here?"

Alleria smiled at him, feigning adoration. Her arms stretched and she rubbed her eyes.

"I woke up in the middle of the night and couldn't sleep again. I thought this would be a good opportunity to study my etiquette, so I can be a worthy queen."

Her answer pleased him; Alleria could see it in his smile. His fingers traced the line from her cheek to her neck and down her chest where he stopped short of her breast.

"I'm glad you are here."

"Where else would I be, My Lord?" She fluttered her eyelashes slightly and tried to maintain her innocent expression. Another smile crossed his lips and she was grateful that he underestimated her. One thing Alleria had learned in her short life was to be obedient, and this night it served her well.

He pulled the cloak away and cocked his head at her. "Were you cold?"

"A little. But to be honest, I mostly just wanted to snuggle under something, and I didn't want to drag the heavy blankets here. The cloak seemed a perfect compromise."

He rubbed his thumb across her cheek again and then over her lips. His eyes fixated on her mouth.

"I have to admit," Gwae said in a deep throaty voice, "my intention to visit you was less than honorable. But I will respect your wishes for etiquette and wait until we are married."

You'll just go down and wake one of your other wives to please you, she thought bitterly, but instead of speaking the words out loud, she lowered her eyes.

"Thank you. I am grateful you will let me keep my honor until our wedding night."

Gwae got to his feet, placed the cloak over his arm, and extended his hand.

"Let me escort you back to your bedroom."

They walked back to the room where four anxious girls were waiting. Alleria saw that they were holding hands. They looked less colorful in their faded nightgowns, and the darkness took away some of their bright charms.

"I'm sorry to cause such upset. I promise I will not leave my bedroom without notice again in the night. I hope I did nothing to displease His Lordship."

Alleria fluttered her lashes at Gwae, who smiled in return.

"Girls, you may leave us, and tell Primrose to return to her room; my bride has been found."

The four women bobbed in unison and hurried out of the room. Gwae led Alleria to her bed. She kicked off her slippers and crawled between the covers.

"You are a good and devoted young woman, Alleria."

Gwae lowered himself and sat on the side of the bed. His fingers played with her hair, a far-off expression in his eyes as he stroked and teased the locks.

"Tumsa taught me compliance."

"She taught you well. I am pleased with you."

"I am glad I can please you, Lord," she said, the meek smile on her face hiding the hatred she felt inside.

"Alleria, you will not be my first wife."

Her eyes widened and the shock she felt about his confession worked in her favor; he mistook it for surprise.

"I don't mean to upset you, but where I come from it's very normal to have more than one wife. However, I have decided you will be my most important wife. You will be my queen."

Alleria graced him with a forced understanding nod and smile.

"Are you a king, Gwae? People call you lord, and not majesty."

"I am a king of sorts, Alleria. But when you marry me and I take over the full reign of the castle, I will be crowned king and I shall have you as my queen. As long as you stay loyal to me, of course."

Her heart sank. Gwae's words frightened her because she had no intention of staying loyal and she feared what he would do when he found out that she meant to betray him by fleeing.

"Of course." Her voice was soft. "But what of the first moon? Does he not reign as well?"

"Marrying you will give me the power of two moons; the third will be no match for my will. All you need do is grant me a son or daughter and we can make our child the vasal of the first moon."

"Will the first moon agree with this?"

"Our union will be too strong for him. Either our two houses will rise against him and destroy everything he stands for or he will take our child as the peace offering, and the three houses will be united into one." He smiled at her, greed simmering behind his dark eyes. "But let's not talk of this now, my love. Let's talk about us. You will be the most beautiful of all my wives, and I look forward to having you by my side for eternity."

The beautiful women, who floated so peacefully within the glass pillars, appeared in Alleria's mind, and her heart cried out to them. Gwae licked his lips, and with the lock of her hair, he traced the shape of Alleria's nose and mouth. Then he leaned over to kiss her. His kisses were always passionate, but more so now, and she felt his hand roam the hem of her nightdress and slide over the bare skin of her leg. His lips moved faster and he pressed his weight against her. Alleria froze, fighting another pinch of panic.

To her horror, her body responded to Gwae's touch.

No, not him. Please don't let him be the one.

The long fingers, cold against her warm thighs, slid farther up, and Alleria bolted upright. Gwae pulled back—perturbed by her sudden jolt—a haunted look in his eyes. He breathed heavily, and for a moment, Alleria thought he would kiss her again, only this time he would not stop with kisses alone. She pleaded with her eyes, watching Gwae struggle with his passions.

"My apologies. I should go. If I stay here, I will deflower you before our wedding night and I promised I would keep your honor intact."

To his credit, he removed himself from the bed, though he moved slowly and with clear reluctance.

"Four days, Alleria, then you will be mine. Four days and I will do exactly with you as I please."

"Four days," she repeated with a forced smile.

Hopefully, I will be gone by then.

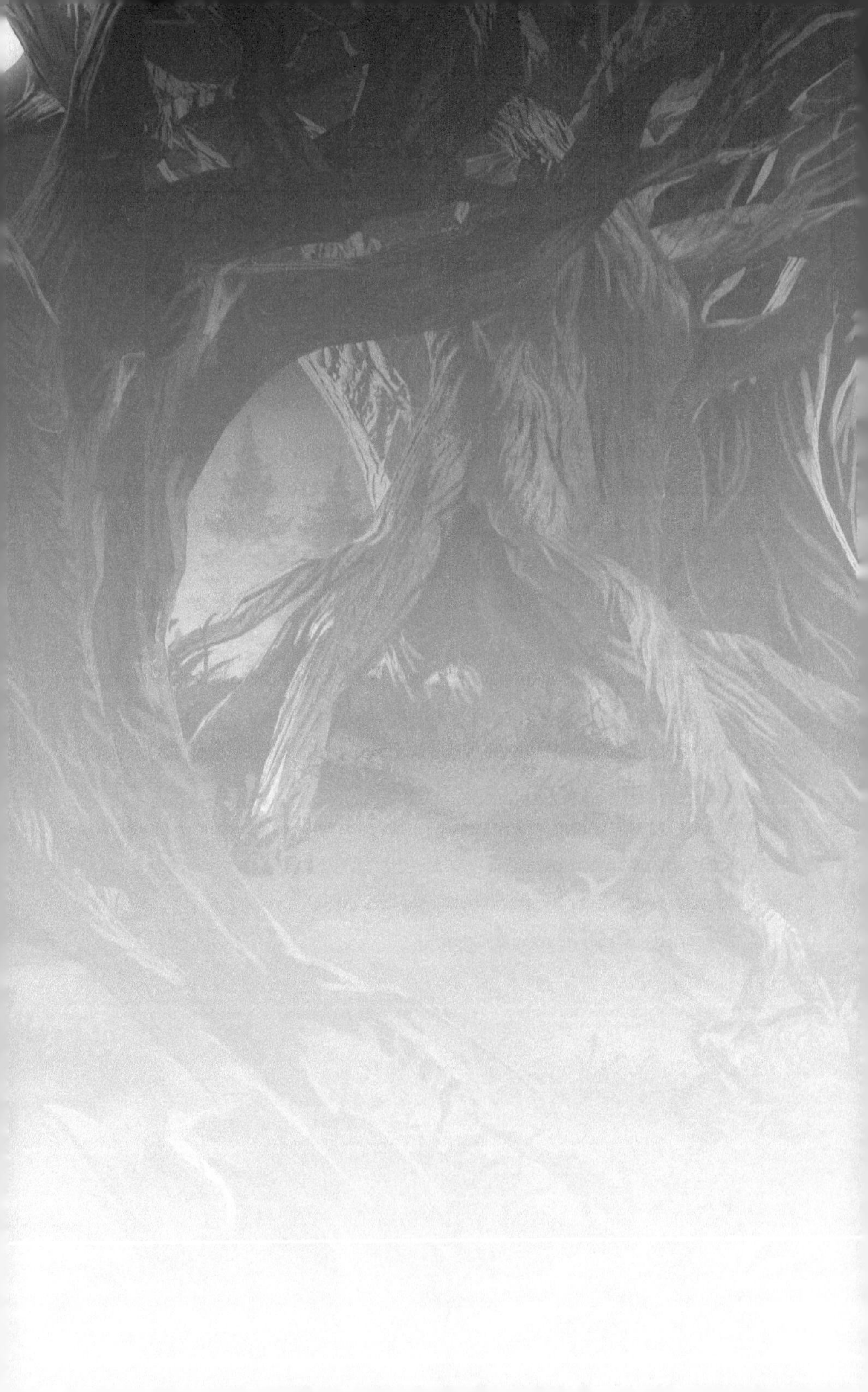

CHAPTER SEVENTEEN

I t was risky to sneak from her bedroom twice in one night. Alleria wasn't sure if she'd convinced the handmaidens with her trick as well as she had Gwae.

To fool the Moonlord proved none too difficult; she suspected he was arrogant enough to believe she was loyal to him. Ideally, Alleria would have waited a day or two, but she needed to find out if it was Jack who was captured that very night. If it was him, his life would be over soon.

Alleria waited a few hours until she felt certain the handmaidens were asleep. Once, she heard one of the handmaidens, she believed it was Poppy, sneak through her room. Alleria could feel her presence and she concentrated on her heavy breathing. Poppy's footsteps moved away, and when she finally dared to open her eyes, the girl was gone.

Now is my time to move. They just checked up on me, so they won't do so anytime soon again... I hope.

The cloak she wore earlier was still at the bottom of the bed where Gwae left it and she pulled it around her shoulders again while she pushed her feet into the slippers.

If they catch me, I will spend eternity in one of those glass pillars, waiting between life and death for Gwae to wake me and have his way with me.

The thought turned her knees to jelly. If she didn't get away now, Jack—if it indeed was him—would die, and within days, she would be Gwae's bride. She thought of his promise to do with her as he pleased. It made her want to scream.

The corridor outside the room was still abandoned. Her steps were light but swift. She reached the door to the southern tower and made her way down.

Please don't let me run into anyone.

For the few weeks Alleria had lived in the castle, she never saw a single guard around the place, and this was the first time she thought of them. There were many servants, most of them female, who were almost invisible and showed themselves when Gwae beckoned them. The courtiers frequented the palace, but they stayed in the heart of the castle, where the dining room, throne room, and ballroom were. They never ventured into the wings. The rest of the castle seemed abandoned and Alleria wondered where the servants lived. She knew her handmaidens had a room next to hers, a room she never visited. Like everything else, they appeared when summoned or when needed and disappeared when they were dismissed. It was almost as if the servants lived in the walls. They were never far. That still didn't explain why a castle didn't need guards.

When Alleria reached the bottom of the stairs, she opened the door that led to below ground. She had no idea where the dungeons would be, but she suspected they would be down below.

Perhaps another door in that corridor? Wherever they are, this as good a place to start searching as any.

The darkness didn't frighten her as much as it did the first time, and Alleria was prepared for the cold. She wondered if there were people down in the depths of the castle, locked in the dungeons... there had to be a dungeon keeper at the very least.

Several doors she passed had no handles, like the room where she found the wives; after a few feet, the corridor changed. Magic light beamed overhead and she recognized it immediately.

I've been here before. Back when I first came, I was held in a room like this.

The doors had little windows in them.

I must be careful; the women with no eyes dwell down here.

But there was no evidence of the women, and Alleria did not hear any sound until she passed the doors and the corridor became less pleasant looking. The stones under her feet were a dull gray, and though the light still covered the ceiling, there was nothing cheerful about this place. The beautiful obsidian walls faded to black stones and the whole corridor breathed an atmosphere of hopelessness. There had to be magic in the air because Alleria's nightdress flared up several times and she knew it wasn't her gift setting it off.

A new door loomed up in the dark, not made of wood, but of black metal bars. Alleria peered through. Inside, there was nothing but darkness, but in the next room there was light, and Alleria saw a female prisoner in a dirty, white shift hanging upside down in the center. She couldn't see what was suspending the prisoner in the air, but her limbs were sprawled out and her face was a mask of pain. Sometimes Alleria saw a glimmer of light ripple through the space around the prisoner. The female was engulfed in magic and Alleria suspected it was hurting her.

Why need guards when you have magic? She understood. Gwae must not feel there were any threats to his castle, none that he could not remedy with magic.

Several of the rooms held prisoners, each suspended by magic, each in their own world of torment. Alleria wondered at the pain and the fear in their faces, if the torture was just physical or if it went deeper than that. She desperately wanted to save each prisoner, but she couldn't risk alerting someone before she found Jack.

I'm sorry; I have to be selfish.

Finally, when she had given up all hope that she would find him in time, she reached a larger cell, and in the center, she saw Jack.

It's him—he's really here.

Alleria was flooded with a sense of relief. Jack was not suspended in the air like the other prisoners; instead, he was chained with shackles that hung from the ceiling.

Is Gwae's magic not strong enough to hold him?

She knew a little about Jack's immunities, but not enough to know what effect the Arallfyd had on them. Jack wore the clothes Alleria last saw him in, only now his shirt hung open, exposing his chest. Trickles of blood ran down his flesh and bruises and burns covered him. There were no open wounds, but the blood looked fresh. A fireplace stood to one side of the cell and the light of the fire tinted Jack's exposed skin.

A noise betrayed the presence of another person in the cell with Jack. It wasn't one of the eyeless women, but a man. He was tall, muscular, and bald, and he was dressed in a plain, black shirt and britches. He held a poker above a fire, and when he turned her way, Alleria saw that he had scars, not only where his eyes were, but over the areas of his nose, mouth, and ears too.

The man moved with the same determination as the eyeless women had done when dressing Alleria and his movements were equally jagged. He pushed the poker against Jack's skin, causing him to cry out in pain. The smell of burning flesh, rich and salty like roasted pork, hit her nostrils, and Alleria felt sick. The burn closed immediately. It left a black mark, but only for a few seconds, for it too faded right before her eyes. She saw the bruises turn from purple to green to yellow and fade with the same speed.

He's healing.

Her hand wrapped around the outer bars, and when she applied light pressure, she found the door open. The faceless man placed the poker on a wooden table and walked to the large wall, which displayed an impressive collection of knives.

How much torture did Jack have to endure? How long has he been here?

The door squeaked when Alleria pushed it open and she froze. Jack was silent now and the cell was quiet. She felt sure the man should have heard her, but he didn't respond. The faceless man picked a knife from the wall and ran the blade past a whetstone, his movements deliberate and jerky. Alleria stepped into the cell and grabbed the poker from the table. At that moment, Jack looked up at her, his face a mixture of emotions. He mouthed at Alleria to go. She shook her head in reply and lifted the poker high above her head.

She sucked in a deep breath, then swung, and the poker connected with the bald head. The skull cracked but the man continued his movements as if nothing had happened. He ignored Alleria as if she didn't exist and she hit him again. The skin ripped open and the skull caved in. This time, the man twitched, but he still ignored her presence.

With the third blow, his skull opened completely and the man fell to the ground. There was no blood, no liquid at all; the skull was pulverized but no organic matter spilled. The body twitched a few times before it remained still and Alleria felt unsettled by the dead creature's presence.

"Jack..."

She didn't even know what to say to him, so instead of words, Alleria chose action and pulled at his shackles.

"That thing has the keys."

Jack's voice sounded weak, and though he was covered in bruises, Alleria saw them healing before her eyes. Blood still covered his chest, but miraculously it seemed to have dried already.

"Around his waist, the keys... they're around his waist."

"Right... sorry."

Alleria knelt next to the creature on the ground and struggled to touch the dead body. Her fingers shook when she pulled a small key chain from the belt, and she returned to Jack to free him from his bonds.

"Why are you here, Alleria? You put yourself in danger for me, and I don't deserve it."

There were tears in his eyes and his body hung like a slack doll. Jack had never acted like this around her before; he looked broken.

Not now, Jack. I need you.

"I'm not saving you; you're saving me. I need to get out of here and you need to be my guide."

Her hands trembled with such force that she struggled to get the key in the lock, and when it didn't fit, she tried the next one.

Luckily, there were only a few keys—though she might accidentally have tried the same key more than once—and eventually one of them fitted. Jack's arm fell down and landed on her shoulder, and it stayed there while she struggled with the second shackle. His body was even hotter than usual and he smelled of sweat—the scent was not altogether unpleasant, a hint of musk and sweetness at its undertone.

When the second bond came off, Jack rested his full weight on her, and although they threatened to topple over, Alleria managed to keep her balance.

"You came for me," he whispered against her cheek and hair. "You came for me."

"We have to go, Jack. When they notice I'm gone again, they'll search for me. And I don't trust how easy it was for me to overpower that guard who was tormenting you."

He leaned on her for a few brief moments, but then straightened up, and she saw him get stronger with every step he took.

"I think Gwae overestimates his own power. He's too reliant on magic. This works in my favor because magic doesn't have the same effect on me. I doubt it would be as easy to free any of his other victims. His magic is stronger than any I know."

"Let's get out of here as fast as we can," Alleria said.

"Where are we going?" He looked at Alleria with shining eyes and she felt a pang of uncertainty about leading him.

"I..."

Behind Jack, a familiar shape appeared.

The spirit of the wife.

The phantom beckoned Alleria and she nodded with determination.

"We go this way."

She grabbed Jack's hand and rushed to follow the four-armed woman.

"What is that shadow thing?"

"It's a long story, but in a nutshell, that's the spirit of one of Gwae's wives."

"One of his what?"

Jack slowed a little.

"We don't have time for this now, Jack. We have to hurry."

"Can we trust her?"

"Do we have a choice?"

He stopped for a moment and then shook his head.

"Trust me when I say she hates him as much as we do. Maybe even more."

The tylwyth teg sighed, but he allowed her to guide him. They followed the spirit through the dungeons. Jack shivered, and from the way he moved, Alleria could see that his internal wounds had not healed as well as the ones on his skin. She slipped her hand around his waist and he shot her a grateful smile.

Alleria hadn't seen this part of the castle yet, and to her surprise, the female stopped at something that looked like a well and pointed down it.

"Portal."

"She's pointing at this well," Alleria told Jack, who obviously couldn't see the figure as well as she could. On her tippy-toes, Alleria peered over the rim, but she saw nothing but darkness, as if the well were filled to the top with a black material.

"Portal," the four-armed woman repeated.

"I know what this is," Jack whispered, and he touched the stone rim. "This is one of the magic travel routes for tylwyth tegs. They were created by the more powerful lords as quick ways across the border or get to other places within the Arallfyd. This one was made by Lord Vynorto, who probably has a lot of spies and messengers. By these routes, his minions can travel through the Arallfyd without being detected by his enemies."

"Have you used these before?"

"Once or twice, though they are quite a difficult magic to operate."

"Does your magic immunity get in the way?"

Alleria glanced at the fabric of her dress and wondered if it would prohibit her from traveling through these portals.

"No, portals are voluntary magic, and they are a different sort than spells. More permanent, and more like a door. You know, armor will protect you from swords, but you can still walk through a door... this is like that. But like with all magic, there are rules we need to stick to." Jack frowned and rubbed his chin. "If I do this wrong, we might end up at the other side of the Arallfyd."

"Does it matter if we do? We need to get out of here."

"I really don't want to be lost. There are a lot of places here where you don't want to wander around. I want to leave this place as quickly as I can. Lord Vynorto will come after us as soon as he finds out you're gone. In the Arallfyd, he'll have the advantage."

Jack didn't look Alleria in the eye when he spoke, which struck her as odd. But time was running out and his arguments were valid enough, she thought.

"Do you know enough to get us through?" Alleria pointed at the well and her eyes pleaded with him. "You know, through this, ehm... portal thing?"

"Yes."

There was doubt in his voice and his face, but Alleria knew this was their only chance.

"I just hope that I know the exit as well as I think I do."

Jack straightened his shoulders—it was hard to believe he had been so injured only minutes ago—and jumped on the edge of the well. He turned and offered Alleria his hand.

"Come on, unless you want to stay here."

He graced her with a smile, but the mirth of his lips did not negate the doubt in his eyes, and Alleria grimaced in reply. She turned to the ghostly apparition of Gwae's bride.

"Thank you for your help. Without it we would have never gotten out. I'm sorry I couldn't do more for you in return."

"You may still help us one day," the female replied. "When it is time for the second moon to reign." She disappeared. Alleria turned to Jack and put her hand in his. With a grunt, he pulled her close to him.

"These portals... they aren't a pleasant way to travel."

Before she had a chance to respond, Jack jumped into the well, his arms wrapped firmly around her. For a second or two, she was completely weightless. Her hair and cloak fluttered around her as cold air rushed past her face. Then pain hit her as they slammed into the side of the well, and despite Jack's efforts to keep her covered with his arms and body, every impact hurt. Jack held her head against his neck with one arm and he pushed them away from the walls as much as he could, but it was in vain, and Alleria's teeth rattled each time the pair connected with the stone.

Without warning, they dropped straight down. The sides of the well were nothing but empty space, and it was so dark she couldn't even make out Jack, though he still held her tight. *"Giât sy'n agor mil o ddrysau, gan fy arwain at fy cyrchfan,"* Jack whispered into the dark.

A tremor of light rippled through the nothing and Jack's face appeared in the brief illumination—his eyes fixed on Alleria's as if he had been able to see her all along. The space around them was so big that it looked endless. The glow outlined what looked like another hole.

The light twisted and twirled around the hole and she heard the wind before she felt it. A loud roar turned Alleria's limbs to pudding, and a pull of cold air tugged at them both as they were sucked in the direction off the opening.

"Jack..."

Alleria's voice was almost completely muffled by the sound of the wind.

"It's okay, Alleria; we're almost out."

His lips brushed her ear as he shouted directly into it. Alleria nodded in response and closed her eyes. Jack let go of her, and before her dress had time to make up for the lack of warmth, she was overwhelmed by instant cold. Seconds later, they connected with ground.

The wind was knocked from her lungs and Alleria lay on her back as she tried to catch her breath. Above her, the sky was bright blue and clouds curled into one another as if they were posing for a painting.

"It's daylight," Alleria wheezed with some surprise. "It was night when we left."

"The journey through the portal takes more time than you think. Also, I'm pretty sure we're outside of the Arallfyd. Time moves different here."

The temperature in their new location was a lot warmer than it had been only seconds ago, and the clothes she wore adjusted accordingly. Instead of warming the girl, the fabric now cooled her skin. Jack crawled toward her on his elbows, his face filled with concern.

"Are you in one piece?"

His light brown skin appeared more battered than Alleria's, but scrapes and bruises healed right under her eyes.

How does he do that?

Alleria lay back and concentrated on her body. She focused on each part and tried to determine if she was hurt. Her limbs and back felt bruised, but the only thing that really hurt was her cheek. She touched it and felt it slick with blood.

"It's not too bad," Jack reassured her. "Just a scrape. You'll find it will heal fast. How about the rest of you? Anything broken?"

"No, I'm actually doing fine. The absorption material must be more than magic and temperature proof." She held up a piece of the cloak. "Not so much as a tear in the fabric, and it's barely even wrinkled. This stuff is amazing."

"This is absorption fabric?" Jack pulled on the dress and rubbed it between his thumbs. "The real stuff?"

Alleria sat up and leaned on her elbows. She pulled the fabric from Jack's grasp.

"It is. Gwae owned a lot of it. He made me wear it to keep my magic under control."

An expression appeared on Jack's face that Alleria couldn't quite place, but it made her uncomfortable. He didn't look at her, but instead just stared at the material. Behind him, Alleria watched the mists swirl.

"Thank the gods we don't have to go through the mists again. I'm surprised we managed to travel outside of the Arallfyd."

"Yes, these portals can be very convenient if we want to have a quick in or out route." Jack winked at her and brushed at his clothing.

"But wouldn't that make it easier for the fath tywyll to travel to the human world?"

Jack shook his head.

"Fath tywyll can't travel this way. Only tylwyth tegs. Their magic is similar to the mists."

"Jack, if these portals were here all the time, why didn't we just take these? Save us the whole journey?"

"It doesn't work like that. The portals actually belong to the Lords They only lead to the portals at the different castles, and the portals outside of the Arallfyd are disconnected from one another. No Lord appreciates uninvited guests, so the magic works one way unless there is an invitation. If there are ways around them, I don't know them, and I don't *want* to know them. If you get caught trying to enter a castle uninvited, it will most surely mean death... or worse, you might have to owe the lord a favor."

He nudged Alleria under the chin and added: "Also, I was afraid they might take my priceless companion from me."

Alleria rolled her eyes.

"Surely someone as clever as yourself would have found a way around that by now." She winked at him. Halfway Jack's eyebrows furrowed and he shook his head.

"Rules, Alleria, it's all about rules. And places like the Arallfyd have a lot of rules. The human world is easier because the rules are often man-made and can be bent or broken. But if you change the rules of magic, it has more dire consequences. That's why the Lords guard the rules very strictly, and the council guards the Lords. That's the only way to control the chaos."

His glance crossed Alleria's face and then he cracked his neck and his arms. "We needed to get out of the Arallfyd, and I'm surprised I found the right door. I didn't realize how much danger you were in until you ran away."

"What happened between you and Brand... I mean, that thing that pretended to be Brand?"

"He got away from me the first time and tried to go after you, but I followed him. After a while I caught up, and we fought again. It was pretty horrible, and when I killed him, I was weakened. That's when those bird things found me and hit me with their webbing."

"Those got me too."

"I suspected as much…" He eyed her. "Alleria… I didn't know who you were. I knew what you were—I knew you had to be of gosgeiddig blood—and I was pretty sure who sired you, but I didn't know you were 'the female heir.' Honestly, I was pretty naive about the importance of you being a female descendent. If I'd known, I would have never taken you into the Arallfyd; it's too dangerous there for you."

"What does that mean?"

"It means that a lot of the kings and high lords seek you as an ally, or they want to kill you. You are the direct bloodline of the second moon, the daughter of Lord Nezmysly. Daughters are rare—I can't remember there ever being one, now that I think of it—and that holds a certain status, apparently. Brand was a servant of one of the Eastern kings—he used his name when he died, but it slips my mind. They're all looking for you, Alleria. I think it has something to do with the mists. That somehow set off an alarm at our arrival."

"How? Are the fath tywyll connected to them? I heard the mists were expanding, and as far as I can tell, that's not a good thing for anyone."

"I don't know exactly what is in those mists, but I'm willing to bet gold on it that there's more than just the brides of the Lost God alone in there. The more cunning of the fath tywyll will have spies or, at the very least, certain spells active on or surrounding the borders. Everyone is very cautious at this time. There are rumors that the Lost God may be returning, and that is bad news for everyone."

"Where did you hear this? When did you hear this? I keep hearing of this Lost God, but no one has explained who he is to me yet. Everyone is being very mysterious."

"Lord Vynorto happened to mention it during one of the sessions where he came to personally stick a poker through my flesh."

Jack waved his hand in a casual manner and Alleria cringed.

"He wanted to know more about the Lord of Ravens, and he wanted to hear it for himself. I got the impression he enjoyed a bit of torture on the side. Unfortunately for him, I really didn't have any information to share."

"Why would he ask you?" Alleria shook her head; she didn't understand. Jack didn't work for the Ravenlord as far as she knew.

"He seems to think I'm one of his offspring."

"Are you?"

"I don't know. It's not unlikely; from what I know of the Lord of Ravens, he gets around. My mother never told me who my father was, only that he was fath tywyll, and I never asked."

"I don't believe you," Alleria said. "Doesn't every child want to know who their parents are?"

Jack shrugged, making it clear he wasn't going to answer her question. Alleria shook her head, but she had more pressing questions. "Who is the Lost God, Jack?"

"The Lost God was one of the most powerful of all the gods. Eons ago, when he still had a name that has now been long forgotten, he sought to destroy the other gods and be the one and only deity. Several gods had died due to his schemes, and he almost succeeded had he not been betrayed by one of his followers. The treacherous minion reached out to the three moons, who in turn managed to thwart the Lost God. They tried to kill him, but only managed to poison him. He was stripped of his name and became the Lost God. There is power in a name, and he was weakened because of the loss of his. Despite his vulnerable state, he made a second attempt to rule the Divine Pantheon. This attempt failed instantly, and this time he was banished. It is said that the Lost God disappeared and has not been seen since. At least that's how the legends go. There are only few who remember the time when the Lost

God was still part of the Divine Pantheon, and even they claim to no longer remember his true name."

"And they believe he has something to do with the expansion of the mists? I've heard say that they call those horrible creatures inside his mistwives."

"Yes, that's the rumor, but the mistwives are new to me. You'll have to fill me in about them later. For now, let's get out of here. I'm feeling a bit antsy standing still. To be honest, you won't be much safer in the human lands either, unless I find a good place for you to hide."

"Jack..."

"We'll think of something. Let's go find a place to rest now. Unless you have a better plan."

"I don't know what *your* plan is yet."

She peered at him, her eyes narrowed.

"We're in the Borderlands. I know a place where we can stay the night and that will give me some time to think. Any plan I have still needs some working on. For now, let's just get us somewhere safe."

Jack pulled Alleria to her feet. His fingers glided over her shoulders and he admired the fabric of her cloak and nightgown again.

"It's good that you have that dress."

"It's not exactly a dress."

He waved her words away with nimble fingers.

"Doesn't matter; it looks like a dress here, trust me."

Little beads of sweat had pearled on his forehead and Alleria realized from the heat on her face that the temperature was stifling. She felt blessed that the absorption material kept her cool.

"Where are we, Jack?"

He didn't answer her; instead, he led the way. Once again, Alleria followed him, unable to mute the uneasy feeling that lay in the pit of her stomach.

CHAPTER EIGHTEEN

The inn sat at the edge of the Borderlands and the area surrounding it was different in every way from the Shadow Marshes. There were no swamps or muddy pools, and the rich flora and fauna that Alleria was used to from her old home made way for a few dry-looking bushes and some unfamiliar creatures that looked like reptilian rodents. The further they traveled, the more barren the landscape became. Jack proved a careful guide; the Borderlands were always filled with danger. Alleria's long months hidden away in the cabin with Jack had almost made her careless, and it was a harsh reality to be back. She never expected that, in many ways, the Arallfyd would be less dangerous than the world outside of it. At the same time, she realized she'd only had a glimpse of it. The winter journey had kept them very much isolated from normal life. Even her time in Gwae's castle only showed Alleria a little of the magical world. Her lessons had been limited to the way of life in the court and she had not had to deal much with the wilderness of the Arallfyd.

As much as she was pleased to be away from Gwae and his entourage, she didn't exactly share Jack's relief to be in the Borderlands again. Tumsa was a distant memory, but she was all but forgotten. Every bird, frog, or other little creature posed a potential threat as they could serve as the old witch's eyes.

The inn was a tall, square building made of white stone. Where usually a roof was topped by a thatch, this one was flat, stone, and square. The entrance—which was little more than a hole in the wall—boasted a sign with a picture of a strange animal that looked like a cross between a horse and a cow with two humps gracing its back. The creature walked on long, spindly legs with knobby knees and it had a dumb expression on its friendly face. A pink tongue protruded from the corner of its mouth. The whole thing looked a little silly, and the bold, black letters of the Fenoshi alphabet spelled: The Drunken Camel.

"What's a camel?"

"It's the creature in the picture."

Alleria cocked her head to examine it.

"I've never seen anything like it. Are they meant to be drunk?"

Jack laughed and put his arm around her neck.

"It is just the name of the inn, you silly girl."

Her face pinched in a serious expression; she didn't like when he mocked her ignorance.

"Excuse me. My knowledge of popular inn names is a little rusty."

With some satisfaction, she watched him flinch, and Jack pulled his arm away from her.

"You're being a bit grumpy today."

"I've never heard of these camels either. They must have not been in my lessons of the Fenoshi."

"Well, your thirst for knowledge about camels will soon be quenched."

"How so?"

He only graced her with a smile. His silence grated her nerves and suddenly she felt entirely fed up with everything. She was tired.

"Where are we, Jack?" she asked. "If this sign is written in Fenoshi, I would say we're either in the south or the east of the Borderlands, right? Isn't Fenoshi the common trade language there?"

"Fenoshi is the common trade language almost everywhere, but yes it's most spoken in the east and the south."

Jack ushered her inside with a warm hand on her back. This place was nothing like the previous inn. The temperature inside was much cooler than outside and the whole common area lay hidden in the darkness. There were several wooden tables lined up in neat rows. Straw and earth covered the ground; from the musky scent, Alleria could tell the straw was all but fresh. Pungent body odor mixed with the sour scent of the straw. Only a few patrons sat around the tables, some drinking from earthenware mugs, others huddled together close enough to share whispered conversations. They were dressed in colorful robes, their heads topped with turbans or ornately embroidered hoods. Their skin color ranged from the soft fawn tone of Jack's skin to a rich, obsidian tint. All of them were human, Alleria was certain of that; she could see it in their features and their body shapes and postures. A beautiful woman with curls the color of gold and skin that looked carved out of mahogany walked up and kissed Halfway Jack on the lips. Her brass action made Alleria blush, and she felt a brief flash of anger, which she managed to control before the absorption fabric flared up.

"Jack..." the woman purred in Fenoshi. "It has been too long since you graced my bed with your presence."

"Tees'ha." Halfway Jack pushed the woman away from him and gave Alleria an apologetic look. "I'm not here for your bed."

The woman named Tees'ha glanced over Jack's shoulder at Alleria, and the contempt was clear on the reddish-brown face.

"Don't tell me you settled down, Jack."

Her dark green eyes looked unusually bright in contrast to her skin.

"I don't need to tell you anything, Tees'ha, except that we would like a room."

Hatred flared across the woman's face. Alleria saw it plain as day.

Does she love Jack?

"Follow me." The woman turned on her heel, her long curls bouncing as she moved. Jack's hand once again found the small of Alleria's back, and he gently pushed her ahead of him. The woman led them up narrow, stone stairs. To Alleria's relief, she noticed the strong scent becoming fainter.

"Room four, *the honeymoon suite*." Tees'ha's voice dripped with sarcasm. She opened the door to reveal a small, dark room with a tiny window. In the middle stood a narrow double bed and there was one little table with a chair and a bowl of grayish water.

A vicious smile curled across the exotic woman's full mouth.

"Enjoy." She sneered and walked off, wagging her hips.

"We've seen worse, right?" Jack smiled at her, but Alleria saw the embarrassment in his eyes.

"Friend of yours?" She nodded toward the retreating image of Tees'ha.

"I have a lot of beds to keep me warm." Jack shrugged and Alleria rolled her eyes. "Let's get some sleep. I know it's early still, but it's been a long couple of days and I wouldn't mind a bit of rest."

"I have no idea how long it took us to get through that portal. It felt like both an eternity and a second at the same time."

"Several hours at least." Jack pulled at the clasp of her cloak and gently took it off her shoulders. "You know, that nightgown is very becoming."

Alleria made a scoffing sound but was pleased with the amused expression.

"Don't take it off here," Jack said, his face more serious. "This gown can save lives here in the Borderlands and out there in the human world. You don't seem like the kind of girl who would appreciate killing innocent people."

"I'm not," she said, barely above a whisper. She glanced out the small window onto the empty courtyard behind the inn. "And you don't have to worry about me taking it off... I can't. I don't know how it works, but I'm sure there is some spell in place that prevents me from doing so."

"Ah... makes sense. Gwae probably didn't want you to discover your powers and be a threat to him. I shouldn't have too much issue taking it off." There was a naughty glint in his eye. "So, when we need to take it off, I can be of assistance."

Alleria blushed.

"I wonder if Gwae knows I'm gone yet," she said, changing the subject.

"Most likely. He'll send his servants after you, I'm sure."

"What are we going to do?"

There is that look again... I don't like it.

"For now, we rest. We need to be sharp for tomorrow."

Jack jumped on the bed, which creaked under his weight, and patted the mattress, an impish grin curled on his lips.

"Come on. We've slept in the same bed before."

He patted the mattress again and Alleria exhaled in mock disgust. Gingerly, she took off her shoes and joined him on the bed, where Jack wrapped his arms around her and pulled her toward him.

"I never thanked you for saving me, Alleria." His voice was thick and muffled in her silver-gold hair. "Thank you."

"You saved me too... more than once. We're not quite even yet."

"I'm sorry for everything."

"At least I'm free."

Hot breath tickled in her hair and Alleria felt safe for the first time in days. When she heard his light snoring, she became aware of her own fatigue and soon allowed herself to drift off into the world of dreams.

When Alleria woke up, she found an empty space on Jack's side of the bed. Her hand touched the place where he lay before she fell asleep. It was cold. He must have been gone for a while. Only a little light from the second moon shone through the small hole in the wall that functioned as a window. Alleria was about to get up when the door opened and she saw the shadow of Jack walk inside. He made no noise and Alleria assumed he didn't want to wake her, but there was something in his body language that made her close her eyes and pretend she was asleep. Jack crawled back in bed and Alleria's body stiffened when he put his arm around her.

I'll bet he was with Tees'ha, she thought bitterly, *sharing the warmth of her bed.*

Sleep proved more difficult this time, but when she finally drifted away, she slept soundly until the morning. Her dreams were haunted by images of Tees'ha and Jack, and of Gwae, who in the dream was actually Tumsa trying to find her. It was a relief to open her eyes and see that the room was cast in a glimpse of sunlight.

"Good morning, sleepy head." Jack lay on the bed propped up on one elbow. His voice was cheerful, but Alleria could tell it was a forced cheer.

"Did you have fun last night?"

Oh, Alleria... why did you say that?

It was too late, and she saw a hint of surprise in his face.

"No. I made some plans last night. That's all. No fun was had."

Alleria grimaced at him and pushed away the blankets. She swung her long legs over the rim of the bed.

"What are the plans, Jack? Because we can't go back to the Arallfyd, we can't stay here, and it's not safe in the human lands either. And what about your own problem? If you don't deliver to your boss in time, you're in as much trouble as I am."

His eyes held hers, and without warning, he leaned forward and kissed her. Alleria's stomach exploded in a sea of proverbial butterflies and her heart danced in her chest. His hand roamed over her shoulder and up her neck, then he cupped her cheek and jaw while his lips moved against hers, his tongue exploring her mouth with a familiar hunger and passion.

She couldn't resist him and reciprocated his kiss, though it surprised and overwhelmed her.

"I'm sorry," Jack whispered against her lips, his breath hot. "I had to kiss you before you wouldn't let me anymore."

His hand lowered a little and his fingertips rested on her hot, clammy throat.

"What do you mean?"

He kissed her again, but she felt something close around her throat this time, and when she pulled back, she spotted the guilt in his eyes. Something tugged at her neck... her hands touched it, and Alleria recognized the leash.

"You betrayed me with a kiss...?" The sadness crippled her and her shoulders sagged. "You're going to sell me on the market as planned. To save your own skin. You won't even consider finding another option that would save me too, even though you know I'll be in danger? Whoever buys me won't be able to keep me away from Gwae, and you know it." Her voice shook with cold disappointment and grief. "If they don't just cut my heart out, that is."

She blinked away hot tears.

"I told you I wasn't your friend, Alleria. I never said I was."

She turned away from him and curled up in a little ball.

"Don't, Jack. Don't explain or apologize; grant me at least that much respect. I just don't want to hear it."

Jack moved away from the bed and straightened himself.

"I'll arrange some breakfast. We leave in a few hours with the south-east caravan. It's only a day's travel to Mtumwa."

She listened to his footsteps as he walked out. The door closed and Alleria was left alone with her thoughts.

He planned this—all along, he planned this. Her dress flared up to absorb her power. *It isn't a coincidence that we came out through the portal near Mtumwa; he never gave up the idea of selling me.*

Tears spilled from her eyes and landed on the straw mattress. She didn't want to fight the flood anymore. She needed to cry.

Stop being such a baby, Alleria. He never lied to you and he never betrayed you, because he always told you what he planned on doing. It's his own life he needs to save, not yours. You had a chance to get away from him. You could have let him rot, but you were too soft and too caring. Will this finally be the lesson that you can never trust this man again?

After her heart was empty and she had no tears left, Alleria got up and washed her face in the dirty-looking water. With as much dignity as she could muster, she put on the cloak and walked downstairs.

I escaped two people who wanted to rule me so far, so perhaps I can escape a third.

Halfway Jack waited for her at one of the tables and she sat without making eye contact. A bowl of exotic fruits and nuts was placed in front of her and they ate in silence.

After breakfast, Jack said his goodbyes to Tees'ha, who looked less spiteful when she saw the chain around Alleria's neck. She expected the dark-skinned woman to look pleased, but there was sadness in her eyes.

I don't need your pity.

It was Alleria's turn to look upon the other with disgust.

Halfway Jack and Alleria traveled through the few remaining miles of the Borderlands in silence. He led the way, and she followed, only this time she held her head up high. She had been many things in the passing of these months—first a beast, then a slave, a companion, and a desirable woman—and that made her different from the timid girl who'd started this journey. Jack would sell her at the market and she considered her life debt to him paid. What happened after, she didn't know, but she would fight to gain control of her life. Alleria never wanted to see Halfway Jack again, this much she was sure of.

At the edge of the Borderlands, they met up with the caravan. Alleria had heard stories about caravans, but seeing an actual one was different from the tales. A long line of canvas wagons pulled by tall horses stood as far as the eye could see. Some of the travelers sat on camels—which looked a lot more dignified from the silly creature on the sign at the inn. All around her, people were packing up the camp and readying themselves for a new day on the road. Muscled men pulled down mud-stained tents and folded them into small parcels. Jack led Alleria over to a group of people who stood around one of the wagons.

"Anvstaheli," he called out and waved his hand. A short, fat man with a grayish skin tone and a greasy beard responded. His eyes were heavy lidded and bulging, and they peered out into the world from under a disproportionally broad turban. The language he spoke was one Alleria couldn't understand, which added to her increasing misery. Halfway Jack engaged in a conversation with the man he called Anvstaheli; the traveler laughed and slapped the taller man's shoulder. Then he clapped his hands, and a pale young man, wrists and feet manacled, led a large camel toward them. The beast was bigger than Alleria expected and she was a little daunted by it. Between the two uneven humps lay a worn leather saddle.

"This will be our transportation." Jack smiled at her, but she gave him the cold shoulder.

"You wanted to know about camels; well, for the next day and a half, you will know more about them than you ever wanted."

The pale boy, his skin almost as light as Alleria's, talked to the camel and the creature obediently kneeled. Despite her anger, Alleria was impressed by the wobbly, careful grace of the large beast as it bent its tall legs to reach the ground. Then the boy laced his fingers together and held up his palms to her. He said something that Alleria couldn't understand and she glanced at Jack for guidance.

"Put your foot on his hands and he will help you up."

She obeyed, but with a sense of hesitation. Alleria's mounting skills left a lot to be desired, and there was no elegance in her movement when she clambered onto the humongous beast. It smelled odd, like a mixture of wet clothes and the straw of the inn. The hard, uncomfortable saddle felt unsteady under her legs, so she held on for dear life. Jack mounted with the same grace as he did everything else, and Alleria felt him slide into the saddle behind her. His arm slid around her waist and he pulled her against him. Alleria struggled for some room, but he held her tighter and took the reins from the pale boy.

"Unless you wanted to steer this thing?" His voice tickled her earlobe and he held the reins out to Alleria.

"No," she answered reluctantly. Jack clicked his tongue and pulled on the reins, which caused the camel to wobble and rise. Alleria grabbed on to Jack's arm for support. The sun was hot, and she wondered what season it was in this part of the world; spring was never this warm in the Shadow Marshes. The absorption fabric cooled her body and Alleria pulled the hood over her head to keep the sun from burning the skin on her face. At any other time, she would have been fascinated with the camels, or even the caravan around her, but now she tried to pull away into her own little world.

There were so many people here. There were plenty of slaves too, in all shapes and sizes. Some walked on their own, while others were transported in large carts that looked like cages on wheels. Watching them made Alleria swallow a bitterness that rose in her throat. There were obvious faerisees and a lot of humans among the slaves, but as far as Alleria could see, she was the only tylwyth teg slave.

She closed her eyes and pictured the slave market, wondering what type of person would buy her.

At night, the caravan stopped and set up camp. Jack and Alleria slept in a tent with some of the other travelers, and he held on to her as if he were afraid she might get stolen. Alleria didn't fight him, but remained cold and uncaring.

The next day, the journey continued until the walls of Mtumwa loomed up in the distance. A part of the caravan split off from the group and the rest continued further south. Left with the other slavers, Jack steered the camel toward the gates of the big city.

The company traveled through the opening in the large wooden wall, and Alleria stared wide-eyed at her surroundings. The smells were overwhelming and she couldn't quite make out what lingered in the air, but it was a mixture of pleasant and foul. Thousands of houses, some made of wood and some of brick, were scattered throughout the town, and in between them ran the stone road they traveled on. The remainder of the caravan continued to the heart of the city and it took at least half an hour to get there.

Everywhere Alleria looked, there were people. Slavers drove hundreds of bound souls across the large market square and customers prodded at the captives as if they were examining horses. A row of women—completely naked save for their manacles—stood huddled together. An obese man with piggy eyes squeezed the breast of a pale woman with red hair. The sight of the women made Alleria understand the gravity of being a slave in a way she had not before.

This was far worse than she imagined and a sob escaped from deep inside her chest. She hid her face behind her hands and let the tears roll over her cheeks.

"Alleria." Jack's voice was soft. "I won't do that to you. This is not the part of the market where you will be sold."

"Does it really matter? You are doing this to me. As soon as I stop being your possession, I'll be someone else's. They can do with me as they please."

His hand balled up around the fabric of her dress, but he didn't respond.

"You might as well just put me up there naked."

She couldn't see his face, but she knew her words affected him as she felt his muscles tense.

Halfway Jack steered the camel toward the back of the market, in the direction of a great, round building with another flat roof. Before the entrance stood a bright orange tent, and if there hadn't been men with large whips patrolling the outside, it would have looked rather jolly. Jack kicked his heels against the camel and the creature stopped. A short boy with long, greasy hair and chestnut skin ran to take the reins. Jack climbed out of the seat behind Alleria. The absorption material adjusted the temperature now that Jack's body wasn't adding extra heat. At Jack's command, the camel lowered its body, and he helped her from the saddle.

She dismounted more gracefully than she had mounted, and Alleria strode away from the camel as if she were a queen rather than a slave. The boy even bowed his head, showing his respect. Jack didn't look her in the eye when he grabbed the chain and led her to the orange tent.

The inside was muggy; the hot canvas of the tent and sawdust floor combined in an overpowering heat and smell. Large men with dark skin and leather straps tied around their waists stood arguing in loud tones. Alleria couldn't understand what most of them said, but some of the traders spoke in broken Fenoshi. She heard words about prices and value.

"Borak," Jack called out as he watched a group of men. A tall, muscular man with black skin and slanted eyes with gold irises walked toward them. He inspected Alleria; his oval pupils reminded her of something feline.

"Halfway Jack, what a pleasure. I see you bring me a real-life gosgeiddig." His catlike gaze slid over Alleria's body without any form of modesty, the smile on his face making her uneasy. "This is a splendid beauty. I think you are not asking enough, Jack."

Jack grimaced and Alleria saw his jaw set.

"Is she...?"

"She's a virgin."

"If she weren't so valuable, I would keep her for my harem." The man named Borak touched the skin of Alleria's cheek.

"Shame about the wound." He rubbed his finger around the sore spot and Alleria winced. "It looks fresh... will it scar?"

"No, a little of your special ointment and she'll look as right as rain for your auction in the morning."

Borak brought his face near Alleria and inhaled the scent of her hair. She, in turn, got a nose full of the strong, musky aroma of sweat and spices. The sour undertone made her feel ill.

"A real beauty," the slaver muttered again.

"You know the deal, right?" Jack's voice was tense.

"Yes, I will not sell her off to wizards. Trust me, I won't need to. Someone like this... I think a powerful faerisee would be eager to pay well for her."

"Keep her cloak on, and that dress. Whatever you do, don't take it off, or she'll be gone. These female gosgeiddig have some tricky powers, and this is a clever one. The clothing will prevent her from using her magic. She can't take it off herself; a fath tywyll made sure of that. And keep her covered as much as you can."

Jack's words were harsh, and they caught Alleria by surprise. She jerked her head in his direction and frowned, but Jack's face was perfectly serious.

How could my power help me escape? It's never done me any good before.

Alleria kept silent, but something nagged at her subconscious. The slaver laughed and pulled at her cloak, then handed Jack a parcel wrapped in cloth.

"As we agreed."

Jack flipped back the fabric and Alleria saw a hint of gleaming steel in the dim light of the orange tent. He looked at her then, his odd-colored eyes holding hers, and she was sure she saw regret in them. The knife disappeared under his dark clothing and he stepped forward.

"You were a pleasure to be with, Alleria. I'm sorry it had to end like this."

He pulled her hood farther up her head and touched her nose with a soft, hot fingertip. "I hope the future will treat you better than I did."

"I hope you fall from your camel and land on that knife." Alleria smiled sweetly at him and Jack chuckled. She wanted to hit him and scream at him, but she kept her dignity and just shot him a haughty glance.

"Take care. And keep that cloak up."

And with those mysterious words, Jack turned and walked out of her life. Despite her anger at him, Alleria still felt her heart sink to her stomach. The tears burned behind her eyes, but she refused to let them fall. The cloak flashed a few times to absorb her power. Borak eyed the fabric and rubbed his chin with an eager smile on his face. After a moment's contemplation, he took the chain around her neck and gave it an experimental pull.

"I don't think I ever had anything as fine to sell as you, little gosgeid-dig."

Alleria turned her head from him and wrapped her arms in front of her chest, her face a mask of disgust.

"Let's find you your sleeping quarters, shall we? Tomorrow is a big day for you. That's when you'll meet your new master." The large slaver pulled the chain and Alleria was forced to follow as he led her through the tent and into the round building. It was even larger than she'd initially thought, built like an amphitheater, with rows of semicircular seats surrounding a round stage and hundreds of people from different cultures sitting together. Most of them were men, but Alleria saw a few women scattered among the crowd. All talked in loud voices. The gathering of so many people made her uncomfortable. She peered down at the stage and saw a line of slaves standing at the back. A ratty looking auctioneer pulled forward a tall man dressed in red robes. Antlers grew from the top of the slave's head and his skin was covered in a thin fur that looked similar to Alleria's before her curses had been lifted. The slave was a faerisee, and she was pretty sure he'd had his hair since birth.

The auctioneer, talking in broken Fenoshi, asked for the bidding to start. People screamed from all directions, waving colorful cards. Borak avoided the crowds and hastily led Alleria to a corridor hidden underneath the third and fourth rows of seats.

"This is a special part of the slave market, beautiful one. Here we sell mostly faerisees. A tylwyth teg is pretty rare as it is, especially a gosgeiddig like you. Imagine how much money I will make from a female. I don't think I've ever seen a female gosgeiddig before. I didn't know they existed."

The corridor was made of stone and light shone in through the gaps in the seats above them. High above were thousands of legs belonging to the bidders, moving and stomping with the excitement of the auction. Alleria was too numb to be upset or angry anymore; her mind was a mess and she reacted in the only way she knew how... she kept her head down and followed.

The corridor led to another building, this one lower and square in shape. There were several large cells filled with all sorts of faerisee slaves. They looked at Alleria from behind their bars with sad, dead eyes.

Will my eyes look like that? Perhaps they once did when I still lived with Tumsa.

"Don't worry, gosgeiddig, I won't put you in with this scum. I want your virginity intact when I sell you. You get a special little room all to yourself, away from the others."

The cells ended and the corridor bent. At the end, there was a metal door—no bars like the other cells, just solid metal.

"This will be your room for tonight."

Borak opened the door, the sound of the metal echoing through the stone, and pointed for her to go inside. A wooden plank with a blanket attached to the wall would serve as her bed and the small, barred window let through a surprising amount of sunlight. On the wall above the bed hung a set of long manacles. At least it was cool inside and the smells weren't as bad as she had encountered in the past day.

"Let's make sure you can't take off those clothes and escape," Borak said. "You know, just in case…" He pulled Alleria toward the plank where he chained the manacles over the sleeves of her nightgown. To test the solidity of the restraints, he tugged on the chain, and with a satisfied grunt, he turned and left the cell. The dark-skinned man closed the door, leaving her alone in the tiny room. She lay down on the wood and wrapped her cloak around her, waiting for the footsteps of the slaver to retreat. Only when the sound died did she allow herself to cry.

CHAPTER NINETEEN

A deep thud woke her from a fitful slumber. Alleria blinked to get the sleep from her eyes. In the middle of her cell, a dark mass lay on the ground. The sun had gone down, casting her surroundings in darkness, yet the moons illuminated just enough of the interior that she could make out shapes and outlines. Voices in the distance indicated nocturnal activity beyond the confines of her cell. The place hadn't been truly quiet since she arrived.

Whatever lay in the center didn't move, and Alleria found the courage to slip from her bunk to approach it. The chain attached to her manacle was tangled and she needed a moment to get the knot out before it allowed her to move far enough from the cot for her to reach the shape. Determined, Alleria turned around and inspected the mysterious object on the floor. To her dismay, she realized she was looking at a woman curled up in a fetal position.

How did she get in here? The door is locked.

Alleria bent over the still woman, her mind groggy from sleep, unsure of what to do next. As soon as she came near the figure, her nightgown and cloak flared up so unexpectedly that it gave her a fright. She bolted upright and took a step back, her nerves frazzled. The woman was obviously magical in some way, because Alleria was sure it was an outside force that set off her garments. The light of the absorption material was so bright, it illuminated the woman completely. Her appearance was similar to Alleria's. Her hair was not quite the same color, but the same length, and she was roughly the same body shape and size. Alleria pushed against the woman's shoulder in an attempt to wake her. The figure moved under her push, revealing her face and torso. Alleria gasped when she saw that the woman was dead.

A gaping hole in her chest revealed that her heart had been removed. Alleria stifled a cry. She didn't dare call out for anyone, afraid of what would happen when they found a dead body in her cell. An unexpected flash of light took all thoughts from her mind and all sight from her eyes. Blinded, she felt a searing heat as the body of the woman burst out into flame. Alleria's instinct kicked in and she jumped back, her arm covering her smarting eyes. She crawled onto the wooden plank. The chains of the manacles rattled, poking her in the back as she moved as closely to the wall as was physically possible. Her eyes had adjusted to the light and she watched in horror as flames spread from the body across the sawdust on the floor, spreading up the stone walls.

Stone can't burn; this is impossible.

Only then did she notice that the flames were not the rich red-golden color of fire, but a strange purple hue, and there was no smoke blossoming from them.

Magic fire.

There was no way out of the cell for her; she was tied down and trapped. The only thing she could think of was to hide under the absorption cloak and hope the fabric was immune to this particular magic too. The flames emitted no smell, and since there was no smoke, Alleria deduced that she at least wouldn't die from smoke inhalation. She had no idea what dangers this magical fire held, other than its heat. She could feel it searing through the little gaps in the fabric and she tried to keep herself protected as much as she could.

The flames licked at her, but the cloak flared up, holding its own and keeping her safe. Through the soft crackling of the flames, she could hear the heavy cell door open, and Alleria felt a glimmer of hope. She peered through a small opening in her hood. Ahead of her, flames parted and a figure walked through. Alleria recognized him instantly.

Halfway Jack... why is he here? Her shock grew as she realized Jack was completely naked. Not a stitch of clothing covered his body. He stood before her and wrapped his hands around her manacles. His muscles rippled as he forced them from the wall. Then he turned to Alleria and reached out his hand to her.

"I'm sorry for my indecent dress, My Lady." The corners of his mouth twisted up in an impish and flirtatious smile. "I might be immune to magical fire, but my clothes aren't. I'm not in the same position of luxury to wear such fine material as yourself."

"Jack... are you real?"

She touched his hand tentatively. He, in turn, grabbed her with confidence and pulled her close. Alleria blushed, more aware than ever of his nudity.

"I'm sorry I had to trick you into thinking that I would sell you, Alleria. But I wasn't sure how good an actress you would be if I let you in on our little secret. These slavers are paranoid people and I didn't want to rouse any suspicion."

"You planned this?"

"Yes. I was thinking about our sticky situation and I realized the only way I could keep you safe would be if everyone thought you were dead. It's not a long-term plan, but at least it will buy us some time. This is the perfect place to fake a death. A lot of witnesses, a lot of suspects. Plus I got to kill two birds with one stone and get my Servantian dagger in the process. I have to admit there was a selfish element to all this too. I told you I wasn't a good guy."

"When did you set this up?" Alleria gawked at him. "How did you find the time?"

"I made the final arrangements at the Drunken Camel, though I've been planning this since the shelter." He pulled her hood further up her head. "I wasn't going to sell you into slavery, not after our journey together. I'm sorry I led you to believe that I was for such a long time. I hope one day you'll forgive me."

Above them, the roof was starting to catch fire and Jack's jolly expression turned to one of concern.

"If you don't mind, I will fill you in on the details later. Right now we just need to get out and get as far away from here as possible. I don't want this fire to spread out of hand; there's no need for innocent lives to be lost. Also, I want to be far away before they find 'your' body."

Alleria nodded with gratitude.

"Keep your skin under that cloak and you'll be fine."

She pulled her hood so far over her face that she couldn't see where they were going, but Jack led her through the flames. The material of the cloak and nightgown absorbed the heat, but because of her movement, Alleria found it impossible to keep her feet and hands covered. The impact of the fire created painful blisters on her skin. They didn't stop her from moving; the thought of freedom almost dulled the searing agony.

Only when she felt the cool of the night air did she pull down the hood and release the hem of the cloak. Thick, white blisters covered her fingers and ankles and the fabric of her slippers was scorched.

"This way," Jack whispered. "Over here."

A canvas wagon stood near the building, a driver in the coach box ready to go. Jack nimbly made his way inside and he reached back to aid

Alleria. Moving with his usual catlike grace, he pulled a gray robe from an open trunk and donned himself in it.

Once dressed, he whistled to the driver who instantly spurred on the duo of horses. Jack leaned back on one of the sacks while he eyed Alleria with a crooked smile.

"I'll bet you don't hate me as much now, do you?" He whistled between his teeth. "You hated me plenty before."

"I wanted to take that Servantian dagger and stab you in the eye," she admitted.

Jack threw back his head and laughed.

"I apologize again for fooling you." He hiccupped, still laughing. "Aside from your acting skills, I've heard rumors there might have been mind readers among the slavers. I just didn't want to take the risk."

"Now what happens?"

"Well, hopefully they will think that the woman in the cell was you. With a bit of luck, they'll assume someone didn't want to wait for the bidding war tomorrow and wanted your heart now. I put a lot of emphasis that I didn't want a wizard to buy you. Now it looks like one stole your heart."

"Who was the woman in my cell?" Alleria asked, feeling a pang of guilt. "Did you kill her?"

"That was no woman at all, but a very bad copy of you. She'll appear as a corpse, but she was never alive. Don't worry, I only kill in defense of myself or others."

He leaned forward and kissed her on the cheek. The move caught Alleria by surprise.

"When you told me your cloak was made of absorption material, the plan finally clicked. That fabric would keep you safe and no one would know about it. They haven't heard of absorption material here."

"You told that slaver about it."

"Not in great detail, and he probably thought it was something magical to keep your powers in check. He would not suspect it to be resistant against magical fire. Not many things are."

"You are."

"Yes, I am. And so is that fabric of yours. Luckily, not many people outside of the Arallfyd know about its properties." He tugged at her cloak. "Word of your death will be carried back to the Arallfyd."

Alleria laughed, feeling positively giddy. "No one will come looking for a dead girl."

"For now. Don't count your blessings yet, for eventually someone will know you are still alive. There will be soothsayers, or some obnoxious magic spell will reveal that you still walk this world. I don't know how long it will last. I wonder how long that hideous witch that raised you will be fooled. She is tenacious, to say the least. I don't believe for one moment she ever stopped trying to find you. Your demise will throw her off the scent for a while, I hope, but outside the Arallfyd, she will always pose a real threat to us."

"Us?"

"Well, I owe you my life, don't I? Without you, I would have never gotten my Servantian dagger, and that would have cost me my life. The only way I can think of paying off my debt is by being your loyal servant and protector." He grinned with such joy that Alleria couldn't help but smile.

"You mean to say I'm no longer your slave?"

"I would say that I am yours."

"Don't be my slave, Jack... I don't want any slave or servant. But I would gladly accept a friend." Tears welled up in her eyes. She laughed and cried at the same time, her shoulders shaking. "I can't believe that after all these years, I'm free."

"Don't get too excited." Jack's face was serious and he rubbed her shoulders with his fingers. "A creature like you can't stay hidden for long.

But at least, for now, you are free. I think it will still be best if you hide for a while. Do you see that man up there?"

He pointed at the front of the wagon. Alleria nodded.

"That's Gallifroid. He is an ally of Merwig and he'll take you to the old man's house. There you can live for a while until we have found you a safer abode. I contacted Merwig that night in the Drunken Camel and told him of our plan. Needless to say, he's on board. That old fool is very fond of you, you know."

Jack winked at her, and his odd-colored eyes sparkled in the dimly lit wagon.

"I like Merwig. I would gladly stay at his house. But what of you?"

"I will travel with you to the Borderlands, and then our ways will part. My mission is to get myself that heart of Odalyn and return it to Boss Metisse to pay off my debt."

"Sounds rather simple."

Alleria was disappointed that Jack wouldn't travel with her to Merwig's house. She realized she had grown accustomed to his company over the last months.

"Well, everything is simple if nothing gets in the way." Jack ran a hand through his hair. "Technically that counts for all things in life. Unfortunately for me, things tend to get in the way."

"What will you do after you've paid off your debt?"

Without warning, Jack pulled at her legs. Alleria lost her balance, sliding forward as she landed on her back on the floor. He crawled on top of her and looked into her eyes. For a moment, there was silence. With one hand, he opened the clasp from the chain around her neck and gently pulled it away from her skin.

Freedom.

"When I'm done paying my debt, I intend to come and find you at Merwig's house... and I plan to earn back your companionship by serving you until I've paid for every tear I have caused. Perhaps one day you might trust me again and I can show how deep my feelings for you truly are."

His voice was hoarse and she saw a familiar passion in his eyes.

"I…" Alleria's heart fluttered against her rib cage. Her fingers tingled and her palms were lined with sweat as she placed her hand against Jack's gray robe.

"If you can forgive me for all the things I've done, that is." Jack wasn't smiling when he said the words, and his face showed a hint of pain and regret. "I've treated you terribly. But you've changed me, Alleria. I'm not sure how, but you have. Spending all that time with you, it made me a better man. Your kindness, your caring nature, they made me fall in love with you. I hope you believe me when I tell you that I'm deeply sorry for all the suffering I caused you."

"I think I can manage to forgive you… in time. You weren't always good to me, Jack, but you were the first person to treat me with kindness. Perhaps you were selfish, but you could have treated me far worse. Otherwise I would have never loved you, and I do." She winked at him and ran her fingertips across his cheek and over his lips. Her touch brought a smile to his face again.

"You love me?"

"Yes."

"Then the world is a beautiful place." He leaned in and kissed her with more passion than he ever had before.

In the depths of the Shadow Marshes, the old witch sat peering into the fire. The thin, white hair revealed a liver-spotted scalp underneath, and only a few teeth remained. The past year Tumsa felt she had aged a lifetime. Without the magic of her gosgeiddig, time was catching up with her. Her scrying spells had failed her, and she was convinced that Alleria was somewhere in the Arallfyd, the only place where the old woman couldn't find her. She had spent her time finding that which could harm the tylwyth teg named Halfway Jack, and she had found an ally who was willing to help, but all her hard work had been in vain. If the girl was on the other side of the mists, the old witch could do nothing. She could not travel to the other world, even if she wanted to. That right was only reserved for the tylwyth teg.

Tired, her heart filled with pessimism, the old witch muttered the familiar spell that allowed her to scry upon a subject of her choosing.

With a vigor she hadn't felt in a long time, she sprang to her feet. In her mind's eye, she saw the young woman she had been seeking. The old witch barely recognized her at first because she had not seen her in her true form since she was a toddler, but she knew who the girl was.

"Alleria," Tumsa whispered, her wrinkled mouth twisted in a malicious grin. "There you are..."

EPILOGUE

"My Lord?" The pale female looked translucent in the mist, nothing more than the outline of a face in the white fog.

"What is it?" The Lost God sat on his throne made of souls, his face and voice betraying his disinterest. The gray shapes that existed within the throne writhed and moaned, and sometimes a tormented face would push through the mass of beings, screaming without a voice.

"A servant of the Ravenlord was caught by guardians. He brings news about the daughter of the second moon."

"News?"

The Lost God sat up with renewed interest. The souls in his throne shifted and their color faded from dark gray to white. The faces seemed more peaceful and their movements were not as agitated as they had been before.

"Tell me this news."

"He claims she is dead."

"It's a lie."

The Lost God leaned back and waved her words away. The souls in his throne turned black and commenced their writhing, the anguish once again marring their faces.

"I would feel it if she died."

"Yes, Lord."

"This doesn't change anything. She will be mine by the next Blood Moon. Mark my words, for it is written. When the borders drop, we will consume the human world. When our bellies and our minds are filled to content, we will turn upon the Arallfyd and consume it with the same hunger."

"Yes, Lord."

The Lost God banged his fist on the throne and the souls cried out in pain—their screams now loud and audible.

"She was supposed to be mine. I had laid claim on her. She was right there, in our domain, and you let her go."

"Something protected her, Lord. We could not get near her."

"You did not try hard enough. She should have been mine." His anger melted away and he smiled at the faces in the mist. "She will come again; her kind can't stay away from the Arallfyd, you mark my words." He rubbed his chin, taking a few moments of contemplation before he added: "If not, I will drag her from the human world myself. With the daughter of the second moon, the child that could not be, on my arm, I will reign all three realms."

The mist swirled and revealed the wicked smiles within.

Soon, they seemed to whisper.

Soon.

ABOUT THE AUTHOR

Chantal Noordeloos has a deep appreciation for storytelling of any kind. Her love for myths and fairytales has only blossomed and grown since her childhood, and now she likes to use elements of them in her own writing.

As a writer, she enjoys dipping her toes into the speculative fiction pool, and she's a self-proclaimed 'genre-floozy'. Her 'go to' genre will always be dark fiction. "It helps being scared of everything; that gives me plenty of inspiration." In 1999, Chantal graduated from the Norwich School of Art and Design, where she focused mostly on creative writing. Noordeloos says: "Reading should be an escape from everyday life, and I like to provide people with new places to escape to and new people to meet." Nothing pleases her more than when she succeeds in surprising her readers or pulling at their heartstrings.

When she's not writing, Chantal spends time with her support-ive husband and supervillain-to-be daughter. They like to go on quirky adventures together, preferably in faraway lands. When far-away lands are not an option, they explore their home country, the Netherlands. If you look close enough, you can find fun anywhere.

www.ingramcontent.com/pod-product-compliance
Lightning Source LLC
Chambersburg PA
CBHW030120010826
48973CB00002B/351